[illegible]
and apart from holidays to very hot places where you can sit by a pool and drink cocktails as big as your head, she wouldn't really want to be anywhere else. *The Secrets of Meadow Farmhouse* is her seventh novel. She is also the author of the Swallowtail Bay series, *Snowflakes at Mistletoe Cottage* and *The Little Theatre on the Seafront*, which was shortlisted for the Katie Fforde Debut Novel of the Year award.

When she's not writing, Katie spends her time with her husband and two kids, and their dogs: Wotsit, the King Charles spaniel, and Skips, the three-legged Romanian rescue dog. (And yes, they are both named after crisps!)

For more about Katie, you can visit her website: www.keginger.com, find her on Facebook: www.facebook.com/KatieGAuthor, follow her on Twitter: @KatieGAuthor or sign up to her newsletter here: http://bit.ly/3gbqMS0

Also by Katie Ginger

The Little Theatre on the Seafront
Summer Season on the Seafront
Snowflakes at Mistletoe Cottage
Spring Tides at Swallowtail Bay
Summer Strawberries at Swallowtail Bay
Winter Wishes at Swallowtail Bay

Everyone LOVES Katie Ginger

[illegible]utifully written. It made me want to move house right now and set up by the sea!'

Tilly Tennant

'A delightful and delicious read for hopeful romantics everywhere'

Sandy Barker

'Seaside, strawberries and a sexy hero – what's not to love?'

Mandy Baggot

'Simply delicious – summer escapes don't come any more tasty!'

Jane Linfoot

'A hilarious romantic comedy that left me with a big smile on my face'

Holly Martin

'A moving, festive, absolutely gorgeous read! Perfect for curling up with this Christmas'

Samantha Tonge

'Does jumping up and down, cuddling my Kindle and grinning from ear to ear count as a review?! … Katie writes with such warmth and humour and I could feel every word'

NetGalley reviewer

'Loved it!'

NetGalley reviewer

'Sweet, heart-warming, and very enjoyable. This book is like a warm chocolate chip cookie, you feel better for eating it, get a bite of exciting chocolate now and again all while just enjoying the experience. Love the book!'

NetGalley reviewer

'The perfect book to enjoy in a few days of quiet downtime'

NetGalley reviewer

'Absolutely loved this book. Couldn't put it down. Wonderful uplifting storyline. Can't wait to see what's next'

NetGalley reviewer

The Secrets of Meadow Farmhouse

KATIE GINGER

ONE PLACE. MANY STORIES

This novel is entirely a work of fiction. The names, characters and incidents portrayed in it are the work of the author's imagination. Any resemblance to actual persons, living or dead, events or localities is entirely coincidental.

HQ
An imprint of HarperCollins*Publishers* Ltd
1 London Bridge Street
London SE1 9GF

www.harpercollins.co.uk

HarperCollins*Publishers*
1st Floor, Watermarque Building, Ringsend Road
Dublin 4, Ireland

This paperback edition 2021

1
First published in Great Britain by
HQ, an imprint of HarperCollins*Publishers* Ltd 2021

A catalogue record for this book is available from the British Library.

ISBN: 978-0-00-842274-5

Printed and bound in Great Britain by
CPI Group (UK) Ltd, Croydon CR0 4YY

This book is produced from independently certified FSC™ paper to ensure responsible forest management.

For more information visit: www.harpercollins.co.uk/green

Marion Louisa Coeburn
(2nd July 1891–23rd March 1975)
and her love
William (Billy) Arthur Davis
(6th July 1893–9th April 1917)

Prologue

June 1959

The wedding dress hung in front of the wardrobe, elegant and beautiful. Premature, some might say as she wasn't even wearing a ring. But Vera couldn't help telling her mother about the engagement, and her mother couldn't help but fetch it for her.

Side by side, they appraised it together, her mother giggling like a schoolgirl, Vera giddy in her excitement. Arty had asked her to keep it quiet until he'd spoken to his parents, but Vera had never been that good at keeping secrets. She was an open book as far as her thoughts and feelings were concerned, wearing her heart on her sleeve. Her half-sister always told her she should toughen up, but Vera had never seen the need, and after the events of the afternoon, when Arty had paused in the middle of the coppice where the ground was lush with green and the tall trees formed a canopy over their heads, taking her hand in his and slowly going down on one knee, it didn't seem the right time to start now. How could she when there was little to no chance of containing her unbridled joy?

'Will you marry me?' he'd asked, with trembling hands and a slight shake to his voice.

As if there were any possibility she'd say no. She loved him more than anything else in the world. She'd never met anyone so kind, so funny or so handsome.

The sun had shone down on them, dappling through the leaves, causing shadows to dance on the ground. She'd replied instantly with a resounding yes that echoed around them and he'd picked her up in his strong arms and swung her about on the spot.

Replaying the moment over in her mind, she'd never felt a happiness like it. All he had to do was speak to his mother and father, which he'd do that very afternoon and who, he assured her, would approve. It didn't bother her that he'd asked before speaking to her father. He was a good man and only wanted her to be happy.

As soon as she'd returned to the farmhouse flushed with excitement, her mother had guessed and Vera admitted the truth without a thought. Even as a child, without hesitation she'd owned up to the things she'd done, having learned early on that lies were always writ large on her face. Her mother had been over the moon. Apparently they'd been expecting it any day now, and they had celebrated with cake. Even her stepfather had raised a glass of sherry to her good fortune. 'He's a fine man. And rich too,' he teased.

Vera giggled because they all knew that money meant nothing to her. It was him she loved. The shy, quiet boy she'd spotted in the fields as a young girl, then grown up with, becoming friends and now lovers. Soon they would become husband and wife, marrying at the small church in the village and picnicking on the green. Content in her plans, after the allowance of a small glass of sherry, Vera had tipsily gone to bed.

The night had been long and restless as her overactive mind refused to cease, unable to sleep for the joy and anticipation pulsing through her veins. She imagined herself in the dress, pictured herself dancing and dreamed of forever being Arty's wife. In the half-light, she stared at the wedding dress now airing on her wardrobe door. It was, perhaps, a little old-fashioned, but she loved that it was her mother's, and her mother wanted her to wear it. The neck was too high and would need taking down; the sleeves, too, were long with frilled cuffs, but overall, she liked it. It would be her something borrowed, or perhaps something old.

A faint tapping at the window drew her attention to the day breaking outside. At first, she'd thought it was rain, but as she listened to its rhythmless nature and growing intensity she realised it was something else. With a thrill of excitement, Vera pulled back the covers and swung her legs out of bed. The cold spring morning penetrated the thin material of her nightdress and she pulled her dressing gown on before silently padding her way to the window.

As she pulled back the curtains, the emerging white light of the sun illuminated the slowly waking world, blinding her. The sky held patches of cloud here and there, harsh and dark, threatening rain. Her eyes dropped to the ground below her window. Arty. Arty had come to see her. A shiver ran down her spine at the romantic nature of this dawn visit, and as quietly as she could, she ran down the stairs, avoiding the patches of old wood that creaked and moaned underfoot, and unlatched the heavy back door.

Vera stayed in the doorway, propriety forcing her to hide. Though her mother had always told her not to worry too much about convention, there were some things that would not be tolerated, and meeting a beau in the early hours of the morning in nothing but your night clothes was one of them. Arty stood motionless in his shirtsleeves, his arms hanging limply by his sides. Goose bumps covered his skin from the chill morning air. 'Arty? What are you doing here?'

'I'm sorry, Vera,' he replied, his voice weak, almost inaudible. He'd been crying. His eyes puffy and red, bloodshot through lack of sleep and marked under with deep blue shadows. 'I'm so sorry. I can't marry you.'

Fear tensed her muscles and a burden of dread rested on her chest. He hadn't said that. He couldn't have. 'What do you mean?' An incredulous laugh escaped her. 'What are you talking about?'

'I can't marry you, Vera. I'm so sorry.' Tears welled in his eyes once more and with a strong sniff he attempted to force them away.

'Why not?' A weight pressed down, tightening her ribs. 'You love me and I love you.'

'You know why—'

She shook her head. 'But you said you didn't care. You said—'

'I know what I said.'

Vera watched the rise and fall of his chest as he breathed heavily. Why was he hurting her like this?

'I have to think of others, not just myself.'

He was saying words that weren't his. He'd never have said anything like this before, when their relationship was purely friendship. It must have been his mother. She must have refused her consent. Vera felt the slow, steady tearing in her heart as it ripped so completely in two.

'You don't mean that,' she whispered, tears now falling down her face. Her heart ached, slowly breaking as his words sunk in. With white knuckles, she held tight to the doorframe, her body no longer able to stay upright. All her strength had disappeared.

'I'm sorry, Vera, but I do. I have to go.'

He turned and walked away, and as loudly as she could without waking the others, she called out to him, but apart from a slight turn of his head, he didn't stop, or acknowledge her anguish.

Vera's hands shook as she closed the door and leaned back against it as though it would stop her from disintegrating. Her legs gave way, unable to take the weight of her emotions. She slid down to the floor, curling her legs up and hiding her face behind them. Tears soaked through the fabric of her nightdress so it stuck to her skin. The grey clouds that had threatened only moments before let loose their burdens and as her life fell apart, the rains came.

Chapter 1

Paris
Present Day

The sights and smells of the Paris flea market were almost too much for Amelia's hungover senses to bear. Only her excitement at living in the city she adored, and a need to be out of her apartment, led her forwards.

Though the baking emanating from the nearby shops smelled delicious, the aromas changed with every step causing her stomach to roil and calm in equal measure. The strong scents of garlic and onion were overtaken by that of sweet pastries and butter. The crowds wove around her, all heading for the farmers' market at the bottom of the tiny street or returning up the hill with bags laden with fresh produce. In between, shopkeepers cast open their windows, displaying the eclectic range of goods they had to offer. Amelia's eyes darted between the numerous chandeliers that hung from the ceilings of one store, onto antique vases side by side on a small side table. Traditional French furniture lined the street outside along with stacks of paintings. On the other side of the street, smaller objects like perfume bottles, vintage jewellery and trinkets glittered as the sun hit the windows.

All around, the sound of chatter penetrated her ears, resonating through her sluggish brain. Fluent in French, Amelia could make out most of what was said, but when so many voices merged and the locals spoke so quickly, she struggled to keep up. Snippets of conversation met her, forming unusual and humorous sentences.

She pushed her large round sunglasses further up her nose to shield her eyes from the sun's strong glare, and her stomach rumbled loudly.

Spring in Paris was a magical affair as flowers bloomed around the city, giving the air an overwhelmingly floral scent. She'd been there for eight years now, but the capital never failed to impress her. Each season affected the city differently, but whereas summer could sear the streets with a hazy heat, spring gave all the golden glow but with a much more temperate feel.

Pausing at her favourite café, with a mix of folding metal and wicker chairs tightly packed around small circular tables, she took a seat and ordered a café crème and a buttery, flaky croissant; the perfect thing to soak up the rest of the wine lingering in her system while she waited for Océanè to join her. She'd want to know all about her date with Bastien last night and by the time Amelia had something to eat and chatted to her friend, she'd feel well enough to look again for the perfect items to finish off the job she was working on. As an interior designer, Paris – with its chic fashions and varied shops – was ideal for her business. Could she have built this career in the tiny English village she'd grown up in? Probably not. Though regret at the way she'd left bubbled inside, causing her insides to roll again.

Twenty minutes later, Océanè arrived and ordered the same as Amelia. Amelia asked for another café crème before the waiter disappeared, knowing the questioning was soon to begin and a second caffeine hit would help her endure it. Her friend didn't exactly mince her words.

'So?' Océanè asked in her heavy French accent. 'How was your date last night? Was Bastien attentive? Did he buy you champagne? You have seen him, what? Five times now?'

'He bought me wine. And lots of it. Too much, in fact,' Amelia said, adjusting her sunglasses once more as the sun moved across the sky, climbing higher. The coffee was helping her headache, but she still felt a little fragile. This morning she had dived to the bathroom and hastily scraped her black hair into a chignon and swiped bold red lipstick over her lips, knowing it would give her pale complexion some colour. Over the years she had tried to absorb the Parisian style of dressing: classic, expensive pieces, simple lines, and most of the time she managed to pull it off, but there were times, like this morning, when fashion wasn't important. She'd thrown on old loose jeans and a jumper but it only took a moment with a real Parisian to make her feel sloppy and slobbish, and as Océanè cast her eyes over her outfit, she knew she didn't approve.

Océanè swiped her blonde hair over her shoulder. 'You do look a little, how do you say …'

'Under the weather?'

'Pasty.'

'Thanks.' Amelia giggled.

'Did you not have a good time? He is very handsome, *non*?'

'We had a very nice time.' For once, Amelia was grateful that she looked so ill any blushing wasn't likely to show as thoughts of his intense and passionate kisses rang through her head. 'And yes, he is very handsome. He wined and dined me, paid me compliments, made me laugh, but I've left him to make his way home while I'm out.'

'You are avoiding him?' Her friend's tone was incredulous.

Bastien was almost perfect and she liked him well enough, but Amelia wasn't very good at the small talk made the next morning. It made her uncomfortable and embarrassed and to be honest, she hadn't had a lot of practice at it. An image of Adam flashed into her brain and she shook it away. Ever since she'd left him back home in the tiny village of Meadowbank, he'd pop up in her mind, most often when she was thinking about or trying to date someone else. No matter how much she tried, she couldn't shake him off.

'But you will see him again tomorrow?' Océanè asked. 'He is in love with you, I think.'

'I don't think he's in love with me. I know he likes me, but—' Amelia paused while the waiter delivered their drinks. She took a sip of coffee and saw the imprint of her red lipstick on the rim of the cup. 'I don't think it's love.' Sometimes, she found it hard to believe that someone would ever love her. Her life had been so destitute of it from such an early age. 'And to be honest, I'm not sure I'm in the market for that sort of thing at the moment. I like him, but …'

The words died on her lips. What could she say? He was another man who over the years hadn't made her feel the way Adam had? Océanè would laugh at her for thinking of a love that happened so long ago. An image of their goodbye at the train station floated before her, causing her throat to tighten. She dropped her eyes to her cup, focusing on the coffee inside it, hoping it would draw her mind and the pain away.

Océanè took a moment to understand the phrase, but realisation quickly dawned. 'You are mad. He has everything a woman could want: money, success, good looks.'

Bastien did have all those things and he was also kind and funny, which is how they'd made it to five dates rather than just one, but despite her best efforts, he still hadn't managed to break through to her heart.

'You are a cold woman. You care only for your work.'

Amelia raised her head at this remark. Was she cold? She didn't think so. She had friends and had been through some decent relationships, but they'd never felt strong enough to last. She wasn't cold, she was just focused on living her life to the full. She'd worked hard to become one of the foremost interior designers in Paris, and she wanted more than just a man who was perfect on paper. She wasn't prepared to invite a man into her life for the sake of it. She'd always done fine on her own and her life was far too busy for loneliness.

Océanè continued. 'I do not know how you can be so immune to his charms. Our men – French men – Parisian men – know how to win a woman's heart.'

'Your French men are pretty charming, but I'm far too busy with work to worry about love.'

'Don't your parents want you to get married? Mine do. They say that I should marry Émile and have children before they are too old to enjoy being with them. They say my eggs will die.'

'Your eggs?' Amelia almost spluttered her coffee.

'Eggs.' Océanè motioned towards her lap. 'Your parents do not worry about your eggs?'

A sharp pain shot into Amelia's chest and a hurt she'd convinced herself had been dealt with stabbed anew. 'My parents are dead. They died when I was a child.'

Océanè's hand paused as she tore off a piece of croissant. 'You have never told me that. We have been friends for years and yet you make no mention of this. Why not?'

Amelia shrugged one shoulder. 'It's never come up before.' That was a lie and she quickly changed the subject, unsure why she had suddenly admitted it. Perhaps she was more tired than she realised. Her temples started to pound again. She'd been out with friends every night this week, and last. Maybe a decent dinner cooked by herself – something hearty and wholesome rather than tiny, minuscule restaurant portions – and a quiet night in were in order. 'Once we're done here, I'd like to take another look around. I'm after some special pieces for an apartment I'm working on in Montmartre.'

'You will have to do that alone; I have to meet Émile. But you must think about Bastien. There are many women who would like to take your place in his bed.'

'He was in *my* bed, actually,' she replied, playfully eyeing Océanè over the rim of her cup.

'You know what I mean.' Océanè raised one perfectly shaped eyebrow. 'You can be too hard, Amélie. Too independent.' It always amused Amelia that Océanè called her by the French version of her name when she was being serious. 'One day, you will push a man too far away and he will not bother coming back.'

Not if he's the right man, Amelia thought, but didn't bother saying so. She hadn't planned on sleeping with Bastien last night and it had been a moment of weakness she was paying for this morning. She hoped that by spinelessly hiding out until he'd left, she'd avoid an embarrassing situation.

'You have a great business, yes?' Océanè said. 'You have a great apartment, yes? But you are never alone. Always you are with friends. A person cannot exist without love. Eventually, you will have to let someone into your heart. Why not Bastien?'

Feeling the prickle of embarrassment inch its way over her skin, Amelia pulled her compact from her handbag and topped up her red lipstick. She'd been without love all her life, since her parents' deaths but she couldn't face talking to Océanè about that now. 'I've done fine without a man so far,' she said light-heartedly, hoping that would be the end of the conversation.

After they had finished their coffees and talked about their plans for the rest of the weekend, Océanè left and Amelia took another walk around the flea market. Temptation sat on her shoulder and whispered into her ear as her eyes fell on different objects that would suit her already overflowing apartment. Some of her clients liked a minimalist style, but when Amelia saw something she wanted, it was almost impossible to resist. As a result, her small flat was now packed with possessions and her wardrobe overflowing with clothes.

Amelia haggled with a vendor to buy an ornate perfume bottle – a finishing touch for the Montmartre apartment – and a vintage copper milk jug for her own place. She'd find somewhere for it to go later. Maybe the bathroom? And made her way back to the Metro.

As she climbed the steps from the Metro station, the cold, fresh air blew through the elaborate dark-green metal bars and under the glass ceiling. The station design was so iconic she had a picture of one in the living room of her apartment. She'd bought it shortly after moving in all those years ago, and though it had been fairly inexpensive, it was still one of her most prized possessions.

Her apartment in Saint Germain was in a typical eighteenth-century block with white shutters and decorative ironwork across the windows. On hot summer days she would cast the windows open and let the light flood her apartment. As she stepped inside the communal hallway, she gathered her post and made her way upstairs. An envelope postmarked from England caught her eye and her lungs turned to stone. It had a company name she didn't recognise. Even worse, the town it came from was dangerously close to Meadowbank; the tiny village she'd grown up in with Great-Aunt Vera who had begrudgingly taken her in after her parents had died.

Curiosity almost forced her to open it there and then, but Amelia valued her privacy and continued upstairs. She pressed the key into the lock, hoping once more that Bastien had left by now. She really didn't fancy talking to him. He'd try to convince her to spend the rest of the day with him and all she wanted was to nap on the sofa as the soft breeze blew over her.

With a gentle push, the door opened and all was quiet inside. No sounds of snoring, no sounds of movement, and sighing with relief, Amelia advanced down the hall and into the open-plan living room and kitchen, anchoring the milk jug under her arm so she could see the envelope again. It nestled among bills, inviting Amelia to ignore everything else and tear it open without any further delay.

'Good morning, *ma chérie*.'

Glancing up, her eyes fell on Bastien, lying naked on her kitchen counter, one leg bent, the other outstretched and all of him on display. The copper milk jug fell from underneath her arm, landing on the floor with a deafening clatter. Bastien wobbled precariously and almost toppled forward onto the floor. His hand shot out, gripping the edge of the counter to steady himself. Amelia nearly dropped the pretty perfume bottle as well, but somehow managed to keep hold of it. She gazed around as if it might help her understand why he'd chosen the kitchen as the best location for his seduction.

'Bastien!' Her neck grew hot. 'What are you … umm—' So much for avoiding an embarrassing situation. Amelia decided the best thing was to pretend everything was perfectly normal, which was a bit of a stretch but doable if she kept her eyes only on his face. 'Wh – what are you still doing here?'

'I am waiting for you,' he replied, regaining his balance and lowering his voice to nothing more than a seductive grumble. In the current circumstances, it didn't really work. Bastien pinned her with his eyes, and his gaze never shifted. Of all the things she thought she might face if Bastien were still here this morning, she wasn't quite prepared for him to be naked and spread-eagled in her kitchen, and she found herself momentarily lost for words.

Amelia placed the perfume bottle on the counter, thanking the Lord it was still intact. Unsure what else to say, she stammered, 'I'm, umm, I'm a bit busy today, Bastien. Sorry.'

'Too busy for love?'

The sound of the L word twice in one day stiffened her shoulders as another image of Adam shot into her brain. Bastien gave her puppy-dog eyes and Amelia's headache intensified. How on earth was she supposed to remove him from her kitchen? It wasn't like she could grab a fish slice and prise him off the counter. 'Bastien, can you please put your pants on and maybe umm, get your bits off my worktop?'

He didn't move. 'Do I not tempt you? Come now.' He held out his hand to her but all Amelia could do was rub her forehead.

'Bastien, please, pants on.'

'Let us spend the day together.'

Amelia sighed and pressed her hand harder onto her head. This was exactly why relationships weren't a good idea. She should never have let her guard down and shared that second bottle of wine. 'Bastien, you're a very nice man and I had a great time last night, but I really can't see you today. Please, I really need you to go.'

'But—'

'No, Bastien.'

Sheepishly, he moved. She guessed the kitchen counter had been too cold to sit on for long because his pants were lying on the floor by her feet. He must have decided to forgo them only at the very last moment for full-on seduction. At least he was committed. Amelia picked them up using the tips of her fingers and handed them to him as Bastien's skin made a horrible squeaking sound as he pushed himself down from the counter. It looked like she'd be spending the afternoon disinfecting the kitchen before she cooked anything and seeing as his pants had been on the floor, she would have to wash that as well.

'You really want me to go?' Bastien tried one more time, attempting to impart some lust into his voice.

'Yes, please. I'm sorry, but I really have work to do.'

'But it is Saturday.'

The letter again caught her attention and curiosity built but as much as she wanted to know its contents, she couldn't open it with Bastien around. Frowning as she placed the letters on the counter, she turned away from him and went to grab a bottle of water from the fridge, hoping he'd get the hint that it was time to leave. Océanè's words that she was a cold woman echoed in her brain. She didn't mean to be cold with Bastien, but how else was she to get this naked Frenchman out of her apartment? Without turning, she was aware of him heading off into the bedroom and a few moments later, he placed a gentle kiss on her cheek and said goodbye.

The cold water slid down her throat and concern mixed with anticipation sent goose bumps over her skin. She didn't normally get letters from England and the company name sounded unnervingly formal. After spraying and wiping down the counter, she sat on a stool and opened the post, starting with the bright white envelope postmarked from England.

As soon as she pulled out the thick white paper, her eyes began to scan the words. An unexpected wave of emotion hit her, and her body shook in response. For a moment, her breathing became hard and erratic and she willed herself to calm down. Great-Aunt Vera was dead and had left her Meadow Farm: the draughty old farmhouse they'd co-existed in for ten unsentimental and lonely years, as well as the land around it. You couldn't even really call it living together because that implied a level of fondness that had never existed as far as her aunt was concerned.

Shaking her head at the memory, Amelia was glad she'd left for university and never returned. Vera hadn't wanted her and if it hadn't been for Adam, the only friend she had in the village, she'd have run away long before then. He'd talked her out of it so many times when Vera had told her off for doing nothing more than being a child. Vera had always made her feel so burdensome and ultimately forgettable.

A moment's respite from such intense emotions came as she thought of Adam again. The youthful face she remembered once more pushed its way into her brain and she swallowed hard. She'd missed him immensely over the years but had never been brave enough to contact him. He'd been her first love and she regretted that she'd left without saying a proper goodbye but there was no possible way she could have stayed in that place forever. He'd have got over it by now, Amelia reminded herself. He'd have forgotten her quickly. He'd probably been happy to be rid of her.

Swallowing down her feelings, Amelia reread the letter. As shock subsided to be replaced by grief and guilt, Amelia took another drink of water. She hadn't even known Vera was sick. Apart from exchanging Christmas and birthday cards, they didn't speak at all and her most recent Christmas card hadn't mentioned anything about declining health. Had it been sudden? The solicitor's letter didn't mention the cause of death.

Though she regretted how their relationship had ended up, unless someone knew Vera – knew how cold and hard she was, how unloving – people didn't understand. Some people were naturally private, and it was a behaviour Amelia herself had learned, but Vera took it to a whole new level, hating everyone. Amelia buried the turmoil threatening to rise and overtake her under the knowledge that she'd made something of herself. She took a breath in, counted to eight and let it out slowly, counting again as she did so.

Despite everything, Vera had left her Meadow Farmhouse and according to the letter, she'd made Amelia the sole heir. Amelia had always found the village hard to handle. The concern when she'd arrived and the constant reminders of why she'd ended up there had been overwhelming. Meadowbank was one of those places where everyone knew everyone else's business and, as she'd grown, she'd longed for somewhere impersonal where no one asked her questions or reminded her of the past.

Would Adam still be there? Would anyone even remember her?

After she'd left, Amelia had never planned on going back and yet now it seemed she had no choice. She had to return to Meadow Farmhouse.

Chapter 2

Meadowbank

After hastily finishing what projects she could and rearranging others, Amelia left Paris just over a week later and made the trip to the tiny village of Meadowbank in Kent. She was unsure of how long she'd be in Meadowbank, but luckily she worked from home and didn't have any staff to worry about except for a virtual assistant she'd hired. It was one less thing to occupy her mind, which had been full of Adam since reading the letter. How long would she be there? A few weeks maybe? Once the place was clear, the sale she could handle from Paris and, eager not to waste time, she had already booked an estate agent for three weeks away. Ever organised, Amelia had also been in contact with the solicitors and someone was going to meet her at the farmhouse with the keys.

Océanè's use of the word *cold* rebounded in Amelia's head as it had since their coffee date. Was she being cold over Vera? It was hard to be sure. It was true she hadn't yet cried over her death, though the evening after she'd received the letter the back of her nose had stung as her brain wandered towards distant memories. Vera had never been one for praise or encouragement, but Amelia was still upset that she had gone before they could reconcile. Perhaps she should have made more effort on that front. Stupidly, she'd always assumed it would happen one day of its own accord. She'd never thought Vera would go without it ever occurring.

Since Amelia had left her apartment and made her way to the

Gare du Nord, her heart had sat like a lead weight in her chest. She didn't want to leave the safety of Paris and return to the small, suffocating village. She couldn't say return home because Paris was her home now. Everything familiar to her was in this city, not the other side of the Channel. Would any of it be the same as the day she'd left? She'd hoped that while on the Eurostar her unease would settle, but it hadn't. It had only intensified as the time ticked by and the distance shortened, bringing her ever closer to her old home and her old life.

Before the darkness of the tunnel, Amelia pulled out her phone and began scrolling through her social media feeds. After a few moments, her fingers twitched. Would it hurt to take a look at Adam's Facebook page again? He wasn't on Instagram or Twitter – she'd already checked – but he was definitely on Facebook. Not that she'd stalked him over the years. It had been a perfectly normal level of interest, but she had searched for him just to see what he looked like. Every time she did, a dull ache would throb in her heart. Adam was one of those people who didn't use it often and of course, without being his friend she wouldn't be able to see all that much, but curiosity forced her fingers over the keys.

Amelia's eyes eagerly scanned the screen as a few photos popped up. There was a cute one of him with his mum, Lynne, at an event but it wasn't clear where the event was. It didn't look like Meadowbank. In another, which definitely hadn't been there the last time she'd looked, he was laughing with his head thrown back wearing the tiniest swimming shorts she'd ever seen. While his choice of swimwear was dubious (Amelia had always associated budgie smugglers with middle-aged men on holiday in Greece), the physique was ridiculous. The skinny youthfulness had gone from his face and his features were more chiselled and rugged. His jaw was square and firm, and his gloriously red hair had ebbed to a less orangey hue. There were hints of brown she could see as she held the phone slightly in front of her nose, and there were toned, flat abs that made her palms a bit clammy.

How had she ever left him behind? Especially when he'd ended up looking like that. Men like that didn't end up with pale-skinned, gothic-haired women with abandonment issues like her. They ended up with women who only had half their eyebrows and dewy complexions. Her heart gave an involuntary double beat and she took a deep breath to calm it. Just as she did, the train rocked, and her thumb slid across the screen, liking the photo.

'Oh no. Oh, no, no, no, no, no.' Amelia's jaw hung loose as she realised what had happened.

Panic rose and she immediately hit the like button again to remove it but knew deep down that the notification would have been sent. Adam Noble would soon know that after ten years, Amelia Williams had creepily liked a photo of him looking particularly sexy in nothing but his Speedos. Why couldn't it have been the one with his mum? That at least would have made her seem less like a pervert. 'Oh God, oh God. Shit. No!' She tried to mutter, but annoyance made her pathetic whine louder than intended and someone across the aisle tutted. 'Sorry for swearing,' Amelia said when she glanced over to see a middle-aged woman glowering at her. 'But I just accidentally liked a photo of my ex. We've not seen each other in ten years.' She mumbled more to herself than the other woman.

The lady softened and sucked air in through her teeth. 'Oh dear. That sounds … embarrassing.'

Embarrassing wasn't the word. Mortifying might hint at what she was feeling but embarrassing didn't even come close. It was a drop in the proverbial ocean. She was quite tempted to throw herself from the train if only it didn't have automatic doors. A wave of heat flew over her and Amelia dropped her phone into her lap before pressing her cold hands to her cheeks. Of all the photos, why did it have to be the one of him half naked?

'I'm sure it'll be fine,' the woman said. 'Do people even use Facebook these days?'

'Some do, some don't.'

'Well, maybe you'll be lucky, and he'll be the type who doesn't.'

'Maybe.' Amelia told herself to calm down. *Just brush it off.* The words drifted around her brain but didn't sink in and she tried again to talk herself down. What did it matter if she'd liked a photo of Adam wearing next to nothing? He probably didn't even live in Meadowbank anymore and as she'd unliked the post pretty quickly, maybe he wouldn't even know. Amelia forced herself to take slow, deep breaths, even though her cheeks were still flaming.

Would he even remember who Amelia Williams was? Just because she still thought of him after all this time didn't mean he still thought of her. Maybe he'd moved on and their years growing up together had faded from his memory. Memory, after all, was a strange thing. There were times when she could barely remember her parents now. Only vague notions of their faces, and the sound of their voices had faded completely. A surge of melancholy forced Amelia to pick up her phone and begin again on her social media feeds – work this time, rather than personal. It was safer that way.

After arriving on English soil and leaving the train station, a taxi took her on the final part of the journey to Meadow Farmhouse. The scenery blurred as they drove through the lane into the village, on towards the farmhouse she hadn't seen in ten years. A brightly coloured ornamental sign proclaimed proudly that she was now entering the village of Meadowbank and below it was a horse and cart loaded with hay. Picturesque thatched cottages lined either side of the road with small picket fences. Everything about this place was quintessentially British from the timber-framed houses, thatched roofs and blossoming front gardens to the small, quaint bakery, butcher's and tiny village school. Old-fashioned, Amelia thought sweetly.

A surprising feeling of nostalgia inched its way into her brain, warming her thoughts. She'd expected to see the place with the eye of a tourist, but the sense of coming home, the feeling of peace – even fondness – hadn't been anticipated. Amelia pulled the collar of her jacket together and reminded herself that Paris was her home, silently listing all the things it had that Meadowbank didn't. Unsurprisingly, after Bastien's display, he hadn't made the list.

It would only be a few more minutes before she saw the farmhouse itself and apprehension grew, mangling Amelia's nerves. On leaving, she'd tried to imagine what it would feel like coming here and not having to see Vera. Easier perhaps but incredibly sad. She was ungrateful and had never hated Vera. She appreciated that she'd taken her in and given her a home, but it had been hard living with someone who so clearly hadn't wanted her around. Vera had only taken her in because she was the last living relative Amelia had, and things had always been tough between them. She'd never been fond of communication and it had left Amelia feeling isolated.

When her parents died without a will and with only each other as next of kin, the police had located Vera and asked her to take in the orphan child. Though Amelia tried to think of the deeply buried memory in detached terms, it was impossible, and queasiness forced its way up. She'd been an obligation, nothing more. It was either take her in or she go into care, and Vera had thought it her duty to provide a home. At least, that's what Amelia had always assumed because it wasn't something they spoke about. Vera didn't talk about feelings and, at times, Amelia hadn't even been sure she'd had any.

Eager to see more of the village, and ignore the melancholy rising inside her, Amelia leaned further to the window, her eyes darting across the scene to take in as many details as possible. Weaving around the village green, where summer fairs and primary school sports days had taken place, and on past the bushy duck pond complete with tinkling stream, the car headed to the other end of the village. Amelia saw the nearest thing they'd had to a supermarket was still operating, looking like something from an old postcard with wicker baskets outside holding fruit and vegetables, and she wondered if it still belonged to the same family. Unlikely, after all this time, but she was glad it was still there.

One of the things she loved about Paris was the small boutique stores. It didn't have just chains and supermarkets. Amelia firmly believed every town, village or city, needed quaint little shops like this. It gave character. The duck pond was the same as ever and she remembered feeding the ducks with Adam and his mum, tossing bread into the water for the hungry birds to chase after. Swallowing down a strange sense of wistfulness, she stared at the scenery.

Down a side road, a wooden board confirmed they now had a deli. That certainly hadn't been there when she was younger, and with an internal chuckle she noted that it seemed Meadowbank had become gentrified over the years. It was strange to think how people and places exist when you're not around. In her mind, it was like Meadowbank had gone into stasis and ceased to change or evolve. Such a silly point of view really. A part of her had assumed it would remain untouched, as it had seemed when she was little – caught in a time capsule – but time never stood still no matter how much you wanted it to. It always moved forward, just as she'd learned to do.

At the furthest end of the village green, the car took the still-familiar left turn and went on towards the rolling green fields. Houses became few and far between and acres of abundant green land surrounded her. The fields dipped and sloped away as far as the eye could see, cut through occasionally with tractor marks. Some were full of sheep lazily grazing, some were fallow, and squiggly lines of hedges criss-crossed the vibrant grassland, illustrating where history had marked out boundaries once upon a time. She'd forgotten how beautiful the place was when caught in the right light, and today was a perfect spring day.

The impossibly blue sky above was scattered with wispy clouds and the sun shone in through the taxi window. Amelia loosened the grey scarf worn over her black blazer and grey jeans. She'd wanted to look smart for her arrival, knowing it would give her courage to face whatever was about to befall her. Her usual red lipstick stained her lips and her hair had been tied into a high ponytail.

The country lanes swivelled left and right, and Amelia tightened her grip on her handbag. They passed over the small bridge that crossed the stream she and Adam had dipped their feet into on hot summer days and on the banks a rabbit scurried away into the undergrowth. It had been a long time since she'd seen such wildlife. It was like being a child again. A minute passed and farms began to appear on her left.

'It's just a little further on,' she said, knowing the driver's satnav would probably miss the turning. 'It's right here.' The car slowed at a crooked wooden sign, the overgrown plants behind covering some of the letters, and Amelia leaned over from her seat in the back. Even though the lettering was faded and the wood rotten, the words were just about legible: Meadow Farmhouse.

She'd arrived.

Sitting back, Amelia hadn't realised that her finger had gone to her mouth, about to chew a painted fingernail. She'd given up that nervous habit as soon as she left for university at eighteen.

The day she left, she'd assumed she'd come home for holidays, but luckily it had only been that first Christmas break she'd returned to Meadowbank for a non-celebration with Vera, who had never enjoyed Christmas. That had really been the last time she'd seen Adam Noble. When she waved goodbye at the train station, holding back sobs. She'd assumed she see him again the next holiday, but after that and for her remaining years at university, she'd stayed in shared houses sometimes on her own when everyone else returned to their families.

A dull ache in her chest lingered as she pushed her thoughts on. Océanè had been wrong. There was nothing wrong with living your life on your own. Amelia had done fine so far, and besides, she wasn't alone, she had friends.

'This it then, miss?' The taxi driver's voice cut through, bringing her back to the moment.

'Yes. You can drop me here if you like rather than go all the way down the drive.'

'You sure?'

'Yes. Yes. Fine.' She'd already begun uncoupling her seatbelt, giving the driver no choice but to stop the car. 'It saves you time and it's easier to turn around here than at the bottom.' She wasn't sure why she was rushing, but something made her want to see the place as quickly as possible. She checked the meter and found the money, handing it over with a thank you. As soon as the driver had taken it, he raced around to the back of the car and hauled out her two enormous suitcases.

Staring at the thin belt of trees to the left of the driveway and the dense wood off to the right on the edge of Meadow Farm's land, Amelia wondered how long the trees had been there. The thick oaks were already mature when she was younger and she and Adam used to climb all around them. They'd been her own personal playground. Their long branches had recuperated from winter, covered now with blossoming green leaves. Birds darted in and out of them, though Amelia couldn't find their nests. She heard them chirping happily and closed her eyes for a moment to meditate on the sound. Of course she'd heard birdsong in Paris, but this sounded different. Unmasked by traffic it appeared brighter and more musical.

The very first time she'd arrived it had been spring; a warm bright day when the police had delivered her to Vera's house after they'd informed her of the car crash that had stolen her family. For all that journey, she'd sat in the back of the police car, her hands clasped tightly in her lap, knuckles white as she tried to stop the tears flowing down her face. A kind policeman – a Family Liaison Officer, she supposed – had sat in the back with her, giving caring glances and attempting to take her hand, but she couldn't release them. The pressure between her palms had been the only thing keeping her terror and grief at bay.

The same fear threatened to climb up and spill out now, and she clenched her jaw shut. She refused to think about the solitary night in a care home while they'd located Vera. The long loneliness of the strange house full of children she didn't know and noises she didn't recognise. Part of her felt a failure for allowing it to distress her as much as it did. She was a grown woman now – a successful interior designer who lived in Paris – not the same scared little girl she'd been before, but the remembrance was visceral and overwhelming. With all her might Amelia pushed the memories down and her feelings with it. It was too painful to even think about. Slowly, she began her walk down to the house.

In the fields around her, daisies danced in the breeze, butterflies skimmed across the petals and bees moved efficiently from flower to flower. To her right, the wood loomed on the edge of Meadow Farm's estate – a dense, tall patch of browns and greens. She and Adam had built camps there and played as teenagers, trying all the things the cool kids did like smoking and drinking. Neither of them had bothered with drugs. They hadn't needed them to escape.

Instinctively, Amelia glanced around for any sign of Adam now, as though her brain was replaying it all. He was most likely married with three kids, two cars and a dog, living somewhere new. He'd always wanted that sort of life, but at eighteen, all she could think of was becoming more than the orphan child dropped here one morning by a stranger.

The wheel of her suitcase caught on a stone in the pot-holed drive and tipped to the side. 'Oh, nuts and bolts.' Amelia righted it, cursing as mud splattered up the back of her jeans. Dirt crept up her ballet pumps, threatening to make its way inside, and Amelia wished she'd worn something more suitable.

Around the bend in the unkept drive, the farmhouse itself came into view and shock forced Amelia's feet to stop. The place had changed beyond anything she could have imagined. To say the farmhouse was ramshackle was far too much of a compliment. Decrepit would have been a better description. Every plant around it was overgrown, as was the ivy growing up it in veins. The tatty loose thatch probably had birds living in it by now, and here and there windows were broken, patched up with wood.

What was that noise? She spun, then cocked her head, turning her ear to the sound. 'Chickens?' So there were still chickens at Meadow Farm. A smile came to her face as she remembered chasing the hens around the garden as a child. She could only have been about ten at the time. Then later, she was trusted to collect the eggs for their breakfast. It had been an age since she'd had runny eggs and soldiers. Thanks to her time in France, she could whip up a decent omelette but there was something infinitely more comforting about runny eggs with salty buttered toast soldiers. Amelia frowned at the mix of emotions whirring inside her, as if she was letting Paris down by remembering so many nice things about Meadowbank. Returning home had certainly been stranger than expected.

What had happened to Vera that she stopped caring so much about the place? She'd always loved Meadow Farmhouse more than any person or thing, claiming it was a name to be proud of. So how had it gone so downhill? From the exterior, it wouldn't be wholly unexpected to open the door and find livestock inside, all sat at the table having afternoon tea like something from Beatrix Potter. Scanning again with her eye for design, Amelia thought how good it would look if she could bring it up to scratch. It had always suited the yellow colour it had been painted, but its brightness had faded now.

It would make someone a wonderful home, but it was going to take a lot of work and more time than she'd allocated to bring it up to scratch. Her plan had been to clear the house of Vera's belongings, spruce things up and sell quickly. She'd counted on it being structurally sound, yet at the moment it seemed anything but. With a twinge of conscience, she thought about Océanè calling her cold. Perhaps it was wrong to treat this like any other job. Though she knew she was only doing so through self-preservation. Perhaps she should invest more into what had been her childhood home. After all, it was going to be the last time she saw it.

As she was assessing the house and picturing it back to its former glory, a black-and-white collie dog bounded around the corner almost running straight into her. When it saw her, it slowed in surprise, its back legs the last part of its body to get the message as it skidded to a halt in a puddle.

'Hello, you.' Seeing the dog's happy face, she let go of her suitcases and scratched him behind the ear.

A giant man with a huge bushy beard and dirty overalls tucked into socks ambled around the corner. 'Who are you?' he demanded. With his size and stature, he was slightly menacing but for all Vera said, Meadowbank had always been a neighbourly place.

'I'm Amelia Williams.' It seemed she'd been right to wonder if anyone would remember her. Seeing the dog, realisation dawned as to who the giant was. 'It's Mr MacMahon, isn't it?' Though she was an adult now, it didn't feel right to try to call him by his first name. She wasn't entirely sure she'd ever known what that was. 'And this can't be Bobby?'

'Aye, it is.' The man appraised her, his left eyebrow quirking as he regarded her. The dog sat with his tongue sticking out, looking almost as though he was smiling, which even Amelia, with her limited canine knowledge, knew wasn't possible.

'You were just a puppy when I saw you last,' she said, stroking the dog who leaned against her legs.

'Grown a bit, hasn't he? So, Vera's niece what upped and left.' Amelia kept her eyes on the dog, feeling awkward. 'Not to speak ill of the dead,' Mr MacMahon said, scratching at his temple.

'But I can see as why you would. She was a hard woman: Vera Cabot. A hard woman.'

What could she say to that? It was true, but Amelia didn't want to speak ill of Vera either. Not to Mr MacMahon who had been their neighbour while she was growing up and still appeared to be now. 'Do you still own Spring Farm?' she enquired, hoping to turn the conversation away from herself.

'I do. I've been checking on the place since Vera passed. Just been feeding the chickens. Sorry I didn't recognise you at first, but you can't be too careful these days, can you?' He took a step forward and paused, swinging the dog's lead by his side. 'I still lives next door to Adam Noble. D'you remember him?'

So he was still here. Amelia wished her chest would stop constricting every time she heard his name or she might have a heart attack. The thought of the Facebook fiasco flew back into her mind. If she saw him and he mentioned it, what would he say? What would she say? *Don't panic. I'm not really a lecherous woman, it was all a mistake.* That wasn't really going to help. Or would it simply be an unspoken embarrassment sitting in the air between them? That was if he spoke to her at all. She wouldn't blame him for blanking her entirely. Amelia cleared her throat. 'Yes, I remember him.'

A wry smile came to Mr MacMahon's face as he walked past her. 'Welcome back,' Mr MacMahon said, walking past her. 'Come on, Bobby.'

The dog glanced at her then shot off after his master. Within minutes they'd stepped through a gap in the belt of trees on the left-hand side of the drive and disappeared.

How was Adam still here? In some ways it shouldn't have been a surprise. He'd always loved Meadowbank. He loved the peace and quiet of being in nature and would never have survived in a cramped, impersonal city. It would have smothered him. She wondered what he'd ended up doing. At the time she left, he'd chosen not to go to university, but hadn't found a career. He hadn't even had a job. Had he settled on something and made something of himself? He'd always been laid-back, but she hoped he'd found a vocation that made him happy, as she had.

A silver car came slowly down the drive and Amelia watched as the solicitor climbed out. 'Hello, there,' he said cheerfully, hopping over muddy puddles with a briefcase in hand.

In his clean, pressed suit and tie, he was as out of place in this wilderness as she was, and she glanced again at her pretty ballet pumps. She had wellington boots in her suitcase but hadn't wanted to wear them for travelling. She'd have looked pretty silly marching through the streets of Paris in those. God forbid Océanè had seen her; she most definitely would not have approved.

'Crikey,' he said, hoisting up his briefcase and leaping over a particularly deep pool. 'You're not dressed for farm work either, are you?'

'No, I'm not,' she replied with a chuckle. His kind face took away any insult from the statement. 'I think we might be in for some rain judging by those storm clouds over there. Do you mind if we head inside?' She pointed to the sky behind him.

'I think you're right. We better do this quickly then. How do you do?' He held out his hand. 'I'm Donald Morris from Morris, Crompton and Peel. You must be Amelia Williams.'

'I am. Nice to meet you.' She shook his hand, then placed her own in her pocket. It was fresher today out of the warmth of the taxi and her fingers and toes were becoming cold.

He unclipped the briefcase and took out the keys. 'Firstly, I'm so sorry for your loss.'

'Thank you. That's very kind.'

'Would you like to open the house? This is your new home after all.'

Amelia's shoulders stiffened. 'Oh, umm.' She hadn't expected to be asked that and given how emotional the journey had been, she wasn't sure what would happen if she did. Would she burst into tears? Would the echo of teenage rows come back to her?

There was also the memory of her first tentative steps over the threshold as the policeman hung back and Vera took her in. Vera had wrapped her arms around her, she remembered now, and gently shushed her tears, but how things had changed as she'd grown. Amelia wasn't sure she trusted herself to open the door in case her fingers trembled even more than they were already. 'No that's fine, thank you. You may as well do it as you've got the key ready.'

He moved over to the heavy wooden door and pushed it to, standing aside for Amelia to walk through first.

It was so dark inside, her eyes had to adjust to the dim light and she almost stumbled, unable to confidently place her foot. A chill emanated from the stone floor, seeping into the thin leather of her shoes. The gathering breeze found its way through every gap in the old, warped windowpanes and draughts crept around her.

Everything was just as she remembered only darker and dirtier. The front door opened into an open-plan living room and kitchen that took nearly all of the ground floor. The paint on the sturdy well-crafted kitchen units had chipped and splintered over time. Already, Amelia could see what the kitchen would look like painted in a bright cream. With the large family-sized table in the middle, it would be a wonderful space for families to bond over dinner, chatting about their day. She started at the memory of quiet dinners after her arrival when the pain was fresh and raw.

The place needed more light, brighter curtains, livelier colours. On the countertops remnants of Vera's life were still strewn around. A thick wooden cutting board and knife sat next to the sink along with earthenware pots full of rolling pins and wooden spoons. Vera had baked, jammed and pickled everything she could. It was mainly to avoid having to go into the village, but she had always seemed most contented in the kitchen. Amelia felt her face tense as grief threatened to bring tears to her eyes. Grief for Vera and, though she hated to admit it, for her parents.

'Oh, Vera,' she muttered.

'I'm sorry?' replied Mr Morris. 'Did you say something?'

'No, nothing,' Amelia said quickly.

Without thinking, she wandered through the living room. It was crammed full of boxes and general rubbish but little else. The only sign of life was an open book resting on the arm of the sofa, the spine stretched out, and a few pictures over the fireplace. The room radiated sadness and Amelia wondered how she could make it feel any different. She studied the size of the room and the sofa. It was old and worn and if she didn't get a new one, she'd at least have to cover it with throws and cushions to give the idea of how cosy Meadow Farmhouse could be. It had the makings of a warm and inviting home with everything an estate agent would want for a country property. There was a huge farmhouse table, wooden beams, a stone floor, even a butler sink. It was the atmosphere that was the problem. A gloom that had settled over everything.

Through a door at the back of the living room was her playroom. Amelia had always thought she was special having a space all to herself; that was until she realised it was because Vera wanted to be as far away from her noise as possible. She remembered hiding in there, trying to play just after she'd arrived but in those first few weeks, she'd found it hard to imagine anything other than the deep, dark hole of her heart. Vera had delivered her hot chocolates and biscuits, she recalled. A forgotten kindness.

Amelia finished wandering and came to rest between the living room and the kitchen where the stairs led up to the three bedrooms and the only bathroom. Her heart and head could barely keep up with the vast array of emotions flooding through her at every turn, or the memories both happy and sad. She kept expecting to see Vera's tall, wiry frame at the sink, peering out into the grounds as she muttered to herself before darting off to complete another task. Everything about Vera had been brusque. From the way she washed up, to the way she spoke. That was probably why she never had any friends. No one in the village liked her and as well as everyone's sympathy at being an orphan child, Amelia had received pitying glances at Vera's lack of manners.

Cobwebs hung in the corners of the rooms and from the timber beams that ran overhead. Even a few spiders danced down silks into the room. The air was heavy with dust and Amelia could feel it clogging her pores and sticking to her skin. She held herself rigid as if readying for a wave of unhappy memories to hit, but nothing more came.

'Do you mind if I sit at the table?' asked Mr Morris.

'No, of course not. Please do. Sorry, it's just a bit strange being back.'

The solicitor's briefcase slammed onto the large wooden table in the middle of the kitchen, helping Amelia gather her thoughts. 'So,' he began, unclipping the shiny metal clasps and digging around for paperwork. 'Are you thinking of living here or selling?'

'Selling,' she told him. 'But I don't know when.' Judging by the internal state of the place, to get a decent price might mean spending more than just a little money and staying longer than she intended. Every surface in the kitchen was crowded with cutlery, crockery and food packets, and the rugs on the dirty stone floor were muddy and marked.

'Well, we can advise you on all those things when the time comes. Right now, it's just a case of signing some paperwork and I'll be out of your hair,' said Mr Morris.

She went to sit at the kitchen table with him. The worn wooden surface indented with nicks and scratches triggered a fierce feeling of nostalgia. The taste of the runny eggs and buttery toast soldiers, the sense of quiet calm that surrounded the farmhouse, removed as it was from the centre of the village. Each mark on the wood represented a memory, an event that had happened here, giving the house a sense of history. As she ran her finger over one of the dents, she asked a question that had been going through her mind since the letter arrived. 'What actually happened to Vera?'

'You don't know?' His surprise at her ignorance intensified the guilt and she couldn't quite find the words to explain herself. He clasped his hands together and laid them on the table in front of him. 'I'm afraid she died of a heart attack. It was very sudden, and she didn't suffer.'

'Who found her?'

'I believe it was the milkman. She was cremated according to her instructions and her ashes scattered on the farm. She'd made a surprisingly detailed will, outlining everything she wanted to happen.' Amelia nodded her understanding. 'So, if you could just sign the deeds, we'll get them filed. Here's my card. Do get in touch if you need any advice.'

Amelia took it and once all the legalities were finished, she said goodbye and showed him out. She supposed she should go and find her old room, unpack her things and maybe even check for supplies. But a sudden hankering for a cup of tea overtook her and as she glanced around to see the kettle in the same place it always had been, she could almost feel Vera's ghost speaking to her. Her harsh voice and the words from her mouth were nearly always universally negative. The row they'd had over her decision to move away had been the final time they'd spoken. The only people Vera had ever been remotely kind to were Adam and his mother, after Adam's dad had upped and left.

Alone, tears sprang into Amelia's eyes and she dabbed at them, fearful they might be the start of many. She wasn't normally one for crying and wondered why it was coming on now. She hadn't cried when she'd read the letter, nor when she'd packed and travelled here. What was different about this moment? She answered the question almost immediately. She missed the safety of her flat and the protection of her usual routine. The farmhouse felt familiar and yet unfamiliar at the same time and a part of her couldn't wait to leave again, while another felt a duty to deal with everything properly. The surge of emotion was overwhelming.

Though they hadn't ever gotten along, Vera had looked after her, saving her from a life of children's homes or foster care, and she felt a sudden rush of sadness for the woman everyone disliked. Amelia had been lucky in many respects, and out of that respect she would do right by Vera. No matter how hard she had to resist the urge to run away this one final time.

Chapter 3

After a restorative cup of tea, black because there wasn't any milk, with nerves more settled, Amelia took another walk around the farmhouse. Some of the doors were hanging from their hinges, the place was dirtier than she'd ever known it and cold from the draughts, but surprisingly, it was structurally sound. Even upstairs, where the bedrooms had old-fashioned iron frames, there was nothing a bit of cleaning and decorating couldn't fix. Amelia peered at the door to Vera's room, wondering what it looked like now. She wasn't quite brave enough to go in there yet, and instead, pulled back the sleeves of her jumper before fetching her suitcases.

An hour later, Amelia had unpacked and hung whatever needed it on the wire coat hangers in her old wardrobe. She'd then stacked the majority of her clothes in the matching mahogany chest of drawers. From her window she could see out to the side of the house over fields and towards the coppice. Did Adam still have that scar on his lip from the time they'd climbed in the wood and a branch had snapped? She hadn't been able to tell from the Facebook photo. As he fell, it had cut his mouth so deeply, spilling blood everywhere; she'd run all the way to his mum's house to fetch someone. The burn of humiliation at liking the Facebook photo rose up her spine again and she shook her head to dislodge it.

Looking around her old spare room, so much of it was the same. The furniture, the bed, they were all the things she'd known from her childhood. The only thing that was different was a painting on the walls that hadn't been there before. On closer inspection, she saw the name on the bottom was Vera's. Amelia had no idea Vera had ever painted and could only think that she'd taken it up as a hobby after she'd left. Vera had already been in her early sixties when Amelia arrived but you wouldn't have known it; she was incredibly active. Though the fields around Meadow Farmhouse weren't farmed, she'd tended a vegetable patch and the chickens who were allowed to roam free always needed rounding up.

Settling a little, Amelia realised the state of the house had shocked her because Vera had also been house-proud to the point of having something to prove. For some reason, she had a chip on her shoulder, though Amelia never understood why. Vera had inherited this beautiful farmhouse and all this land from her parents. She'd grown up in the village and everyone knew her well. It wasn't like she'd ever felt inferior the way Amelia had. Vera had always declared she had everything she needed, within the four walls of Meadow Farmhouse.

The drawer of the bedside table creaked as Amelia stowed away her toiletries, and as she straightened, a voice rang through the open window, coming from the front of the house.

'Cooee? Hello?'

Though she peered out of her bedroom window Amelia was unable to see anything as it had a view to the side, rather than the front of the house. She dashed to the other spare room to look out. An old woman stepped back from the front door, gazing up at the house, her features hidden by wispy grey hair.

'How did you even know I was here?' Amelia asked. She couldn't tell who it was from the top of her head alone and a prickle of tension mounted as she considered what to do. Amelia herself was never very good when people had lost someone, unsure what to say or how to act, so fearful of making things worse, and it was just as hard to be on the receiving end of condolences.

Another memory played out, of a trip into the village shortly after her arrival. The sad but kind glances of the villagers as she shuffled along with Vera, all stopping to say how sorry they were for the poor child and how Vera was a good person to take her in. She couldn't remember Vera's reactions to them, only marching along briskly by her side, her hand tight in the older woman's. Having remembered Vera's embrace earlier, she wondered now if the strength in her hand had come from anger at their questions or protection, but she grew uneasy at the memory, worried that the same feelings would return if she heard kind words and condolences.

'Yoo-hoo? Hello?' The woman called again and with no choice but to open the door, Amelia dashed downstairs, grabbing her scarf and throwing it around her shoulders before opening the front door.

'She's gone.' Amelia stepped off the worn stone step and peered around. A moment later, the old woman emerged from the side of the house, an expression of kind concern on her face.

'No, I haven't.'

The dark clouds from earlier had blown over to be replaced by bright white ones and as the sun shone between them, Amelia shielded her eyes from the light.

'There you are, dear.' The older woman came towards her. 'I was worried you'd run away again.'

The hairs on the back of Amelia's neck lifted. Not only was it disconcerting that people seemed to remember her, but all they were remembering her for was leaving. The lady was plump with rosy cheeks and a mop of curly grey hair fading to white. She thrust forward a wicker basket.

'Mr MacMahon told us you'd come back, and I thought there won't be any milk in that house after all this time. At least not any that's fit to drink, so I'd best take her some. And some tea and biscuits.'

'Oh, okay, thank you.'

A chicken jauntily crossed Amelia's path, pecking at the ground as it went. It remained completely oblivious to the two people who paused their conversation to watch it. Somehow it had escaped from the run and was now taking a gentle stroll around. Amelia wondered if she should she pick it up? Would she remember how? It seemed a lot bigger up close than when they were naked and frozen on her kitchen counter. The chicken stared at her, cocked its head, then went on its merry way. How had she not been more afraid of them when she was younger? But the chickens would have to be dealt with later, and turning back to the woman, she suddenly remembered the face from her youth. It was Mrs Bostock, her primary school teacher.

'Is that your chicken, dear?'

'Yes, I suppose it is,' Amelia replied still unsure what to do about it.

Mrs Bostock offered the basket. 'We're very sorry for your loss, dear.'

Amelia stepped forward and extended her hand to take it. 'Thank you. It's very kind of you to think of me.'

'Nonsense. It's what you do for neighbours, especially poor lambs such as yourself.'

The reference to her past was clear and Amelia tried a small smile of appreciation but from Mrs Bostock's confused expression wasn't sure it had worked. Just then Mr MacMahon stepped out from the line of trees to the side of the house.

As he grew closer, he said, 'I know Vera wasn't one for generosity but that doesn't mean we all aren't.'

'It's lovely to see you, dear,' Mrs Bostock added. 'Aren't you a beautiful young lady now? But then you always were with that lovely long dark hair of yours. Though the first time I saw you your eyes were red raw with crying, poor love.'

Amelia worried her emotions were written on her face. She didn't want to seem ungrateful, but her memories had been too much for her already today and the reminder she'd just been given made her step back. As she tried to think of something to say, the words failing with her discomfort, another person appeared from between the trees, rambling towards her.

It was Mrs Claribold, the dentist's receptionist and she'd arrived with a man Amelia didn't recognise. She was another person from Amelia's childhood who it didn't seem right to be overly familiar with. 'Hello, my dear. We brought you a little something to help you settle back in.'

'I was just saying,' said Mrs Bostock, 'how lovely it is to see Amelia back again. And how sad it was the first time she arrived.'

'Oh, yes,' Mrs Claribold agreed. 'You were a sad, bedraggled little thing, weren't you? It fair broke my heart to see you. Such pain. Too much for a wee young thing and so unfair.' She held a dish covered with a tea towel and Amelia tried to focus on the mouth-watering smell coming from it. She couldn't think any more about those first, intensely painful months at Meadowbank and it was unnerving how her return was shaping up to be the same. Luckily, Mrs Claribold saved her from having to say anything by thrusting the dish at her and declaring, 'Beef and red wine stew. Just the thing to feed you up a bit and warm you on a chilly day, especially in that house. Those draughts.' She shuddered at the thought and pushed the dish towards Amelia.

With everyone staring at her, Amelia placed the wicker basket at her feet and in bewilderment stepped forwards. 'It smells delicious.' They all, including the chicken, watched expectantly. 'Well, thank you, everyone. I'd best get back to it. There's lots to sort out.'

'I bet there is. I don't know how Vera let the place get so bad—'

'Now, now, Mrs Claribold,' Mr MacMahon said, slowing her head of steam. Mrs Claribold quietened only for Mrs Bostock to take over.

'It's about time you came home,' she added fondly.

How did so many people remember her? Amelia hadn't expected anyone within a ten-mile radius to be pleased to see her, given that she was Vera's relative. Whether Vera had intended to or not, she'd always made Amelia feel so unimportant and small that she'd assumed she was easily forgettable. Just a minor character in everyone's lives rather than a main. Even in her own life there were times she didn't feel special enough to take the starring role.

'Are you going to get hold of that chicken?' asked Mr MacMahon as it pecked at the ground at his feet.

Amelia stifled a laugh at the absurdity of the situation and wished again she'd worn more suitable shoes. If she tried to shoo it away with her foot it might peck through the leather and she'd lose a toe. Mr or Mrs Chicken – she remembered something about combs and feathers being bigger, but she couldn't remember which way round it was. It was probably the man. That would be typical, wouldn't it? – but whatever sex it was, it was enormous and had a dangerously large, pointy beak. Though chickens weren't exactly known as one of life's predators, it still managed to look somewhat menacing.

As Amelia glanced at the chicken then back at Mr MacMahon, the plain and simple answer was no, she wasn't going to get hold of it. Not right now, anyway. She was going to wait until everyone had gone and then find a broom or something to chase it back to the little chicken house with. The run must be in a mess if they were escaping like this. It certainly hadn't happened in her youth. Or had it? She had a vague memory of chasing chickens with Vera and her actually smiling for a short time. 'Umm …'

'Here, I'll take it.' Mr MacMahon strolled forward, and in sure and certain hands scooped up the bird. It appeared so much smaller in his grasp and Amelia felt silly for being afraid of it. She never had been as a child. 'We're mighty glad you're back, Miss Amelia, but you'll have to – what's the phrase? Man up? When it comes to chickens.'

Amelia giggled. 'Yes, I think I will.' She bent to pick up the basket as a louder, angrier voice full of vitriol and bitterness rang out.

'She'd have been better staying away.'

The assembled group gasped and turned around to see who had spoken.

Amelia's fingers brushed the handle and she straightened up again, leaving it on the ground. The lady stepped forward, matronly and with her arms crossed over her chest. She hadn't brought anything with her and the scowl on her face showed that the thought hadn't even have crossed her mind. It was Adam's mother, Lynne, and she was not best pleased to see her. She must have arrived while Amelia was staring at the chicken.

Amelia paused like a rabbit trapped in headlights. She thought of Adam, of the Facebook fiasco – of his abs – and now this, in front of all these people. She didn't need a mirror to know her cheeks were a vivid pink.

'All these years when Vera was alive you never bothered coming back. Not even to see my boy. No letters, no email things. No nothing. And now she's gone you're straight in like a … like a vulture.'

Everyone gasped again.

'Now, now, Lynne,' said Mr MacMahon still holding the perfectly contented chicken in his arms. 'There's no need for that. It's not young Amelia's fault she inherited the farmhouse, is it?'

His support was gratefully received as Amelia battled for some words to defuse the situation, but Lynne wasn't done yet, and she jabbed a finger towards Amelia. 'Broke my son's heart she did. Used him. Straight off the moment she could and didn't bother coming back. Ten years it's been. Ten years. I bet you're going to sell the place, aren't you?'

'Well, I—' She shook her head and half-shrugged, searching for a response that wasn't going to fuel Lynne's anger. Was it better to just be honest now? 'I think I probably will. I live in Paris now, you see.'

'Course you do.' Lynne sneered. 'Too high and mighty for here.'

The remark stung. She didn't think she was better than anyone else. That wasn't at all why she'd left in the first place and Amelia feared Lynne's attitude was shared by the village and that kinder people like Mrs Bostock were in the minority. It was why she'd always been so reticent about returning and now her concerns were proving well founded. Again Amelia sought for something to say but Lynne's angry gaze took the words from her mouth. Any time a half sentence formed, the words died on her lips as everyone watched her.

'You have no idea what you did,' Lynne snarled. 'Don't you all remember? And it wasn't just Adam. We all know it affected Vera too, especially towards the end.'

Amelia waited, hoping she'd say that it had all turned out for the best as Adam was now married with an adoring wife and house full of red-headed children. And what did the remark about Vera mean? It was true that when Amelia had left for Paris after university, they hadn't separated on good terms, but Vera had never tried to clear the air between them. Her angry words that she was ungrateful and that nowhere in the world compared to Meadow Farm still sent a shiver down her spine. It was ironic, really, considering Vera disliked the place and most of the residents intently. In rebuttal, and full of defiance, Amelia had argued that she was spreading her wings like children were supposed to. Her attempt hadn't ended well, and in an effort to wound, Vera had said that as she wasn't her child she could do as she wished, but there would be no crying to her when it all went wrong.

Amelia hadn't even realised that memory existed with such clarity in the deep recesses of her mind. She'd buried it under happier ones created in her new life, but feeling it now – seeing it now as it played out – was like a slap to the face. Had Vera regretted her actions or simply hated Amelia even more?

Lynne glared at her, and amid the haze of other memories trying to surface, Amelia readied herself for another attack, but she didn't add any more. Instead, Lynne glowered then turned on her heel and marched off.

'There, there, dear,' Mrs Bostock said, patting her arm. 'I'm sure she'll calm down eventually.'

Eventually? That didn't bode well. Mrs Bostock walked away with Mrs Claribold following behind, keeping their eyes averted like Amelia was Medusa and might turn them to stone if they made eye contact.

'I'll put old Red here away and be off,' said Mr MacMahon, ambling away with the chicken under his arm.

Mrs Claribold's friend, an old man, stayed behind for a moment, staring between her and the house. His heavily hooded, watery blue eyes darted around, and his white hair lifted in the breeze, blowing into his face. A sadness swept his features and she wondered if he was about to offer his condolences too. It took a moment for her to remember him. He'd aged badly, like life had been hard for him these last ten years, but it was Arthur from the village. Amelia had never known his surname.

'You look strangely like her, you know,' he said and the words stopped her in her tracks as a note of melancholy lingered in the air.

'Come on, Arthur.' Mr MacMahon had reappeared now minus a chicken. 'Let's head back and leave Miss Amelia alone.' With a fleeting glance, Arthur began to walk with Mr MacMahon. Mrs Bostock, Lynne and Mrs Claribold were already entering the gap in the trees, which led to a shortcut to the village.

Tears threatened again but Amelia widened her eyes, willing the water to dry. She balanced the glass dish in one hand before picking up the wicker basket in another. She hadn't looked forward to returning and if the afternoon's events were anything to go by, she'd better get back to Paris as soon as possible before any more painful memories forced their way to the surface or Lynne decided to come after her with a pitchfork. And if that was how she felt about her after all this time, what the hell was Adam Noble going to say?

Chapter 4

'There you go, Lorraine,' Adam said, standing up and checking the cupboard door to make sure it was hanging properly. 'That's the last cupboard fitted. It's looking lovely, isn't it?' He peered around the newly fitted kitchen, pleased with his handiwork.

'You're a wonder, Adam. Really.' Lorraine passed him his cup of tea and a cupcake, gazing from under her spidery eyelashes as she did so.

He'd been working on her kitchen for the last few days and was sure he must have put on about a stone. Lorraine had told him that having the kitchen changed was the first bit of work done on the house since her husband had upped and left. Every time Adam had been there, she'd plied him with cakes and sandwiches as if he needed feeding up. Between her and his mother, he hadn't had to cook at all which, while useful, did make him feel a bit silly at twenty-eight years old.

Only Lorraine's motives didn't seem to be that motherly. He was sure she'd been eyeing him flirtatiously and her hair had definitely become blonder since he started on her kitchen. She never seemed to go anywhere when he was working in the house, chatting to him endlessly and alluding to how lonely she was. He tried to answer supportively but in a way that showed he wasn't in the least bit interested. Lorraine was a lovely woman, but she was a good ten years older than him and he wasn't really looking for a relationship right now. Not after the debacle that was Philippa and her rather dramatic exit from his life, not to mention the scars that had never quite healed from Amelia. Even thinking of her name made the hairs on his neck stand on end.

'I might have some more jobs for you,' she said, and he was sure there was a flirtatious undertone to her voice again. She licked the cupcake icing from her fingers whilst staring at him.

Feeling mild panic rise, Adam shoved the rest of his cupcake in his mouth and began to tidy away his tools. When he'd finally swallowed, he said, 'Well, just let me know, Lorraine and I'll fit you in, but I've got to get back to the workshop now.'

'Really? Couldn't you just stay and do this one little thing for me?'

'You need to tell me what it is,' he said gently, looking at his watch to show he couldn't stay long.

'It's … umm … well … I wanted to talk to you about those figures your mum mentioned. The ones you make yourself. Yes, that's it.' She clapped her hand together before offering another cupcake. Adam politely declined. 'I was thinking of getting some for the garden.'

In embarrassment, he turned away. He had asked his mum not to say anything about the strange little sculptures that were a cross between an artist's mannequin and Groot from *Guardians of the Galaxy* because he wasn't sure what he was going to do with them all. He wasn't even sure what they were for. They were just a hobby. A way of passing the time and exploring this niggling need to do something a bit more artistic with the wood. He didn't mind fitting kitchens, and he didn't want to be a sculptor either, but he wasn't quite ready to tell everyone what he was doing. The trouble was, he didn't have anywhere else to store them so right now they lined the walls of his workshop. All twenty or so of them. Like a little wooden army ready to march.

'Tell me about them,' Lorraine purred, leaning against the counter with her cleavage on display.

'Well.' Adam scratched the back of his head, embarrassment tingling his scalp. 'They're kind of like scrunchy-faced wooden gnomes. I've actually got one that looks like Danny DeVito.'

'Oh.' Lorraine's face said it all. It had frozen and her mouth formed a pinched line that tipped up slightly at the corners.

'Or like Groot from *Guardians of the Galaxy*,' he continued.

'Who?'

'You know Baby Groot?' Adam waved his arms doing the famous Baby Groot dance. Lorraine backed slightly away. This was exactly why he hadn't told anyone else about them. He should have found somewhere to hide them in the workshop too. Maybe under a giant dust sheet or something, though knowing his mum she'd have just gone nosing about anyway. 'They sound … lovely. Do you have some pictures?'

He did, but he didn't really want to show them to her now. The look on her face had been enough of a rejection for one day. Clearly, he needed to work on his sales pitch. 'Sorry, no. So, was there anything else you wanted me to do before I go?'

'No, no. That's fine.'

At least his strange little sculptures were good for something, he thought. They'd certainly quelled Lorraine's desire to spend time with him. As it was already nearing six, he made his way back to his workshop. Even though Lorraine didn't like the sound of them, he could feel his fingers tingling with the need to make another one. There was something wonderful about working with the wood so the figures emerged and their own personalities came out. Somehow he instinctively knew what expression to give them. Some were cheeky, some were grumpy, some were laughing and yet he never really planned what to do before he started. The wood just spoke to him. He scoffed to himself as he packed away. He could just imagine the ribbing he'd get in the pub if he said that to any of his mates.

He'd read somewhere that he should start a Facebook page for his business, or an Instagram account. He didn't even have a website, but then, he'd never needed one. All his work came from the village or from neighbouring ones based on word of mouth. For such a small place there was always something to mend, a new kitchen to fit, or a commission to make. He'd never needed to advertise and as the only carpenter in Meadowbank he often had more work than he could manage. There'd never been a need to do all the modern stuff and he didn't particularly like it either. He didn't use it personally. If he wanted to talk to someone, he rang them or saw them in the pub.

As he drove through the quiet, darkening village and out towards his farmhouse, Adam gazed at the scenery around him. He loved Meadowbank and had never felt the need to go anywhere else. Carpentry had turned out to be in his blood. When his mum had told him to find a career – anything to stop his lazing about moping after Amelia Williams – he'd been apprenticed to old Trevor Sims and taught a craft that he'd naturally taken to. Mr Sims still lived in the village and even now Adam would ask him questions when he had a difficult commission. Sometimes he'd even drop by Adam's workshop to see what he was working on and they'd share a pot of tea and set the world to rights. That's what you got in a place like Meadowbank: kindness and support. There were always some people who liked to gossip or thought they were better than others, but they existed everywhere, and were generally the type of people who didn't bother getting involved in community events.

The gravel grated under his tyres as he pulled into the drive of Willow Farm and stopped in front of the workshop. Opening the door, Adam inhaled the strong smell of wood, savouring its earthy scent. He turned on the radio as the last of the evening sunlight spilled in through the windows. Over the low hum of the music, he could hear Mr MacMahon's lambs bleating in the field next door and the cows lowing behind him.

A few years ago, Adam had sold some of his farm to Mr MacMahon, knowing that the smaller plot of land his house and barn would sit on were more than enough. He liked the sounds of the animals waking him in the morning. Mr MacMahon's tractor was a bit much sometimes, but when you worked the land the way farmers did, you had to beat the heat and rise early. Even if Adam was forced out of bed at dawn, he could always nap in the afternoon, or have an early night. Having his own business meant he wasn't beholden to anyone and he could start and end when he chose. Especially when he was working on commissions, like the rocking horse resting in the corner of the workshop, or indulging his love of sculpture by making his strange wooden figures. As he studied them now, he thought the Groot description was pretty accurate, better than Danny DeVito.

Adam walked to the other end of the barn and began working on the rocking horse, determined to smooth out a troublesome knot in the wooden neck of the horse. The converted barn was far bigger than he required, but it had been easier to refurbish the old outbuilding attached to the farmhouse he and his mother had shared, than find somewhere new. That would have meant looking out of the village, which he really didn't want to do. And where he was, he had enough room to make his own furniture and indulge his passion projects, like the coffee table he was making out of an old tree stump from Meadowbank Wood. Behind him, at the back of the room, ran another workbench littered with tools. Chisels, different-sized hammers, planers, power tools; everything he needed was to hand and he felt naturally at home here.

Carpentry wasn't the most exciting career in the world, but he was happy, and it was a relief not to live with his mum anymore. She'd moved from the farm to Ivy Cottage in the centre of the village as soon as he'd earned enough money to buy it for her. Adam had known how much she loved it ever since he was little, and it had been his way of saying thank you for supporting him through his years of learning the trade and then building his own business.

The barn door burst open and the woman herself flounced in bearing a huge casserole dish full of food, muttering under her breath. No matter how many times he told her that he was able to cook for himself, she still insisted on bringing him something when she'd 'accidentally' cooked too much. She had a lot of accidents.

Normally, his mother was happy and cheerful, her voice lyrical and soft, but today her shoulders were tense and her tone angry. Considering that yesterday she'd been placid and sharing jokes with him, the change was jarring. 'Everything all right, Mum?'

She put the large red cooking pot down on the table and began tidying his other workstation, stacking bits of paper and moving his stationery around. She either tidied or cooked when she was annoyed and as she seemed to have done both, it must have been something really bad. Adam couldn't quite make out a sentence from the random assortment of words she was grumbling under her breath and animating with flailing arms. Leaving the wooden horse, he unravelled to his full height, stretching his back and neck. At six foot two he did struggle to get under sinks and into small spaces but he always managed it, even if he ended up with bumps and bruises. He still wouldn't choose to do anything else. 'Mum, you okay?'

She continued her outraged tidying. 'I don't know what she thinks she's doing.' He couldn't make out the next part as her voice lowered, then it picked up again with such velocity he jumped. 'But still. Who does she think she is?'

'Who? Mum, what are you talking about? Is it Mrs Fowl again?' He leaned against the counter, amused at the village's goings-on. 'What's she done this time? Tried to take over the spring fair committee again? Is she organising a coup or arguing about who's running the tombola?'

Lynne picked up the red casserole dish, then placed it back down in exactly the same spot. Turning to Adam, she thrust a hand onto her hip. 'Amelia Williams is back.'

Hearing his mum say her name sent a bolt of ice through him that chilled his core. The hairs on his arms rose as remembered feeling washed through his veins. Should he pretend he didn't care? Make out that it didn't bother him that after all this time she'd finally come home? Over the years, he'd dreamed and hoped but those wishes had never materialised into anything. Not even so much as a postcard. As far as he could see, he had two options. He could pretend he was fine, but it would be pointless. His mum remembered only too well the state he was in after she left. It had taken him far longer to recover from Amelia's leaving than he'd thought it would. Far longer than it had taken him to get over his last break-up. Or he could just be honest about how he was feeling. The chances are his mum knew that already.

Caught in the moment, his body flooded with the same heartbreak it had the day they had stood at the tiny train station saying goodbye. She'd been home for Christmas and as she hugged him, her face wet with tears and him holding his own back with all his strength, she'd promised to stay in touch. Only she hadn't.

Back then the feeling of loss had taken him by surprise. Not so much for the day she left, but in the months that followed when he realised he was never going to hear from her again. That the text message or email he'd always hoped for was never going to come. Slowly, he'd come to understand that their relationship hadn't meant that much to her when it had meant everything to him. It had left a hole in his heart. Shock was now replaced with anger and frustration at the way things had turned out and, pushing his hand into his unruly red hair, he tried to let those feelings go.

As soon as Vera had passed, there'd been a small chance Amelia would return to deal with the farmhouse, but no one was sure Vera had even left it to her. As she hadn't returned over any of the last ten years, they'd assumed she'd do everything from afar if indeed Vera did allow her to inherit. There'd been every possibility the bitter old woman would leave Meadow Farmhouse to an animal charity or something just to spite the closest thing she ever had to a daughter. She was a hard woman, and it was a desperate shame but there was nothing to be done about it now, and it wasn't like the village hadn't tried. Every offer of help made to Vera Cabot had been thrown back in their faces. His mother, he realised, was staring at him, awaiting a response.

'Has she?' He tried to keep his voice light and easy, but it ended up sounding like he had tonsillitis.

Lynne scowled. 'Now don't give me that.'

'Give you what?'

'All that *has she?* nonsense, like it's all fine and dandy.' He cocked his head at the way she lowered her voice and mimicked him. Then her manner softened. 'Are you all right about it?'

'Yeah.' He shrugged. 'Why wouldn't I be?' Adam wondered if the anger he felt was clear on his face. For a moment, he could have been standing at the train station on a freezing January day, wrapping Amelia in a hug, telling her he loved her and that he couldn't wait for her to return. Had she known when she kissed him it would be the last time she'd do it? He wanted to hope not, but the anger inside told him she had. Lynne raised her eyebrows. 'What? Honestly, Mum, I'm a grown man now. Not a teenager.'

'Well she'd better not go showing her face in the village, that's all I can say.'

'She's going to have to at some point. Or maybe she'll prefer to stay away from everyone. Anyway, it was all a long time ago. Try and chill out, okay?' He placed a hand gently on her shoulder. He was doing quite a good job of pretending his body wasn't on fire with anger and resentment. He almost believed it himself.

'I would if she hadn't been looking so … so—'

'So what?' *Ill? Upset? Gorgeous?*

'Like herself.' *What the hell did that mean?* 'Do you know what she said earlier—'

'Earlier? You saw her today?' As soon as he said it, he wished he could take it back. He also wanted to ask again what she looked like but that would mean showing and admitting he cared. Lynne turned away, a little shame-faced and with a tinge of pink on the apples of her cheeks. 'Mum, I know that look.'

'What look? I don't know what you mean.'

'Yes, you do. It's the look you get when you've got leery. When did you see her and what did you say?'

'Well …'

'Mum?' He sounded like a stroppy teenager but could already picture her reaction. She wasn't great at hiding her feelings. She'd been exactly the same after his last girlfriend, Philippa, left him on Valentine's Day the year before. That had sucked big time, but after experiencing such a monumental heartbreak at such a young age he'd learned to take things in his stride. Philippa had moved to a neighbouring village now, but her parents still lived in Meadowbank and his mother had flat-out blanked them after it happened. Adam loved that she cared about him, but she really needed to stop getting so involved in his life.

He'd bounced back from Philippa surprisingly quickly. The humiliation of the way she did it had been the worst thing to deal with. As usual, the village had rallied round. They hadn't taken sides, but as he'd become a single man, the ladies delivered food to keep his spirits up while the men gave a strong pat on the back. The thought of all that support brought a warmth to him, but it quickly faded. 'What did you say to her?'

'Nothing much.' Lynne fiddled with the hair at the back of her head.

'Mum?'

She glanced back at the door. Was she considering making a run for it? 'I heard she was back at Meadow Farmhouse and I … umm …'

She hadn't even finished and already he was hoping the ground would swallow him up. 'Oh, Mum, what did you do?'

'I just mentioned that she should have stayed away and that her coming back now, when she hadn't bothered to see Vera in all these years, was a bit like one of those birds …'

When she let the sentence die, he prompted, knowing she was

stalling. 'What birds?' With any luck she'd called her a bluetit or a swallow or something nice, but judging by the look on her face, she hadn't.

'You know the ones you get in the desert,' she mumbled.

'Which ones?' Trepidation made his limbs heavy. His mum knew exactly which birds she was talking about but was obviously too ashamed of herself to say it out loud.

'The, umm … the ones who pick over carcasses. The big evil-looking things.'

'Vultures?' he squeaked. 'Mum! What did you go and do that for?' Adam couldn't hide the shock from his face.

'I was just a bit cross.'

'A bit?'

Lynne dropped her chin and shuffled about on the spot. 'I might also have mentioned what a mess you were after she left.' The tinge of pink grew stronger and her cheeks were now bright and shining.

'To Amelia? You told her that I—' He took a breath and lowered his voice. 'That I found it hard after she left? Great. That's – wow – that's just awesome. Thanks, Mum.'

'Mr MacMahon had to pick up one of her chickens and put it away for her.' He wasn't quite sure how this was related but the randomness of the remark didn't bother him.

'Mr MacMahon was there? Anyone else?'

More shuffling. *Oh Lord.* 'Can't remember, exactly.'

'I reckon you can, Mum. Come on, out with it.'

'Just Mrs Bostock and Mrs Claribold. And—' She began tidying up again. 'And Arthur.'

Adam took a step backwards so he could look out of the large window above the workbench and see the lambs in the side field, anything to distract himself from the humiliation of his mum's actions. Heat prickled the back of his neck. This was even worse than Philippa dumping him in the pub on Valentine's Day. No one wanted their mum making a public address about their private life. She might as well have stood on the village green with a loudspeaker.

'Sorry,' Lynne said, finally looking at her son. 'I didn't mean to embarrass you.'

Seeing the regret on her face, he held in a sigh and pulled her into a hug. 'That's all right, Mum. Come on, what have you brought me for dinner today?'

'I made you a lovely sausage casserole. I know cooking for one can be a bother. If I hadn't had you to cook for you when your dad left, I'd have lived on beans on toast.'

Whatever his mum had said earlier, she'd always been there for him, and it's not as if Amelia would be around for long. With any luck, he wouldn't even see her. The embarrassment would fade, just as it had last year after Philippa had left. He couldn't even pretend his heart had broken, because after Amelia, nothing yet had come close. Amelia would probably only be there a matter of days to collect any important things and then leave again. Though his heart pulsed with pain, he ignored it. The chances of seeing her were slim and even if he did there was nothing to say.

Adam decided he wouldn't bother telling his mum about the curry he'd put in the slow cooker that morning ready for when he finished work. It would keep until tomorrow and her sausage casseroles were always the best. 'Sounds delicious, Mum. I'm looking forward to it already.'

Chapter 5

Despite her tiredness, Amelia found it hard to sleep that night. Memories of Adam and of Vera kept flooding her brain every time she closed her eyes. Her bed was as comfortable as it ever was and the room felt familiar enough, but she'd forgotten how eerie night-time was in the countryside. An all-encompassing silence swallowed her up, and it magnified every other noise. Even her breathing sounded heavy and loud like she'd been out running. The thatch rustled in the wind and birds called and crowed as she closed her eyes and tried in vain to sleep.

After tossing and turning, she eventually dozed off, only for a strange, frightening noise to wake her with a jolt. Amelia shot upright and shivered in the darkness. What was that? She rubbed an eye with the heel of her hand and strained to hear, turning her ear to the sound. A shaft of moonlight penetrated the curtains and spilled onto her bed. For a second, she'd thought she was back in Paris, safe in her apartment, and with a groan she remembered where she was and shivered in the midnight cold.

More strange noises met her ears, and she cocked her head. What sounded like hundreds of chickens were running around the farmhouse. How many did Vera have? When she'd nipped out at dinner to feed them, she hadn't actually counted them, just thrown down some food that instinctively felt enough. And what were they up to? Were they doing laps? Why were they up at this time of night? A chorus of clucking, squawking and milling mixed with the ruffling of feathers sounded deafeningly loud in the quiet night.

Amelia flopped back down, closing her eyes and rolling over.

The safety and warmth of the bed pulled her back in. Couldn't she just leave the chickens to their own devices? Vera had during the day but never at night. It wasn't safe. There were too many things that could happen to them. They could wander off and get lost, or get eaten by a fox. Amelia grabbed her phone from her bedside table. It was gone two o'clock in the morning.

The last thing she wanted to do right now was chase excited poultry around the farmhouse, but what other option did she have? What if they were running from a fox right now? Maybe that's what they were doing. She sat up straighter, trying to identify if they sounded scared but it was impossible to tell. All the clucking sounded the same. Nothing particular screamed, 'Help! I'm being attacked by *Fantastic Mr Fox*!' They could just as easily have been saying, 'Well isn't this lovely! Where are you off to now?' Mr MacMahon, who seemed to have an affinity for chickens, might be able to tell the difference but she certainly couldn't. If there really was a sharp-toothed hungry fox out there, was she really going to nip into the darkness and scare him off? What with?

Amelia pulled the duvet up around her, grimacing at the cold, but as much as she wanted to stay in bed, her conscience pricked. She couldn't let those poor chickens fend for themselves or wander off. Throwing back the covers, Amelia grabbed her dressing gown and put it on over her silk pyjamas. They were her favourites and worked fine in her Parisian apartment with underfloor heating, but here in rainy England, in the draughty old farmhouse, they weren't quite up to task. 'Stupid,' she cursed herself. She should have brought her trusty snuggly ones. Maybe she'd been in more of a flap when packing than she realised.

With bare feet Amelia padded downstairs. Her ballet pumps were by the front door where she'd kicked them off after saying goodbye to the welcome party, as was an old torch. 'Has this happened before, Vera?' Amelia turned on the torch but paused before opening the front door. How exactly was she going to get them all back inside the chicken run? Looking around, her tired eyes focused on a broom at the back of the kitchen. That would do to poke them with and, hopefully, shepherd them back to relative safety.

The cold wind swept over her as she stepped outside, and her toes froze inside the thin leather of her shoes. The light from the farmhouse spilled over the ground as half a dozen chickens enjoyed a midnight stroll on the muddy ground, stopping to peck here and there as if they were all on a jolly holiday. Perhaps Mr MacMahon was right, and she needed to just man up. They were only chickens after all. Amelia put the torch and broom down and tried to pick one up. The chicken squawked and hopped out of her reach. The second time she tried, it walloped her in the face with its wings.

'Ow!' she screeched, backing away to the broom. 'Fine. Mr MacMahon has Bobby the sheepdog, I've got Bobby the broom.'

She tried a semi-circular motion to shepherd them around the side of the house. The trouble was, that although chickens don't exactly have long legs or huge wingspans, they are surprisingly nippy and when approached by a broom are inclined to either run in the opposite direction you want them to go in, or angrily flap their wings. The one Amelia approached did the latter and she resisted the urge to run back inside.

'Why are your wings so big? It's not like you ever go anywhere.' She stood back for a second. 'And, why do your wings look humongous but chicken wings in restaurants are tiny? Hmm? Answer me that.'

Unsurprisingly, the chicken didn't answer.

'What was that?' Amelia spun on the spot as a horrid rustling sound came from the side of the house. The noise emanated from near the chicken run and with mounting terror she followed it, trying to see if a fox was there.

Goose bumps rose on her skin and she shivered with both cold and fright. Everyone knew what happened when people went outside in the dead of night. They went to have a look at something and boom! Someone grabbed them from behind, dragging them into the undergrowth. She'd watched *Children of the Corn*. All this needed was spooky music. She spun to look at the wood that bordered Meadow Farm and frightened herself even more as the shadows reached out towards her. 'Bugger this,' she muttered gripping the broom tighter.

Something moved in the long grass of the field behind the house. She paused, her heart pounding in her chest. There it was again, a rustling or snuffling like a giant boar searching for scraps of food. Whatever it was it sounded big – huge – enormous, and it was coming towards her. The blood pounded in her ears and she backed away as the long grass parted. She drew in a breath, ready to scream as her eyes searched the gap to find what it was.

Suddenly, she closed her mouth and frowned in confusion. There was nothing there. She watched for a moment longer, imagining a giant creature leaping out and attacking her, but then a small, ridiculously cute hedgehog waddled through a gap at the bottom and Amelia almost fell backwards with relief. She leaned on the broom and a sudden burst of laughter escaped. How ridiculous she was being all because it was night-time. She wouldn't have acted like that in the day, nor as a child when she lived here. The sights and sounds of Meadowbank, day or night, had never frightened her before.

Returning to her quest to round up the chickens, Amelia continued prodding and sweeping with the broom. After more than an hour of toing and froing, she'd managed to secure all but two of the chickens in the run through either inelegantly wrestling them to the ground or poking them up the bum with the broom. The last two, who she'd decided to name Bonnie and Clyde, were proving a little more reticent than the others.

'Right. That's enough,' she said forcefully, but only the wind blustered in response and the two chickens ignored her completely. They were out-and-out flouting the threat of the broom and when she actually made contact with one, giving it a very gentle shove, it stubbornly refused to move and stared at her challengingly with an expression that said, 'What on earth do you think you're doing to my bottom?'

Taking a deep breath and rolling her shoulders back, she lunged at the chicken and swiped with her arms but it hopped out of her way, leaping into the air as if it could fly away, if only it could be bothered. The second attempt resulted in her pulling out a few tail feathers and apologising profusely.

'Oh shit, sorry! Sorry, Bonnie. I didn't mean to do that.'

Finally, she caught Clyde and Bonnie seemed to give up, following along behind. With a sigh, Amelia fastened the chicken house door and folded over the wire that had come loose, hoping it would hold until morning. A piece of wood nearby must have been used to prop it up and Amelia angled it so it wouldn't tumble again.

Circling around to the front door, she trudged inside. Amelia wiggled her toes to bring them back to life. They were so frozen she wasn't sure they'd bend enough for her to climb the stairs. Thank God she didn't have to do things like this in Paris. She thought of her apartment and what she'd be up to the next day if only she were there.

After a moment, her circulation returned and once in her room she put on a pair of socks before she climbed into bed.

'I hope I don't have to do that every night.'

In the darkness and cold, her mind raced with thoughts of Vera and Adam – even Lynne's words rumbled around her head. With the thick duvet wrapped around her like a cocoon, Amelia squeezed her eyes shut and pictured her apartment in Paris, imagining herself in her soft comfortable bed. It wouldn't be long and she'd be back, she told herself. It wouldn't be long at all.

***

Amelia awoke eager to begin redecorating the farmhouse and bringing it back to life. Of course, she'd have to clear it and work room by room, but the sooner she got started, the sooner she'd be home and there was a lot to do before the estate agent came. She didn't want to have to put him off or delay her plans. Last night's jaunt with the chickens wasn't exactly how she'd imagined her first night back, and though she felt tired this morning, she knew the best thing to do was to plough on and not stay in bed for another five minutes.

Dressing in her old, comfortable jeans and a warm jumper, she made her way downstairs. Seeing it with fresh eyes, and without the shock of yesterday, Amelia could already picture the place completely renovated. The walls should be plain white because the dark timber beams gave enough accents of colour. The old sofa could be hidden under thick woollen blankets and scatter cushions in pastel spring shades to create a feeling of cosiness. And on the old wooden table in the kitchen, an enamel jug of flowers would take centre stage. If Vera didn't have one, she'd be able to find one pretty easily. All the kitchen units needed was repainting and the stone floor would shine fine after a good scrub.

After a fortifying cup of tea and some toast, courtesy of Mrs Bostock's wicker basket that had contained a loaf of delicious freshly baked bread, Amelia talked to herself as she set to work.

'Right, time to get on.'

Her plan was to begin in the living room. It was by far the darkest room in the house and she wanted to see how much lighter it would look if she cleared it of all the rubbish. First though, she had to organise a glazer to fix the broken windows. After searching online, she found one based in the larger town nearby and booked him to come out in a few days. That was one job ticked off her list already.

The living room had two large windows, one on the front wall facing out over the yard and driveway down which the welcoming party had marched only yesterday. The other window on the side of the house had views out over the fields that belonged to Meadow Farm. They weren't farmed anymore and were nothing more than grassy fields, though they were full of pretty wildflowers. Amelia remembered Vera talking about her younger days when all the fields would be used for something.

For a moment, Amelia wondered what it would be like to tend your own vegetable patch as Vera had, and pull up carrots, potatoes and onions then come inside and make a dinner fresh from the garden. It was an appealing thought in some ways; simple, uncomplicated, harking back to older times. She shook the thought away. It would probably get boring pretty quickly, even if her cooking skills would improve.

Dust sprung from the thin curtains as she pulled them back, the motes glinting in the spring sunshine that filled the room. As Amelia began to sort through Vera's possessions, she noticed that her guardian had never been one for trinkets or sentimentally collecting the things other old ladies did, but she had kept a random assortment of crap that she could only have thought would come in useful one day. Things like old newspapers and a stack of empty cardboard boxes that reached as high as the old faded floral sofa. Amelia took one and began to fill it with everything she didn't intend to keep. Starting with the large bureau in the corner, Amelia methodically went through the contents.

'What was the point of this, Vera?' she asked the air, holding up a biscuit tin filled with buttons. No two buttons were the same, so they weren't really useful for anything and as far as Amelia remembered, Vera had never darned. It went into one of the cardboard boxes.

After clearing the bureau, Amelia moved on to the bookshelf in the corner. The bottom half had a cupboard and the top half was shelved, though there weren't many books and the ones with creased spines were psychological thrillers; a genre she hadn't expected her great-aunt to read. Amelia sat on the dusty rug and opened the cupboard door. A heap of papers fell out spilling everywhere and Amelia paused, her arms in the air, helplessly watching the cascade of detritus. She'd never have expected it of her great-aunt who she always remembered as being fastidious.

Slowly, she began to sort through the mess. Most were bank statements and other regular post. Though there were more gardening magazines than she'd expected given the state of the place. One thing that seemed really odd was that there were no personal letters to or from anyone and Amelia was struck again by how isolated Vera had made herself.

'You must have been lonely, Vera. No matter what you said, how could you not be?'

By the time Amelia had worked on the living room, the sheer amount of dust on her clothes was incredible. Even her hair felt dry and dirty when she ran her hands through it, but at least the heating and hot water worked so she could have a long, hot bath when she'd finished. Right now, Amelia ached to sink into a bath full of hot water scented with her calming bath oil and allow the heat to relax and unwind her knotted muscles. It would be bliss, but there was still so much to do first.

Sadness filled Amelia that there was nothing truly personal in the room. It was clear someone had lived here for a long time, but there was nothing to tell who Vera really was. There were no porcelain shepherdesses or ornaments to show the things she'd liked. Instead, there were only piles of decade-old newspapers for the fire and drawers of faded utility bills with *paid* written on them in Vera's spidery hand. Nothing to show it was a home rather than just a house. Considering the age of the house it must have had some history.

Vera had told her that Meadow Farmhouse was one of the oldest farms in the area. The only other building supposed to be as old as Meadow Farmhouse was a large manor house not too far away, called Highfield. It sat in the highest position overlooking everything else but had never been closely connected with the village as far as Amelia could remember. She supposed once upon a time it would have been staffed by local people, but those days were long gone.

Most buyers loved the history of a house. She herself did, adoring the architecture and monuments around every corner of Paris. But there wasn't any history among Vera's possessions, only rubbish. Looking around it was, quite frankly, unbelievable that Vera had accumulated so much useless stuff and crammed it into every nook and cranny of the room. And yet, the place still felt bare.

Amelia's phone rang from where she'd left it on the kitchen table and she hurried over to answer it.

'*Bonjour!*' Océanè said cheerily. 'How is your aunt's house?'

Where to begin? 'It's an absolute state,' she said with a half laugh, though sadness crept underneath it. 'I can't believe Vera let it get this bad. I'm going to be here at least three weeks while I get everything sorted out.'

'That sounds ...' Océanè searched for a phrase and Amelia tried to help her out.

'A big job?'

'*Oui*, but I was going to say dull, yes? Boring.'

'Oh.' Amelia frowned at the unexpected reply. So far returning to Meadowbank and being in the farmhouse had been far from boring. The change of routine was disconcerting. Her life in Paris was busy but she often did the same things over again. Dinner dates with clients, drinks with friends or people Océanè said she must meet. How strange she hadn't realised until now. 'How are you?' she asked, eager to move on.

'Urgh, Émile wants us to go and see his parents again.'

Océanè had not been impressed by Émile's family who lived in a small village outside Paris. Though Émile was kind and she could see his mother being so too, Océanè had said repeatedly that the trips were tedious and unexciting. When Océanè had finished listing all the reasons the visit was a bad idea, she asked, 'How was your first night in the spooky ghost house?'

Amelia paced while she told her about the welcome party and the chickens in the night. Océanè giggled. 'It's not funny,' Amelia said, laughing too. 'It was the middle of the night and I was terrified. Do you know how many noises there are in the countryside? Things rustle and creak and chirrup and snuffle.'

'I can just see your face! It is the thought of you in your dressing gown, running after chickens. For all you try, you are not so sophisticated, eh?'

Amelia's laugh faded, unsure how to react. When they spoke, she often felt that she was at a disadvantage to the chic Frenchwoman who sometimes sneered at her very English friend.

Outside, the strong breeze pushed along the dull white clouds, herding them together ready for rain. If she listened intently, the bleating of lambs and sheep from nearby fields carried on the air. She hadn't heard it in so long and had forgotten how close to nature she had once been. Nowadays, her ears were full of the sounds of traffic, heavy French accents and the hum of the Metro.

'You must hurry back,' Océanè said. 'Before your nose turns red like all these Englishwomen who live in the country.'

'No, they don't.' Whether it was the physical distance between them or something else, Amelia found a courage she hadn't had before.

'They do. They have thread-veined cheeks and wrinkled skin. Men like Bastien will not want you if you come back looking like that.' Absent-mindedly, Amelia touched her nose. It had turned red from cold last night, but that had faded by the time she'd got up. 'You must hurry back. I miss our café dates.'

With a sigh, Amelia bid her friend goodbye. Being surrounded by mess made her wish she was back in Paris right now. Drinking café crème and eating delicious food. That reminded her, she needed to walk into the village and get some more supplies. It would be good to clear her head and get some fresh air. She wouldn't go far. It was probably best, after Lynne's words, that she kept away from everyone in case they felt the same. Though she was a little interested to know what the village was really like now. Would it feel different because she was older? Seeing as it had a deli and goodness knows what other shops lurking in the small lanes off the green, some things had clearly changed, but her curiosity would have to wait until she'd got through more of this room first.

'How could you live like this?' Amelia asked the air again, staring around her at the mess. Even after all these years she could hear Vera's terse response.

'How I live is nothing to do with you.'

The thick wooden mantelpiece over the log fire held the same photographs that Amelia remembered from her childhood, and these were the only personal items on display. From a gold-plated frame spotted with black, Amelia's grandmother and Vera's sister, who had died before Amelia arrived, smiled out. Vera's mother and father on their wedding day posed stiffly in another. Though the arrangement was formal, they looked adoringly at each other, and it raised the question: how had Vera ended up alone when she'd been surrounded by love? To her shame, Amelia didn't know. Great-Aunt Vera had just been Great-Aunt Vera; the indignant, guarded woman who had provided a house for her to live in but had never been affectionate. Amelia had never considered the events of her great-aunt's life before.

Most painful of all, there were no pictures of Amelia anywhere. None of her with her class at school, no pictures of her and Vera at the spring, summer or Christmas fairs held in the village. There was simply no evidence she'd ever existed here. Adam's house had been littered with pictures of him and his mum, and even a few with his dad before he'd left. That familiar feeling of being insignificant – of being nothing more than a burden – welled up inside and Amelia's throat tightened. She reminded herself of all that she'd achieved through hard work and dedication. Of her apartment and life in Paris. She'd made something of herself.

Thinking of Adam, would Lynne have told him that she was

back? Would he even want to see her? Probably not if Lynne's words were anything to go by. Had she really hurt him that much? Amelia closed her eyes for a second, trying to swim in the sea of emotions that threatened to drown her.

'This will all soon be over,' she told herself, taking slow deep breaths.

The few paintings on the walls were quite pretty, she mused, trying to cheer herself up. Vera had painted a watercolour of Meadow Farmhouse before it began to fall apart, and she'd captured the colours perfectly. The farmhouse was bathed in a golden glow from either sunrise or sunset, Amelia couldn't quite tell. The bright green of the ivy climbing up contrasted with the dark thatched roof and the faint yellow of the walls. Another was of the coppice that separated Meadow Farm from the grounds of Highfield. Somehow Vera had depicted the way the light dotted through the leaves shining onto the floor of the clearing. Spots of light lit the earthy, leaf-covered ground and thick ancient tree trunks. That was where she and Adam had played as children. It was also where they'd had their first kiss one summer's evening.

She'd been fifteen and he sixteen, both shy and restrained. A smile pulled at her lips as she remembered it and warmed her against the cold of Vera's loneliness. It had been one of the hottest days of the year and she'd worn her bikini top and denim shorts. They'd cooled down by spraying each other with the hosepipe and then gone for a walk into the shade of the woods. As they sat below a huge tree, sheltering under a dense canopy of green, he had turned to her and said, 'I really like you, Amelia.'

'I like you too,' she'd replied, hoping he meant it in *that* way, but too scared to say it first.

'No, I *like* you, like you.'

When he'd leaned over and kissed her gently, his lips barely brushing her own, she'd been filled with euphoria. So chaste. So pure. For a moment at least. And then they'd made out like teenagers do. Now, in the cold, gloomy living room, she put a hand on her stomach to stem the intense fluttery feeling. It was silly that her memories were having such an effect on her. Adam had always lived in her dreams, often when she wasn't expecting it, but being back was intensifying her reactions.

The easel in the corner of the room caught her attention and she moved to it, examining the picture still leaning against it. Beside it sat a box full of watercolours and brushes and as she knelt to study them, her eyes fell on the black pin mould climbing the corner of the room. Another repair to add to the list. She stood back up, unsure what to do with the art box. The colours in the painting were remarkable, and she hoped the hobby had brought Vera some enjoyment. Amelia's fingers traced the edge of the canvas. Meadow Farmhouse still seemed to be the only love in Vera's life, but it didn't feel right to throw out something like this. Maybe she could take one back to Paris and hang it in the flat? Maybe Adam would like one too? Especially as he'd stuck around and, she supposed, continued to see and talk to Vera.

After a loud rumble drew her eyes down to her stomach, Amelia stopped and checked the large L-shaped kitchen units for supplies. The first door she opened let loose a waterfall of pots and pans.

'Christ, Vera. Have you booby-trapped the place? That only just missed my toe.'

As her search for food continued, the drawers and cupboards of the kitchen were the same as the living room: full of items that should have been thrown out. Saucepans with missing handles, broken wooden spoons and cracked bowls had all been kept for no discernible reason. Thanks to her time trawling through Parisian flea markets, Amelia identified some tarnished antique silver cutlery that she'd keep and clean up, but everything else was simply tatty and old. As she opened a high cupboard, the door came completely off in her hand and she only just managed to keep hold of it as cereal boxes fell onto her head.

'Oh, for goodness' sake, Vera!'

Of course, she didn't get hit by fluffy Sugar Puffs or Rice

Krispies, it was brick-like Weetabix that bounced off her skull. Something that would definitely leave a lump. A low growl escaped from her mouth and she resisted the urge to cry.

Thankfully, there were some food staples like pasta, rice and tinned tomatoes, so she wouldn't have to buy too much at the shop, but everything fresh was out of date.

By the time she'd finished clearing the overflowing cupboards enough to close them, there was a stack of pots and pans to go to charity and another of things to be taken to the local tip. Taking a rest at the kitchen table, Amelia gazed around her. The two rooms looked even worse than before and she'd now discovered that as well as cupboard doors that needed fixing, the bathroom door was so warped that if you managed to close it, it wasn't certain you'd get it open again. She desperately needed a carpenter.

'How have I managed to make the place look even worse?' Amelia asked, slumping into her chair. As she huffed out a breath, she stared at the enormous mess and went to make a cup of tea. A flyer half stuck to the kitchen counter caught her eye. It was for the spring fair. Perhaps she could donate some of the unbroken things to that? She didn't need all these pots and pans and couldn't exactly sell the place with them. She needed to clear everything as quickly as possible and dress the house so it showed prospective buyers the type of lifestyle they'd have if they lived there. Little touches like some designer wellington boots by the door, just dirty enough to give the impression of country walks, and old-fashioned pots and mixing bowls to give a homely feel. She really liked that idea actually, and in a way, Amelia knew she was creating the type of country home she'd always hoped to have as a child. All the makings were here; she just needed to change the atmosphere.

It was March now and the spring fair wasn't until the third of April – Easter Saturday – so there was plenty of time to get everything sorted in the farmhouse and find out who to give the donations to. A telephone number for the festival committee had been printed on the bottom. Maybe she'd give them a call later when she'd plucked up enough courage. If they were anything like Lynne Noble, they might not accept anything from her at all. But the dread caused by that was nothing compared to Amelia's next job. The one she knew she had to do now before her nerve failed her altogether: checking on Great-Aunt Vera's room.

Chapter 6

Teetering on the threshold of the doorway, it took a moment for Amelia to summon enough courage to step inside. Vera had always been adamant that her room was a no-go area from the very first moment she'd arrived.

'My bedroom is entirely off limits, do you understand?' Amelia shuddered at the memory.

Walking in now, with the bare floorboards covered in rugs, it was like entering a forbidden palace. One of the boards creaked underfoot and Amelia hoped all these scrapes and moans wouldn't put off potential buyers. She'd grown used to them over the years she'd been here and already had a feeling she'd be able to ignore them tonight.

A large pine bed dominated the centre of the room and over the other side of it Amelia could see the rocking horse she had loved as a child.

'Huh. I can't believe you've still got this, Vera.'

She'd always assumed her great-aunt had thrown it away as soon as she'd outgrown it and finding it now was more than a little surreal. Given that downstairs was so empty, Amelia had expected the same of Vera's room and it sent a sting into her heart to think Vera had kept it or even thought to do so.

In the corner, under a window that faced the front of the house, was a dressing table complete with large mirror and old-fashioned, possibly antique, three-piece vanity set. The bright sunlight spilling in reflected off the upturned hand mirror while the enamel flower design on the spine of the comb sparkled. The hairbrush faced upwards, and as Amelia went to it, she could see some of Vera's pale white hairs caught in the soft, fine brushes. Overcome by a potent sense of loss and guilt at their parting, the back of Amelia's nose stung and tears sprang forth.

'Oh, Vera,' she murmured to herself. 'Why did you have to be so difficult to be around? Things could have been so much better—' The words died as grief overtook her.

She'd never felt before the enormity of how different things could have been if only Vera hadn't hated having her around. Over the years, there had been odd occasions where they'd laughed together or worked side by side in the kitchen, mainly as Amelia had grown and become more independent. Not many, but a few. How odd that such strange things like the hairbrush were setting her off now.

Amelia hadn't anticipated feeling any of the emotions currently coursing through her, least of all such a level of loss and sadness. It was almost as if the house itself was soaked with Vera's grief as well as her own, and it filled the air around her. Over her years in Paris she had shielded herself from thinking about it all by keeping busy, but now, unnamed emotions were surging through her, burying her under a weight of grief and the realisation of what could have been, if Vera had only let her in.

Desperate to move away from her feelings, Amelia dried her eyes and went to the wardrobe, casting open the doors.

'Get a grip,' she told herself, wiping her cheek. 'There's work to be done.'

Vera had never cared about fashion and, as Amelia had expected, most of the space was filled with thick corduroy trousers and jumpers, the clothes she most remembered her wearing. But then a faded white dress caught Amelia's eye and she pushed the other coat hangers away.

'What's this then, Vera? You once boasted you didn't own any dresses. What's this gorgeous thing hiding at the back of your wardrobe?'

Amelia reached a hand to the hanger, the delicate fabric soft beneath her fingers. She pulled it out and her eyes roved over the exquisite lace adorning the high neck, down the long, sheer sleeves and over the straight floor-length skirt. With a gasp, she realised what it was.

A wedding dress. Vera's mother's wedding dress.

She recognised it from the picture of Vera's mother and father downstairs on the mantelpiece. Vera had never been married and more than once had bitterly described how the village thought her the spinster of the parish. Amelia had never had any idea that she'd kept such a thing and found it surprisingly sentimental.

Amelia stood back. This was part of her heritage and part of her family history. Having lost her parents so young, it was a history she'd never really considered before. Though Vera's mother was her great-grandmother, Amelia had no knowledge of her. She'd died before Amelia came to Meadowbank and, ever tight-lipped, Vera never spoke of her. But it felt wrong to just cast it aside. The fabric was so delicate it might fall apart if she dared shake out the creases. Taking the very ends of the skirt in her fingers, she examined the rips and tears in the pale white material wondering how on earth they'd got there.

'You poor thing,' she whispered to the dress, but in the silence of the room her words echoed around her. 'You clearly haven't been cared for properly, have you?'

It wasn't really Vera's fault. She wasn't one for dresses, or make-up, or even moisturiser. She'd even told Amelia not to be so vain when she was eleven and trying it all for the first time.

'You should have been protected from the elements,' Amelia declared. Though it seemed unusual for that many rips and tears to split the fabric.

She'd have to get a clothes bag, so it wasn't damaged any further. How sad that it had ended up in such a state. After the paintings and now this, there were more things to keep than she'd expected. Would there be room in her small Paris flat that already overflowed with possessions? None of them carried the same sentimental value as this. Confused at finding such an object, Amelia decided to put off her trip to the village a little longer and continue to search Vera's room.

At the base of the bed sat an old wooden trunk with a curved lid. Amelia had once played pirates with Adam shortly after making friends and they'd pretended it was a treasure chest. When Vera had heard them running about upstairs in the general area of her bedroom, she'd charged up, shouting furiously at them for going into her room. Amelia hadn't been there a year yet and remembered the shock of it as Vera's voice thundered around the old house, bouncing off the walls.

Amelia didn't really remember her parents shouting at her. As she'd grown older, she'd found it harder and harder to remember them at all. Now, it was more like a dream that she'd ever lived anywhere else. She'd been given photographs of her parents and Vera had passed on all her mother's jewellery – she was wearing a piece now – but it was no substitute. Amelia gazed at the silver ring on her finger, and though she had no particular memory of her mother wearing it, it was still comforting to know that she had.

Amelia tried to shake the feeling that she was doing something wrong by looking inside the trunk and almost checked over her shoulder before lifting the lid. The hinges squeaked and she leaned over to see inside. At first, all Amelia could see were blankets, but after taking them out and laying them on the floor she spotted a small polished wooden jewellery box. It must have belonged to Vera's mother as Vera never wore any jewellery. Reaching in, Amelia took it out and gently lifted the lid. Nestled into the red velvet lining were some beautiful cameo necklaces and jewelled brooches. How odd that Vera had kept such things.

'What other secrets have you got, Vera?' she whispered aloud.

Amelia moved to Vera's bed, leaning down to open the bedside cabinet. The top of it was covered in a lacy cloth marked with tea stains and another pang of guilt hit her that it was too late to apologise that they had argued so fiercely before she left. She opened the cupboard door expecting to find nothing more than a book or perhaps a notepad, but the only thing in the empty cupboard took her breath away.

A large oval gold locket sat in an open wooden box. The gold had tarnished with age, but the carved filigree pattern caught the light from the window. Amelia sat cross-legged on the floor in front of it, holding it carefully in her hands. It was an exquisite piece. Definitely antique, though she didn't know how old exactly. The word *beautiful* escaped her mouth before she could stop it. She ran her finger over the pattern, her brow furrowing as she tried to remember if she'd ever seen it before.

A vague recollection came to mind, the picture focusing in her mind as she replayed the memory. Amelia had come upstairs looking for Vera to find her sitting at her dressing table, holding something that could very well have been the locket. Yes, it was. She remembered the chain looping over her fingers. She'd called out to her and Vera's head had spun, an angry scowl on her face.

'What do you want?'

Amelia couldn't remember now why she'd gone upstairs, but she remembered asking what it was she was holding.

'None of your business and don't go prying into people's private things. It's wrong. This village might think everything is their business, but it's not. Do you understand?'

All Amelia could remember was backing away, apologising. The rest of the memory faded, and Amelia was sure that was the last time she'd seen or indeed heard about the locket. With care, she ran her thumb down the side, finding the clasp, and after applying a little pressure, it opened.

On one side was a picture of a baby in a large, old-fashioned christening gown and on the other was a handsome man in army uniform. He had a square, clean-shaven jaw and a rigid straight back. In the sepia image it was impossible to see the colour of his hair and eyes though the youthful face showed he was young. Perhaps it was the light reflecting off the small glass cover, but

Amelia had the feeling that fear was present behind his stern expression. There was something in the dullness of his gaze. A strange tightness at the corners.

Though she studied the picture, there was no sign of who this man was, and Amelia was certain Vera had never mentioned a family member being in the army. She remembered Vera saying that her own father hadn't had to fight in the Second World War because as a farmer he was in a reserved occupation. Amelia had once done a project on her family history at school and it was one of the only times Vera had been forthcoming with any information, though she only spoke about her father and mother and refused to mention anything else. Knowing how private she was, it hadn't seemed odd at the time. Vera hadn't produced the locket then. Amelia was sure she would have remembered something so special and beautiful.

'Who are you?' Amelia asked, hoping somehow the house would answer.

And who was he to Vera and her family that she'd kept this? Had she known him or had it belonged to a different member of her family? A family she never enjoyed talking about. It seemed Meadow Farmhouse, like other old places, had secrets of its own. A spark of excitement flickered into life under the layer of sadness that had settled on Amelia since her return. Could she find out who this man was? Perhaps there was something else here in Vera's room that could help? Or maybe she'd find some information somewhere else in the house?

Even though the only memory attached to the locket wasn't a pleasant one, the thought of giving it away was unthinkable. It was one of the only tangible reminders she had of her time here. This, the paintings, and the wedding dress were her replacements for the happy memories most people had.

Unsure what else to do with the beautiful piece of jewellery, and feeling light-headed with emotion, Amelia closed the locket and placed it carefully back in the bedside cabinet. But as she moved away, her steps were drawn back to it and she took it out again and examined the picture inside.

The emotions it had stirred made it impossible to place it back in a dark, empty cupboard. It felt like neglecting a child – someone you had responsibility for. She caressed the cool metal, running the chain through her fingers and it somehow felt like a link to Vera. A positive connection in the gloom of their past. Could she wear it? Would Vera hate it if she did? She'd certainly not wanted her to know about it when she was alive, but she was gone now and the question of the who the man was had already taken hold of Amelia's mind.

Holding it in her hands, it seemed that, of all the items left in the house, this was the one possession she had of Vera's that had truly meant something to her and because of that it meant something to Amelia too. Coming back to Meadow Farmhouse, Amelia realised she didn't want to just say goodbye to Vera. She wanted to understand her too.

In some way, it felt gaining an understanding of her might make up for the way they had parted and lift the burden of guilt she carried before saying goodbye to the farmhouse one final time. Mr Morris had said Vera left a detailed will so she must have known she'd left Amelia the locket. Amelia tentatively placed the long chain over her head, careful to tuck it under her jumper. The face of the man inside, flooded with repressed fear, had imprinted on her brain. She had to find out who he was. After all, if she sold Meadow Farmhouse, she'd never get the chance again. Or should that be *when* she sold Meadow Farmhouse?

Amelia glanced at her watch. Another hour had gone by already. Staring at the remainder of the room, there didn't seem to be anything more to search through, and with her emotions spent she stood up, taking a deep controlled breath. Swallowing down her apprehension, she braced herself for her last nerve-racking task of the day: a trip to the village and the kind-hearted but gruelling questioning of the Meadowbank villagers.

Chapter 7

'Time for a walk,' Amelia declared, tutting as she slipped her feet into her new yellow flower-patterned wellington boots. She barely spoke to herself in Paris, but now she was back this disconcerting habit needed addressing. She placed the strap of her bag over her chest and checked she had cash in her wallet. Would the village shop take cards? She wrapped her large scarf around her neck, took the keys and closed the house.

Time was of the essence after all. She hadn't made quite as much progress on the house as she'd hoped and wanted to get back and see what else she could discover about this locket. Surely there must be some more family photographs or letters somewhere.

With the afternoon sun paling and the breeze growing stronger, creeping inside the fabric of her blazer, Amelia hurried on. The air smelled different here in the country: fresher, earthier. She passed through the gap in the evergreens and found the path – a small dirt track trodden into the greenery. Here and there, where the ground was still rain-soaked, the smell of mud filled her nose so pungently she could almost taste it. Shaded by the trees it was cooler, but the sun came through at every opportunity, highlighting the spring flowers bursting open. On the edge of the path, Amelia ran her hand over waist-high satiny petals, enjoying the feel of them on her skin.

With a pang, she recalled the parks and gardens of Paris with their structured flowerbeds and distinctive design. The peace they gave was somehow different to here. Maybe because it punctuated such a volume of noise, offering respite from the busy world around it.

Everywhere she looked were varying shades of verdant green, from the leaves on the trees high above her, to the dark ivy climbing up the trunks, and the tufts of grass edging the path at her feet. Soon the trees were left behind, and she stepped onto a country lane that opened up before her. The side of her foot scraped a small milestone, but the distance and locations had been worn away by time. Over the fields on either side, flocks of birds danced and soared on the breeze. A resonant sense of calm surrounded her, and the world seemed to exist in a special kind of harmony. The land was farmed according to the seasons, the birds lived by nature's timing.

After such an emotional day, Amelia's shoulders eased down, and a sense of peace relaxed her tightened muscles. She took a breath of the fresh spring air, allowing it to blow the dust from her skin. She chastised herself for betraying her beloved Paris.

Spring Farm, Mr MacMahon's place, appeared on her right. His farmhouse was a lot like Meadow Farmhouse but in a much better state. Tubs of flowers lined the driveway and Amelia took a quick snap on her phone, a reminder to copy it. Not only did it look lovely, but it would be a nice touch when she came to sell the place. She continued and her pace sped up as she passed Adam's old farm, not wanting to run into him. She wasn't prepared for that yet and with her emotions heightened, there was no telling how she'd react. She might burst into tears at seeing him like a complete idiot, or he might mention the Facebook fiasco and then she'd have to hide behind a tree until the embarrassment wore off.

Continuing down the lane without a car in sight, she stubbed her toe on a lump in the road. The roots of a huge ancient tree reached out, pushing the tarmac up. It seemed nothing could keep nature at bay in Meadowbank. You either worked with it, or against it and if you chose against it, it would get its own back. The road wound sharply to the left and she followed it, staring at the acres of fields around her when with a painful thud she collided with something or someone rather tall.

'Ow!' she proclaimed, then straightened up rubbing her head and laughing in embarrassment. 'I'm sorry. I wasn't looking where I was going.'

Her words floated away on the fresh spring air as she immediately recognised exactly who it was, and from the frown on his face it was obvious he'd realised who she was too. His expression had changed from a relaxed grin that raised his cheeks to something far more irritated. His mouth formed a thin line, and the brightness of his brown eyes dulled. A tingle of shame ran down the back of her neck but competing with it was an instant, electrifying attraction. The Facebook photo had nothing on the real thing.

Adam's face and frame had filled out as he'd grown from a boy to a man, and his arms and legs had become muscular and toned. She remembered the flat abs from the photo and heat built in her chest. Christ he was impressive. As she'd noticed when she'd seen the photo, his hair had deepened in colour to a burnt red rather than the brighter, more orange tone it had been at school. Amelia's heart thudded like someone was pounding on her back. Sexy, in a rugged, unpolished way, he was the exact opposite of the Parisian men she normally dealt with. Men like Bastien who wanted cashmere rugs to match their cashmere coats. The scar on his lip had faded but there was still a silver mark visible and Amelia's breath caught once more. Heck, that was sexy. He'd changed so much and yet, in his eyes, she could still see who he was or at least, who he had been.

'Adam!' she exclaimed, dropping her hand from the top of her forehead.

For a moment he didn't speak, staring at her before dipping his eyes to his shoes. 'Amelia.' She couldn't tell if he'd said her name as a statement or a question.

'Hi. How – how are you?'

'Fine. Yeah. Great.' Adam thrust his hands in his pockets and rocked on his heels. 'All fine.' Another awkward pause. 'You?'

'Fine,' she replied, knowing how ridiculously English their encounter sounded. She wondered how many times either of them would say *fine* in this excruciating moment. She'd always wondered what it would be like to see him again but hadn't expected her body to react in such a profound way. Her heart was thudding and her insides had knotted.

'So …' Adam glanced around as if he couldn't wait to get away and Amelia searched for something to say.

'It's nice to see you.'

His eyebrows quirked. Was he surprised that she felt that way? 'Right. Yeah. You too.' Adam checked his watch.

Amelia tried again to get something out of him. 'It's been a long time.'

'Yeah. Sorry, but I have to get on. Stuff to do. Loads of … bits and bobs.'

And before she could say any more, he walked away back towards Willow Farm. Was it anger that radiated from him with such a burning intensity? Or was it hurt? Whatever it was, she could only assume it felt similar to stepping onto the surface of the sun as her body burned with the after-effects. Guilt sprang through every nerve as she watched him go. She deserved it and he had every right to be angry with her. She'd never meant to hurt him, especially as much as Lynne had said she had. She'd always assumed he'd have forgotten her quickly and moved on with his life. It was surprising her now to learn how hurt he'd been.

For a time, she thought about going after him, but what could she say that would make it right? That wouldn't make matters worse or more painful for them both? With no other choice, she turned on her heel and headed towards the village. At least it was done now. She'd seen him and survived. With any luck, the ache in her heart would begin to fade because she knew for sure there was no way back. He'd made that abundantly clear.

Finally, Amelia emerged at the edge of Meadowbank proper and continued towards the green. Cottages now lined either side of the narrow lane, picture-perfect with small flint-stone walls or picket fences marking front gardens. Nearly all were well tended and those that were a little untidier gave the impression of wild-flower meadows growing free.

Meadowbank had always looked like something from a post-card, and it had only ever increased Amelia's feeling of not fitting in. The village was made up of happy families and helpful neigh-bours, none of whom had been like her and her dysfunctional 'family' of one crazy great-aunt who sneered and snarled at passing strangers and a grief-stricken orphan.

'Well, look who it is.' An older woman stopped opposite Amelia, but Amelia didn't recognise her, her mind still dwelling on the encounter with Adam. 'Amelia Williams. My word, look at you now. So grown up.'

'Th – thank you,' she stammered, fearing a repeat of yesterday.

The woman leaned her grey head in closer. 'Don't remember me, do you?'

Amelia tried once more but couldn't place her. Drawing on her tact, she said, 'I'm afraid I don't. Sorry. It's been a long time since I've been here.'

'That it has. And no offence taken, dear. I'm Mrs Edwards. I taught piano at your school for years, though you weren't one of my students. But I remember you. Poor thing. I remember the day you arrived.' Amelia stiffened. Please don't let her have to listen to this again. After the emotions of yesterday's arrival, of the locket now pressing against her skin and the shock of seeing Adam, she wasn't sure she could cope with another reference to her parents and tried to find the words to stop her. 'So quiet you were, all except for your tears and sobs, but look at you now. Pretty as a picture.'

'Th – thank you.' In the cool air, Amelia stammered and her skin prickled. Any sense of space vanished, and the houses loomed in her peripheral vision.

'Have you seen Adam Noble yet? You two were thick as thieves and he's still here. He didn't leave.'

Was it her imagination, or had Mrs Edwards stressed the *he*? Yet she was grateful for the change of subject. 'Yes, I have. Well, just briefly in the lane.'

'We were sorry to hear about Vera. I can't pretend she was a well-loved woman, but I'm sure she was dear to you in her way. And after losing your parents at such a young age. So hard for you.'

Amelia had to get away as anxiety prickled her skin like a thousand tiny needles.

'Yes – umm—' She couldn't have felt more awkward if she'd wandered into town naked. As the expression of the man inside the locket once more fluttered through her brain, a part of her wanted to take the chance to ask about him, but as Mrs Edwards continued to speak of Amelia's anguish, she knew she couldn't listen to any more. 'It's lovely to see you, Mrs Edwards. I really must get some shopping and head back to Meadow Farmhouse.'

'Of course. I'm sure there's lots you need to do. You get on then, dear. Toodle-oo.'

The village shop came into view at the end of the lane and Amelia crossed to it. Old-fashioned wicker baskets lined the outside and as she drew closer, she saw bright green apples, earthy-covered potatoes fresh from the ground and round juicy tomatoes. They were so appealing, like the fruit and vegetables in the farmers' markets in Paris. Amelia let out a heavy sigh. How desperately she wanted the safety of the city and, anxious to escape the feeling, she darted for the door. As she entered, her shin collided with the front of a buggy. She really needed to stop thinking so much and start paying attention to where she was going.

'I'm so sorry. I've done it again,' she said, holding up her hand in apology for a second time that day.

'Again?' came a pleasant younger voice than she'd heard recently. 'Oh dear. Sounds like you're having quite a day.'

Amelia glanced down at the buggy and the rosy-cheeked girl who seemed put out that her biscuit had been knocked from her hand. She was just on the verge of crying when the mum leaned down and pulled it from under her pudgy thigh.

'There you go, darling.' Her voice was warm and soft like honey and she glanced up at Amelia.

'I'm really sorry. I wasn't looking where I was going. Is she okay?'

The young lady's eyes flitted over Amelia's shoulder and she followed her glance. Mrs Edwards was still there talking to a gentleman, but she nodded her head in Amelia's direction and Amelia knew she was being talked about.

'Ah,' the woman in front of her said knowingly. 'Mrs Edwards?'

'Yes.' A wry grin pulled at Amelia's mouth.

'She can be quite direct sometimes, can't she? I'm not surprised you were scarpering away as quickly as possible.'

'I'm sure she meant well but it just—' *Touched a nerve? Hurt like hell?* She couldn't bring herself to say either. 'I never took her piano lessons, but I remember hearing her teach. It was terrifying.'

Amelia's eyes roved over the woman who was about the same age as her. She wore a short sky-blue jacket over a white T-shirt and skinny jeans. She had a slightly rounded tummy from the little one, who Amelia guessed at being around eighteen months old. Her dark blonde hair hung in waves around her face and she wore barely any make-up. With such lovely peachy skin, she didn't really need to. The toddler, who was dressed as cutely as her mum, began gurgling and talking to her biscuit.

'Are you new to the village?' the young woman asked. 'I don't think I've seen you before.'

'Not exactly. I used to live here a long time ago, but I've had to come back.'

Her smooth brow creased a little as she thought. 'Sorry if this sounds nosy but are you Amelia Williams?'

Amelia shifted from one foot to another, some of her ease vanishing. She couldn't bear another reminder of her parents' deaths. 'Yes, I am.'

'I've heard all about you already but nothing bad, I promise.' With Adam's reaction just now and Lynne's greeting the other day Amelia found that hard to believe. She relied on her usual defence of cracking a joke.

'I remember how news used to travel around here. It's better than Royal Mail. Much easier just to tell someone something and wait for half an hour for it to make it around the village.'

'That's true.' She giggled, reaching down and stroking her daughter's hair. 'But everything I've heard has been very nice. I'm Sophie. Sophie Gladstone. My husband is a partner in the doctors' surgery here.'

The previous doctor, the one Amelia remembered, had been very old-fashioned with a rather blunt bedside manner. He always wore a black suit and Amelia had been terrified of him because he was dressed as if he was off to a funeral, which didn't instil much faith in his doctoring abilities. It was hard to trust a man whose patients clearly died so rapidly he had to be ready to go at a moment's notice. Looking at Sophie, Amelia couldn't imagine her husband being like that.

'So you're new to the village too?' she asked.

'Yes. Though I've been here for a while now.' Sophie glanced down at her little girl, then back up to Amelia. 'I'm surprised you need any shopping. When I arrived, people kept giving me things.'

'I was greeted with a few bits yesterday.' She laughed. 'I just need a couple of essentials. The supplies Mrs Bostock gave me were wonderful but woefully short on wine. Thankfully no one has given me any eggs. I've got more than I know what to do with.'

'I can totally understand the wine issue. And I don't envy you having chickens. I'm not keen on keeping chickens,' Sophie said with a shudder. 'My husband wants to, but I really don't fancy it.'

'Well, he may not when he hears that last night I had to get up at stupid o'clock in the morning and chase them back into their run.' Amelia replayed some of last night's antics in her mind. 'I really need to find someone to fix it, actually.'

'Adam Noble might be your man, then.'

'Adam?' Amelia tried to keep her voice calm, but the quiver betrayed her.

'Yes, he's a carpenter. The only carpenter in the village actually. And he's terribly, terribly, good.'

'Oh.' Amelia had only just stopped thinking about him after their encounter earlier and now here was his name again. The coldness of his greeting and the resentment he so clearly felt towards her were more than just painful. They were torturous. She desperately needed a carpenter for Meadow Farmhouse, but hopefully there was another in a nearby village she could ask for. 'Well, if you want to put your husband off, tell him all about my chasing the chickens around with a broom last night. It took about an hour and some of them aren't in the least bit afraid of brooms. I'd completely forgotten how bolshie chickens were.'

'I will definitely tell him that, because if I ever give in and that happens, he'll be the one out there in the night getting them all back in.' Sophie chuckled, then paused. 'Listen, would you like to grab a coffee or something? There's a little café down Mill Lane. It doesn't close for a couple of hours yet.'

Taken by surprise, Amelia stuttered. After seeing Adam all she wanted was the security of the farmhouse, but she'd liked talking to Sophie and was enjoying her company.

'If you can't, I understand. You may not feel like it right now with everything you've got going on. It must be a really hard time for you. Sorry if I was insensitive.' Sophie blushed and she began pushing the buggy past Amelia. 'Actually, we'd better get going.'

'Wait!' Apart from Adam, she hadn't had many friends in the village and something about Sophie's expressive and sweet demeanour made her want to stay. 'If you've got time, I'd love to. I just need to grab a few bits from the shop first.'

Relief flooded Sophie's features and the pinkness faded from her cheeks. 'Great. I'll meet you there.'

Sophie went on her way and Amelia took a breath before

heading inside the shop. As soon as she strode in she saw Meredith, an old school friend and daughter of the owners behind the till in the corner.

'Amelia!' Meredith exclaimed cheerfully. 'It's so lovely to see you back.'

Though she and Meredith had never been best friends, they'd been in the same class and always gotten along at school. 'Hi, Meredith. How are you?'

'I'm well. Really well.' She patted her protruding belly. 'Just waiting for this one to come and join us.'

'Is it your first?'

'Fourth actually.'

Amelia's eyebrows lifted of their own accord. 'Wow, congratulations.'

'Who'd have thought when we were little we'd end up where we are. I heard you've been living in Paris.'

The shop was small, and Amelia began to gather the things she needed. Where was the wine? She definitely needed a bottle or six of wine after the last two days. Amelia found quite a decent selection and added a few to her basket. An old man nearby glanced over as she added the seventh bottle for luck, but she ignored him and carried on with her shopping. 'Are your mum and dad still working?'

'Only when I need them to. I took over the shop a little while ago when Dad got sick.'

Amelia popped her head above the shelf so Meredith could see her face. 'I'm sorry to hear that.' Now she thought of it, Pat – Meredith's dad – had always been kind to her when she stopped in for sweets on the way home from school. Once he'd even let her have one for free when she didn't have enough money. Had he known that Vera didn't have sweets in the house? Again, she hadn't actively recalled that memory but still it had popped to the surface.

'He's okay now. But he retired a bit early to have more time to relax and I took over.'

Amelia went to the counter and paid for her goods. 'I'm glad he's doing okay.' She thought of asking Meredith about the locket. If she'd seen Vera wearing it since she'd left, or if her mum and dad knew anything about it, but as she tried to form the words, Meredith leaned forwards.

'So … I heard you're selling Vera's place?'

'Yes, I am.'

'That's a shame. We thought it'd be nice if you came back. Dad was pleased to hear you were home.'

'Your dad was always lovely. I don't suppose you know any local carpenters? Some bits of the farmhouse need fixing.'

'There's only Adam Noble, but he is very good. You must remember Adam? You two were a thing before you left, weren't you?' Amelia's cheeks and neck began to burn. Luckily, Meredith carried on. 'My dad said he's got an affinity with wood.'

How did she ask if there was anyone else without it getting back to Adam? Someone was bound to pass on that she'd refused to employ him and then what would he think? And God forbid Lynne found out. She'd be back with a pitchfork. She didn't think he could hate her any more, but that might just do it.

'So have you?' Meredith asked.

'Sorry, have I what?' Amelia stalled for time as she tried to control her voice.

'Seen Adam?'

'Yes, I bumped into him about half an hour ago.' *There, that wasn't too bad. Nearly normal.* She left it at that.

'Got even more handsome, hasn't he?'

'Yes. Yes, he has.' Amelia hoped her voice wasn't ringing as audibly with sadness as her heart was. 'Nice to see you, Meredith.'

'You too.'

Amelia headed out of the door as quickly as possible, as her head began to pound. She refused to think of how her heart ached. Even her ribcage felt bruised and sore. Why did everyone keep mentioning Adam?

Mill Lane had always been full of nothing more than the usual pretty cottages you found in every other street in Meadowbank. So as Amelia walked down, she was surprised one of the cottages had been changed into a café and was even more surprised at how busy it was. With outside tables covered in red-chequered tablecloths, it reminded her of the cafés of Paris. She thought of her busy social calendar and the noise and bustle of the city. There no one stopped you in the street asking questions and you could go quietly about your day. Meadowbank was taking some getting used to again. In a way, she appreciated everyone's well-wishes and concern, but being the centre of attention was unnerving and she pined for the solitude of city life.

A painted sign above the door proclaimed the café was called *Annie's Tearoom*. On closer inspection, the café was made up of two cottages knocked into one. The two small front windows had been enlarged and in what had once been the cottage front gardens nestled behind a low flint wall and a myriad of flowering plants, were even more small round tables. Through the right-hand window, Amelia could see a counter with a large glass cake stand next to it. Sophie waved at her as she fastened the belt on her little girl's highchair. With a deep breath, she pushed the door open and cast her eye over the interior. It was cute with pink bunting criss-crossing the ceiling, and milk bottles of flowers on each table. Just like in a movie, it went quiet as she entered and, avoiding everyone's gaze, Amelia made her way to Sophie.

'How did it go in the shop?' she asked.

'Not too bad.'

'Lots of questions? I always get quizzed on what Isla's up to. "Is she walking yet? Has she said her first word? Is she napping? She should be sleeping through the night by now, shouldn't she?" I know everyone means well but it can be a bit overwhelming.'

'I know exactly what you mean.' Overwhelming was the perfect description for how the last two days had been.

'I can see from your shopping we're going to get on well. I

normally get looks when I buy that many bottles, but I don't have any other vices.'

Amelia laughed. She was already growing to like Sophie. 'Sometimes, a glass of wine is the only way to relax. The shop has a good selection actually.'

'I bet the wine's amazing in France.'

'It is pretty good.'

A middle-aged lady bustled over to take their order. Amelia had hoped it would be the younger waitress who was currently slicing into a delicious-looking coffee cake. She wouldn't have any clue who Amelia was and would be unlikely to ask questions. Instead, they had Annie, the tearoom owner whose light brown hair flecked with grey was tied into a tight bun. 'What can I get you ladies, then? And how's Miss Isla today? Is she talking yet?' She leaned over and began talking to the child. Sophie and Amelia shared a see-what-I-mean look.

'Can I have a latte for me and some milk for Isla please, Annie? What would you like, Amelia? My treat.'

At the mention of Amelia's name, Annie shot upright. 'Amelia Williams of Meadow Farmhouse? My gosh how you've changed.' She peered at her closely. 'Actually, I should have recognised you straight away from your hair. You always had lovely long dark hair. I was sorry to hear about Vera, dear. She wasn't the easiest woman, but you've had a hard enough time as it is, haven't you? What with your poor departed parents and everything. Are you here to stay or are you going to sell the place?'

With two sets of eyes on her and God knows how many others judging from the silence in the tearoom, Amelia balked and tried to ignore how her palms were growing clammy. 'I'm thinking of selling, yes. Can I have a black coffee, please?'

'Coming right up, dear.'

When she'd gone, Amelia saw the concern on Sophie's face, and worried that she too would start asking about her parents. It wasn't that she hadn't dealt with their loss, Amelia told herself, but having it brought up so many times over the last couple of days had been … difficult. Without realising it, her hand went to the locket, fiddling with it under the thin wool of her jumper. Could she ask Sophie about it? No, she was new to the village and wouldn't know anything about it.

'Are you okay?' asked Sophie, gently.

'Yes, I'm fine. Honestly.' Amelia relaxed a little. 'Like you said before, the questioning can be a bit much sometimes. You said you'd heard about me. Do you mind if I ask what you've heard?'

'A couple of people mentioned that you're the only relative Vera had but they weren't sure you'd want to come home. I only met her a few times. She was very … blunt, wasn't she?'

'She certainly had her moments.' Amelia hoped that would be enough of an answer. Thankfully, Sophie sensed her discomfort and didn't ask any more questions. Their drinks were delivered, and she sipped her coffee even though it was scaldingly hot, buying some time to think. 'You said you came here recently too?'

'Yes. We lived in Chichester before, but Michael, my husband, had been looking for a practice in the country for ages. We wanted Isla to be brought up somewhere quiet, with lots of fresh air, so as soon as his partnership was confirmed we sold up and moved. At the time I was heavily pregnant, and it was all a bit stressful, but we soon settled in.'

'I bet all those food parcels helped,' Amelia joked.

'Yes! They did, actually.' Sophie poured the glass of milk into Isla's sippy cup and handed it to her. Isla popped it into her mouth, joyfully dribbling it down her chin. 'It felt a bit weird to accept such generosity from absolute strangers. After living in Chichester where we didn't really speak to our neighbours, it was really odd to just be chatting with people and them being so kind. But it was such a godsend. It meant Michael and I ate actual food. As I'm sure you know, there aren't any takeaways here so we probably would have starved.'

Her own first night would have been radically different if Mrs

Bostock and Mrs Claribold hadn't been so generous. 'It sounds like you've had a lot on your plate. I hope you've settled in okay. Whereabouts are you?'

'Do you know Lynne Noble?'

'I do,' Amelia confirmed.

Sophie blew her coffee to cool it. 'I live next door to her. She's in Ivy Cottage; I'm in Magnolia Cottage.'

'She doesn't live at Willow Farm anymore?'

'No. But then Adam's our age, isn't he? It'd be a bit weird if he still lived with his mum. You do know Adam Noble, don't you? I think he's always lived here. You probably went to school together.'

'Yes, we did,' she replied, her chest growing tight. They'd more than just gone to school together, but whatever relationship they'd had before was lost now and she felt the familiar sting in her nose heralding tears. Amelia took another sip of her coffee focusing on the heat of the liquid in her mouth.

Just then, a group of teenage boys on mountain bikes came speeding down the lane towards the duck pond, leaving angry shouts in their wake and walking sticks being rattled in the air behind them. They peeked back over their shoulders, jeering and laughing.

'Those boys!' Sophie groaned. 'They can be real terrors. They nearly ran into the buggy the other day. I had to yank it back so fast, Isla nearly catapulted out of the front. Luckily, there aren't many groups of kids like that around here. That's one of the good things about Meadowbank, but their parents really should do something. If you really are looking for a carpenter, you won't get better than Adam. He's amazing. He made me a wonderful cot for Isla and it's so much nicer than anything I could have bought from a shop. What work do you need doing?'

'Just a few doors are sticking – that's all.'

'I think I've got his number somewhere.' Sophie rifled in her bag and pulled out her wallet. Instead of handing over the business card Amelia had expected, Sophie pulled out a scrap of paper.

If she called him would he answer? Would he talk to her once he knew who it was? From his behaviour earlier, she wondered if he'd ever forgive her for what she'd done. And now she knew the extent to which she'd hurt him, she was pretty sure she'd never forgive herself.

Chapter 8

The red towelling beer mat underneath his hands was suddenly very interesting. Studying the pill of the fabric, moving it this way and that with his fingers, Adam stared down, anything to get the image of Amelia Williams out of his brain.

He'd been too busy trying to decide if the bird ahead was a hawfinch when she'd knocked into him. Not knowing who it was, he hadn't cared at first, smiling apologetically at who he presumed was a neighbour out for a walk. But as soon as he'd seen her eyes, he'd realised who it was and where she'd come from. Of all the bad luck. He'd only nipped home to get his wallet. The idiot he was, it had fallen out of his jeans when he was getting dressed this morning, but he needed it for the pub. Now he had to sit with his friends while these terrifying emotions whirred within him.

Adam scoffed audibly and then dropped his eyes as the landlord looked over, wondering what on earth he was doing.

'You all right, Adam?' Dean, the landlord, asked.

'Yeah, just a cough. It's nothing.' But it wasn't nothing. It was an earthquake that had shaken his world. Seeing Amelia had been almost overpowering. From the moment his mum had mentioned she was back in the village, he'd imagined what it would be like to bump into her again but nothing had prepared him for it being so literal. Adam raised his hand to his chest where her head had hit him. Immediately after the bump, he'd pushed his hands into his jacket pockets and balled his fists, trying to rein in his emotions. She'd been so polite. So … awkward.

He'd felt exactly the same and as she'd tried to speak the prospect of conversation had panicked him and he'd bailed, studying the dirty, muddy lane to keep from turning back to her. Walking away was supposed to provide freedom from the hurt inside but now he was suffused with resentment and disappointment.

Anger surged within him as he remembered the way she had cast him aside. The long, slow goodbye of wondering if today would bring a call, a text message, or an email. An answer to his own attempts to contact her, only for it never to arrive.

'Adam?'

Unaware he'd even been spoken to, his head shot up. Dean was smiling at him. 'Wow, didn't know I had such interesting beer mats. Usual?'

Heat built in his cheeks. 'Yes, please, Dean.'

'You sure you're all right?'

A rill of annoyance tensed his muscles. He had to get control of his feelings. Adam knew he couldn't stand here being angry forever and hoped a normal conversation would help shake it off. 'Yeah – fine – no worries. Just lost in my own world for a minute.'

'Well, here you are.' He lifted the pint of amber ale onto the bar and Adam's mouth watered in anticipation. The local brewery made the best beer around. If anything was going to fix his mood, this would. 'That'll sort you out.'

He took it gratefully and ambled to the large fireplace his mates were gathered around. They were like him – decorators, electricians, roofers. He'd met most of them after Amelia had left, when he'd decided to become a carpenter. He'd been apprenticed to Mr Sims and he'd also gone to college. All these lads from the village had too. They'd been friends for years now and were like his family.

'Hey, here he is!' Rob cheered. 'We thought you'd forgotten your wallet on purpose. Again.'

'What do you mean *again*? Cheeky bugger. It's normally you who's never got enough for a round,' Adam replied but underneath his happy demeanour his emotions were still veering from shock to anger and on to something he wasn't quite ready to admit to yet.

He sank into the chair. Though he'd always known she'd grow up to be beautiful, he hadn't been prepared for how stunning she was. Her pale grey eyes shone out like glittering stars, glowing in the dark. Amelia had always had this piercing way of looking at him no other woman could match, cutting through all his layers of bullshit: all the teenage bravado and macho angst. From the lack of contact over the years, he'd been surprised she recognised him so quickly. The low fire of anger he'd been harbouring for years blazed and engulfed him. It had been so easy for her to leave him and his sorrow had almost proved too much.

'What's wrong?' asked Pete. He'd always been the more emotionally astute of the bunch, but as Rob had the emotional range of a cucumber that wasn't saying much. Still, Adam wasn't ready to say just yet.

'Ah, nothing, mate. Honestly I'm fine.'

Rob gave a quick raise of his eyebrows. 'So it's nothing to do with your mum trying to flog some weird wooden statues you've been making on the sly? What's all that about?'

Adam sat up paying more attention. 'What?'

'Oh, yeah. She's out in the garden trying to tell everyone about them. She could work on a market stall, your mum. "Come on, folks, you know you want one. Three for a pound".'

Adam nearly lost his pint as the glass clattered on the table. It spun in a circle but somehow managed to stay upright, though most of the contents spilled down the sides. He leaped to his feet and made his way outside. Sure enough, his mum was chatting merrily to a table full of people, trying and failing to describe his sculptures to one of the old regulars.

'I think they'd look lovely in your front garden, Nigel. And Adam does all sorts. Some are a bit short and squat with ugly squished-up faces and then he's got tall ones with extra-long arms and legs. They're like weird misshapen wooden bodies, but in a nice way. They're ever so nice, really.' Nigel rubbed the nape of his neck. 'Or you could have them in the house, in your conservatory or something. Shall I get Adam to show you some? He's got photos on his phone and he said he'd be here this evening.'

Nigel shook his head and Adam didn't blame him. The way his mum had described them they sounded horrendous. He couldn't think of anything less he'd want in his garden. 'Mum,' he managed to say through his clenched jaw. 'Let's leave Nigel to his pint, shall we.'

He placed an arm around her and shepherded her towards the door.

'What's the matter?' Lynne asked, glowering at him. 'You're not going to sell any of these bloody things if you don't actually tell people you're making them. You can't just have an army of them in your workshop that sit there gathering dust.'

'I know, Mum. I just need to figure out how to talk about them, that's all.' In reality, he needed to do a lot more than that. At the moment, his artistic ambitions were like a dirty little secret and he had to get over himself if he was ever going to explore this creative aspect of his personality. Trouble was, he was still too afraid of what people would say. Would they think he was getting above himself? Probably not if he was painting or doing something normal like pottery. But his crazy-faced sculptures weren't going to be to everyone's tastes. 'I need to research how to sell them. They're a bit …'

'Weird? Scary-looking? Unpleasant—'

He rolled his eyes. 'I was going to say different or unusual, but yeah, I suppose weird is as good a word as any. Come on, Dean was looking for you.'

'Was he?'

Adam felt a twinge of guilt at fibbing to his mum, but it wasn't just for his own sake, it was for Nigel's too. No one deserved having his mum in their ear trying her unusual sales pitch. After Adam deposited his mum at the end of the bar, she headed into the kitchen to find Dean and Adam made his way back to his pint. The warmth of the open fire hit him, and he rubbed a hand down his face, preparing for the ribbing from his mates.

'So, what's all this then, Leonardo da Vinci?' Rob teased. 'What have you been up to? Or should I call you … actually, I don't know the names of any sculptors.'

'It's nothing.' Adam gave a one-shouldered shrug. 'I've just been messing about with some wood, that's all.'

'Your mum said something about Groot and an artist's mannequin.' Rob could barely speak for laughing and Adam's neck burned with embarrassment. Aside from the day he'd realised Amelia was never going to contact him again, this was without doubt the most painful and humiliating.

'I think they sound kind of cool,' Pete said, and Adam shot him an appreciative glance. 'Did you know Amelia Williams was back? Mrs Edwards saw her in the village earlier. I was painting the outside of Marigold Cottage and she stopped by and told me. Amelia was at school with us remember? You and her had a bit of a thing, didn't you?'

Adam took it all back. Pete was as emotionally astute as a cucumber, which was a bit unfair on cucumbers. If he'd seen the look on Adam's face he'd have realised that this was the last thing he wanted to talk about. The fiery rage from earlier sent heat through his veins as it ignited once more and he edged away from the fire.

'Oh, yeah,' said Rob. 'You two were thick as thieves at school then when she hit uni – whoosh – she was gone. Here one minute then off the next. Never came back. I think she had the right idea, personally.'

'Shut up,' said Pete. 'You've lived here all your life. You wouldn't know what to do if you went anywhere else. The furthest you've ever gone is Shagaluf.'

'Even then you were crying for your mum after a day,' Adam added.

'That was the hangover.' Rob grinned and giggled at the

memory of what had certainly been a memorable holiday. Among his friends' teasing banter, the fire inside faded for a second.

'Didn't take it very well, did you, mate?' Rob said, softening for a moment.

Adam shrugged. 'One of those things, wasn't it? But it was a long time ago. To be honest, I'd forgotten all about her.'

He stared into his pint hoping they bought the lie. As long as he didn't think about it too much, he'd be able to keep himself under control. Usurpingly, he didn't have any plans to visit Meadow Farmhouse so with any luck, he wouldn't see her again.

Chapter 9

After a quick search of the other bedrooms, it was clear the bulk of her work would be downstairs in the living room and kitchen. The spare bedrooms were sparsely decorated with basic furniture and no personal belongings, whereas the living room and kitchen were still full of a surprising amount of trash.

From her seat on the floor of the living room where she was emptying and scrubbing a sideboard that could be beautiful if it was cleaned and polished up, Amelia wiggled her foot. It had gone to sleep from being pinned beneath her. She'd been working solidly on the living room for two days and black sacks filled with paper now lined the kitchen. She had to find somewhere else to store them because it was getting harder and harder to get to the cupboards, but on the bright side, it wouldn't be long, and she'd be able to start painting.

After careful consideration through the long, lonely evenings, she'd changed her mind about the bright white and decided something with a hint of cream would be better. A stark white would feel too cold and what the place needed was warmth. Amelia sat back, wiggling her toes as a startling realisation struck her. The last two nights she'd been alone. Her ever busy social life in Paris meant that she was hardly ever at home alone. Completely alone. She'd always felt that was a sign of success. If she wasn't meeting clients, she was out with friends and acquaintances. When she was home, her apartment felt stifling and yet, here, where she'd expected to feel trapped, the feeling had been something else entirely. Yes, the past still weighed heavy on her, but being back as an adult the farmhouse offered an innate sense of peace. Or at least it was as she grew more used to being here. Before she returned to Paris, she would at least have stripped away the layers of sadness that had built here over time.

Nights alone in Paris always brought a fear with them. A fear of missing out and of not making progress. She'd always worked hard to drive her life forward. The last few nights here and being away from Paris had shown she didn't need to worry quite so much. The world hadn't fallen down around her ears and, to be honest, she hadn't actually missed it all that much. The shift in her perspective brought a frisson of fear and she rebuked herself for not being more positive about her life back home.

'I get the feeling, Vera,' she said to the air, 'that you should have more personal stuff for a life of nearly eighty years. It's like you existed rather than lived.' Obviously, no answer came from the silent house and Amelia continued to work. 'I mean, even I, who grew up in an era of tiny mobile phones and text messages have got some keepsakes.'

They were things Adam had given her, friendship bands from university friends, and pictures of her parents they'd discovered when they had cleared her parents' house.

Another long-buried memory replayed in her mind. She hadn't wanted to even enter the house that day, loitering on the doorstep as she had Vera's room the day before. Her home had seemed suddenly intimidating and imposing, like something from a horror novel. Vera, with uncharacteristic kindness had led her inside and helped her to pack. She remembered watching from the doorway as Vera placed her parents' clothes into black sacks.

Sadness flooded her heart now and Amelia reached again for the locket, opening it once more to look at the picture. Apart from taking it off to sleep, she'd worn it every day and the connection it gave her to Meadow Farmhouse was driving her to make the house as lovely as it could be. Whoever she sold the house to, she wanted them to be happier than Vera had been here. The picture of the man seemed to spring into her mind as soon as it wasn't preoccupied with more practical thoughts. When she let her guard down he was there, along with Vera's chastisement that she wasn't to pry. But it wasn't prying. For Amelia, it was a way of saying goodbye, of putting the pieces of Vera's life together so that she could respectfully lay her to rest. If only older, more powerful memories wouldn't keep surfacing.

'I seriously need to stop talking to myself,' Amelia said out loud, whisking back some hair that had fallen from her ponytail. 'They say it's the first sign of madness, but I think talking to chickens in the middle of the night is probably worse.'

Seeing Vera's name on one of the letters, Amelia realised she hadn't checked the back of the locket to see if a name was written on the photograph. That was quite a common thing to do, wasn't it? Her fingers scrambled to get the locket open and take the photographs out. She held her breath as she turned them over but there was nothing written on the back to give a clue as to who these people were – the baby or the man – but as she turned the photo of the man upright, Amelia couldn't pull her eyes away from his. She felt she'd seen those eyes before. Taking out her phone, she took a picture, enlarging it to see if there was anything that could help her identify where the man was from. As a soldier, there might be a medal or insignia pinned to his jacket.

With mounting excitement, her eyes focused on the soldier's arm where a shape appeared to have been stitched on to it. Unfortunately, there wasn't enough of it to make out exactly what it was, and Amelia let her phone drop to her lap with a sigh.

'Who are you?' she asked in barely more than a whisper.

She didn't know of any soldiers being stationed around here. Where could she get that information? 'A little search online might help.' Taking up her phone again, she typed in soldiers and Meadowbank but nothing particularly helpful came up. Her village was so tiny, she wasn't surprised it wasn't mentioned anywhere. The library would have some information though.

Having worked since half past seven that morning, Amelia

stood and closed the window she'd opened to let the fresh air in. A stretch of her legs would revitalise her for a busy afternoon of finishing the clear-out of the living room and moving the furniture into the centre. Tomorrow, she had to clean the walls of the pin mould and air it all out before she could paint.

Before leaving, she went to close the door to the playroom that was now an extra sitting room with an ancient television inside it, but as she swung the door to, the entire thing came away from its hinges. 'Arrgh! Bloody hell!' Instinctively she stopped it falling and was somehow able to catch it before it crushed her toes. There was no getting around it. She definitely needed a carpenter. The bathroom door was sticking too and last night she'd got trapped inside. After nearly freezing to death in her towel, she'd managed to yank the door free and break out.

Then just as she'd dressed and warmed up, two of the chickens had made another escape attempt. She wasn't sure if it was Bonnie and Clyde as most of the chickens looked the same, but they hadn't even blanched as she'd branded the broom and, in the end, she'd had to grab them and carry them back to the run. Clearly, it too needed some work and though her skill with design and even a paintbrush wasn't bad, she wasn't that good with a hammer and nails.

If the only carpenter around was Adam, he was unlikely to accept any work from her. After their run-in she didn't even know how to ask. It would be excruciating being in the same room as him with hate radiating off him while shame radiated off her. With any luck, another solution might present itself.

Casting the thoughts from her mind, Amelia left the farmhouse and strolled into the village through the belt of trees and along the country road that felt so familiar it was as if she'd never been away at all. It was here she'd bumped into Adam yesterday. If the man in the locket wasn't popping into her thoughts, Adam bloody Noble was. Knowing now how much she'd hurt him her throat closed and guilt bit at her. She'd been wrong to let so much time pass between them but every time she'd thought of getting in touch, she'd let fear stop her and as more and more time passed, it had become harder and harder. She'd been a coward and now he would never forgive her. How could he? Their relationship seemed unrecoverable. There was no chance of making amends.

Amelia swallowed as the reality of the lost chance sunk in. All the while she'd been in Paris, there'd been the possibility that should she return and he still be here, she could apologise and explain. But knowing now that that chance was gone tore at her heart, more than she realised it would.

Aware that her eyes were misting with tears, Amelia stared at the rolling green fields to her right. A tractor made its way across the crest of a hill and on the tree-lined lane to her left birds hopped and darted in the branches.

Striding down the path to the centre of the village she wondered if she'd run into anyone else today, but the road was quiet. As she passed the village shop and crossed the green, a few people waved, and she waved back. In some ways, she preferred this sort of contact. She didn't have to speak. It was when people talked to her and mentioned the painful moments of her past that she faltered and lost all ability to form sentences. No matter how hard she tried, when the past came back to haunt her, she could never think of anything to say. Which was silly really because all her awkwardness and embarrassment did was prolong the situation.

Situated on the other side of the village, beyond the green and near where the stream widened, Meadowbank village library stood proudly. Only a small road separated it from the trickling brook, and on the grassy bank opposite, a couple of wooden benches sat for those who wanted to enjoy the peace and quiet. The small, thatched-roof building seemed more like a village hall and it didn't seem possible it could hold a great deal, but Amelia remembered it being particularly well stocked and organised. Though she wasn't overly bookish, she had come to hide here when Adam hadn't been allowed out to play and she didn't want to sit with Vera's misery. She'd read so many books on cold, wet days, sat in the children's section.

A small green sign outside confirmed the library's opening times and she took a moment to appreciate the beauty of the place. The wide windows down the side reflected the sun under the dark roof and the green paint appeared inky from last night's rain. It would soon dry to a paler, more inviting hue and Amelia followed the path to the large door.

The library was much how she remembered it and the smell of books and paper filled her nose. The quiet serenity of the place was instantly refreshing. A few people browsed the MDF bookshelves and Amelia couldn't help but think that, from a style point of view, they were entirely out of place. The old building called for something like the village shop had; a vintage vibe that illustrated the quaintness of the place. What they needed were proper hand-crafted bookshelves. Something with character. Either that, or something super modern to act as a juxtaposition of old and new, though the rest of Meadowbank probably wouldn't agree with that one.

After a second, Elsie Martin approached her. She'd always had amazingly pale skin, but it was so white she could have been carved from marble. Her brown frizzy hair curled around her shoulders and her eyes were hidden by a pair of glasses, but her smile instantly brought life to her face. 'Can I help with anything?' She took a step back. 'Amelia?'

'Hi, Elsie.'

It wasn't a surprise that Elsie Martin, who had been in the year below her at school, had ended up working at the library. She'd always loved books and at every break sat on a bench in the playground reading. She'd only had a few friends, and they too had loved books as much as she had. It goes to show, Amelia thought, that once you found your people, you didn't need masses of friends. Was Océanè one of her people? She'd called her cold, but sometimes it seemed to be the other way around. Adam had always been a big reader, trying to encourage her, but it had never really taken. Though she did enjoy a beach read when she was on holiday. A romance or an adventure story that intensified the feeling of escapism a holiday always gave. It was odd how returning to Meadowbank was feeling less like a holiday and more like coming home. She shook the thought away.

'I'm surprised you remember me,' Amelia joked.

'Of course I do! Why wouldn't I?'

'Memory's a funny thing isn't it?' she replied, shaking off her surprise. Her memories of her mum and dad – the most important memories she could have – had faded with time. She'd always supposed other people's memories of her would do the same till she'd become nothing more than a ghost.

Elsie tipped her head acknowledging the sadness in her statement. 'My friends and I thought you were so cool.'

'Me? I don't know why.'

'You just were. How are you? It must be strange being back.'

'It is a bit. I was looking for some information actually.' Elsie tilted her head slightly. 'I found this when I was clearing Vera's room.' She reached under the neck of her jumper and pulled out the locket.

'Oh, it's lovely.'

'I don't suppose you know anything about who this man might be?' She flicked open the locket to reveal the photographs. 'Vera never mentioned anything to me, but you know what she was like. She didn't talk to people unless she had to and even then, she wasn't always polite.'

Elsie peered at it, and her pupils flicked around as she studied it. 'I'm sorry, I don't. He's not familiar to me. And I was sorry to hear of Vera passing away. If she came into the village she would pop in sometimes. She quite liked thrillers I seem to remember.'

'I found some in the house actually. I'll have to check if they belong to the library.'

Elsie waved a hand dismissively. 'Don't worry too much. I'm sure you've got enough to think about.'

'Do you know of any soldiers being in the village? Or how this man might have come to know of the Cabot family?'

She pushed her glasses up the bridge of her nose. 'I'm afraid Vera didn't speak to me more than anyone else, but our local historian wrote a pamphlet on the links between Meadowbank and a local military hospital. Well, we call him our local historian. I'm not sure he's actually qualified, and he is a little bit odd, but he's very enthusiastic.'

'Do you have a copy?' Amelia resisted the urge to bounce on her heels at the prospect of new information, even from an enthusiast.

Elsie frowned and shook her head. 'I'm afraid we've run out and my colleague' – she turned and peeped over her shoulder to see a bored-looking woman scowling at some children – 'spilled her coffee on our reference copy. I've been waiting for him to get back from holiday to request some more.'

'Oh, okay.' Amelia couldn't hide the disappointment in her voice.

'Sorry that doesn't help. He should be back soon though. There are some local church records over in the reference section through there.' She pointed through a magnificent, beamed archway and Amelia couldn't help but smile at the beauty of the place. 'They probably won't help until you have a name or something, but maybe the census records for Meadow Farm will lead you somewhere? That's generally where we advise people to start with family history searches. That or certificates for births, deaths and marriages.'

'I'm afraid I don't have any of those yet. Vera's place is full of the most remarkable rubbish but nothing particularly personal. But thanks, Elsie. I'll take a look.'

'Let me set you up with the microfiche.'

Amelia followed with no idea what a microfiche was but hoped it wouldn't be too difficult to figure out. It was better than nothing and it was certainly better than going back to the farmhouse and sorting through more of Vera's decades-old post.

Elsie pulled open one of the locked drawers of a huge wooden dresser and searched through. 'Do you mind if I look at that picture again, Amelia?'

'No, of course not.' She pulled out the locket once more and showed Elsie. As she closed it and silently put it away, she told herself that she'd find out who he was and say goodbye to them all before she left again. It was the least she could do. She owed it to Vera to know her better than she'd been able to in life. As the farmhouse had yielded nothing useful, perhaps this was the way to do it.

'I can't tell whether that's a picture from World War One or World War Two. The latest census you can look at is 1921, but as that's after the First World War it might not be much help. You could try the census from 1911 first?' Amelia nodded, not sure either option was going to be particularly useful, but she had to start somewhere. Elsie continued. 'The census is only available one hundred years after it's taken, and the 1931 census was destroyed by a fire in 1942, and no census was taken in 1941 because of the Second World War.'

'Your knowledge is really impressive,' Amelia said, and Elsie blushed. 'They're both before Vera was born so why don't we start with 1911 and I can at least see who's lived at Meadow Farmhouse. It should list her grandparents, shouldn't it?'

'Good idea.'

A moment later, the microfiche was reeled into the machine and Amelia began to search. It was filed by street and surprisingly hard to read. She'd thought she'd be able to whizz through because the village was so tiny, but half an hour later and with aching eyes she sat back, yet to find Meadow Farmhouse.

'Hello again.' Sophie appeared in her peripheral vision with her daughter by her side. Isla was holding a stack of books tightly to her chest.

'Sophie! Hello. Hi, Isla.'

'Books!' Isla said, holding them out for her to see.

Amelia gasped and pointed. 'Look at all those books you've got. You can't possibly read them all?' Isla giggled.

'How are you settling in?' Sophie asked.

'Not too bad, thank you. You wouldn't believe the amount of stuff Vera had. I'm going to have boxes and boxes of pots and pans.'

'You should think about donating them for the spring fair.'

'I saw a flyer actually, but I haven't got around to ringing.'

'Well, I'm on the committee and I'm on the bric-a-brac stall this year, so let me know when you've sorted it and I'll come and get it. You don't have a car, do you?' Amelia shook her head. 'That's fine. I don't mind, just let me know when suits you.'

'Thanks. I'm just taking a break and doing a bit of research on the house.'

'That sounds fun. I researched the history of Magnolia Cottage just after we moved in. I just had to know who'd lived there and what they did.'

'Did you find out anything interesting?'

Isla began wiggling on the spot. 'Do you need the toilet?' Sophie asked her.

'No!'

'She does. Sorry, I better go before she has an accident and I have to apologise to Elsie … again. But I was wondering if you fancied another coffee sometime?'

'I'd love to.' Amelia beamed. 'Feel free to drop by the farmhouse anytime you want some company. You can bring your books,' she said to Isla who waved them before continuing to wriggle.

Sophie began to lead her away. 'Don't forget to ring me if you need anything.'

'I won't. Thank you.'

Amelia went back to her searching, but the records were so faint in places and the writing so squiggly it was getting harder and harder to make out the street names let alone decipher the name and occupation of the person who'd lived there.

'Well, look who it is,' came a kindly voice from over her shoulder and Amelia turned to see Jocelyn Carmichael. She had been the Girl Guides leader when she was at school and had always been rather fierce.

'Hello, Jocelyn. How lovely to see you.'

Amelia had pestered Vera for months to join the Girl Guides when she was about ten and with Vera's loathing of the village it had been a huge victory when she'd finally agreed. Only Amelia hadn't enjoyed it quite as much as she thought she would and attended a total of four sessions. It seemed she wasn't very good at cooking, baking, or being prepared, and even as a grown-up couldn't hold in a giggle when someone mentioned bushcraft.

Hanging out with Adam and exploring the woods and hills had been far more fun. In some ways, Vera had given her freedoms unknown to some of her friends.

'What are you up to in the library?' the white-haired old lady enquired. Though older than Vera, Jocelyn's eyes sparkled with mischief.

'I'm just trying to find some information on Meadow Farmhouse.'

'What is it you'd like to know, dear? If anyone knows it, it'll be me. I've been here a long, long time.'

'Oh, well—'

'Actually, I was just dropping these books back and going home.' She held a copy of *Fifty Shades of Grey* under her arm and Amelia tried to stop the giggle growing inside her. 'I whizzed through this one and now I need the others. You can keep all these literary classics. Give me a good bonkfest to pass the time. Why don't you come and join me for a nice cup of tea and some cake.'

Amelia didn't know whether to accept after Elsie had gone to such effort for her and glanced back at the microfiche then Jocelyn. 'I was just—'

'I haven't got all day, dear. Do you want to come or not?'

Feeling like the ten-year-old Girl Guide she'd been before, Amelia didn't really feel she could say no. After all, a list of names on a census wasn't the same as hearing from someone who had known Vera and her family. Jocelyn was far more likely to have useful information than the old microfiche. 'If you're sure, Jocelyn – I don't want to put you out.'

'Nonsense. Come along.'

While Jocelyn took some books from her wheelie bag and went to the still bored-looking woman at the counter to hand them back, Amelia found Elsie a few bookshelves down. 'Elsie, I'm sorry but—'

'Didn't you find anything?' She looked mortified, like she'd failed in her duty as a librarian.

'No, it's just that Jocelyn has invited me for tea and to talk about Meadowbank. How do I take all that down?' she asked pointing to the microfiche.

Elsie shook her head, her frizzy hair bouncing. 'No problem. I'll do it. There's a bit of a knack anyway.'

'Thank you so much, Elsie, you've been really helpful.'

'The best thing about places like this is the oral history and hearing people's stories. I'm sure Jocelyn will be able to help you more.'

'You always did love history,' Amelia said kindly and Elsie blushed again.

'Come on, dear,' said Jocelyn now moving towards the exit with surprising speed. 'You can't keep an old lady like me waiting. I haven't got time to loiter.'

'If you want a tip,' Elsie whispered, 'Jocelyn is partial to some nice shortbread. You could dive into the shop and get some on your way. I'm sure it'll make her even more keen to talk, but don't bother with chocolates. She'll think you're creeping.'

'Thanks,' Amelia said with a giggle, grateful for her advice.

These were the type of idiosyncrasies people had in Meadowbank.

In Paris, all her friends were the same – stylish, a bit posh – they talked about culture and ballet even though many of them never went to the theatre. Océanè would praise the latest play or opera to be performed but when Amelia suggested they go, she'd never be available. She was sure it wasn't a French thing; people were the same the world over. When she thought about it, she didn't have that much fun with Océanè sometimes. It was always very serious. The short time she'd spent with Sophie had been radically different to that already and they barely knew each other. She really hoped she stopped for a coffee. Meadowbank felt freer somehow, and the sense of nostalgia sent a judder down her spine.

'Do you remember where I live, dear?' Jocelyn called as Amelia hurried to catch up.

'Are you still in Dairy Lane?'

'I am.'

A renewed sense of hope began to flutter in her tummy. Was she now about to get some answers?

Chapter 10

Jocelyn was perfectly happy for Amelia to nip into the shop on their way home. When Amelia had suggested it, she'd cheerfully informed her she needed a wee and from the size of her incontinence knickers it would take a while to get them off and on. Apparently, one of the signs of ageing was developing a bladder the size of a thimble but one you couldn't control. And she wanted time to put some bits in the freezer before they sat down for tea and cake.

The village shop was far busier than the first time Amelia had stopped in, and she weaved her way through the crowd. Meredith waved to her after saying goodbye to the customer she was serving.

'Amelia, we haven't seen you for a few days. Everything okay?'

'Fine, thanks,' she replied, feeling a strange sense of trepidation and excitement at what was to follow. 'How are you? How's the bump?'

'Bump's fine. Counting down the days now.'

'It must be very exciting.' She checked around her. 'Meredith, have you got any biscuits? Some really nice shortbread or something?'

Meredith pulled a face. 'No. Sorry. I've only got the family packs on your left. Would this be for Jocelyn, perhaps?' Amelia's mouth hung open in shock and Meredith laughed. 'I saw you walking along the street together.'

'Right. Yes, they are. I was told she likes shortbread.'

'If I were you, I'd head to the deli. They sell some lovely tins of Scottish shortbread she's quite partial to.'

'Isn't it bad for business sending me off there? Shouldn't you try and sell me something from here instead?'

'No.' Meredith laughed again. 'We support each other. They send people here for the basics and I send them there for something a bit fancier. To be honest, I think Jocelyn eats their entire supply of shortbread. Do you know, we even talk to each other about what we're going to stock? It's worked well so far. Especially at Christmas.'

An old lady plopped her basket by the till. 'That's what this village does, Amelia Williams. Supports each other. Always has.'

'Of course,' Amelia replied, though she felt a little told off.

She said goodbye and dashed to the deli, eager to get something to show her thanks, and trying not to keep Jocelyn waiting. A large glass counter ran the length of the shop filled with different meats and cheeses and to the sides were thick wooden shelves lined with pretty packets and fancy goods. There hadn't been a shop like this when she was younger, and she was surprised the village had developed such tastes. They even stocked some of the brands she'd seen in her local shops in Paris.

'Can I help?' asked a woman behind the counter. She was about the same age as Amelia with a youthful complexion and blonde hair, her clothes covered by a black apron.

'I'm after some Scottish shortbread, please. Meredith at the shop said you stocked some.'

'Just over there, my lovely.' She pointed to a large wicker basket in the corner, crammed full of tins of biscuits.

There were expensive French madeleines, baklava, and Scottish shortbread in traditional tartan tins. Next to the basket, on the shelf, were some plastic-wrapped biscuits that the label said were made locally. Amelia grabbed a tin of the French madeleines for later. As she picked them up she expected to pine for France but it didn't wash over her as quickly. The mystery of the locket was clearly taking over her mind.

How had it only been two weeks since she'd heard of Vera's

death and a few days since she arrived in Meadowbank? In some ways it seemed she'd made little progress on the farmhouse, merely moving rubbish from one room into another, but she'd worked on jobs that had felt like that and they'd turned out all right in the end. Change always made her unsettled and restless, maybe that was why she was focusing on this locket? It stopped her thinking about the fact she was not only an orphan but now had no living relatives. The word *orphan* rebounded in her ears and loss over her parents threatened to overrun her. Her time at Meadowbank was proving emotionally exhausting, dealing with things she never intended.

Taking a box of the shortbread for Jocelyn, and some madeleines and locally made chocolate cookies for herself, Amelia made her way to the counter. She had a feeling she'd need a sugar boost after today and she hadn't had any lunch.

As Amelia paid for the items and the woman placed them into a bag, she popped in an extra pack of hazelnut cookies. 'Oh, I didn't need those.'

'Our treat, my lovely. You've just lost a loved one and nothing helps more than one of these with a cup of tea. That's how I got through my mum passing last year.'

She seemed so cheerful, Amelia was momentarily lost for words. 'I'm sorry to hear that but I'm happy to pay for them.'

'No, I won't hear of it. It'll make me feel better knowing you've got one of these to nibble on when it all gets too much.'

'Oh, umm, thank you.'

'You're very welcome.'

The kindness brought a rush of endorphins that eased away the tension in her shoulders and slowed the mounting trepidation. It was a moment of peace in what had been a hectic and emotional week. Checking her watch, she hurried on to Jocelyn's house thankful that the village was so tiny it would only take a minute to get there. Fresh air filled Amelia's lungs, refreshing her eyes after the harsh strip lighting in the library and the squiggly microfiche. How did historians do it? Her hand went to the locket once more when it bounced off the skin of her chest.

When she turned down Dairy Lane, another tiny street filled with pretty cottages, she almost stumbled as she spotted Adam talking to someone over one of the garden walls. When he saw her, he stared down at his feet. Butterflies swirled inside her. He was talking to another young man whom she recognised from school – Rob Batten – but she and Adam had never really been friends with him while she was here. Rob grinned at her as she drew near.

'Amelia Williams. The disappearing woman. Nice to see you back.'

Rob had always been a bit of a dick, but Amelia hardly noticed him. Under Adam's gaze her breathing was unsteady but no matter how hard she tried she couldn't pull her eyes away. He kept his eyes down but they drifted up to her from time to time. That he couldn't bring himself to look her in the eye hurt and she forced herself to turn to Rob. 'Hi, Rob. You look well.'

'Adam, look! It's Amelia.' Rob's tone was strange and a mischievous glint had appeared in his eye.

'Hi.' Adam's words were like lead weights dropping heavily to the ground between them.

'Hi. Listen, umm, sorry about the other day—'

'What happened the other day?' asked Rob, clearly enjoying himself.

'She bumped into me,' said Adam matter-of-factly. 'It's fine. No problem.'

'Right. Okay. Still, I wasn't looking where I was going. Sorry.' He finally met her gaze and his brow furrowed, his expression pushing her words away.

'Thanks.'

'Where are you off to?' asked Rob, glancing between them. Had Adam mentioned her to him? Or did he remember how close they had once been?

'I'm seeing Jocelyn.'

'Jocelyn?' Adam asked, then he dropped his eyes once more as if he hadn't meant to speak in the first place.

In the awkwardness, which Rob the dick was clearly enjoying, humiliation burned and she said, 'She's waiting for me, so I'd better go. Bye.'

She had no idea if Rob had said anything as she'd left because all she could hear was the blood pounding in her ears, but he was now talking to Adam like nothing was wrong. Adam even laughed at something he said and the sound of it forced her head to turn back to them. He was watching her from the corner of his eye. If only she knew what he was thinking. On second thoughts perhaps it was better not to; she doubted it would be complimentary. She pushed open the gate to Jocelyn's house, now cursing that the village was so tiny she'd run into him again. It was far too painful. When she turned away one final time, Jocelyn already had the front door open for her.

'Are you coming in or what, dear?' asked the well-padded old lady in her slippers and a giant cardigan. 'Come along in then.'

Amelia had wondered what her cottage would look like. Would it be as dated and dark as Meadow Farmhouse or as lively as she was? The bright and airy hallway wasn't anything like Vera's. Jocelyn led her into the living room and, as with most houses, every surface was covered in photographs and items collected over a lifetime. Again, Amelia wondered why Vera had kept so much rubbish, but had so few personal items. And when she thought of the photographs she did have on display, none of them were of her. Was she really that much of a disappointment to Vera? She'd been wondering if Vera had felt the same regret she had that they had ended up so at odds, and cursed herself for being too proud to make the first move to reconcile.

'Thank you for letting me nip into the shop. I wanted to get you some biscuits to say thank you for your time.' Amelia took them out of the bag and handed them to her.

'Thank you, dear.' She studied them then eyed Amelia. 'Did Adam tell you they were my favourites?'

'Adam?'

'Yes. He did some work for me recently near my birthday and I told him they were my favourites. You two were always together when you were younger. I know we never heard hide nor hair of you when you left, but did you keep in contact with him?'

She wondered whether to admit the truth but couldn't bring herself to say out loud how stupid she'd been to think he would just forget her. The trouble was, every time she began to think of herself as memorable, a voice in her head made her feel like she was full of herself to even imagine it. It wasn't that Vera had beaten her down. Not intentionally. It was just that, being such an inconvenience to someone had a way of making you feel you were an inconvenience to everyone. She deflected the question by saying, 'It was actually Elsie who mentioned about the biscuits.'

'She's a good girl. Right, you take a seat and I'll bring in the tea tray. The pot's all made.'

Amelia thought about offering to fetch it but didn't think Jocelyn would like that. She wasn't in any way infirm and the last thing Amelia wanted was to insult her. A moment later, she returned with a pretty pink teapot that must have been generations old and proper cups and saucers. Jocelyn had also put some of the biscuits onto a plate.

'I can't say Vera and I ever saw eye to eye. We mostly left each other alone. Not that that was hard as she barely came into the village unless she absolutely had to, but I am sorry she passed. She was younger than me, you know.'

'I know Vera wasn't everyone's cup of tea,' Amelia replied, sitting down on the sofa. She placed her handbag at her feet.

Jocelyn sat opposite her in an armchair that faced the television. She took the remote from the arm of the chair and turned the sound down. 'Do you like James Martin?' she asked, directing her gaze at Amelia.

'I don't know who that is, I'm afraid.'

'The cook.' Jocelyn prodded the remote at the television. 'Him. James Martin. I quite fancy him. Isn't he handsome?'

'Yes, he is,' Amelia said with a chuckle. 'What's he making?'

'I've no idea, dear. I stopped listening ten minutes ago. I just like watching his hands. I used to get my kicks with a double dose on a Saturday, but now he's only on in the evenings, just before Dinner in a Dish arrive.'

Dinner in a Dish must be the Meadowbank equivalent of Meals on Wheels and Amelia checked her watch. She hadn't realised how time had moved on. 'Would you like me to wait until he's finished before I ask you some questions?'

Jocelyn adjusted her posture and sat a little straighter in the chair. 'No, that's fine. So, you've inherited Vera's farmhouse?'

'I have.'

'And how do you feel about that?'

There was so much to pack into that answer she wasn't sure she'd be able to get it all in in an hour. 'I'm not entirely sure.'

'It is what it is, dear, sadly. According to Adam's mother, after running away – oh, ten years ago – you've come back and are interested in the place all of a sudden. I heard you were selling and couldn't wait to get back to Paris.'

Amelia felt a mixture of embarrassment and guilt pulse through her and she clamped her hands together in her lap. She needed to practise answering some of these more difficult questions before she ventured out again. It was surprising Lynne hadn't been mentioned before now. 'I am selling,' she said quietly. The woman's kind eyes made her carry on, though she wasn't sure what words would come next. 'Vera's been described as hard and difficult and unfriendly and she was all of those things. She was never motherly, which is why I left as soon as I could.' Biting back the sea of emotion threatening to jumble her brain and steal her words, she carried on. 'But coming back, I've realised that there must have been more to Vera than the side I saw, and I'd like to know more about her before I sell Meadow Farmhouse and return to Paris.'

Amelia had dealt with her grief over the years, but it didn't stop the pain that shot up inside when she thought of it. Though it was humiliating, she wasn't at all surprised that Lynne had said what she'd said. She probably didn't think Amelia had any feelings at all after the way she'd left Adam. Jocelyn's eyes roved over her and Amelia had a feeling of being analysed by a psychiatrist. 'I can't just up sticks on my old life and move here because Vera left me Meadow Farmhouse.'

'Why can't you?' Amelia stared. 'You can if you want. What you mean is, you don't want to. Which is fine.' Jocelyn relaxed back in her chair. 'What have you come to ask me then?'

Amelia began to ramble in shock as Jocelyn's words reverberated in her head. 'I was hoping to learn some more about Vera.' Reaching down, Amelia took the locket from under her top and opened it. 'And do you know who this man is? Or why Vera might have kept his picture?'

Jocelyn frowned, then leaned forwards and poured the tea from the large ornate pot. 'I'm sorry to disappoint you, dear, but he doesn't look familiar.' Amelia slumped backwards. 'All I can tell you is that there was a hospital the other side of the village during the Second World War, at Highfield.'

Amelia listened intently sitting forwards in her chair.

'They weren't far from you, or at least far from Meadow Farmhouse. Those at Highfield weren't best pleased about it but needs must. Everyone had to do their bit. They had Americans as well as English servicemen.' Jocelyn seemed to be enjoying her reminiscence with a faraway look in her eye.

'Do you think that's an American uniform?'

Jocelyn looked again. 'I think it is, dear, but my memory is not what it was. Some were French too. Those Americans were ever so handsome in their uniforms. I was only, oh … thirteen or so when they started turning up.'

'They must have been quite a sight with their movie-star accents.' She could just imagine the ladies of Meadowbank swooning at these exotic creatures.

'They were, dear. There wasn't a girl in the village who wasn't in love with one of them.' She pulled her cardigan closer together as if her words had pulled up a particularly chilling memory.

Amelia frowned, but carried on. 'You said you were older than Vera. Do you remember her as a child?'

'Yes, she was the same as the rest of us. Happy, as far as I can remember.'

'Do you know why that changed?'

A slight coldness came to Jocelyn's features. 'Like I said, I didn't know Vera very well.'

'Is everything all right, Jocelyn?' Amelia asked. 'If Vera did something, you can tell me. It won't change anything now and it's not like I don't know how she was. I don't mean to sound heartless, but you don't have to pretend she was wonderful when we both know that she wasn't.'

Jocelyn nibbled on a biscuit, but her manner had changed from the sparkling, open woman Amelia had first encountered. 'As Vera grew, she became more and more angry.'

'But you don't remember a particular event?'

Jocelyn shook her head.

'What were her parents like? There was a picture of them on their wedding day and they seemed very happy. Did Vera have a happy home?'

'Very,' Jocelyn replied, but when she didn't add anything else, Amelia continued hoping something else might prompt more of a response.

'I remember doing a project on my family tree at school. She didn't tell me much about them, but she did say she was proud of her father and that, as a farmer, he was in a protected occupation.'

'Herbert Cabot was a decent man.' She said it as though it

was something to remember. 'And he came from good honest farming stock.'

'Did he originally own Meadow Farmhouse?'

'No. It belonged to Vera's mother's side, but he worked on the farm as a labourer before they married. There and others. He was a good farmer, and after they married, he made the most of that place.'

'Thank you.' Amelia dropped her eyes to the locket, feeling the cold gold under her fingertips. 'There are all these people connected with Meadow Farmhouse and I have no idea who they really were. Vera hardly ever spoke about anyone. In fact, that school project is the only time I remember her mentioning her dad.'

Jocelyn's hand reached across and took Amelia's. When she spoke, her voice was soft. 'Margaret Cabot, Vera's mother, was a good woman. She loved her children very much and worked hard all her life. Do you know much about Vera's sister – your grandmother?'

Amelia shook her head. 'No, but I saw a photograph of her at the farmhouse. She was very pretty.'

'She was. She was a very happy young lady.'

'What happened to her?'

'Vera never said?' Amelia could see the disapproval in Jocelyn's eyes. 'We always knew she'd keep her life private, but I'm surprised she didn't mention any of them to you.'

'If she did, I don't remember it, and I don't remember my mum or dad talking about them, but then I don't remember much about them at all.'

'I'm not surprised, dear. You were so young when they passed.' The weight of sadness those words carried caused Amelia's breath to catch. 'Vera's sister – your grandmother – was named Imelda.' Amelia felt her eyes widen as the name sank in. 'She was only forty-four when she died and it was a great loss to the village. She was always getting involved in community events.'

'Unlike Vera,' Amelia replied, and Jocelyn nodded her agreement.

'I'm afraid so. Imelda married a local man, Edward, your grandfather, and they had your mother. Your mum left for university and moved away when she met your father, but they always came back to visit. Such a shame,' she said sadly, clearly referring to their early deaths.

The room began to close in around Amelia and she felt the tension in her cheeks as she struggled to keep her expression neutral. The feeling that she might burst into sobs at any minute grew in her chest.

'Apart from that, there isn't much else I can tell you.'

'And you're sure you don't remember anything about the soldier, or anything to do with Meadow Farmhouse?'

Jocelyn's eyes sharpened, and her voice had taken on a defensive tone. 'What does it all matter now?'

Amelia wasn't sure if that was a yes or no. 'Do you think Vera preferred being on her own?'

'Of course she did, dear. It was easier, wasn't it?'

'Easier than what?' Were they finally going to get somewhere?

Jocelyn paused then cleared her throat. 'Life's hard, isn't it? Losing people is hard. You of all must know that. Now, I must get on.'

Though the words were said kindly, Amelia recoiled. She was right. It was hard being on your own, but sometimes it was safer that way. People couldn't be replaced like objects could. Perhaps Vera had decided after losing her own parents and her sister, that life was easier if she didn't care about anyone. Perhaps that was why Vera had never shown Amelia the sort of love and affection she'd craved. From Jocelyn's stance and expression she realised the conversation was over and it would be rude to push for more information.

'Thank you for your time, Jocelyn. You've been really helpful.'

'You're very welcome, dear.' The older woman stood. 'I do hope you'll stay a while and not rush back to Paris. I've a feeling a slower pace of life might suit you for a bit. I can imagine you're all go in the city but being all go all the time can be exhausting.'

Amelia was enjoying the slower pace of life of these last few days, but all holidays and breaks from the norm felt like that. No doubt tonight when she settled on the sofa for another meal alone she'd start missing being out, wined and dined and talking with friends. Jocelyn led the way to the front door and Amelia said a final goodbye before making her way down the path.

It had been a long time since she'd spoken so honestly about her family and how much she knew about them. She hadn't even known her own grandmother's name. That that was strange hadn't occurred to her before now. It must have at some point as a child, but she couldn't remember any particular circumstance. Yet, she still didn't know anything about the man in the locket or why Vera had kept it. The desire to solve that mystery grew fiercer with every step towards Meadow Farmhouse. From the way Jocelyn had changed during their conversation, Amelia had the feeling that she knew more than she was willing to say. People of her generation still lived by the saying 'don't speak ill of the dead' but maybe there was someone else she could talk to or records she could look up.

She began the walk back, circling around the village green and off to the shortcut that led out onto the country road in front of hers and Adam's houses. Surely the chance of running into him again was slim. As the fresh air chilled Amelia's skin, lifting the hairs on her arms, it felt like she'd learned everything and nothing today. She learned who her grandmother was and who her great-grandmother and great-grandfather were. That was a lot more than she had when she started. It was information some people took for granted. Those who had family to speak to and relatives to ask. She was already at a disadvantage in her search, but as she opened the locket to see the eyes of the soldier staring back at her awash with fear and, she realised now, pain, she was determined to find out more.

Amelia hurried along the shortcut as the light began to fade. The canopy of branches framed glimpses of navy and mauve streaks in the sky and as Meadow Farmhouse came into view, she saw Arthur, the old man who had lingered after the welcoming party a few days ago.

'Hello, Arthur. Is everything okay?'

He jumped as her words carried on the mounting breeze. 'Oh – I – yes. Everything's fine.' He wrung his hands together and turned to walk off in the opposite direction.

He seemed confused or upset. 'Can I call someone, Arthur? Do you need some help?'

'I came to see Vera,' the old man said. His voice was so low that at first Amelia thought she'd misheard.

'Oh.' Did he not know Vera had died? She didn't know Arthur all that well and had never really spoken to him as a child. Was she in danger of upsetting him further if she stated too coldly what had happened? Perhaps he had an illness or dementia. She didn't want to frighten or upset him. Arthur dropped his eyes as if realising Vera wasn't there.

'Where do you live, Arthur? Is there someone I can call? Would you like to come in for a cup of tea?' It was growing colder, and she couldn't leave him out here.

'I live in the old people's home in the village now,' he said seeming much more relaxed. 'You look like her.' Arthur had said that before when she'd seen him, and it unnerved her.

'Vera?' He nodded. 'Do I?' Without thinking she touched her long dark hair, pulling it over her shoulder. Thinking of the photograph of a young Vera on the mantelpiece, she probably did look like her a bit. They both had long dark hair and pale eyes. And she supposed, Arthur, like Jocelyn, would have known the young Vera.

'I'd better head back,' he said quietly.

'Are you sure you wouldn't like a cup of tea or something to warm you up first?' She had no idea how long he'd been there but she couldn't send him on his way without offering again.

'No, no.' He waved a finger towards the ground as he headed off in that direction.

'Do you have a torch or something? It's getting dark.'

The only reply she got was a shake of the head as he carried on his way. Amelia took another glance up at the sky. Clouds were gathering, speeding the descending darkness. The walk to the village was only a short one. He'd be there in a few minutes, though she might ring the home just to make sure he got back okay. Opening the front door, Amelia edged inside her childhood home wondering how she would ever sleep after so much had happened in one single day.

Chapter 11

Adam unpacked the last few sculptures from the back of his van whilst checking over his shoulder in case anyone passed by.

Why had he ever thought this would be a good idea? This wasn't the kick up the bum he needed. He was basically signing up for six hours of humiliation. This had been a stupid thing to do and he was bitterly regretting it now the day had come. Signing up to the monthly arts and crafts market at Highfield had seemed like such a good idea at the time. After a couple of pints, powered by embarrassment at Rob's ribbing and at his mum's attempt at flogging them, he'd signed up as soon as he got home. Part of the decision was based on a need to get rid of as many of them as he could. The number in his workshop really was quite frightening. His mum had described them as an army and she wasn't far off. Another reason was his stubborn streak kicking in and a wish to show everyone they were works of art and not just a silly hobby. Now he was parked at Highfield, he wished he'd never filled out the online form and paid the money for a pitch. It was Saturday. He could still be in bed.

'Adam,' said Mrs Motley, the wife of the top human rights lawyer who'd bought Highfield a few years ago. They didn't really come into the village much but would occasionally hold events like this. His mum thought it was to keep the village onside, but he liked to think it was because they were as busy as everyone else. They didn't need the money from something like this. Highfield wasn't like a lot of country houses that were falling apart. Its high-end opulence was more like a spread in an interior design magazine. More likely, they just didn't have time to hold lots of events but joined in when they could. 'Adam, darling, how lovely to see you here. I was surprised when I saw your name on the list. Have you got some more of your marvellous furniture to sell?'

'A bit. Yes.' Adam had the foresight to bring the coffee table he'd made from an old tree stump in an effort to stock something he could actually describe and talk about without blushing. 'I've also got some sculptures I've been working on.' He pulled one of the larger ones from the back of the van and placed it on the floor in front of him. It was actually one of his favourites, the one he described as naked Pinocchio. Mrs Motley's eyes widened but her mouth stayed in a tight grin.

'How lovely.'

She hates them, he thought with a sinking feeling. If that was to be everyone's reaction, it would be a very long day.

'Do follow me into the house.'

After following her inside the house and finding his pitch in the enormous ballroom that had been expertly restored, he set up his stall. He gave the coffee table pride of place and put some of the cuter sculptures behind. They looked a bit like they were having a tea party. It might have been a little presumptuous to bring a cash box and a notepad for those who wanted to buy one or place a commission, but he added them to the table nonetheless.

At ten o'clock the doors officially opened and the first few visitors came in. As he watched from his spot in the corner, Adam wrung his hands together. Perhaps pacing behind the stall would keep the nerves at bay. Marching back and forth, he received a wary look from the lady on the crochet table next to him. He sat down again.

People were drawing nearer as they made their way around the room. Was it just him, or was it incredibly hot in here? Could he ask Mrs Motley to open a window? He'd forgotten to bring a flask with all his dithering about, hesitating as to whether to come or not. Now his throat was dry and scratchy but that was nothing compared with the cold that swept over him as his eyes were drawn to the couple who'd just entered. It was Rob and his girlfriend, Jessica.

'Oh, for f—' Crochet lady cleared her throat and glared at him. 'Sorry, stubbed my toe. Don't worry, I was going to say flipping. I wasn't going to say fu—' She held her hand up to stop him and edged a little closer to the far side of her table.

What was he doing? He'd just sworn at an old lady. Okay, not quite at her, but as good as. And now he was talking to himself in his head. Today was definitely not going well.

As soon as Rob saw him, he made a beeline over. 'Adam! What are you doing here? Are you selling those weirdo sculptures your mum was going on about?'

'Rob!' Jessica admonished. 'Don't be mean. I think they're cute. I like that one.' She pointed to one of the smaller, cuter ones. 'It looks a bit like Baby Groot.'

'Thanks, Jess,' Adam said, relaxing a little. There, not everyone hated them, but he didn't yet have the courage to say how much it was or push for a sale. He couldn't risk a rejection, sticking with the compliment and waiting for her to ask if she was interested was enough for now.

'Well, maybe if we don't see anything else, we'll come back and get it,' Rob said. 'They're not my type of thing, but nice craftsmanship, mate.'

'Cheers.' It was better than nothing and to be fair, Rob was gobby but he wasn't always an idiot.

The next two hours passed much the same way. Some of the people he met had come from other nearby villages, others were from Meadowbank. All his conversations with his neighbours were the same. They'd heard his mum mention his 'weird little men' and though they admired the skill and artistry, no one actually wanted one.

After getting a cup of tea from a drinks stall in the grounds and taking a break from the barrage of surprised reluctance, Adam came back willing the last few hours to pass quickly. He was beginning to worry that today was doing more damage to his reputation than good. Would everyone now think he was a weirdo and not hire him? Even with his mum's vocal efforts, they clearly hadn't known he had such artistic aspirations. Maybe he should stick to carpentry and furniture making from now on.

Adam pottered behind the stall. He hadn't thought the day could get any worse when a face entered the hall that he immediately recognised, and the surge of emotion inside made his jaw tighten. Amelia Williams was talking to Mrs Motley and she was showing her around. Amelia hadn't seen him yet and though he didn't want to be caught staring, Adam couldn't pull his eyes away. Her long dark hair swung about her face, rested on her shoulders, and her pale grey eyes danced as she smiled. Mrs Motley didn't show everyone around, and he wondered what Amelia was doing here. At nights he'd tried to imagine her face ten years older but it had surprised him just how lovely she was. There was a softness to her features that he hadn't remembered from their youth, particularly her lips.

After she'd called into Jocelyn's the other day, he couldn't help but swing by and try to find out what she was doing there. Being the sprightly old woman she was, Jocelyn had teased him, immediately seeing through his surprise visit to check the banister he'd fixed over a month ago. She hadn't yielded any information though and as her tormenting had grown more intense, he'd taken the chance to escape.

Panic rose as Mrs Motley showed Amelia around the stalls. In a matter of seconds they'd be here, at his, and then she'd see his weird half-Groot, half-mannequin sculptures. If she reacted the same way most of the others had, he'd die of embarrassment – actually drop dead on the spot. If you could die from fright, he was pretty sure you could die from humiliation as well. Adam tried to plan an escape route. Could he just leave? No he couldn't because a customer was coming over. Why did someone have to start showing an interest now? He'd spent all day being mocked. Actually, that was an exaggeration but why did it have to be now?

The customer wasn't a woman he had seen before so she must have come from one of the other villages. He forced himself to make small talk. 'Good afternoon.'

'Good afternoon, young man. These are lovely. I like that little guy on the end. How much are you selling him for?'

'Danny DeVito?'

'I'm sorry?'

'Nothing. That's just what I call him. Umm ... twenty-five pounds.' He hadn't known what to charge and though this didn't reflect the hours it had taken to make each and every one, it seemed a reasonable price. From the corner of his eye, Adam saw Amelia edging closer and closer.

'He's lovely, but that's a bit steep. Would you take fifteen?'

Though Adam knew he could haggle, his first reaction was to hug the woman for not running away screaming. With the threat of Amelia coming near, he gratefully, and quickly, accepted, hoping he could offer to carry it to the woman's car for her, giving him an excuse to leave. 'Yes, definitely. Thank you.' He took the cash and thrust it into his pocket. 'Where's your car. I'll take him for you.'

'No, that's fine. He's only diddy. I can manage. I think I'll call him Martin. I don't know who Danny DeVito is and I think he looked more like a Martin.' The woman was sturdy enough to carry a steel girder, but Adam double-checked, hoping she'd change her mind. 'Well aren't you a lovely young man, but no, that's fine. Hand him over.'

Adam did as he was told, anxiety gripping him again. Even if Amelia saw him, he wasn't going to talk to her; he'd already decided that. There was nothing left to say and there was every possibility his anger would grow, and he'd tell her how destroyed he'd been after she'd left. She was almost on top of him, so to speak. Best not to focus on that thought too much – he was hot enough. There was nowhere to go. His only option was to hide. He bent down behind the table, pretending he was searching for something in his rucksack. With any luck, she'd pass by quickly.

Mrs Motley's voice grew louder and he could see from their feet they were the other side of the table. 'As you can see, we're very busy today, but you're welcome to come back next week. Maybe on Monday? About ten?'

'That sounds perfect. Thank you.'

'Fabulous. Well, I'll leave you to look around. See you next week.'

Mrs Motley's feet left in the opposite direction, but Amelia stayed put. He waited for her to leave and when she didn't move, he remained crouched down.

'Adam?'

This time he whispered the swear word he wasn't going to use earlier. There was no escaping it now – she'd recognised the top of his head and as much as he'd love to, he couldn't hide under there forever. Taking a deep breath, he straightened up. The sweetness in her eyes almost melted his heart but he called on his reserves to protect him. 'Amelia. Nice to see you.'

'Are these yours?' she asked, pointing to the sculptures, and as the first prickle of embarrassment took him, he tapped his fingers on the table. 'I heard you were a carpenter, but I had no idea you made things like this too. These are fabulous. I—' She faltered as his gaze shot to hers. Quickly, he dropped his eyes, surprised at her reaction. 'I love them.'

'Oh. Umm, thanks.'

A tinge of pink crept into the apples of her cheeks and Adam reminded himself again he was not going to soften. 'They're beautifully crafted. Fabulous. They've got so much character.'

Stunned by her compliments, Adam didn't know what to say. No one had ever described them so nicely before. Possibly because before today he'd never been brave enough to show anyone apart from his mother, but still, he appreciated her words.

'I'm an interior designer and I know some people who'd love these. Did you make all of them yourself?'

She was trying so hard to strike up a conversation that he couldn't in good conscience continue to respond so coldly, but after holding on to so much hurt for so long, he was struggling to answer her compliments.

As he searched his mind for any useful words, Amelia took his silence as a rebuttal. Pain flitted across her face before she said, 'Well, bye, Adam.'

'What are you doing here? At Highfield I mean,' he blurted before she could move off.

Amelia turned back, her nerves clear on her face. 'When I saw it was open, I thought I'd take a break from decorating and come in. I—' She hesitated, clearly thinking about whether to go on. 'I found something at the farmhouse – a locket that belonged to Vera – and I've been trying to find out a bit more about it.' She pulled it out from underneath her scarf and showed it to him. He never recalled Vera wearing anything like that, but then she wasn't really one for jewellery.

As he leaned forward to look, getting closer to her, the air felt charged with emotion. The aromatic smell of her long dark hair came to him and before he could get carried away, he reminded himself of the promises she'd made. That she'd email, text, keep in touch after she settled into life at university. A part of him knew even then that a new life called her on and he'd be left behind, nothing more than an afterthought.

'Good luck, then,' he said, pulling back. 'I'll see you around.'

Her face fell and he wished it didn't have to be this way, but he needed to put some distance between them both physically and emotionally before she had even more of an effect on him.

'Bye, Adam,' she replied quietly before tucking the locket away and moving on.

The noise of the crowd seemed to surge in his ears, and he turned to stare at his sculptures. She'd described them so well.

They did have character. For a moment he replayed the feeling of embarrassment he'd had at each and every jibe from Rob or other people today. It was easier to feel that than recognise the pain, and yearning, in his heart.

Chapter 12

Amelia dropped the paintbrush back into the tray and admired her handiwork.

'Not too bad at all. Even if I do say so myself.'

With only a couple of weeks until the estate agent came, she was pleased with her progress. Now the living room was clear, and even on this rainy day, more light spilled in through the new windowpanes, the light cream paint was brightening the room. She'd ordered most of the stuff online and it had been delivered with perfect timing the day before. Being without a car wasn't a problem in Paris. It was one of those cities you could easily get anywhere but Meadowbank was different. Thankfully, the delivery driver had found the property without much trouble.

The old threadbare rugs that had covered the living-room floor were outside, ready for the tip, and the stone floor had been swept and washed. New curtains framed the two large windows in the living room against the walls she had already painted. After working in interior design for so long, she was a dab hand at rollering and cutting in, and it didn't take her long to get a room finished. On one, she had placed Vera's half-finished picture from the easel. The colours worked well and even though it was incomplete, it added to its charm. For some reason, it spoke to Amelia of how Vera had half-lived her life, though the questions it raised about her own were unnerving. The more she looked at it the more she wondered how happy her life in Paris really made her. That the answer hadn't immediately come to her was even more unsettling.

Above the fireplace, she had hung the painting of the coppice.

This would be one of the things she'd take back to Paris. She couldn't resist the reminder, however painful, of the beautiful place and the memories of Adam associated with it. She'd faced him now, and though he had again rebuffed her efforts at conversation, she couldn't stand the thought of someone else looking at the picture. It belonged here, or at least, with her. She'd considered asking Adam if he wanted Vera's painting of Meadow Farmhouse but as they weren't likely to speak again, and he clearly hated her, she hadn't actually contacted him to make the offer.

The heavy woven curtains in a pale lemon added a splash of colour and matching throws with contrasting scatter cushions tied the sofa in nicely. All in all, she was pleased with her progress and though Vera hated change of any sort, Amelia liked to think she would have been pleased it was turning into a home to be proud of once more. Every time she closed her eyes and imagined it finished, Amelia had to pull herself back from seeing it how she wanted it. Strangely, separating her professional and personal thoughts about the place was growing harder and harder.

A knock at the door gave Amelia the perfect excuse for a quick break and she went to answer it. As rain battered the windows, she was pleased she'd taken the chance to visit Highfield yesterday during the arts and crafts market, though she hadn't expected to see Adam there, or to speak to him. It had been the longest conversation they'd had, but with it had come the most tension.

'Morning,' Sophie said, as Amelia opened the door, happy for the mental change of subject. Isla literally jumped inside, launching herself from the front step over the threshold with gusto. She had a backpack in the shape of a pink pig, and wellington boots that were almost as long as her legs. Sophie followed, quickly closing the door behind her. 'It's horrible out there today. All that spring showers nonsense can jog on. It's torrential.' After shooing Isla further inside and removing her backpack and boots, Sophie lifted her head. 'It's lovely to see you. We thought we'd stop by and say hello if you've got time.'

'Of course. It's lovely to see you, too.' Her burgeoning friendship with Sophie was a surprising aspect of her return home. She hadn't expected to meet someone she clicked with, but Sophie had a warmth to her that swept you along. Totally unlike Océanè, she thought, then scolded herself for wavering in her loyalty. 'Hello, Isla.'

'Wow,' said Sophie, seeing the living room. 'It's looking amazing already. You have a real eye for design.'

'Thanks. Good job I'm an interior designer then,' Amelia joked.

'Are you? That sounds wonderful. I'll have to get you to help me decorate our bedrooms. It's certainly looking brighter in here. What's with the door though?' She pointed to the playroom door.

'Ah, yes. I need a carpenter.'

'Did you not call Adam?'

'Not yet.' She'd been putting it off for as long as possible but there was no way she could continue to do so. How that would go after yesterday didn't bear thinking about. 'Would you like some tea? I was just about to take a break.'

'Tea sounds good. I'm gasping. Michael's gone out for his usual Sunday morning run, so I thought I'd pop by.'

'In this? He's brave.'

'He's a lunatic, but it helps him deal with stress.'

Amelia made two cups of tea and took some of the biscuits she'd bought the other day to the table. Sophie joined her.

'Wozat?' asked Isla, trying to climb onto a chair. Amelia pulled it out for her so she could clamber onto the seat.

Sophie translated. 'What's that? Amelia's letting us have some biscuits.' Isla turned to her mum and grinned toothily. She had Sophie's blonde hair and it was curling from the damp air.

'Would you like some?' Amelia asked, offering her one. Isla took it and began chomping away, saying a full-mouthed equivalent to thank you after Sophie reminded her.

'S'rain,' Isla said, pointing to the window and speaking with a ball of food in her mouth.

'I know,' Amelia replied. 'It's raining lots, isn't it? Is that why you wore your boots?'

Isla nodded emphatically.

'What else have you got for Amelia, Isla?'

She climbed down off the chair and opened her backpack, retrieving a piece of paper before climbing back up and presenting it proudly. 'F'you.'

'What's this?' Amelia asked, smiling broadly as she studied the picture.

'It's a welcome to Meadowbank card. Isla made it this morning.'

'Ah, thank you, Isla. It's fabulous. Is this me?'

Sophie peered over to where Amelia was pointing. 'Yeah. Sorry you look like a cross between a horror movie clown and a hot air balloon. I promise you don't look like that in real life.'

'I'm glad to hear it. She's nailed my red lipstick though. Is that a – a penis?' she whispered.

'I think it's supposed to be your handbag.'

'Right. And I've got—'

'Three boobs, yes. Or they might be udders. I hope she doesn't think mine look like that.'

Amelia laughed as Sophie patted her chest. 'Well, thank you, Isla. I love it.'

'So,' Sophie said, cupping her hands around the warmth of her mug. 'When we saw you at the library, you said you were finding out about the house. Anything good? Have you got ghosts?'

'Only Vera's,' Amelia joked, but then, under Sophie's open gaze, she gave in to a surprising burst of honesty. Sophie wasn't at all like Océanè and Amelia was sure she wouldn't think she was going crazy being so interested in it. From their text exchange yesterday, Océanè couldn't have cared less and simply encouraged her to come back to Paris as soon as possible.

'How fascinating,' Sophie said after listening intently to all that Amelia had found.

'And I found a wedding dress in her wardrobe.'

'A wedding dress?'

She nodded, handing Isla another biscuit. 'It's all so confusing. It was damaged. But why leave it that way? Why not fix it? Vera kept so little personal stuff. I mean, I can't even find her birth certificate, so it feels like whatever she did keep must have been really important to her.' Amelia sighed. 'I just feel like I didn't even know Vera. I had no idea she'd kept any of these things. It's like the Vera I grew up with – the Vera I knew – wasn't the real Vera at all. Or at the very least there was another side to her. She was always the woman who didn't want me and to think there was more to her than just that is, well … shocking.'

'I suppose we all think like that about our parents – or guardians—' she added hastily. 'To a certain extent,' Sophie said. 'We forget they had a life before we existed.'

Amelia sipped her tea. 'I just don't want to sell this house without knowing more about her or the rest of the Cabots. Once I've sold it, I can't just come back and knock on the door, asking to have a look around. Once it's gone, it's gone. And when I've gone back to Paris—' The thought of never coming back pierced her heart unexpectedly. 'I can't just rock up and ask to come in for a look around.'

'I'm not surprised you want to know. It's important. Once you've got rid of these things you can't always get them back. Gosh, it's like an episode of *Who Do You Think You Are?*'

'It is a bit. I wish I had their skill though. At the moment I'm just bumbling around in the dark, trying to figure out what to do next.'

'What *are* you going to do next?'

'I'm off to Highfield tomorrow to see what I can find out there. If nothing else, it'll be nice to get a feel for the place. I stopped in the other day when the arts and crafts market was on.' Could she mention him? Could she talk about Adam? Emboldened by the wonderful conversation they'd had so far, and how freeing it had felt to be open and honest with someone, she said, 'I ran into Adam there.'

Sophie leaned in. 'I don't mean to pry, but I've been told there's a bit of an atmosphere between you two. And I've heard the mention of *history*. Are you okay?'

Amelia continued chewing her biscuit, trying to think of a response. Even after a year of friendship with Océanè, she hadn't admitted to her about her parents' deaths, or really given away any personal information someone couldn't get from her website bio. Not because it all still hurt, she told herself firmly, but where had that sort of closed-off attitude led Vera? Sophie didn't seem the type to gossip. Would it hurt to admit how things had ended between them and the regret she felt?

After a breath she said, 'I think history might be putting it mildly. Adam and I were really close when we were younger.' Regret rang around the room, beating the echo of the rain outside. 'He was my first love really and I was his but then …'

Would Sophie judge her as harshly as Lynne had?

'Isla, why don't you play with your dolls? They're in your backpack.' Isla hopped down and plonked herself on the floor next to her bag as she began to play. 'What happened?'

'I left.'

'And you didn't keep in touch?'

'I didn't really even say goodbye.' Sophie's eyes widened and guilt stabbed at Amelia. 'I went to uni and then every time a holiday came up, I just didn't come back. I didn't want to stay with Vera, and I had nowhere else to go.'

'Didn't Adam keep in touch with you even if you didn't text him?'

'He tried and—' A heaviness filled her ribcage. 'So many times I wanted to respond, but I couldn't. We lost touch after I went to uni and stopped coming back for holidays. Vera was so angry with me for going. She felt like I'd let her down. Like I'd used her.'

'That's horrible.' Sophie was truly appalled and Amelia felt slightly vindicated. Unless you lived with her it was hard to know the true extent of her temper. 'I know she wasn't your mother, but she was your guardian. How could she say that?'

The pain of some of their more animated exchanges flew back as fresh as they day the wounds had been inflicted. 'I was getting top grades on my course and my lecturers were really proud of me. It was a type of encouragement I'd never had before. Vera always told me to work hard and not let her down after all she'd done for me.' Saying her name now in the dim kitchen made even darker by the heavy clouds outside, a ghostly feeling of disapproval hung in the air and Amelia shivered. 'All these new people were saying how clever I was, how bright and golden my future would be if I kept at it, so I did. When I was in a house on my own in the holidays, I'd read the reading list for the next year, get work experience and internships. By the time I finished uni, I had so much work experience I landed a job straight away. When I said I was moving to Paris, she told me to never bother coming back. At the time, I was so proud I was moving my life forward – I was going to be someone and do something – I wasn't just an orphan appendage – that I just said fine and left.'

'And that was the last you saw of her?'

Amelia nodded. 'I sent Christmas cards and birthday cards over the years, and I sometimes got them from Vera, but not always.'

'And Adam?' Sophie's voice carried no judgement for which Amelia was incredibly grateful but voicing her feelings to someone for the first time engulfed her with shame.

'It's my biggest regret. But the more time that went by the harder it became to try and get in touch. I knew he'd be angry with me, and rightly so – I deserve it; I know that – but I just couldn't bring myself to face it.' Regret didn't feel enough of a description right now, and for the first time she allowed herself to realise what could have been. 'At the time I thought I was doing the right thing by leaving my past behind and I honestly thought he'd just forget about me.'

'From what Lynne said, he didn't. Did that surprise you?'

'Yes,' she exclaimed. 'I'd never have lost contact if I'd have known how much I'd hurt him. I honestly just thought he'd find someone else pretty quickly. He was always cute and so many of the girls had crushes on him. I never thought I'd have such an impact on someone's life.'

'Oh, honey,' Sophie said reaching out. 'I'm sorry Vera made you feel that way.' The soft touch of Sophie's hand warmed her heart.

The truth was, Amelia's heart had been filled with him all her life. Every time the agony and longing had flared up, she'd buried herself deeper in the life she was building and the idea of all that was ahead of her. It had numbed the sorrow until it was so lost underneath plans and ambition that it couldn't resurface. Knowing how he despised her, the familiar desire to run away began to take hold but deep down she knew it wouldn't help this time. All she could hope was that the physical distance would mask the pain until she became busy enough to quell it.

'Anyway,' she said, brightening. 'By about Thursday I should have some stuff for the spring fair. You wouldn't believe the number of pots and pans Vera had.'

'Lovely. We should make a decent amount this year, then. I'm hoping we can get enough to upgrade some of the playground equipment. It's not very inclusive.'

The warmth in Sophie's face spread to Amelia. 'You really like living here, don't you?'

'I love it. Why?'

'I don't know, you just seem to be so …'

'So …?'

'So young and busy and happy for a place like this.'

'Villages aren't quite as full of old fuddy-duddies as the TV would have you believe.'

Maybe that presumption was just a remnant of her childhood. 'Tell me more about how you came to be here. You've heard all about me and my tragic past. I'd like to know about you.'

'My story is a very quick one. I always wanted children and it took us a while to conceive. I'd been on the pill for years and it took ages for it to work through my system. When we found out I was pregnant, I was really eager to find somewhere as perfect as this.'

'What did you do before?'

'I was a teacher, but it was super stressful. The school was so big it was hard to keep up with the work and give the kids the pastoral care they deserved.'

She could see Sophie would have been an amazing teacher. 'Do you miss working?'

'Sometimes.' She shrugged. 'But I want to make the most of Isla being this young. I'll look for a job as soon as she goes off to nursery or something.'

'That sounds like a good plan. She's a lovely little girl.' Some of Isla's dollies were now propped up inside the shoes and boots lined up by the door, and Amelia wondered what Isla's imagination was creating.

'We'd better get going,' Sophie said apologetically. 'I'm sure you'll be wanting to get on and Michael will be back from his run soon. You do know you're going to have to get Adam in to fix that door though. There really isn't another carpenter in the village. There might be one in one of the neighbouring ones, but I can tell you they won't be as good as him. He's a lovely man and really easy-going. I'm sure he'll say yes, even with your past.'

'I know I can't keep putting it off. It's been lovely to see you. Thanks for stopping by.'

Sophie gathered Isla and all her belongings together then helped her into her wellies. As they went off in the car, Amelia waved, grateful to feel the air on her face. The rain had stopped and though the clouds were still grim and grey, tiny patches of blue were breaking through. The air smelled so fresh and cold Amelia could feel it filling her lungs and clearing her nose of paint fumes. She turned to head back inside, and her eyes fell to the coppice that separated Meadow Farmhouse from the estate of Highfield.

A figure lingered under one of the outer trees, holding an umbrella. Sharpening her gaze, Amelia saw that it was Arthur and she wondered again if she should call the home. He was straying further and further from the village, but, she supposed, he wasn't a prisoner and could go where he wanted. Amelia waved and he returned the gesture before turning and heading into the woods.

Taking her phone from her pocket, her fingers trembled as she contemplated a conversation with Adam. It seemed she had no choice but to ask him to come and work on the farmhouse. The trouble was, she was almost completely sure he was going to say no and the thought of that made her shove the phone so deep into her pocket the seams strained. Perhaps she'd do it later after a large glass of wine. Or three.

Chapter 13

That evening, rain battered the windows and whistled through the gaps in the panes. It was pitch black outside and even the stars were absent, obscured by heavy clouds tinged with purple and grey, but with the brighter walls and the fire roaring in the grate, providing a deep orange glow, the farmhouse felt cosy and snug. Amelia had purchased a new television and placed it in the corner of the living room, leaving the playroom as a second sitting room. Apart from some decorating it didn't need much. It had been even barer than the living room, but some soft furnishings would make it an inviting and restful space. Whoever bought it could do as they pleased. On the TV screen in front of her, Nigella Lawson buzzed around her kitchen making a delicious-looking cake that had Amelia's mouth watering.

As she remembered the enormous block of aged electronics she'd watched when she was younger, Amelia admired the slim TV now stood in its place. Vera had always enjoyed cookery programmes and Amelia had watched a few with her. She took a sip from the glass of wine she'd been nursing for an hour as she laid her head back against the cushions. Nights like this were increasingly confusing. A sense of peace relaxed her muscles and her mind slowed to a more sedate pace rather than racing on to the next task as it did in Paris. She enjoyed the restfulness now coming into her life, but then, on the other hand, she missed going out to dinner and sitting in bars talking to people. She missed using the language that had become second nature to her, the lyrical, eloquent sounds rolling off her tongue. Would she forget how to speak French if she didn't get back soon? She'd worked so hard to learn it, so hard to build her life, that effort couldn't go to waste.

As she snuggled under the blanket across her knees and enjoyed the rhythmic tapping of the rain against the glass, she glanced back over her shoulder at the playroom, considering what colour to paint it. The door was still off its hinges, leaning against the wall, and after another near miss earlier when the bathroom door stuck after she'd had a wee, she knew she couldn't put it off any longer. She had to call Adam. As always, when thoughts of Adam came into her head, which they did more often than she cared to admit, they made her long for the simplicity of her life in Paris. Being nothing more than a face in the crowd offered a sense of freedom far removed from the raw emotions that came with Meadow Farmhouse.

A gust of wind blustered around the house causing a draught to whistle through the walls. A crash from behind made her jump and Amelia bounced in her seat as the playroom door fell to the floor.

'Jeeeesus!' Wine dripped down her fingers where she'd flung the contents upwards. She wiped her fingers down her pyjama bottoms.

One of the perks of a quieter life was that she could wear her pyjamas in the evenings rather than having to remain dressed and in full make-up for dinner. Considering her thoughts earlier had drifted to what she missed about Paris, her confusion intensified. Standing, she placed her wine on the mantelshelf and went to pick up the door. Luckily it hadn't scratched the newly painted walls or damaged any other furniture.

'Was that you, Vera, telling me to get on and fix it? I know I keep putting it off.'

As much as the thought of seeing Adam brought her out in a cold sweat, she needed a carpenter. With the estate agent due in just a couple of weeks, she really couldn't wait. Resuming her seat, she took her phone and searched the internet for local carpenters. There weren't any in the villages nearby and the handymen from the nearest city didn't have very good ratings. One had apparently almost set fire to a kitchen when welding a pipe and another had flooded a living room after the shower above it hadn't been installed properly. Even thinking about problems like that made her shudder. She couldn't afford to spend money getting something fixed because she'd hired the wrong person. She had to make sure it was someone who'd treat the farmhouse with the level of respect it deserved. It was, after all, one of the oldest buildings in the village and she had a duty to look after it properly. But that meant only one thing: Adam Noble, carpenter extraordinaire.

Amelia sighed and eyed her mobile phone. Why did Adam have to be the only carpenter in the local vicinity? Why couldn't he have become a pilot or a ski instructor? Someone she wasn't likely to come into contact with? A sudden image of Adam pulling off a ski helmet in a snowy log cabin shot into her brain and as her body tingled, she cast it aside. 'Not helpful.'

At a loss as to what she'd even say, she laid the phone beside her. Perhaps another glass of wine would give her the courage to call. She went to the fridge and topped up her glass, staring at the contents for a moment. She wasn't hungry, but she wanted to do something other than think of Adam and hoped a slab of locally made cheddar cheese would help. She took the scrap of paper with his number on from the front of the fridge and as she closed it, nibbled as she went back to the sofa.

Just get straight to the point, she told herself. *Just be professional.* All she had to say was that he'd been recommended by every single person who'd ever lived in the village and that she had some jobs if he's interested. It wasn't like she had to recite Shakespeare or unravel a particularly difficult maths problem.

But what if he says no? she thought. It would be horribly embarrassing. Then again, it's not as if things were easy between them now. Could they get worse? Probably not. Every time they talked the air seemed filled with unspoken words and painful emotions, and if seeing him in the village proved too much, she could always throw herself in a ditch to avoid him. What other choice did she have? She didn't have the tools or the know-how to fix the doors, and as every other local handyman was apparently incompetent, there wasn't any other option.

Amelia slugged back the cool, crisp wine and nibbled the cheese. This was it; she was going in. She lifted the phone and typed in the number. It wasn't until Adam answered that she realised she'd been holding her breath.

'Adam!' she squealed, sounding surprised that she was ringing him. Amelia gasped in a breath and cringed. Christ, she sounded like an absolute lunatic. And he must wonder what she was doing to be so out of breath. Why was she so out of breath? She placed a hand on her heart to steady it. Unable to stay still she began pacing, tidying the sides of the kitchen putting empty crisp packets into the bin (the sum total of her dinner). 'Adam, hi. It's Amelia … Amelia Williams.'

'Oh.' The line went so deadly silent Amelia looked at her phone to see if he'd rung off. Obviously, he hadn't been expecting her to call. 'Hi, Amelia. What can I help you with?'

Thank God she didn't have to say her plumbing. His voice was so rich and silken she had to concentrate. 'I need a carpenter for Meadow Farmhouse, and you've been highly recommended.' She placed a tea towel back into a drawer and went to close it. It didn't budge and Amelia shoved it with her hip, making an ungainly oomphing noise as she did so. Had Adam heard that? Her cheeks grew hot. Perhaps she'd be safer in the living room.

Walking away, she looked down at her saggy pyjama bottoms. The arse was swinging around like a heavy nappy. Not the most confidence-boosting outfit to make this call in. Still, getting changed into a date-night outfit would have been weirder.

'Right. Who recommended me?' She couldn't tell from his tone if he was happy about it or not. She loved to be recommended to new clients. It was a great vote of confidence that never failed to give her a thrill, but she'd probably be reticent if everyone was recommending her to a past love she wasn't particularly keen on seeing again.

'Sophie did and pretty much everyone else I mentioned it to. They all said you were the best around and when I checked online they were right.'

'You checked online?'

Shit! Why had she said that? Now she looked like she didn't want to employ him, which was true but not because she didn't trust him to do a good job. Bugger. 'Err, only to find your number.'

'But I'm not online,' he said quietly.

'No. That's true,' she gabbled. 'I just – I forgot where I'd put it. Sophie gave it to me.' She really had to stop talking. To everyone. From now on, she'd talk to the chickens and that was it. Since returning to Meadowbank she'd lost the ability to have a conversation without putting her foot in it. Amelia powered on, trying to sound like a professional. 'I've got a few doors and cupboards that need fixing. They're not huge jobs. They're just ones I need a professional for. I can paint and hang wallpaper and stuff, but I'm no good with hammers and nails and … tools.' *Tools? Oh my Lord, just stop talking!* 'So … do you think you can help me out?'

The only thing louder than the beating of her heart was her breathing and she manoeuvred the phone slightly away hoping Adam couldn't hear her. She sounded like she was hyperventilating. The line had gone incredibly quiet again.

'Adam?'

***

Adam stared at the row of sculptures lined up along the wall of the workshop as if they might give him the answer he was looking for. He suddenly missed Danny DeVito. He'd have been able to help him out. All he needed was a thumbs up or down.

Just a slight movement of the limbs he'd made for them. They stubbornly refused to move, and he knew he had to make the decision for himself. Should he take the job or not?

Why had he answered the bloody phone?

He was used to receiving calls from unknown numbers – it was a regular part of his job – but he hadn't expected to be hearing from Amelia. Perhaps he should have. The last time he'd been at the farmhouse when Vera was alive, he'd seen a cupboard door in the kitchen had slipped down on its hinges. Knowing how Vera was letting things go he should have expected there to be more to do. It was wonderful the village had recommended him but right now he wished there were other people she could call.

Being around her, being near her, brought to the surface far too many emotions and muddled him up. Her face the other day – when he hadn't engaged in conversation – haunted him, but how close could he get without losing control?

'Adam?' Amelia asked again, her voice echoing in his ears as he drew his eyes away to the shadows dancing on the ground outside the workshop. She sounded nervous and he wanted to ease her anxiety but he also had to protect himself.

'Umm, let me check my diary.'

You don't have a diary! He placed the phone on the bench and walked around, his hands on his hips. Most of the time he kept his to-do list in his head. He knew full well he was pretty free on Tuesday. Lorraine, whose number he'd entered into his phone having been caught off guard by her before, had rung him about another job, but he was trying not to go as soon as she called. He had a feeling she was getting a little carried away and didn't want to encourage her. Adam glanced over at the phone. He needed more time to compose himself. More time to think about what he wanted to do. Could he call her back? That would just prolong the agony, and a small part of him was pushing him towards her again, eager to make up for his shortness before.

He paced some more, staring at the beams of the workshop

ceiling. He had to answer her soon. Maybe he'd say he was too busy, but there wasn't really anyone else he could recommend. And he didn't want shoddy work at the farmhouse. No, he wouldn't do that. If the village had put their faith in him and Amelia had the courage to call, he'd treat her the same as any client. He'd never let anyone in the village down before no matter how busy he was or how late he worked and he wouldn't start now. Taking a deep breath and marching back to his phone he said, 'I've just checked and I can swing by on Tuesday if that's okay?'

Her words came out in a garbled rush of relief. 'Tuesday would be great, thank you. I'm not going anywhere.'

Yet, he thought bitterly.

Weird rustlings came from the background and he wondered what she was doing. He hoped she hadn't called him from bed. The very thought made his heart pulse. 'Is about nine o'clock okay?'

'Yeah, great. I'll have the kettle on.'

She was trying to be friendly, to put him at ease, or maybe put herself at ease, but right now he couldn't relax into the conversation. A tension had straightened his spine and pulled his shoulders uncomfortably high. He'd been to strangers' houses so many times before and made conversation about the weather or popular TV shows, but the idea of being with Amelia again and finding something to talk about was terrifying. Could he keep his resentment under control long enough to get the job done? Unsure how best to sign off, he said, 'Right. Tuesday nine o'clock then. See you later.' And hung up before she could say another word.

Adam tapped his phone against his chin and stared at his sculptures. 'Thanks for nothing, guys.'

Switching off the lights he retreated back to his farmhouse and, judging by the sea of emotions raging inside him, a long and sleepless night.

Chapter 14

Once more, Amelia stopped at the threshold of Vera's bedroom. Before she left for Highfield to continue her search, she needed to sort through some more of Vera's room in case there were any more clues. She'd had a cursory look in between bouts of decorating, but there just didn't seem to be enough time to do everything and the clients waiting for her in Paris were always on her mind, forcing her to focus on decorating and nothing else.

In all honesty, she'd been putting it off, not wanting to really sort through Vera's room, knowing it was the final goodbye. It felt wrong to remove someone's possessions from their home and though Vera didn't have many, it was still going to be a horrible job. With the living room finished after Sophie left yesterday and the kitchen on the list for later, now was the best time to tackle Vera's room. The ache in her arms and legs told her the break from painting and shifting furniture would be worthwhile, but she wasn't looking forward to it. She just hoped it uncovered some new information so she could think about that and not how final this was.

Amelia blew the air out through her cheeks. 'Right, better get cracking.'

She began with the bedside cabinet, the floorboards creaking as she stepped around, but found nothing else. The empty space where the locket had been was a haunting reminder of Vera's private nature and Amelia tried to shake the feeling that she was becoming the same. She cleared the tea-stained cloth from the top and put in the box marked 'rubbish'. Another box sat next to it on the bed for keepsakes.

Next, she cleared and searched the dressing table. Vera's vanity set went into the keepsakes box. The first drawer held nothing but some slabs of soap and a bottle of talcum powder. The scent of lavender wafted into the air and filled Amelia's nose. As she opened the second one and removed some more toiletries, a small key rolled around the bottom.

'What's this for then, Vera?'

Glancing around the room she couldn't see a lock it matched and, frowning, she put it back into the drawer. Perhaps she'd come across something later.

With the unusable items in the rubbish box and a few in the keepsake box, it was time to start on the wardrobe. Amelia paused, eyeing the roll of black sacks she'd brought with her. She'd known this moment would remind her of the day she cleared her parents' house, gathering her teddies together for the move to Vera's. She sucked in a breath.

'Come on,' she said, sniffing. 'You can do this.'

As she began, she frowned. It had never occurred to her before how Vera had tried to keep her downstairs, urging her to watch some television while she 'did some jobs' in the bedrooms. Amelia hadn't known what those jobs were until she snuck upstairs and watched her. It had been heart-breaking. Now she thought of it, she was sure Vera had rubbed her face while she'd been gently folding clothes. Had she been crying?

Amelia stepped back and flopped onto the edge of the bed, her ribs constricting. Perhaps Vera hadn't always been the monster she'd made her out to be over these last ten years. She'd been wrong to think of her as a pantomime villain.

'Right, that's enough,' she told herself, shaking her head. 'Just get this done.'

When she opened the wardrobe door, her eyes were immediately drawn to the wedding dress. Its poor tattered material moved in the breeze from the open window and she caressed the end of a lacy sleeve in her fingertips. After stripping the clothes from the hangers and bagging them up, something hidden at the back of the wardrobe caught her eye. At the bottom of the wardrobe, the corner of a cardboard box stuck out, hidden under blankets and clothes that had fallen from the hangers.

Amelia knelt and pulled it forwards, hope rising. Slipping her hand around the side, she edged the box out, careful to brace underneath in case the contents fell over the floor. She searched through, hoping she'd at last find Vera's birth certificate. As she pulled back the lid, a small smile came to her face. The box was full of photos. Some were loose but an old, faded cream album filled her with excitement. Amelia opened it and began carefully turning the thin, delicate pages.

Most of the photographs had handwritten labels underneath and many pictured Vera and her family through the years. There was Vera as a baby, Vera as a toddler with her sister, Vera as a young girl. Teenage Vera smiled at the camera as she celebrated her eighteenth birthday. They were all smiling as her mother presented a cake complete with candles. Amelia's heart lurched to think of how miserable and lonely Vera had ended up. Though she never admitted to such a thing, she must have been at times. Who wouldn't be, being alone all their lives?

Amelia stared out of the window for a second, eager for air. Her flat had pretty ornaments, paintings on the walls and was immaculately designed, but there were no photographs out on display. She had one of her parents that she kept in her bedside cabinet, just how Vera had kept the locket. Everything else was in a box under her bed. A pretty box rather than an old cardboard one, but the similarity was shocking.

Amelia continued to search through the photographs, enjoying seeing the happiness of her relatives. There were ones of the Cabot family together and though everyone else was smiling, Vera's thin lips never turned up. Amelia leaned in closer, studying a new picture. The label underneath had Vera and her sister's ages written down. Vera was nineteen. It was an impromptu shot taken on the farm and while everyone else was grinning from ear to ear, Vera stood away from them, her eyes cold and hard. Amelia's hands sped up as she found more and more photographs, in all of which Vera's face remained hard and cold.

Laying out the photographs on the floor, Amelia spoke to herself as she thought things through. 'Up until the age of eighteen, you're all smiles, Vera, and then afterwards, nothing. It's like your mouth literally can't move. Why were you always scowling or – I don't know – sad?'

Something had happened to Vera when she was eighteen that stopped her smiling. And Amelia didn't mean it in a poetic, she got slightly miserable way. She literally stopped smiling. What could it have been to have such an effect?

Nothing in the box helped to identify the man in the locket. Seeing the images laid out before her, Amelia couldn't help but feel that all the pieces of Vera's life needed slotting into place for her to understand what had happened and why she had become so unhappy. Amelia was sure that, given how everyone had remembered her when she came back and nearly all had been kind, the Meadowbank residents would have liked Vera if only she'd let them.

But time was getting on and Amelia had this unhappy task to finish before she could go to Highfield. As she placed more and more tatty old jumpers and threadbare trousers into black sacks, she took a deep breath, feeling a weight lifting from her chest. Coming back to Meadowbank had been like exorcising her demons, or at least facing the ghosts of her past.

Though Adam hadn't forgiven her he had at least agreed to come and work on the house and she expected him the next day. Her stomach filled with nerves and a heavy sense of anticipation. It would be an awkward and tense day but once that was done and Vera's room was clear, she would be free to move on.

***

Having been to Highfield before, Amelia knew it would take her about half an hour to walk there. With the last item of clothing in the bag, she glanced at her phone to check the time. She'd have to set off soon or she'd be late, and she didn't want to rush and arrive all hot and bothered. She found a photograph of Vera, and took it with her just in case it would prove useful. She wasn't sure Mrs Motley would know who Vera was.

Closing the front door behind her, Amelia headed towards the coppice where she and Adam had played as children and where she'd seen Arthur yesterday. The thought of Adam working at the farmhouse, in the same room as her, sent a wave of emotion over her body. Even her scalp prickled with apprehension and fear. They had a lot to catch up on if only they could forget the past and start afresh. He must know how much she regretted what had happened. To her, the feeling seeped from every pore when she was near him. Did he really not know how ashamed of herself she was? How much she'd missed him?

The waist-high grass tickled her palm as she ran her hands over it, walking the dirt track across the fields to the house. The echo of cows lowing in nearby fields filled the air and the sun beat down on the earth, drying the rain of yesterday. With nothing else but the birds singing and sporadic hum of a car in the distance, all was quiet and peaceful. It was so different to Paris where she seemed to dash and run everywhere. The city imbued a feeling that, if you weren't madly hurrying, filling each hour, you weren't living as good a life as everyone else. Being busy was a mark of success and one she'd worn as a badge of honour for most of her life, from her early days at university, right up until ten days ago when she'd left Paris.

Highfield appeared before her and she followed the low flint wall that marked the boundary of the estate until she reached a gate. Edging through, she had come out at the side of the house and roamed to the grand entrance at the front.

It was built of an imposing dark grey stone, with squat, square aspects. Tudor or possibly even medieval. From a distance, the grey made it stand out on the horizon but up close it looked dark and intimidating. The flowerbeds around it softened it somewhat and Amelia could see they had been added fairly recently. When she'd arrived on the day of the market, the many grand rooms had been impressive, but also surprising, considering the house was an enormous oblong. With a slight raise of her eyebrows at the enormity of the building, she knocked.

Mrs Motley answered the door a moment later. 'Miss Williams, how lovely to see you. Do come in.' Amelia followed her inside, unable to stop herself admiring the decor of the hallway. When she'd arrived the other day, she'd expected something in keeping with the historic nature of the exterior to be reflected inside, with walls covered in rich tapestries or heavy wooden panelling, but the hallway was illuminated with bright yellow hues, giving it a sense of light and space. It was big enough to hold a gold velvet sofa against one wall and various tables held lamps and family pictures. 'It's a bit quieter today. Thankfully,' Mrs Motley said. 'Would you like to follow me to the library? We can talk in there.'

Amelia ambled along behind Mrs Motley who was a young, elegant woman in her thirties. Her hair had been piled on her head in a messy bun and the jeans and crisp white shirt combo suited her lithe frame. The only surprise had been her Ugg boots, but then if this house was anywhere near as draughty as Meadow Farmhouse, they were a must.

The cold stone floors of the hallways and subsequent corridor were covered in a plush deep-red runner. When Mrs Motley opened the door to the library, Amelia had been expecting a small study type room, but the space before her was as big as the library in the village. The great circular room, lined floor to ceiling with books, smelled of beeswax. A tall ladder, which ran on rails encircling the shelves, had been stopped near the window. The parquet flooring gleamed and gave a sense of warmth. 'Wow!' Amelia sighed, unable to stop herself.

'It is a beautiful room, isn't it? It was quite dilapidated when we bought the house, but my husband and I have worked to bring it back up to scratch.'

'Are either you or your husband descendants of the original family, Mrs Motley? I thought I saw on your website that you bought the house a few years ago?'

'Do call me Jennifer. And no, we're not Highfield descendants. We never met the family. It was all done through agents. The daughter who was selling was abroad.' She led them to a circular chestnut-coloured table in the centre of the room and motioned for Amelia to sit. 'Now, I understand from our brief chat the other day you were looking for some information on Highfield during the Second World War?'

'That's right.' Amelia's nerves jangled, clanging together like a bunch of keys. 'I don't know if you've heard, but I recently inherited Meadow Farmhouse from my Great-Aunt Vera. Among her possessions, I found this locket.' She opened it, showing Jennifer the picture. 'I'm trying to find out who this man is and how he's connected with my great-aunt's family – with my family. Did you know my great-aunt at all?'

'No, I'm sorry. We don't go into the village much. Our son keeps me busy most days. He's with his au pair today, and my husband works abroad a lot. Sometimes we go with him but often I like to stay here. I'm a freelance journalist and though I don't work as much as I would like to, it works well with my family. I'm afraid they think we're all quite fearsome because my husband's work can be very high-profile. That's partly why we keep ourselves to ourselves. Though I do love Meadowbank. It's a beautiful village.'

'It is,' Amelia replied. Though she had forgotten quite how beautiful until recently. 'I know that Highfield was requisitioned as a military hospital and I wondered if there were any records from that time that might help me identify him.'

Jennifer cocked her head. 'I'm sorry, Miss Williams—'

'Amelia, please.'

'But from what I know, most of the records from around the time were destroyed in a fire after the war.' Amelia felt the fall of her shoulders. 'The only thing we do have left from around that time are some old photographs that belonged to the family and a couple of household accounts. I should offer to ship them to the daughter, though I'm not sure she'll want them. The last time we were in contact with her agent, I got the impression the house had become somewhat of a burden, and she was keen to be rid of all of it. You're welcome to have a look at those bits if you like?'

Amelia made sure to hide the disappointment from her voice as Jennifer was being so kind. 'That would be wonderful, thank you.'

Jennifer went to a short cabinet near the furthest end of the room and opened a cupboard. She pulled out an old white box and carried it over to Amelia.

'As I said, there really isn't much, but feel free to take a look, and if there's anywhere in the house you'd like to look, I'll take you on a tour.'

'Thank you so much. I'd like that. It really is a beautiful place.'

'I'll be back in a minute with some tea.'

Jennifer was true to her word and stopped in a few minutes later with a mug of tea. Amelia accepted it gratefully as the aged paper had sent dust into the air, drying her throat. She'd only taken a couple of things out of the box – two books of household accounts from the early Twenties – and the air was thick already. Amelia placed her mug over the other side of the table, careful to protect the objects she was lucky enough to look at. They smelled of old paper and the excitement of glimpsing into lives lived long ago tingled her nerves. It was exactly the same feeling she'd had when she'd begun to work on Meadow Farmhouse: an honouring of all the lives that had passed through the place before her.

Though the household accounts weren't going to help in her search for the American soldier, she couldn't help but look through them, studying the costs and amounts and imagining the daily running of a great house when it was filled with servants and staff. After flipping through a few pages and drinking her tea, she cleared the table and took out the next stack of paper. Though she had no hope of finding anything, Amelia determined to enjoy the experience. She couldn't imagine many people would get to look at these precious things.

The first few photographs were ancient images of Highfield. She couldn't tell exactly when they were from but from the clothes, she estimated the early 1900s. There was one of all the servants lined up in front of the house. Both the building and the servants appeared bleak and daunting in the sepia image.

As she turned the next one over, excitement began to mount. It was of a farm being worked by lots of different men, but Amelia couldn't tell which farm from the small picture. The Highfield estate was huge and without a landmark it was impossible to place it. They weren't in army uniform but there were so many of them they couldn't all be labourers. She supposed if it was harvest time they might be or perhaps they were the most able-bodied patients. She put that to the back of the stack and as her eyes swept the image in front of her, she almost cried out loud.

Hurriedly removing the locket from around her neck she found the clasp and opened it, though her fingers shook so fiercely she was hardly able to hold it. Dropping it down on the table, Amelia placed it next to one of the men's faces.

It was the soldier. 'It's you,' she whispered.

He was standing in a row with others clad only in their pyjamas. His arm was in a sling and in his other hand, he held, or rather leaned, on a cane. In front of him, a number of other soldiers were in wheelchairs, blankets over their knees. In the middle, a doctor in a white coat grinned to camera. Amelia gasped, and her cheeks could barely contain the smile spreading over her face. Her body seemed to float with elation at the find.

'It's you!' she said louder, half-laughing, half-gasping. 'It's definitely you.'

He'd unquestionably been one of the soldiers convalescing at Highfield. She studied his eyes. They were so different from the locket. He looked happy. Happier than he had been when the other photo had been taken. Perhaps that had been taken at the start of the war when fear of what was to come seized him. He must have been happy to be away from it all. Mentally crossing her fingers, she turned the photograph over, praying there might be a list of names. The back of the picture was bare but for a date: 1942.

As speedily as possible she checked through the remainder of the box but without any further success. There were some more photographs of convalescing patients, but none were dated, and her soldier wasn't in any of them. Neither could she find any more information about the house, or those who had stayed there, that was of any use to her. When Jennifer reappeared a little while later to check on Amelia's progress, she had stacked the remaining items back into the box, leaving the picture out on the side.

'Did you find anything?' Jennifer asked as she came back in.

'I did actually.' Amelia pointed to the photograph on the table. 'It's him. I can't believe that there was anything left. I feel incredibly lucky that of all the soldiers who came here, there was a picture of him.'

She clapped her hands together. 'How marvellous. You must keep it.'

'Really? But it's part of the history of the house. Surely—'

Jennifer held up her hands. 'It is part of the history of the house but all that's going to happen is it'll go back into that box and then into the cupboard. It clearly means a lot to you and if that man is tied up with your family history too, then it's as much yours as it is ours.'

'Are you sure?'

'Positive.'

'Thank you so much. I can't tell you how much this means to

me.' Taking the photograph in trembling hands, Amelia placed it carefully in her bag, making sure not to curl the corners or bend it. 'I still don't have a name, but at least now I know for sure that he was here at Highfield. And from the sling on his arm and the cane, I know that he was hurt in the war, which may help if I can find any of the military records.'

'I'm so pleased we were able to assist you. We did have a local historian asking some questions a while ago, but I hadn't found that box then. I only came across it recently when we were getting a mouse out of one of the attics. That's the trouble with a house like this. They really do get everywhere. Was there anything else you wanted to look at?'

'No, thank you. The way my heart's beating I'm not sure I'd be able to take any more today.' Amelia placed a hand to her chest, feeling the locket once more around her neck, and knowing it was close to her heart soothed her.

'It must be very exciting.'

'It is actually. And though I'd love a tour, I'd better get back to Meadow Farmhouse. I still have a tonne of work to do.'

'Then I'll show you out.'

On the walk back to Meadowbank, Amelia held her bag tightly. There was no reason the photo should come flying out as she'd made sure to zip it closed three times, but she wanted to protect it. It was a shame that tomorrow she'd have to put her search aside and focus on the house once more.

Deep down she knew she was turning it into the home she had always wanted it to be rather than a home to attract buyers, but the longer she stayed there, the less she could help herself. Tomorrow though, with Adam there to fix the doors, she'd focus on clearing and decorating the kitchen ready for whoever would eventually buy it. She just hoped that whoever did, would value Meadow Farmhouse's history as much as she was beginning to.

Chapter 15

For the first time in years, Adam hesitated as he dressed. Normally, he'd throw on his old jeans and whatever T-shirt happened to be lying at his feet. Today though, he actually chose something to wear, picking out his nicest jeans and a shirt Philippa, his ex, had bought him for his birthday two years ago. The collar pinched at his neck and he ran a finger around it, easing it away. He pretended it was because he was seeing a new client and wanted to make a good impression, but the reality was that her calling him, however briefly, had sparked something other than hurt and frustration.

After dousing himself in a cologne he only wore at Christmas, Adam went to Meadow Farmhouse. The front door was already open as he rounded to it and he could understand why. It was a bright and glorious spring day. The sun's rays poked through thin wispy clouds, spotlighting the fields. It was the type of day you open all the windows and let the breeze blow the cobwebs from the house. The air smelled of fresh-cut grass.

Before Vera had died, Adam had borrowed a rocking horse from her. He'd been commissioned to make one and wanted to use hers – or should he say Amelia's – as inspiration. He wondered if subconsciously he'd chosen it to remind himself of the times they'd played with it together as children. She'd remained in his brain since the day she left, and over the years, memories of her had threatened to come to the surface if he didn't concentrate and push them down.

When he'd returned the rocking horse, the farmhouse had been dark and musty, as Vera's own gloom cocooned the place.

Over the last few years more than any others, she had receded further and further into her shell, only coming into the village once a week for her shopping. If the farm needed anyone's touch, he supposed an interior designer's was the best thing to bring it back to life.

Adam called out as he stuck his head through the open doorway, ensuring he didn't reveal his anxiety at seeing her again. 'Amelia?'

'I'm in the kitchen.'

He wiped his feet on the new cheerful welcome mat as he stepped inside. He'd worn his normal work boots, not wanting to look like he was trying too hard impress her, but the nerves were mounting already. The place seemed so much brighter since Amelia had come and livened up the place and not just in terms of decor. A sense of love, care and attention now filled the atmosphere of Meadow Farmhouse and it seemed lighter and more welcoming because of it. It would sell quickly, no doubt, he thought. A family would move in and Amelia's last tie to Meadowbank would be gone forever. He cleared his throat. 'Morning.'

Amelia turned back from putting the kettle on, appearing like she belonged somewhere far more elegant than Meadowbank. Her legs were about ten feet tall in dark denim skinny jeans and she wore a short-sleeved black jumper that sat just at her waist. If she lifted her arms up, he'd probably get a flash of belly button and the idea of seeing an area of skin so personal made his hands clammy. 'Hi.'

An uncomfortable silence threatened when Amelia said, 'Would you like some tea before I show you what needs doing?'

Everyone he worked for made this offer and yet for them, it seemed like a giant step forward. 'Er, yeah, please.' He noticed the radiance of the living room now it had been painted and with it the growing homeliness of the worn old building. Stacks of boxes sprawled over the kitchen floor, open and with old saucepans and crockery sticking out and he was grateful for a topic of conversation to pounce upon. 'How's it going here?'

'Not bad, actually.' She ran a hand over her hair and down the long length of her ponytail, pulling it over her shoulder. Her eyes were on the boxes and she clearly had no idea how attractive the move was. At least it was to him. 'Vera kept so much stuff it's unbelievable.'

'Is there anything you're going to keep?'

'One or two things. I—' She cut off the sentence and Adam worried that they were about to descend back into awkward silences. 'I wondered if you'd like one of her paintings. You've known her as long as I have, and I thought you might want something to remember her by.'

'Me?' Adam asked, visibly shocked at the question. He'd known Vera had taken up painting, having seen her in the fields sometimes with her easel and paint box, but he'd never imagined that Amelia would want him to have something like that. His mum had been adamant Amelia would put everything into a skip and sell the place empty.

'There's one in the living room I thought you might like. Here.'

She led the way, and the intoxicating smell of her perfume filled his senses. It wasn't a gentle floral scent like his mum wore, but something far headier with the sweetness of vanilla. His body reacted and his muscles tensed. He followed her into the living room. She'd placed a painting of the coppice over the fireplace and memories of their more intimate moments brought a warmth to his cheeks he hoped didn't show.

The painting she wanted him to have was a watercolour of Meadow Farmhouse before it fell into disrepair. It rested on an easel in the corner of the room and somehow added to the character of the place. He could already tell Amelia was good at her job. Adam didn't know anything about art or how accomplished someone was, but he liked this in the same way he liked his own little sculptures. He knew immediately where it could go and though Vera was a hard woman, she had been kind to him and his mum, and it would be nice to have something to remember her by. 'I'd love it. If you're sure you don't mind.'

'Of course not.' Her expression softened and some of his hard edges fell away. 'I … you—' She recomposed herself. 'I think she'd have wanted you to have it. I'm giving the rest of that lot to the spring fair. Sophie wants it for the bric-a-brac stall.'

'I'll let Mum know.'

Amelia's eyes widened. 'She's on the committee too?'

'Head of.'

Amelia's eyebrows lifted in surprise.

'You didn't expect anything less from my mum, did you? She loves to organise things.'

'I'd have thought she had her hands full with you.'

'Not anymore. She's given up on that, I think.'

Silence filled the air and a part of him hated how they'd fallen into teasing chatter like old times. And was there anything more unattractive than a twenty-eight-year-old man talking about his mum? The kettle boiled and Amelia went back to the kitchen. She motioned for him to have a seat at the table and after making two mugs of tea, joined him. Silence filled the air and the tension soon grew. He could feel it surrounding them like an encroaching shadow wrapping them in darkness. They had to talk about something. If she was a normal customer, he'd make small talk to put them both at ease. It was professional.

'So … Paris? It's a beautiful city.' *Nice. Start with the city she left you for. That won't be at all awkward.*

'It is,' Amelia replied, not lifting her eyes to meet his. 'Have you been?'

'Yes. Don't be so surprised,' he said jokily trying to lighten the tone. 'I have left the village on occasion, you know.' As a furious blush covered her cheeks, he wished he'd chosen a different topic.

As he'd worried, she was overpowering his senses. With the changes she'd made to the house, he couldn't help but wonder if

Meadow Farmhouse was becoming the type of home they could have had if only she'd stayed. With that thought came a cascade of hurt and frustration at the unsaid words between them, but the anger at least wasn't as strong as before. He tried to calm the tension before it grew too much again.

'So where are these doors that need looking at?'

'There's the playroom door and the door to the bathroom is a bit sticky too. I got trapped in there the other night after my bath.'

Adam focused on what he'd need to do to the playroom door that was leaning against the wall rather than on the thought of Amelia in the bath. Maybe it would be best to start down here until he'd got hold of himself. After throwing back the last of his tea, he examined it and decided where it needed adjusting, and Amelia led him upstairs to the bathroom.

She took a bottle from the side of the bath and reached up to place it on top of the small wooden cabinet on the wall. As he'd expected, when she lifted her arm it exposed a hint of stomach, the skin pale against the stark black of her jumper. Adam examined the door thinking technical thoughts. Anything to stop picturing the snow-white skin he'd just seen. 'Is there anything else you want me to look at?' She shook her head. 'Then I'll make a start on the playroom door.'

They went back downstairs, and Amelia retreated to the kitchen while he moved back and forth to his van finding the tools he needed to rehang the door. She popped the radio on so the room filled with the gentle hum of music and it lessened the awkwardness of the situation.

For more than hour he worked on the door while she sorted through the kitchen cupboards, cleaning and reorganising as she went. He didn't mean to keep looking over, but his head often moved of its own accord. Her almost jet-black hair hung like silk and he wondered how it would feel in his fingertips, then yelped as the screwdriver twisted from his grip and bashed into his finger.

'Are you okay?' Amelia asked quickly.

'Fine,' he replied with a chuckle to hide his embarrassment. 'Just a threaded screw.' *Must not talk about screwing*, he thought to himself, picturing her skin again.

More work ensued and he went upstairs to begin fixing the bathroom door. He'd just taken it off its hinges ready to bring it outside to plane when Amelia screeched from the kitchen. Shoving the door to lean against the wall, he rushed downstairs. 'What is it? Amelia? Are you okay?'

In the sea of boxes, Amelia stared at the top of a kitchen cabinet where a blackbird perched, watching her. She pressed a hand to her chest as she began laughing. The joy in her pale grey eyes filled his heart with something other than pain. 'It flew right past my head and frightened the life out of me. I'm sorry, I didn't mean to scream.'

'I'm not surprised you did.'

She turned to look at him and as he held her gaze, the affection in her eyes took the words from his mouth. 'How do I get him out?' she asked after what seemed like a lifetime.

'Who? Oh, the bird. Umm, I guess we need to try and shepherd him out somehow. Have you got a broom?' He looked around and spotted one by the back door.

'That's Bobby. My chicken-catching broom.'

'You named your broom? I'm not even going to ask.' Adam clamped his mouth shut, reminding himself he shouldn't be joking with her that much. Having fetched it, he held it aloft and wafted it at the blackbird. The blackbird ducked, but otherwise didn't move.

'What if we make it bigger?' Amelia asked.

'Bigger?'

'Yeah, like, put some clothes on it so he thinks it's a person. Like a scarecrow or something.'

It sounded bonkers but as he didn't have any other ideas, he agreed. Amelia sped off upstairs coming back a moment later with an old jumper of Vera's. They placed it on the top of the broom, and he began wafting it towards the bird again.

'It's not working. Hang on. We can use my cape.'

'You have a cape? Like a superhero?'

Amelia's eyes narrowed slightly. 'It's more like a jacket but it's cape-shaped. It's very stylish, actually.'

'Okay,' he replied, smiling.

Now complete with added cape, he wafted Bobby the broom once more and they both shouted at the bird, trying to scare him out, Amelia making ghostly oohing noises as she went. The blackbird watched on like he was at a dinner show and these humans were all very amusing, but apart from a quick glance around he didn't do anything else.

'He's a stubborn little bugger, isn't he?' Adam said, finally giving up on the broom still wearing Vera's jumper and Amelia's cape and putting it back in the corner. 'What about using some of that newspaper?' He pointed to a stack of papers to the side of a box with old crockery wrapped in it.

Amelia frowned. 'What exactly are you going to do with it?'

He shrugged. 'Throw it at him?'

'Worth a try.' And the two of them began throwing balls of newspaper at the bird. Adam's heart leaped as it opened its wings but all it did was shuffle slightly sideways. 'I've got an idea.'

Adam watched as Amelia found some biscuits and laid a trail of crumbs to the open front door.

'Do you think it'll work?' he asked.

'Who doesn't like biscuits?' she replied with a dazzling smile. His heart skipped. 'And I tried this with the chickens the last time they escaped, and it worked a treat.'

They'd been so busy trying to get the blackbird out, it hadn't occurred to him how well they'd been getting on. Their exchange had been like old times and he was surprised Amelia still had the same silly sense of humour. A part of him wanted to hold on to this feeling but another part felt the need to restrain himself. She would, after all, be leaving again soon.

The bird eventually flew towards the crumb nearest the door, pecked it up and flew off outside. Amelia turned to him with a triumphant grin on her face, but a second later it faded as she too seemed to realise there was too much hurt between them for it to be so easily replaced. Distress swept her features before she dropped her eyes, and for a moment he wondered if she regretted the pain she'd caused him. He shook off the feeling. He couldn't think like that. If she thought she'd made a mistake he'd be tempted to forgive her, and he knew exactly where that would leave him. He would *not* fall in love with Amelia Williams all over again.

'I'd better get on,' he said coolly and went back upstairs, leaving her alone in the kitchen.

Chapter 16

When Saturday rolled around, Amelia approached the village green, her nerves growing so strong queasiness rose up her throat. Whilst she hoped the village had become used to seeing her around, the thought of running into Lynne Noble or Adam again gave her palpitations.

She'd enjoyed their conversations at the farmhouse far too much and being near him, whilst extremely awkward and torturous at times, had made her feel more alive than she remembered feeling at any moment over the last ten years. At times he'd look at her, and it was as if he could see how much she regretted their parting. When they'd relaxed into conversation, the attraction she felt towards him flourished and she couldn't deny her heart hoped it had been the same for him.

As Amelia walked on, the comparison of the village fair to the flea markets of Paris ran through her thoughts. She missed buying creamy French cheese and eating it for lunch in her apartment. She missed gorgeous French wine. But it hadn't escaped her notice that lately, all the things she was missing were objects and possessions rather than people and feelings. But what did that mean? The thought was too terrifying to think about too deeply.

The village green came into sight and Amelia inhaled at the sight before her. Brightly coloured bunting had been strung around it and it criss-crossed the air, decorating the trees. The poles that held it up were planted in square white plant pots and fresh yellow daffodils sprang around them. A mass of people filled the space and a strong wave of wistfulness washed over her, bewildering her senses. A vague memory of Vera bringing her to a few of the fairs came to mind and despite her loathing of the village, they'd had fun. Or at least, Amelia had. She was sure Vera had enjoyed Amelia taking part in a game or staring at the cakes in rapture. She'd almost forgotten Vera had the capacity to smile, but now she thought on it, there had definitely been a few occasions when she had. Why had she forgotten that about her? Perhaps it had been easier than trying to understand.

Stalls had been laid around the edge selling homemade goods and traditional fare on tables laid with pretty pale tablecloths. In the centre were games for the children. Giant Jenga and Connect Four had been laid out along with an enormous teddy bear in a striped bow tie, ready to go home with whoever named him. Already kids were flocking to it. Grumpy ducks wandered around, darting in and out of people's feet, quacking as they went, clearly annoyed at having all this noise disturb their usual slumber.

As the day was bright and mild, Amelia had worn a navy dress with white polka dots and a long khaki cardigan with the sleeves rolled up. She'd worn tights and flat brown ankle boots wanting a change from her dusty, now paint-smattered jeans. It was, after all, a day off, of sorts. Amelia made her way through the crowd, avoiding one or two ducks who didn't seem to know which way they wanted to go.

She began at the stalls nearest the duck pond and perused her way around the outside of the green. Every few yards, someone would wish her well and give their condolences. Sometimes they asked if she really was an interior designer and if she'd be interested in any work. Each time she worried her usual awkwardness and embarrassment would haunt her, stealing her words or adding to her guilt, but with each conversation it seemed to lessen. And though she couldn't take on their design jobs, she was happy to share some advice.

Arriving at the food section where the deli and Annie's Tearooms both had stalls, there was more food on offer than even she could eat. Giant doorstop sandwiches sat next to fat pork pies with dark, flaky pastry, and enormous rolls with thick slices of ham were piled next to jars of pickle. Some of the village ladies shared a cake stall full of the most delicious-looking cakes in all types of flavours: coffee and walnut; Victoria sponge; lemon drizzle; deep, dark chocolate; white chocolate and raspberry; toffee … Her mouth began to water. Fancy elaborate cakes, like the ones she saw in Paris patisseries, were all well and good and an art in themselves, but there was nothing quite like a homemade cake that was a little bit wonky with uneven buttercream. The love they were made with just made them taste better.

Again, a memory shot into her brain of Vera taking a cake out of the oven and making buttercream icing ready to go on top. She hadn't been a huge cake eater, Amelia remembered now, so, she must have made the cakes just for her. Where had all these memories come from? As she took a moment to watch the heart of village life beat before her, she realised they had always been there, but she'd buried them under the easier to remember more unpleasant ones. Probably because the powerful feelings they evoked were harder to ignore.

Amelia cast a glance over her shoulder, checking to see if Sophie was at the bric-a-brac stall. She was, and was happily chatting away to the row of customers in front of her.

'Morning, Mrs Douglas. Can I have the chocolate cake please?' The white-haired lady pushed herself out of the camping chair she'd been resting in.

'The whole thing or just a slice, dear?'

'The whole thing, please.'

'Marvellous.' Mrs Douglas's eyes beamed at the other ladies manning the stall. She caught Amelia looking over her shoulder again. 'If this is for Adam Noble, you'll want some of Mrs Doyle's carrot cake. It helps to mend a broken heart.'

'I'm sorry?' Amelia knew her face had flushed as heat flew into her cheeks.

'When his ex-girlfriend left him – Philippa Ormrod; you won't know her, she moved to the village long after you'd left – I delivered him three of these: one a week until he started perking up again.'

'Oh. Right.' The cake was placed in a white cardboard box and Amelia pulled out her wallet and paid.

The idea of Adam having an ex shouldn't fill her with jealousy but the idea of him being with someone else had always tormented her over the years, only being back in Meadowbank made the feeling even more powerful. She had no right to feel anything like that about him, she reminded herself but for some reason it still stung.

Mrs Douglas said, 'Now, I heard you were an interior designer. Is that right?'

'It is.' Amelia nodded.

'Good because my daughter-in-law lives in Little Bingham down the road and as lovely as she is, she has terrible taste in cushions. Would you be able to give her a hand, do you think?'

'Oh, I don't know,' Amelia stuttered. She hadn't anticipated her job leading to her being welcomed with so many offers of work. 'I'm sure I could give her some tips if she'd like to email me.'

'Well, you'll have to be subtle because I always say how lovely her choices are even though the place looks like there's been an explosion of some sort. I don't want to upset her.'

Amelia smiled. 'I promise I will.'

'Lovely. It's nice to see you back, dear.'

'It's nice to be back,' Amelia replied and, surprisingly, she really meant it.

Cradling the cake box, Amelia went to the bric-a-brac stall and though she was busy, when she spotted Amelia, Sophie came over.

'Hey, you! You look fabulous. Far too glamorous for our little fair.'

'Really?' Self-consciously, she asked. 'Do I look silly?'

'Not at all. I love your dress.'

Amelia relaxed and held out the box for her. 'Here.'

'What's this?' Sophie took it and opened it, her eyes widening as she saw the enormous chocolate cake inside. 'I wanted to say thank you to you and Isla for making me feel so welcome.'

Sophie beamed. 'You didn't need to do that. Isla, come and look.' She called over to the middle of the green where Isla was playing with Michael. 'Michael, this is Amelia. Isla, look what Amelia gave us to say thank you for looking after her.'

Isla's eyes nearly popped out of her head she was so thrilled at the prospect of so much cake.

Michael said, 'That's so nice of you, Amelia. Thank you. I'd better get some first before Sophie and Isla get started on it or there won't be any left.'

'Hey!' Sophie protested, but the look they shared was one of intense love. She placed the cake box on a chair behind the table.

'Sophie, dear?' called old Mr Morton from the other end of the stall. 'Where did these lovely dessert forks come from?'

Sophie glanced in Amelia's direction before lowering her voice. 'They umm … they were a donation from Meadow Farmhouse.'

'Were they?'

Amelia held her breath, worried that he might refuse to buy them now he knew where they'd come from. Knowing how Vera was, there was every chance people might not want anything from her. 'They're lovely,' the man said and gathered them up to pay before heading off to another table.

Amelia's shoulders dropped. 'How's it going?' she asked Sophie.

'Brilliantly busy. We're going to make lots of money to help the village. All this kitchen stuff is going down a treat. You'd be surprised at the number of people who say "Oh, I need another saucepan," or "That's a nice serving platter." They don't care who donated it,' she added as if reading Amelia's mind.

'Fuck!' Isla squealed, and everyone spun to look at her. Sophie's face flamed while Michael leaned back on his heels laughing.

'I think you mean duck, darling.' He chased after his daughter as she followed a rather put-out mallard making its way back to the duck pond.

Amelia burst out laughing as a deep resounding chuckle reached over her shoulder. She spun to see Adam, and her breath caught in her throat. His muscular frame was encased in a tight jumper and jeans, and testosterone seemed to leak from every pore. Amelia suddenly wished it was colder because her heat levels were rising uncontrollably. He brushed a hand through his burnt umber hair as he continued to laugh.

Sophie darted back to Amelia, and now Adam. 'God, I'm so embarrassed.'

'Don't be.' Amelia placed a hand on her shoulder, aware of everything she did and said now Adam was listening. 'Everyone knows what she meant. No one thinks you're teaching her swear-words before her ABC's.'

'Why does she always have to do these things in front of everyone? She never does it at home, just saves it up for a crowd. At toddler time the other day she was saying can't but it came out sounding entirely different and I went as red as a tomato.'

Adam laughed. 'That's kids I suppose. And see, no one cares.' He motioned around him to show everyone looking fondly at Isla or going about their business.

'Do you think everyone will talk about us?'

'No,' Amelia said lightly, but there was a slight tension to her voice. 'I'm sure they'll go back to asking me about selling Meadow Farmhouse in a minute.'

'Does it make me a terrible friend that I'm glad?'

'Yes!' Amelia replied, her brows pulling together as she pretended to frown. Sophie was called to serve a customer and gave an apologetic look before departing.

'Hi,' Adam said, his hands in his pockets.

Left alone with him the village green felt suddenly smaller and more intimate. She wondered if his heart was beating as hard as hers was.

'Hi.' *Man up*, she told herself, but it was hard to meet his eye knowing how he was affecting her. She twisted her mother's ring on her finger. 'Thanks so much for fixing the doors. I was finally able to go for a wee without fear of being trapped.'

Wee? You're talking about wee? Of all the things she could have chosen to say, why had she started talking about bodily functions? She could have just stopped after thank you for fixing the doors, but no, she had to keep going and chat about urinating. She nervously pushed her hair from her face.

'I'm glad to hear it,' Adam replied. He sounded so utterly confused that she'd mentioned something so intimate, her shame intensified.

'Right, so I'm going to have a walk around then. Yep? Bye.' She had only taken a small step away when an uneasy feeling knotted her stomach.

'Are you okay?'

'Yeah,' she answered without thinking, but then turned back as she noticed Arthur staring in their direction, wringing his hands. 'Does Arthur always hang around like this?'

'Arthur? Sometimes. Why? He lives in the care home in the village, but he likes a wander too. He's as strong as an ox. Always hiking here and there.'

'I'm sure I saw him at the wood the other day. The one that separates Meadow Farmhouse's land from Highfield.'

'Like I said, he likes a walk, and it's lovely scenery out that way.'

Reassured, Amelia nodded. She knew she should keep on moving but despite her embarrassment was eager to remain talking with Adam. Every time they did it felt like he forgave her a little more, or was that wishful thinking on her part? 'Have you got a stall today? For your sculptures?'

'No.' He shook his head emphatically. 'Christ, no.'

'Why not?'

His cheeks flushed with colour, the vulnerability making him even more handsome. He scratched the back of his head. 'Umm, because people hate them?'

'I'm sure they don't.'

'Oh, they really, really do.'

'Maybe they just don't know what to do with them or how to use them?'

Adam's eyebrows drew together. She didn't think she'd said anything that amazing, but it was almost as though a comedy lightbulb should be above his head. His vulnerability was making her tingle. 'Do you really think so?'

'Definitely.' She pulled her mind away from the sexual tension mounting inside her. Bastien's kitchen display had nothing on Adam. Even a fully clothed Adam. 'It's something I've discovered with artwork and decorative objects. I'll show them to a client and they'll hate them, but when I dress a room and include that piece, they suddenly love them. People like unique things, but sometimes they need help in understanding where best to put them.'

'That's amazing. Thank you.' The smile that came to Adam's face warmed her heart just as her stomach gave a very audible grumble.

It was coming up to almost one o'clock according to the church clock the other side of the green and Amelia needed food. Most days she'd been too busy working to think about eating, stopping for quick snacks or meals she could throw together in minutes. Today though, without the renovation or the locket to keep her mind busy, she was ravenous.

'I think I'll get something to eat. All this fresh air is making me hungry.'

'No fresh air in Paris?' he asked with a grin. This time though, the reference to Paris didn't carry the same unspoken accusation or she thought it didn't.

Amelia chuckled. 'Not really. Cities aren't known for their clean air.'

Right now, standing in Adam's company with a conversation burgeoning between them, she wasn't particularly missing Paris or the life she had there. She'd been so sure that leaving would make her love the city even more and make her eager to return, but the opposite was happening lately. The peace and quiet of Meadowbank, the slower pace of life, had been just as refreshing as Jocelyn suggested it would be. She'd missed being here and even the farmhouse was growing in her affections as she transformed it, removing the darkness that had shrouded it for years. It would make someone a wonderful home, she reminded herself. Someone else.

Adam's voice penetrated her thoughts. 'I was going to get some lunch too. Were you going to the pub or Annie's stall?'

'I thought I'd get something from one of the stalls. You can't not at a fair.'

'Do you mind if I walk with you?'

Adam shuffled his feet and though his gaze was broken, flitting between her and the ground, her heart soared. ''Course not. That'd be nice.'

They walked in silence to the stall for Annie's Tearoom that was already busy with people. Annie was just sending the young waitress back to the café for more supplies and Amelia could see why. Everything looked so enticing. Next to Annie's was the booze stall, and after grabbing sandwiches and cake, she walked over to look at Mr Gardener's rosehip wine and plum gin.

'I'd forgotten all about the booze stall,' she said wistfully.

'It's always the busiest one. Don't you remember the year we got legless on Mr Gardener's homemade rosehip wine?'

Amelia's eyes widened. 'Oh God, I do! You pretended you'd been sent by your mum to buy it. I was too nervous to come over with you in case anyone told Vera, and we legged into the woods as soon as we were out of sight. We drank it in the coppice by our tree,' she added quietly.

'You were grounded for a month,' he recalled, smiling at the memory. 'How did you think Vera wouldn't notice you'd come home drunk?'

'What do you mean *you*? You were just as much to blame, and as far as I can remember Lynne wasn't overly chuffed either.'

'No, but I didn't get grounded for as long as you.'

Amelia gave a rueful nod. 'Your mum was always far too soft on you and Vera far too harsh on me.'

The air carried the echo of their laughter and after catching his eye once more, Amelia dropped hers to the ground. Surely, he must feel this too. There was still something special between them. An unbreakable bond, an understanding that went further than just knowing and loving the other person. Even if they could never be anything more than friends, surely he felt that they still had a connection? A shred of friendship worth saving. The niggling thought that she'd be leaving again soon – leaving it all behind again – tried to take hold, but she thrust it down, refusing to acknowledge it.

Just then a woman came bounding over to him. Her hair was a vibrant white blonde from the roots to the tips, with dark brown, fashionably square eyebrows underneath. Amelia only put her about ten years older than them but blushed at the cleavage on display.

'Adam,' the woman announced, standing incredibly close to him. Had she deliberately chosen that spot to block Amelia out? A stab of jealousy hit her as the woman stroked Adam's arm. 'I really need you to come and hang a cabinet for me in my bedroom.'

Adam's rather terrified expression immediately overtook any stab of jealousy and Amelia had to try not to laugh. He shouldn't be surprised women were reacting to him in this way. He'd grown from a cute boy into a strong, sexy man and sexiest of all, he didn't seem to have any idea of it himself. He took a small, fearful step away.

'I promise I'll give you a call this week to sort out a time.'

The corner of the woman's eyes fell slightly, but her rictus grin stayed intact. She slid her hand down Adam's arm, resting at his wrist. Amelia didn't know if she was trying to hold Adam's hand, but Adam pressed them further into his pockets. 'Now do you promise?'

Really? Amelia cringed at the babyishness in her voice. Seeing Adam's panic as she held him so tightly, Amelia felt the need to save him. 'It's my fault, I'm afraid. I've needed Adam to work on the farmhouse.'

As the woman turned to face her, Adam took his chance to escape. He pulled his arm away and rounded to Amelia's side. 'Lorraine, this is Amelia Williams. Amelia, this is Lorraine.'

'Hi,' Amelia replied, followed by a cheerful wave. From the narrowing of Lorraine's eyes. She was clearly not impressed with Amelia's presence.

'Ah, you're the one who has inherited Meadow Farmhouse, aren't you?'

'I am.'

'And I heard you're selling. When will that be do you think?' Amelia shot a glance at Adam. This reminder of her possible leaving thickened the air between them as if any progress they'd made so far had vanished. Lorraine continued. 'Only I might be interested in buying. Not for me of course. I have the most beautiful little cottage, but I'd love a rental property in the village.'

Amelia tried to keep her voice even. 'I'm not sure when it will be yet.'

She didn't think mentioning the impending estate agent's visit would be at all helpful right now, but she couldn't escape the thought that she really didn't want someone like Lorraine to own the farmhouse. Not that she could really choose who it was sold to. The point was just to sell it and move on.

'Well, you must let me know. And, Adam, don't forget to call me, okay?' She batted her eyelashes at him as she left.

Adam was the first to speak following her departure but only after Amelia's stomach gave another loud and hungry gurgle that made her cheeks flame. He chuckled, but his tone matched his tentative glance. 'Do you fancy sitting by the duck pond to eat?'

She couldn't believe that he was asking her, especially after Lorraine's kindly reminder she was leaving soon. Was this the olive branch she'd been hoping for since their first meeting? She tried to sound casual, like the offer didn't mean the world to her. 'Sure.'

A few of the ducks had found their way back to the pond, tempted by the children throwing crusts into the water. The tall rushes hid a corner of the duck pond from the hustle and bustle of the fair and muffled some of the noise. They hardly spoke while eating and Amelia worried that the easier atmosphere was already dissipating thanks to Lorraine. When Adam said, 'I'll be back in a tick,' it seemed hope was lost and she worried he wouldn't come back at all. An icy shudder charged down her spine, rocking each vertebra in turn. To her relief, he returned a second later with a bottle of rosehip wine, pushing up the swing top stopper. The fragrant smell of boozy fruit hit the air.

He offered it to Amelia. 'This'll take the edge off the cold. That breeze is getting chilly. Want to see if it's as potent as we remember?'

She gave a carefree laugh. 'Go on then.'

He took a sip. 'Duck, that's strong.'

Amelia giggled then grimaced as she drank. 'Duck, that really is.'

The sounds of the spring fair carried on the growing breeze. They'd been lucky to have a royal blue sky over them today, but it seemed that rain would be with them by tonight. Amelia was grateful for the familiarity growing between them and guilt hit her that she didn't deserve it yet, but she'd try to make herself worthy of his forgiveness.

'I was thinking,' Amelia said, 'I wondered if I could help you write something to describe your sculptures. Help you sell them to people.'

'Yeah?'

'Of course. I'd be happy to if you don't mind.'

'Thanks.'

She wanted to ask if he had a Facebook page for his business, but that would risk him seeing that she'd liked his post. It wouldn't seem as creepy now, as long as he didn't notice the date, but she didn't want to bring it up if he hadn't mentioned it. 'I might buy a couple for the farmhouse, actually. I think they'd go beautifully in the bushes out front, peeking out to welcome people.'

'I never thought I'd hear the words welcome and Vera's farmhouse in the same sentence.'

'Neither did I.'

But nevertheless, the farmhouse, and in fact, Meadowbank village, had been far more welcoming than she ever imagined it would be and saying goodbye to it all was going to be a lot harder than she ever thought possible.

Just then Elsie Martin from the library wandered over. 'Hi, Amelia, how's your research going?'

'Slowly,' she replied, moving over to make room for her, but Elsie shook her head.

'Research?' asked Adam, looking between them, but then he caught himself. 'If this is private then I can go.'

'No, it's fine.' She wanted him to know what she was up to and today was proving they weren't quite strangers anymore. 'I've been researching the farmhouse and trying to find out some more about Vera's childhood. I wanted to know more about the place before—' She was going to say before she left for good, but the words were physically painful to form. 'Before I got here,' she added, covering her tracks.

Elsie said, 'Don't worry you'll get there. I wanted to let you know that Mr Hoffelmeyer is back from his holidays tomorrow. I'm sure he'd be happy to see you. Here's his number.'

'Elsie, thank you.' Amelia took the ornate business card and read it before placing it in her bag. It stated *historian* in large gold lettering so despite Elsie's reservations, he must have had some qualifications. She hoped.

Elsie darted away back into the crowd and Amelia was aware of Adam sitting closer to her. 'Is this to do with the locket?' he asked, and Amelia remembered showing it to him at Highfield.

She took it out again, admiring the photo once more. 'It is. There was a wedding dress hanging in her wardrobe too.'

'A wedding dress?'

She nodded. 'It was tatty and damaged. I think it must have been her mother's or something. Do you ever remember Vera talking about her family or someone being in the army?'

'No, I don't, but she wasn't really a talkative sort of person. How far have you got?' She told him about her visit to Jocelyn and the photo discovered at Highfield. 'Wow, you've managed to do all that and redecorate the place?'

'To be honest, I'm not any further on with discovering who this man is, or why he was important to Vera, but at least with Mr Hoffelmeyer back I can go and talk to him. I just want to know as much as I can about Vera. I mean, she was a little girl once, and a woman my age, but I have no idea *who* she really was. What she hoped, what she dreamed, that sort of thing. I'm hoping if I know more about her, I'll be able to say goodbye to her properly. We didn't part on good terms and I hate that we never made up. I just always assumed there'd be tomorrow to do it.'

As they talked it was like the years fell away, like she was seeing a glimpse into what could have been if she hadn't run away. Would she be sitting here as his fiancée or his wife? Even though it terrified her, she somehow knew they could have gone the distance if she hadn't robbed them of the opportunity. But for all his words, did Adam feel it too?

'You must be feeling a whole range of emotions about her and it's okay to feel those things,' he replied softly. 'When Dad left, I felt relieved he and Mum wouldn't be arguing anymore, angry that we weren't enough for him, pleased that Mum could finally be happy. It's okay to be conflicted.' He paused. 'Would you like me to come with you?'

The offer astounded her almost as much as the gentle tone of his voice. She hadn't expected any more from him than a pleasant conversation that would soon end, but to think that he'd want to join her in her search was crazy. It was so much more than she ever thought possible. When she didn't speak, Adam continued.

'Before Vera died, she lent me the rocking horse you and I used to play on. I had a commission and she agreed to me using it for inspiration. I only took it back a week before she died. And you remember how nice she was to my mum after my dad left? However mean she was to everybody else, she was always good to us and I agree, there was a lot about her and her family none of us knew.'

'She lent you the rocking horse?'

Adam was lucky she'd done that for him. She remembered sitting on the horse in the middle of the living room, rocking backwards and forwards on cold rainy days. As she'd grown, she wanted to learn to ride and Vera had arranged riding lessons with a farmer nearby who owned horses. She hadn't taken to riding, being a little too afraid of the real-life creatures. They were much taller than she'd anticipated at ten years old. Big enough to crush you with one hoof. But Vera hadn't minded. She'd said that she hadn't enjoyed riding either. Amelia's throat tightened. Odd moments had perforated their gloomy existence, and as she'd discovered, quite a few memories like that had been forgotten over time.

Realising she hadn't responded to his offer, she said, 'I'd really like you to come, if you're not too busy.' Amelia balled her hands inside her jacket pockets until the skin on her fingers tensed. Was he really starting to forgive her? 'Do you need to check your diary?'

A hint of pink came to his cheeks. 'No, that's fine. I know what's happening this week.'

'Okay. Do you mind if I ask you something else?' He shook his head, but reticence was clear in his posture. 'You must have seen Vera a lot with staying in the village. How was she near the end?'

'The same as she always was. Maybe even grumpier. I don't think she knew she had a bad heart, so she didn't suddenly start being nice to people.'

'Is it still just you and Lynne?' She hoped it would sound like the genuine curiosity of two people catching up and not anything to do with the weight pressing on her chest. Océanè had always found it strange that Amelia hadn't had any long-term relationships, but she simply never felt strongly enough about someone to let them in to her life. Perhaps because her heart had only ever been filled with Adam Noble.

'Yep, just me and Mum still. She's seeing Dean, the landlord of the Drunken Duck.'

Once again Adam's deep brown eyes met hers. Seeing this grown, handsome man in front of her sent a thrill through her body. She'd always loved Adam, but the feeling inside her was something more profound and infinitely more powerful than it had been ten years ago. Was it simply a reminder of the bond that had existed between them or something new? Something based in the present and not just the past?

Whatever it was, she couldn't explore it. She'd be leaving in a matter of weeks, but as they fell into stilted conversation, she determined to find out as much about him as she could before that time ran out. She didn't need to add any more regrets to the load she already carried. It was heavy enough.

Chapter 17

Mr Hoffelmeyer lived in a large old house on the other side of the village and Amelia had spent the last few days preparing her questions for him.

It had been three days since the spring fair, and though she'd kept herself busy painting kitchen units so the dusty and marked cupboards now shone in pale lemon, and oiling the wooden worktops so they gleamed in the sun, it hadn't stopped the nerves somersaulting every time she thought of Adam and the time they'd spent together at the duck pond. He'd seemed so much more relaxed in her company, yet below the surface of their tentative probing conversation, a tension simmered. She'd wondered if it was best just to come out and apologise, and talk about the way she had left him, but there was never a good time and she hadn't wanted to scare him away. Perhaps they could move on without having to actually confront the past? She wasn't sure. All she knew was that today, he was going to visit Mr Hoffelmeyer with her, and she was glad of his company.

Amelia met him at the top of Willow Farm and could tell he was nervous too. After seeing her approach, he scuffed his shoe against the ground, sending a pebble flying towards the bushes. 'Are you okay?' he asked, frowning as she approached. 'You look pale.'

His concern sent her chest fluttering. The attraction she felt every time she was near him was hard to ignore. A knot formed in her stomach. 'I've been working pretty hard on the farmhouse. I think I'm just a bit tired.' Truth be told, she was possibly a bit under the weather with a stuffy nose and a headache growing behind her eyes, but she didn't want to moan to him and set the day off on the wrong foot. Whatever time they had left together was precious. 'So, this Mr Hoffelmeyer seems an interesting guy.'

Lame. Internally, Amelia rolled her eyes. She didn't have this problem with conversation in France. In France she could meet someone for the first time and chat endlessly, asking questions and covering a myriad of topics, but with Adam she struggled for every word. She didn't want to ask too many questions in case she seemed nosy and invasive, but likewise she didn't want to talk about herself and seem self-absorbed and egotistic. The situation was impossible. And every time she mentioned something to do with the village, her abandonment of him seemed to follow her insinuating things, which left very little to talk about.

'I take it you haven't met him before?' Adam asked, with a slight twinkle in his eye.

'No, I haven't. He wasn't here when we were little, was he?'

'No, he moved to the village about five years ago. He's quite a character.'

The way he said it she wasn't sure if she was looking forward to seeing him or not. *Character* could mean anything. It could mean something as innocent as he wore pyjamas all day or collected glass ornaments in the shape of books, or it could be something far more sinister. Whatever he was like, she still hoped for some answers. The locket remained fastened around her neck and the picture of the soldier was in her handbag, ready to show him.

'He's nice though,' Adam replied after consideration. 'A bit mad, but harmless.'

'Mad but harmless? Sounds great.' Nerves bubbled up once more. That really didn't bode well. 'Sounds like he fits right in in Meadowbank.'

They rounded the village green, where the ducks had decamped from the pond. Families were kicking balls back and forth, while younger children toddled around, chasing the ducks, holding out bread and giggling. It was a lovely sight and Amelia found herself wondering how she had never felt this way about the village before. She was going to miss Sophie when she returned to Paris. She enjoyed spending time with her, more than she did her friends there. Amelia felt like she was always on duty with them, unable to really relax and be the truest version of herself. With Sophie she could just be. Taking a tissue from her bag, she blew her nose. The fresh air was helping her breathe, but she was also beginning to feel decidedly cold despite the layers she'd put on.

'So how's the kitchen coming along?' Adam asked.

'Good. Thanks to the spring fair it's all cleared out and I've been painting units and oiling worktops.'

'I bet it looks great.' Adam's voice rang with regret and Amelia immediately knew why.

Yet again they'd wandered towards her leaving again, which she didn't presume would have any sort of impact on him now, but it was a deafening reminder of all the hurt she'd caused. Why did every conversation end up here? Amelia drew them to safer ground and commented on the fields and the weather, all the traditional subjects that meant they could talk without saying anything of importance.

Adam took them down one of the small lanes leading off the green and after weaving through tiny pathways at the end of the road, they emerged onto another larger country road that circled the village. This was where most of the larger, older houses were situated, all with long driveways taking them back even further from the centre of Meadowbank.

The Old Vicarage was surrounded by green lawns and encased in a brick wall topped with a heavy privet hedge. They followed around the edge to find the waist-height gate that had a shiny bronze name plaque attached to it, and above their heads was a small, thatched porch. It was cute and the brass name plaque dated the house to 1920. The gate creaked on its hinges as she pushed it open. A verdant green lawn circled the house with a curved path reaching a gravel area directly in front.

'Are you sure you're okay?' Adam asked, gently. 'You're very quiet.'

'Honestly,' she replied, trying to reassure him. 'I'm just nervous.' And not only about seeing Mr Hoffelmeyer. Being with Adam made her jittery but she gripped the handle of her bag and tried to hide it. 'Finding out about Vera – the soldier – it means so much to me.'

'I'm sure Mr Hoffelmeyer will be able to help. He's very knowledgeable.'

'Just possibly a lunatic,' she joked, and Adam grinned in return.

'Yeah, possibly. But don't worry, I'll protect you.'

Amelia reached inside her bag and pulled out and a sheet of paper. 'By the way, this is for you. I've been working on some ways you can explain your sculptures to people. I thought they might be helpful for promotions and websites and things.'

When Adam took it, his fingertips brushed hers and though his were warm and hers cold, she instantly ignited at his touch. The thought of his solid arms around her, warming her on cold dark nights made her swallow. He'd said he wanted to find out more about Vera too, that he had a sense of obligation towards her, but was that really true? Could she dare to think that despite everything he was there just to be with her? That he was beginning to forgive her?

Even after taking the note, he didn't move away. 'Wow, thanks.' Adam glanced at it, smiling, before folding it over and placing it in his back pocket. 'I'm surprised you had time with everything else you're doing.'

'Well, I said I would, and I've had time in the evenings. It's been nice to think in design terms again.'

They approached the front door. Amelia looked away as his smile faded, the implication being she couldn't wait to get back to Paris and use her skills again.

The house itself was a little more modest than the name and entry made it seem. Built of red brick with two windows on each side of the door, the panes divided into four, it was pretty, but to Amelia it lacked some of the homeliness of a slightly dishevelled farmhouse. This was the type of house you had to remove your shoes before entering. Lately, since Isla had come to the farmhouse really, Amelia had imagined children running in leaving muddy boot prints and clods of mud on the stone floor and her sweeping it up with a grin. Even without imaginary children, she'd been enjoying the freedom that came from not having to maintain a picture-perfect apartment. She hadn't realised the pressure had existed before, having been too busy living her life, but now she stepped back she could see the demands she often placed on herself to live the perfect life. When she returned to Paris, she'd have to make a few changes, and build in more time to relax and just be.

After knocking, the door was opened by an extravagant-looking man in a matching tweed jacket and waistcoat with bright red pocket square and green velvet trousers. His grey hair, like a ball of fluff on his head, tufted out from behind his ears. Amelia expected him to have a monocle or carry a magnifying glass, but instead a pair of small, gold-framed glasses perched halfway down his nose. He was clearly in his late sixties, and his skin was deeply tanned from wherever he'd been holiday. 'Good day. Good day. You must be Miss Williams, and Mr Noble, how lovely to see you again. How wonderful of you to contact me. Do come in.'

'Hi, Mr Hoffelmeyer,' Amelia replied. 'It's very kind of you to see us.'

'Why of course,' he enthused, clapping his hands together. 'Absolutely my pleasure. Please, come in, come in.'

The dim hallway led into a living room that was even more dated than Vera's farmhouse had been, but somehow it suited Mr Hoffelmeyer and wasn't at all gloomy. Three of the walls were lined with dark overflowing bookcases filled with densely packed paperbacks and pamphlets. A stack of open hardbacks marked with scraps of paper lay on a round table near the window.

Mr Hoffelmeyer ushered them inside. 'Vera's descendant, hey? Returned to her homeland.'

He said *return-ed* like a Shakespearean actor and Amelia pressed her lips together in amusement. 'Something like that.'

Mr Hoffelmeyer motioned to the centre of the room between a chintzy sofa and armchair in front of a large fireplace. 'Would you like some tea? Coffee? Jammie Dodger?' He picked up a plate of biscuits from the small circular table in front of the window and offered them around.

'Tea would be lovely, thank you,' Adam replied, holding his palm up to the biscuits. Amelia did the same also asking for tea.

Mr Hoffelmeyer flitted off and returned a remarkably short time later with a tray complete with teapot, cups and saucers, and matching sugar bowl and milk jug. 'My good lady wife already had the kettle on. Luckily, she saw you arrive. She was out pruning her bush.'

'Right,' Adam replied. The word carrying a slight laugh that he hid as well as he could.

'Shall I be Mother?'

Amelia nodded. 'Yes, please.'

'So, what is it I can help you intrepid historians with?'

'I was wondering what you know about the American soldiers who stayed in the village during World War Two.' Amelia shuffled to the edge of her seat. 'Elsie at the library mentioned you'd written a pamphlet on it.'

'Such a fascinating topic, my dear.' Mr Hoffelmeyer went to fetch one from a bookcase and handed it to her. She'd expected a folded sheet of A4 but the substantial document he gave her was more like a small book. She'd have to read it later. 'There's lots of detail in there but just to give you a rundown, when World War Two was well underway, with so many men being wounded in battle and then sent home, both field hospitals and hospitals here were overrun. Because of that, the government started requisitioning country houses to be used not just as hospitals but as depots to store goods and in some cases, military headquarters. I can see why you of all people would be interested.'

'What do you mean?' she asked, hope flowering in her chest. Adam glanced over at her.

'But do you not know?' Amelia shook her head and Mr Hoffelmeyer adjusted his glasses. 'Why, when Highfield was requisitioned as a military hospital some of the soldiers of all nations tended Meadow Farm's land while rehabilitating from wounds sustained in battle. When the men were fit enough, they liked to make use of them – for their own sakes too – and so, many of them worked on the farms around here. Being so close, I believe Meadow Farm was a particular favourite.'

She knew about Highfield being a hospital from Jocelyn, but as she replayed the conversation, she hadn't mentioned they actually worked on Meadow Farm. Her brow crinkled as she wondered why not. Perhaps she had simply forgotten to say it. A twinge of excitement bubbled up. If that was the case, the soldier must have known the Cabot family well, but why give them a photograph? It wasn't an answer but it was another link in the chain.

'Do you know *who* worked the farm?' Amelia mentally crossed her fingers, hoping he'd pull out a piece of paper with a list of names.

'I'm afraid not. Many of the records were destroyed when a fire broke out at Highfield after the war had ended.' Her shoulders rolled with disappointment. She already knew about the fire from Jennifer Motley but had hoped Mr Hoffelmeyer had some other sources of information.

'Are there copies?' asked Adam. 'Perhaps the Americans have some? Or the National Archives?'

Mr Hoffelmeyer shook his head. 'Whilst some records are available, many are still covered by the Data Protection Act and held by the Ministry of Defence.'

Amelia tried to hide the regret in her voice. 'So, you don't know who exactly stayed at the hospital or worked on Meadow Farm?'

'No. I'm terribly sorry. I realise that must be very disappointing for you. That's the trouble with family history research; it's often two steps forwards, one step back. But I do know that our country air did them the world of good and many of them returned to service rather quickly. Can you imagine recovering from an injury in this wonderful, peaceful place, then shipping back out into God knows what battlefield? Poor chaps. Who knows where they ended up?' He pushed his glasses back up the bridge of his nose. 'More tea? Garibaldi? Custard cream?'

'Oh, no, thank you.' Though she was eager to continue her questions, she drank her tea before pulling out the locket and the photograph. 'I know this may seem a silly question, and I know it's a long shot, but I don't suppose you recognise this man from your research, do you?'

She took off the locket and handed it over with the photograph. Mr Hoffelmeyer studied it carefully. 'What a beautiful piece. But I'm sorry, I'm afraid I don't. This photo's rather brilliant. Where did you find it?'

'I visited Highfield. Jennifer mentioned that she very recently found a few bits.'

'How amazing. I'll have to pay her a visit. But apart from this and a few others, there aren't many photographs around from that time. I asked around the village when I was doing some research and everyone was very generous, but the ones with the soldiers in were quite rare. Do you know some of the troops were sent over with special pamphlets telling them how to behave with us strange Brits?'

'I'm sure they caused quite a stir,' Adam said as Amelia refastened the locket around her neck. She was aware of his eyes on her, unshifting.

'Did you know my great-aunt at all, Mr Hoffelmeyer? Or have any idea why she might have kept this?' She motioned to the locket again.

'No, I'm sorry, Miss Williams. I didn't know her very well at all, but some of the servicemen did strike up lasting friendships with local families. I tried to talk to her about Meadowbank when I was researching the pamphlet to see if she had any recollection of the men who worked on the farm. Though she would have been too young to know them personally, I wondered if her parents spoke about them, but I'm sorry to say she got quite cross with me and made me leave.'

Age-old embarrassment at her aunt's behaviour surged. 'She never enjoyed speaking about her family. I'm sure it was nothing you'd done.'

Mr Hoffelmeyer smiled, obviously grateful for her understanding. 'I'm so glad you said that because I've been interviewing people for a long time and I always felt that Miss Cabot knew something and didn't want to tell me. Perhaps I was wrong.'

Though Amelia had hoped the question of who the man was might be answered, she at least knew a little bit more than she had before. She would obviously have to curb her expectations. Every time she hoped for a great leap in her understanding, she could only make a tiny step forward. She'd never known genealogy was so frustrating, but at least she was moving in the right direction.

The possibility of never really knowing who the soldier was or how he was connected with her family seemed to be looming on the horizon and it begged the question: if she didn't have that to focus on, would her emotions get the better of her? The mystery and the practical renovation of the farmhouse had been the only things keeping the sense of loss at bay. Since the discovery, she hadn't given herself time to sit down and think about her changing feelings for Vera, Meadowbank and the farmhouse, and as the emotions began to mount, tears threatened, obscuring her vision. Amelia dropped her eyes, eager to escape Adam's gaze that remained fastened on her. Mr Hoffelmeyer, though, hadn't seemed to notice as he finished eating a custard cream.

'Was there anything else I can help you with?'

'Just some advice, really,' she said composing herself. 'Do you know of any way we could identify who this man is? The records are so sparse, where do we go from here?'

'Without the local records I'm afraid there isn't much hope. The pictures you have are helpful, but one's so small it's almost impossible to see anything except for the fact that it's definitely an American uniform and with many war records still unavailable … I am sorry, my dear. It is frightfully frustrating.'

'That's okay. Thank you, Mr Hoffelmeyer. I do appreciate you speaking to me. I think we'd better get going.'

'You've been very helpful. Thank you,' Adam added as they were shown out.

The walk back to Meadowbank was another quiet one with Amelia lost in her thoughts as she tried to process all that Mr Hoffelmeyer had told her. With his usual kindness, Adam didn't press her. It didn't seem like they'd made much progress, but if the man had worked on Meadow Farm, then Vera might have heard him mentioned. He must have meant something to her mother and father to give them a photo. Why had Vera kicked Mr Hoffelmeyer out? Why did she have to be so closed off from everyone? If she'd taken the time to chat to Mr Hoffelmeyer, he might have had more to pass on to Amelia now. Closing yourself off from those around you had repercussions long past the ones you immediately thought of.

'Well,' Adam said encouragingly after a time. 'We got a bit more information at least. We know that this American soldier probably worked on Meadow Farm and that's how he knew Vera's family. Maybe they all grew fond of him and he gave them a picture to keep? It would have been when Vera's grandfather ran the farm. That's a long time ago. I guess that's the hard thing about family histories, unless you have actual records, it's just theories and ideas.'

'Secrets and stories,' she added. 'I just really thought getting to know a bit more about Vera and the farm would help me feel like I'd done right by her. Maybe make up for how we said goodbye. She was so angry with me when I left, I – oh, I don't know – I thought it would make up for not contacting her as much as I should.' She glanced at Adam. His face portrayed no emotion, like a wall had gone up behind his eyes. Could she be brave enough to apologise and face their unspoken past? She opened her mouth to speak, but he cut her off.

'She was a very difficult woman.'

Amelia nodded. If there was ever a sign he didn't want her to mention it, or that he wasn't ready to forgive her, that was it. Whatever progress they'd made, it clearly wasn't far enough. 'I quite fancy some cake now,' she said cheerfully, trying to move the conversation on.

'I'll walk you to Annie's then.' She wanted to ask him to join her but was probably facing another rejection if she did. A walk by his side would have to do. She wrapped her blazer around her as she shivered again.

Annie's Tearoom was busy with families as they approached. She'd savoured every step with Adam knowing their day together was about to end. The locket swung about her neck and she ran her fingers up and down the long chain.

'Hello, Arthur,' Amelia said, pausing at his side. 'Are you okay?'

'Hey, Arthur,' Adam added.

'Just catching my breath,' he replied, turning his face up to the sun.

Amelia stared at the sun too, enjoying the warmth on her skin. 'It's a nice day today, isn't it?' Arthur's face wrinkled as he frowned. She followed his gaze as it fell to the locket. 'Is everything all right?'

'Vera's locket,' he said, his eyes widening in surprise.

'It is.' How did Arthur know it was Vera's? She never wore jewellery and Amelia couldn't imagine her showing it to anyone given how she had told her not to pry. 'Do you know about it?' she asked gently.

Arthur didn't answer but began edging away from the wall and into the lane. Both Amelia and Adam turned at the same time as the yells of teenagers grew louder. It was the same group of kids she'd seen with Sophie. They were on their bikes again, winding down the lane at speed. Arthur stepped away, but without realising he was moving further into their path. They'd be colliding with him in no time. Adam yanked Arthur away and within seconds the gang flew past, whistling and jeering as they went.

'Those kids,' Adam said through gritted teeth. 'They need to find something better to do with their time. Are you okay, Arthur? Do you want to sit down for a minute?'

As Arthur moved away from Adam, Amelia motioned to a table the other side of the wall. 'Would you like to join me, Arthur? Would you like a cup of tea? I was just about to have some cake and would love to talk to you about the locket.'

He shook his head. 'No. No, thank you. I'd better be going.'

Despite his reticence, Amelia couldn't hold herself back. She asked, 'Do you remember Vera wearing the locket, Arthur? Did she perhaps show it to you sometime?'

Arthur stared at the locket fearfully and then, suddenly, walked away without answering. She thought about catching up with him, but it was obvious he wasn't in the mood for talking and Amelia didn't want to upset him. Still, she couldn't help but call out, 'Arthur? Did Vera ever talk about the locket or the pictures inside it?'

The faint sound of his muttering carried on the breeze. She wasn't sure, but it sounded like he said, 'Stupid, stupid, Arthur.'

What could he be talking about? He was only a little older than Vera. Maybe he knew her better than they thought? Now she came to think about it, the few times she'd seen him, he hadn't reacted the same way everyone else had about Vera, saying how hard and cold she was. Yet, she was sure Vera had never mentioned Arthur during her years at home. She turned to Adam. 'Did Vera ever mention Arthur to you or vice versa?'

He shook his head. 'No. But that was a strange reaction.'

When Adam moved to save Arthur, he'd ended up incredibly close to her. She could see faint red stubble on Adam's chin and smell his earthy aftershave. The light reflected off his red hair and her heart began to pound, not only from the strange encounter she'd just had with Arthur, but also from the effect Adam was having on her physically.

For a second, his gaze locked on hers, exploring her face, searching for something. The world around them shrank and she wished she could be brave enough to touch him. Adam opened his mouth to speak when a rush of tingling tickled the back of her nose and she turned and sneezed. Adam stepped back.

Thanks very much, useless body, she thought as she grabbed a tissue and blew her nose. The stuffiness was reaching further into her head, filling it up, and the pounding behind her eyes had spread to her temples. She placed a hand there and was surprised at the heat emanating off her. It was only just lunchtime, but the weariness in her bones made her ache for rest.

Adam took another step back, and her heart fell, but she couldn't blame him. She wasn't exactly at her best or most attractive right now. Sneezing and sounding like a walking, talking germ wasn't sexy. 'Adam, I'd better go home. I'm feeling a bit under the weather.'

His eyes roved over her. 'I'll walk you back.'

She didn't deserve his kindness and, feeling tearful, she nodded confirmation then let him lead the way. More than anything she wanted to take his hand, and when he absent-mindedly placed his on the small of her back, a fire shot through her. Frighteningly, her fear of returning to Meadow Farmhouse to face her past was replaced by the terrifying thought that her mistake might have been to leave Meadowbank, and Adam, in the first place.

Chapter 18

The sheet of paper crinkled as Adam laid it out onto the table, smoothing out the creases from where it had sat in his pocket. Pete had messaged to say they were going to the pub this evening but for once had hadn't wanted to join them.

Since the moment Amelia had given him the note, he'd wished to open it up and read it, but he hadn't wanted to take the focus away from her search. It meant so much to her. He'd been so sure she'd come back, clear the place and sell; it was surprising she was taking the time to do this. She had an exciting life in one of the most beautiful capital cities in the world to get back to, didn't she? Not to mention a stack of friends and possibly boyfriends. He hadn't actually asked her about that, not sure if he wanted to know the answer.

Willow Farm's kitchen was the same shape as Vera's with L-shaped units running around it, but the kitchen table was much smaller. His small circular affair had only ever seated him and his mum, or his mates when they came round for night of poker and curry. Obviously Philippa had joined him there too, but thinking of Amelia's search he wondered how many people had sat around Vera's ancient wooden table, tapping the surface while they talked. He could understand why Amelia would want to know. Vera had been an enigma to them all and once the farmhouse had been sold, there was no going back. Amelia would be gone forever.

With a sigh, he put the kettle on and cursed himself for the reticence growing inside him that Amelia would soon be leaving. After the time they'd spent together at the spring fair and seeing

Mr Hoffelmeyer, he didn't want her to go. He'd seen flashes of the girl he'd loved so deeply, but also the tantalising prospect of the woman she'd become. There was a lot to discover about this new Amelia and he wanted to explore how her personality had changed, understand the experiences she'd had over the last ten years and know her again. Know her as well as he had before.

The whistle of the kettle drew his attention away from the handwritten note and he begrudgingly made his way to the tea caddy, tossing a teabag into a cup and adding the hot water. As he added the milk and sugar, he glanced again at the handwriting that had always been so familiar. Amelia's writing was large and sloping with flowery tails; exactly what he remembered from their youth. As kids, they'd write notes to each other if they were unable to spend time together, dropping them through letter boxes if one or the other was ill. Back then, she'd dotted her I's with tiny love hearts or smiley faces depending on her mood. It was the writing he'd longed to see after she left for university, though he knew she wasn't likely to send an actual letter.

Now, though the writing had lost that special touch; it was the words she'd written that drew his attention. Somehow, Amelia had made his weird Groot soldiers sound amazing. She described them as 'unique, hand-crafted statues made from locally sourced wood' and 'characterful, artist-designed figures perfect for the home or garden'. They were combinations of words he'd never have thought to use. As creative as he was with his hands, that talent hadn't extended to his use of English. It felt strange to have Amelia consider him an artist. It felt strange to consider himself one. She'd also listed some ideas for photographing them, and had made a note about how important it was to show prospective buyers how they might have them in their own home.

After a big slurp of tea, Adam pulled open his laptop. Perhaps now was a good time to start a Facebook page for his sculptures. He didn't really need one for the carpentry work; he already had more jobs than he could handle. But as he thought about his future and what he wanted to achieve, he realised that he would like to focus on something more rewarding. If he was the type of person to have a five-year plan, which he wasn't, it would be to spend more time making furniture and exploring this artistic side. Would he feel that way if Amelia hadn't written these words for him? He'd always considered ambition to be a dirty word. For too long he'd associated it with his negative feelings over Amelia leaving him behind to charge headlong into her new life. Those feelings hadn't dissipated yet, but he realised now he'd been holding himself back. Ambition, he had thought, meant being cruel and cutthroat or missing time with loved ones and friends all for the sake of a pat on the head. If he was honest with himself, it was how he'd imagined Amelia had ended up and that he, boring country-boy Adam, just hadn't fitted in with her plans. Had he been wrong?

Amelia wasn't like that. Neither was Annie who ran her own business and had ambitions for the tearooms. It seemed he'd been blinded by his own prejudices. And if nothing else, as the village already knew about his work – whether they liked them or not – he didn't have any reason not to promote them.

Facebook appeared on the screen and Adam scowled at the notifications icon. They were always a nuisance but because he hardly ever went on it, masses awaited him. As usual, most of them were nonsense but one caused him to peer in closer.

In a strangely robotic voice he read, 'Amelia Williams reacted to a photo of you. What the actual fu …?' He let the word trail away with his breath. As he clicked to see which photo she'd reacted to, he leaned back in his chair, his eyebrows lifting.

After a second, Adam rested his arms on the table and ran his hands over his stubble. Heat began to rise in his chest. She'd liked a photo uploaded the other year of him in the garden of the Drunken Duck. It had been such a hot summer they'd cleared all the tables and blown up a huge inflatable swimming pool. He, Pete and Rob had taken it in turns to be on lifeguard duty and here he was in his Speedos with his head thrown back laughing. They didn't leave much to the imagination and though he'd not been keen on the idea of wearing them, they'd all joined in as a joke. Normally he was a board shorts kind of guy, something that gave a little more coverage.

Adam brought his eyebrows down only to lift them again as he puffed air out through his cheeks. The idea wouldn't even compute. Amelia had liked a photo of him in his budgie smugglers. Embarrassment inched up his spine and he buried his face in his hands for a second.

After all the years of radio silence why was she was now liking photos of him? This strange new development was worrying on two fronts. Firstly, from the date, he could see she had been looking him up the day she returned to Meadowbank. Had she hoped to see him or had it just been curiosity as to whether he was still there. Had she been happy at the prospect of running into him? On the times they had bumped into each other, she'd tried to talk but he'd been unyielding in an effort to protect himself. If she wanted to make amends, perhaps it was time for him to soften too? Could he bring himself to forgive her if she'd be leaving again soon? A grown-up voice inside him told him he should, while another whinier one told him it still hurt too much. If he did let go of that barrier of pain, there was every possibility his heart would run away with him again.

Secondly, Amelia had actually liked the photo, and not just in social media speak. She had *liked* the picture. She'd liked what she'd seen. Did that mean she liked the man he'd grown into or just the fact he was smiling and happy? He was quite different to the skinny adolescent she must remember. Did she find him attractive? At times it had seemed there was still a spark between them. Their connection was like an indelible line. Like when you write on a notepad and pull the page off. Underneath there was still a trace of what had been there before. The thought sent a shiver down his spine. What exactly did that mean for them?

As he stared at the screen for a second more, not seeing the photo, but thinking only of the fact that Amelia had liked it, a knock at the front door was swiftly followed by the turning of a key in the lock.

'Only me,' his mum called as her red hair appeared around the door before the rest of her face followed. 'I brought you some dinner from the pub. I saw Dean was doing a special on steak and ale pie and I thought, oooh, my Adam loves a bit of steak and ale pie, so I nabbed you some. What you up to?'

Holding two plates, one stacked on top of the other protecting the food, she made her way towards Adam and his screen. He quickly flicked it shut and rested his hands on top. The speedy action hadn't escaped his mum's eagle eyes.

'What are you being so shifty about?'

'I'm not.'

'Yes, you are.' She put the plates down. 'Are you looking at porn? Because if you are, I can dump this on the side and go.'

'Mum!' Adam's cheeks burned. 'Sweet Jesus, how do you even know about pornog— actually, don't tell me. I really don't want to know.'

'You don't need to be embarrassed, son. You're a normal red-blooded boy. And you've been single for ages. It's perfectly natural that without a girlfriend you should—'

'If you continue that sentence, Mother, I'll make you leave even if I have to sling you out myself.'

Lynne chuckled. 'All right. But if it's not porn then what are you looking at?'

Adam sighed but admitting to setting up a Facebook page for his strange wooden sculptures was far more preferable to his mum thinking he spent Wednesday evenings looking at porn if he wasn't in the pub. 'I'm setting up a Facebook page for my sculpture business. I've decided to start trying to sell them more widely and actually treating it like a business rather than a hobby.'

'Really?' She grinned. 'That's marvellous.' Lynne trundled over and gave him a hug. 'I'm so proud of you. To be fair, it's about time. I don't know why you haven't done it before. You could have shifted more of them before now and then you'd have more space in your workshop too. I'm sure your creepy wooden goblins will sell like hotcakes.'

'I wouldn't be too enthusiastic, Mum, but thanks to Amelia I've got a decent way of explaining them to people now.'

'Huh, really?' Lynne crossed her arms over her chest.

'Really. I love you but weird creepy goblins isn't exactly how I want to explain them. Look, Amelia gave me this.' He handed her the piece of paper and watched as Lynne's eyes grazed over the various phrases.

'That's very helpful of her.'

'See. Maybe she's not as bad you think.'

'I'll wait until I'm proved wrong about that, thanks. Word has it she's already booked an estate agent to come next week.' Adam focused on keeping his face natural. She'd not mentioned that. 'So I was right that she's selling the place as quickly as possible.' Lynne glanced at her watch. 'Well, I'd better get back to the pub. It'll be getting busy and you know how I like to help out.'

The mention of the estate agent hit him like a slap to the face. He hadn't realised she'd already booked one and what that meant sat heavy on his shoulders. He wasn't naive but for some reason, with their visit to Mr Hoffelmeyer, he'd imagined her staying for longer. 'I don't know how you have so much energy, Mum,' Adam said, eager to show he was unaffected by her news, and placed a kiss on the top of her head.

'The Duracell bunny has got nothing on me. Right, I'm off.'

She disappeared in a blur of activity and, even with the after-effects of her bombshell, he couldn't help but smile. Porn indeed. But he was a red-blooded man and thoughts of Amelia started to flash through his mind. The idea of kissing her, of running his hands through her long black hair, or winding it around his fingers as he pulled her in for a kiss … Heat built inside him despite the ache in his heart at the thought of her leaving.

He sat down and reopened his laptop. Time to concentrate on something else. 'Right. How do I do this, then?'

He clicked and typed, and before long a page for Adam Noble Sculptures – not the most imaginative name but the only one he could think of right now – had been born. As he sat back, proud that he'd achieved something he'd always been afraid of, he couldn't help but think about Amelia Williams and the photograph she'd liked. It was ridiculous how much it meant to him and he closed his eyes, trying to rebuild the barriers he'd felt cracking over the last few days and patch up the holes before he saw her again.

Chapter 19

A knocking at the door awoke Amelia from her place on the sofa. She hadn't intended to fall asleep. She'd got up as normal and tried to work, pottering about and tidying because she couldn't face lifting a paintbrush. After an hour, her head had been throbbing so aggressively she'd had to lie down.

At first, Amelia had thought it would be impossible to sleep on the old wire-sprung seats even though she'd covered them in blankets and cushions. No matter what she did she couldn't get warm, and the plan had been to close her eyes for a moment before having a nap upstairs. As every muscle ached and the pounding behind her eyes intensified, she'd managed it.

Amelia had never suffered from migraines before, but she figured all the stress, worry and, let's face it, emotional turmoil of the last two weeks had brought one on. After she'd flopped on the sofa it was simply comfier to curl her legs underneath her and lie down. Bleary-eyed, she grabbed her phone to see the time. It was nearly two, which meant she'd been asleep for hours. Why didn't she feel any better? The rapping at the front door started again, and squeezing her eyes shut, she pushed herself up to standing.

Weird bits of her were throbbing. Muscles she didn't normally feel unless it had been a particularly unpleasant session in the gym were aching, almost burning. Her triceps pulsed, even her calf muscles and ankles burned. As she reached to open the door, the skin around her knuckles felt uncomfortably tight.

'Hey, I thought – blimey, are you all right?' asked Sophie. 'You look really poorly.'

'I don't feel so well, actually.' Considering she was virtually hanging on to the doorframe for support, that was an understatement. Amelia was willing to accept now that she'd never felt so ill in her entire life. Another shiver shot through her, causing her whole body to shudder, then a sweep of nausea closed her throat. 'I was just going to have a hot bath then get into bed.'

'E'lo,' said Isla, smiling up at her from beside Sophie's knee.

'Hello, Isla,' Amelia replied.

'It's not even two – you must feel really bad.'

'I do.'

'Then let us help you.' Sophie looked down at Isla. 'Shall we help make Amelia feel better?'

Isla nodded before turning back and placing her hands on her hips. 'Go bed.'

'No, it's fine.' Amelia chuckled. 'I can manage. Honestly, if I'm contagious I don't want to give this to either of you.'

'Oh hush, my husband's the village GP. If anyone was going to make us sick it'd be him and besides, I cram Isla full of those chewy multivitamins because I'm such a shoddy cook. She's chock full of vitamin C. It's the only way I'm ever going to make sure she gets all her vitamins and minerals until they start adding them to chicken nuggets. Come on, there's nothing worse than being unwell on your own. I know what it's like. Everything feels like such an effort. You probably won't eat anything if I leave, will you?'

Amelia reached a hand up and rubbed her eyes. 'I think I've got some biscuits left. I can nibble on those.'

'Biscuits?' Sophie's incredulous squeak echoed in her ears. 'Isla, Amelia wants to have biscuits for dinner.'

'Biscuits!' she chanted, raising her arms in the air in celebration.

Sophie scowled. 'That's not very helpful. Amelia, you can't just eat biscuits in your state. You need something good for you that's going to give your body the strength to fight.'

'That's such a mum thing to say.'

'Amelia.' Sophie reached out and placed a hand on her shoulder. 'Let me help you. Please?' A stinging in her sinuses caused Amelia to admit defeat and she opened the door wider. 'Thank you.'

Sophie made her way into the house and Isla followed behind. She toddled off to the sofa and climbed up as Sophie headed for the kettle. 'This place is looking so different already.' Amelia made it to one of the chairs at the kitchen table and flopped down. 'I mean, it just feels so different. There's so much light in here now, and these kitchen units are beautiful, you can feel the weight of the wood.' She ran her hand over them. 'I love the lemon colour. This place feels so much more loved. So happy.'

She had been happier here than anywhere else recently. She was growing to love the farmhouse with its large L-shaped kitchen and butler sink, and the thought of putting it on the market stabbed into her heart. She didn't really want to let it go, but Amelia reminded herself Paris was waiting for her and the estate agent was coming next week. Should she rearrange? No, she'd be better by then and she didn't have the energy to call right now. With clients waiting, she couldn't delay her plans unless absolutely necessary.

'So, what's actually wrong?' Sophie asked after putting the kettle on.

'I've got a headache and the shivers. Everything hurts and I feel a bit sick but not all the time. It comes and goes.'

'Have you got a thermometer?'

'I don't think so.' Sophie walked back and lifted her chin with one hand, while placing the other on Amelia's forehead. 'You're very hot and pale as milk. I think you've got the flu.'

The word *flu* sent another shiver through her and not just because her body was failing. 'I can't have the flu. I need to get this place sorted and I need to find out more about the locket. I have to get back to Paris and my clients. I can't get ill. There's too much to do. Maybe, I'm just tired.'

'Tiredness doesn't give you a temperature or send you shivering, and you're a bit clammy. It's definitely flu. Michael's seen a lot of people with it in the village this season.'

'Maybe a good night's sleep will make me feel better.'

'That I can agree with. It'll be the best thing for you.'

The kettle boiled and Sophie made them both some tea after searching in the cupboards for everything she needed. Amelia wanted to help and direct her to where everything was, but she just couldn't manage it. She'd never felt so exhausted in her life. Perhaps Sophie was right. If flu was going around, she could have caught it. A flurry of concern sent her head pounding again. 'Do you have Jocelyn's number?'

'Jocelyn? Why?'

'I went to see her, and I'm worried she could have caught it off me. She's quite old. It could really knock her for six.'

'I'll get Michael to check in on her. Does that make you feel better?'

'Thank you,' Amelia replied.

Sophie sat back in her chair and Isla toddled over, climbing up onto her mum's lap. 'Here's the plan, then. I'm going to run you a bath to warm you up then you're going to get straight into bed. I'll bring you up some dinner and make something you can heat up tomorrow morning for breakfast. Do you have porridge oats or something?'

Amelia nodded and immediately regretted it as her brain hit the back of her skull and the muscles of her neck stiffened, supporting her head. 'I can run a bath though. You really don't have to stay.'

'I get the feeling, Amelia that because of Vera, you're the type of person who's used to doing everything on her own.'

In amazement, she stared at Sophie and a tear escaped her eye. She brushed it away not wanting Isla to worry something was wrong. Stupidly, it was an aspect of her personality she was only just coming to understand herself.

'You don't need to be embarrassed,' said Sophie gently and Amelia wasn't sure if she meant about needing help, or having her personality nailed so completely. As she carried on, she was relieved to find Sophie was referring to the bath. 'I'll just run it and come back downstairs. I won't see you naked or anything. You can give me a shout when you're in bed and I'll bring you some food up. I'll also bring some snacks as well in case you get hungry later. Isla will help me, won't you, darling?'

Isla gazed at Amelia across the table. 'Are poorly?' Amelia nodded. Isla climbed down and ran around the table to hug her. Amelia's eyes welled with tears once more.

'Thank you, darling.' She sniffed, stinging her sinuses.

'Oh, honey, don't cry.' Sophie leaped up and wrapped her arms around Amelia so now everyone was hugging her.

'Sorry.' Amelia wiped the tears away and Sophie released her, moving back to her seat. 'I always get emotional when I'm unwell and it's been a bit emotional coming back.'

She genuinely couldn't bear to speak more than necessary and hoped Sophie wouldn't ask her any more questions. How could she even describe it all? Every movement of her body took a monumental effort. She just needed to lie in a silent, dark room.

'I get really emotional when I'm ill too. I had a C-section with Isla and once I was home, I cried at an advert for tea.'

Amelia managed to smile.

'I'm going to get this bath run for you. You sit and drink your tea. Isla, keep an eye on Amelia, please.'

Amelia stared at the liquid circling in her mug as Sophie made her way upstairs and Isla watched her from across the table. The old staircase creaked and moaned as Sophie ascended and a moment later, the sound of the water hitting the bath sent anticipation through her body. Her fingers felt a little better from the heat of her cup, as thoughts of Adam jumbled together with thoughts of Vera and the locket, but they were hazy and unformed.

A few minutes later, Sophie came back down. 'Right, the bath's run. I like mine so scalding hot I come out looking like a lobster, but I wasn't sure you would, so I've made it a bit cooler. Do you want me to help you upstairs?'

'No, I can manage.' Every movement seemed to be happening

in slow motion, but Amelia pushed herself up and Sophie tucked the heavy wooden chair back under the table for her. 'Thank you.'

'Get straight into bed afterwards and I'll bring you up some food. I'm not sure what you've got, but I'll try and make something comforting.'

'Thanks, Mum,' she joked without thinking, and the reference to all she'd missed out on with losing her parents brought tears to her eyes again. When Amelia had been ill as a child, Vera had looked after her, but it had often felt like she'd thought it was an inconvenience. That her bothersome throwing up disrupted Vera's ordered life. She'd been surprisingly understanding when a bad cold had stopped her seeing Adam one summer. And there had been times when she'd cooked her special meals after a hard time at school, or when she had exams. This time the happier memories were harder to swallow back down than they ever had been before.

The bath was beautifully hot. Just the right temperature to ease some of the aches and pains, and the steam gave temporary respite from her stuffy nose. Amelia sank down into the water. She'd scrubbed the bathroom clean the other day and its whiteness reflected the mid-afternoon sun in a dazzling brightness. She squeezed her eyes shut. She'd never relaxed like this with a virtual stranger in her house before. Even in Paris, Amelia couldn't unwind until Océanè had left and the flat was her own once more. She'd never been good at sharing her personal space, but in Meadowbank it felt okay to do that. She'd been invited into Jocelyn's and Mr Hoffelmeyer's homes and it hadn't felt strange or awkward. She closed her eyes, savouring the warmth and ignored the realisation that Meadowbank was getting further and further under her skin.

After climbing out of the water and finding some pyjamas, Amelia put on her dressing gown and called to Sophie that she was getting into bed. She was shivering more now as her body adjusted to the change in temperature and she curled into the foetal position under the duvet. Her wrists had started aching and the thumping in her head returned more ferocious than ever.

Sophie edged open the door with her bum and turned, carrying a full tray of food and drink. She'd brought up some bottles of water, the biscuits Amelia had mentioned earlier and a tomato soup with pasta added. It was a simple dinner, but exactly what Amelia wanted right now. She didn't know when the queasiness would return, and she didn't want to eat too much in case it did. Sophie had been right that she needed to eat. She edged out from under the duvet and as she moved, her body juddered from the shivers pulsing through her.

'Thank you so much, Sophie. You've been so kind. This looks brilliant.'

The tray had little legs that stuck out and Sophie placed it over Amelia's lap. 'I'll hang on until you've eaten the soup, then I'll leave you with these nibbles, okay? I found some tissues so popped them on the tray. I think you're going to need more than this lot though, and the cough medicine I found in a kitchen cupboard must have been there for decades, so I'll get you some of that too.'

'I haven't got a cough yet.'

'No, but you might get one and the last thing you need is to suffer. I'll get you some supplies and drop them off tomorrow, okay?' She hesitated for a moment brushing her blonde hair back from her face. 'If you want, I can take a key. I'm not trying to overstep or anything, but it'll mean you don't have to get out of bed and let me in.'

Amelia took a spoonful of the thick tomato soup and the taste soothed her senses. This wasn't from a tin. Sophie must have made it from scratch using whatever she could find in the kitchen. The sweetness of the tomatoes was like a comforting hug and the starchy pasta would help her body stay strong. 'This is delicious, Sophie. You're definitely not a shoddy cook. Isla and Michael are very lucky.' Sophie smiled at the compliment. 'There's a spare key hanging by the front door. Feel free to take it. I don't think I'll be going anywhere for a few days.'

'Neither do I. Make sure you drink lots of water, okay?' She picked up one of the bottles. 'Fill this up whenever you get up for the loo then you won't run out. It's really important you stay hydrated and get as much sleep as you can.' She turned around, looking at the room. 'I see you've got a TV and DVD player. Want me to bring you some DVDs?'

'Yes, please. I'll need something to watch. I can't just lie here doing nothing.'

'No, you're not the doing nothing type, are you? Vera didn't have Netflix then?'

'No and I didn't sign up as I wasn't going to be here that long. Is Isla okay downstairs?' Amelia asked, eager to make the conversation less one-sided.

'Yeah. She's colouring at the table. I'll go back down in a second.'

By now Amelia had eaten half of the soup and the queasiness was growing inside her. She didn't want to leave any because it was delicious, neither did she want to offend Sophie, yet she couldn't ignore the signals her body was sending. Her teeth chattered as she put her spoon down and tried to snuggle further into the duvet without knocking everything off the tray. 'I'm so cold.'

Sophie picked up the tray and put it on the floor. 'I wish I didn't have to leave you. Do you want me to ask Michael to pop in?'

'No, it's fine. If it is the flu, there's nothing he can do anyway. I just have to ride it out.'

'That's true. I'll leave you to rest now and pop back tomorrow with something else to eat. I found some porridge oats and have made you some in a saucepan and popped the whole thing in the fridge. You'll just need to reheat it, but you've got something to eat first thing. I'll bring you some lunch and dinner too. I would bring microwavable meals but if the rest of Meadowbank found out I'd done that instead of cooking something myself they'd be mortified and never let me back on the village committee.'

Amelia shook her head. 'You've got your own family to look after; you don't need to worry about me.'

'I'm not worried,' she said with a reassuring lightness. 'You'll be all right in a week or so, but for now it's no bother to make a little bit extra and drop it round.'

'You're so kind. Thank you.' Amelia's head sank into the pillow and her eyes closed of their own accord.

'I'll see you later, okay?'

She tried to nod in acknowledgement but wasn't sure her head had moved at all. As she tried to think of something nice rather than the pounding in her skull, she was vaguely aware of Sophie leaving and the front door closing a moment later.

The last thing she remembered before she fell asleep was a vision of the wedding dress in Vera's wardrobe and Adam standing at the altar waiting for someone to marry him. In her half-asleep state, she couldn't be sure, but it was as if he was waiting for her.

Chapter 20

As silently as possible, Adam let himself and his mum into the farmhouse. Since Sophie had let him know that Amelia had a nasty case of the flu, the image of her pale unwell face had ricocheted around his brain. The afternoon he'd brought her home after seeing Mr Hoffelmeyer's and touched her back, the feelings he'd concealed for so long ago came flooding back with an intensity that made Niagara Falls look like a lazy trickle of water. However much he wanted to pretend he didn't care about her anymore, he did, more than ever.

'Come on,' whispered his mum from behind him. 'It's steak night at the pub and I want to get you a plate. It looks bloody lovely. Make sure you heat it properly in the microwave though and give Dean back the plate.'

Adam checked his watch. 'Mum, it's literally one minute past twelve. The pub has only just started serving lunch let alone dinner.'

'I know. That's why I want to get there and get you the best bits first before they go. Steaks always go well at lunchtime. Don't say I don't do anything for you.'

He laughed, scrubbing his hand through his hair. 'You do loads for me, Mum and I'm really grateful, but let's get this stuff unpacked for Amelia without disturbing her.'

As quietly as possible, he began unloading stacks of dishes from the overflowing bags he'd been carrying. News of Amelia's illness had flown around the village and everyone had turned out with good wholesome food to aid her recovery. Even his mum had made a few things for her, softened by Sophie's description of her tired eyes.

'Get out before I call the police!' came a frightened cry from the foot of the stairs.

'Amelia Williams,' shouted his mum, spinning to face her. 'Put that toilet brush down this instant and go back to bed.'

Adam, who had been too busy in the kitchen to realise she had come downstairs, turned to see her wielding the weapon of choice above her head. Trying not to find the whole thing funny he said, 'It's just us, Amelia. Sophie asked me to stop in and check on you. Didn't she say?'

'No,' her voice quivered. Realising she was still brandishing the toilet brush, she lowered it. 'Or maybe she did, I don't know. The last few days have been a bit blurry. Sorry. Sorry, Mrs Noble.'

Lynne tutted and stepped forwards, holding out her hand for the brush. 'Honestly. What did you think you'd do with this? Un-hygiene them to death?'

'There wasn't much else upstairs.' Amelia shuddered and pulled her dressing gown around her. Her dark-rimmed eyes looked glassy with exhaustion, and the apples of her cheeks glowed red.

After depositing the loo brush outside, Lynne came back and examined Amelia, placing her hands on her shoulders and turning her head left and right. 'Sophie's right, definitely this nasty flu. I can tell you've had a temperature you smell like a men's locker room.'

'How do you know what a men's locker room smells like, Mum?' Adam asked, pausing with a cake tin in his hand.

'Never you mind. Now, back to bed with you.'

To see his mum being kind to her after the welcome speech she'd given was having quite the effect on Amelia. Her jaw hung loose in surprise until a racking shiver shook her body. 'What are you two doing here?'

'When—' Adam tried to speak but was cut off.

'When Sophie said you were unwell,' Lynne interrupted, 'I decided to cook you some things to help you recover.'

'Then when Mum saw Mrs Bostock in the village shop and

told her you were poorly, she decided you needed cake to speed your recovery and made you a Victoria sponge. She dropped it into Mum's this morning.'

'Oh,' Amelia replied, too stunned to say any more.

'Then,' Lynne began, 'Mrs Carmichael – Jocelyn – heard too and said she'd make you a nice chicken stew and dumplings. Apparently, she had the flu terrible when she was twenty and the only thing she could face eating was her mother's stew. That's in the green pot over there.' Lynne pointed to the table and Amelia's eyes widened at the number of pots, dishes, tubs and tins laid out for her.

'Then everyone else started joining in, making you things and dropping them round to me.'

'But enough of that now.' Lynne started flapping her hands towards Amelia. 'Back to bed with you. I'll make you some scrambled eggs and Adam can bring it up while I sort out this lot. Do you know how disgusting Vera's fridge is? There's some green goo in there that I think started out as a head of broccoli but I'm not entirely sure. It looks like it might have come to life of its own accord. The whole thing needs a good clean before I put anything in there. I'm surprised you haven't done it already.'

'Thank you,' Amelia said softly, and Lynne ran her eyes over her once more before turning and signalling to Adam he was to take her upstairs.

'Don't forget the tissues,' she added as they stepped away.

At the top of the stairs, Adam caught a glimpse of her unmade bed covered in dirty tissues. There were even a few on the floor, and as Amelia glanced over her shoulder in panic, he dipped his head to hide his mirth. She lunged forwards and grabbed handfuls, stuffing them into the pockets of her robe. Adam pretended not to notice.

'Sorry about the mess,' she said in a muted voice. 'I've never felt so ill in my life. At one point I thought I was going to die because my elbows were sweating and I didn't even know they could do that.'

'I can imagine that was unnerving. Here, you get into bed and I'll clear up.' As she flopped onto the mattress, he began cleaning the room.

'You don't have to do that. I'll do it after I've eaten. I'm sure I'll feel better then. Besides you might need some kind of protective equipment. You really don't want to catch this.'

'Judging by the state of you, you won't feel better for a few days yet. And if I don't do this before Mum comes up, we'll both be in trouble.' He took four new boxes of tissues from the carrier bag Lynne had asked him to bring up and put them on the bedside before filling the bag back up with dirty tissues.

'I'm so gross,' Amelia moaned, covering her face.

'You do look a bit rough,' Adam conceded.

'I meant the tissues.'

'Oh.' It was his turn to blush. 'Yeah, that's a bit gross too but you're really ill, so we'll forget about it.'

She nodded, but muttered a pathetic-sounding 'Sorry' once more.

His lips twitched in amusement and the small scar on his lip puckered. 'Don't worry, we'll look after you. I've been feeding the chickens by the way, and Mr MacMahon will stop by and feed them for the next few days.'

'Can't you do it?' she asked, and he wasn't sure if it was because she was afraid of Mr MacMahon or because she wanted him. The thought that it was the latter punctured another hole in his armour. 'He'll just sort them out and leave. He won't come into the house to bother you.'

'None of you need to do all this. Sophie said she'll pop in when she can and from what you guys have brought, I won't need any food for a week.'

'*We* isn't just me, Mum and Sophie, Amelia. *We* is the entire village – and you try and stop them. Mrs Bostock has already said she's going to ask Mrs Norris to make you a shepherd's pie because hers is the best and Mum's pretty much organised a cooking rota so you get three meals a day for the next week.'

'Everybody's being so kind,' she said, blowing her nose. Adam held open the carrier bag and she popped the tissue in. 'I don't know why.'

'Because people care, Amelia.'

'But why do they care about me?'

Her words shocked him. 'Why shouldn't they?'

'I don't know. Vera made me feel such a burden. I always thought everyone would forget about me. I thought you'd forget about me.'

There were tears in her eyes and he was tempted to reach out and cup her face. Instead, he drew his eyes away.

Right now, he'd never felt angrier with anyone than he was with Vera Cabot. As if Amelia hadn't been through enough losing her parents. All Vera had to do was make more of an effort and put Amelia first. It wasn't that hard an ask, and it wasn't like she'd been a tearaway child. She'd been well behaved, worked hard at school and made something of herself. Any parent would have been proud of that, but Vera always acted like Amelia had let her down in some way. Had Amelia really thought he'd just get over her?

For the first time, Adam had an inkling of what Amelia had been through. He'd always sympathised with her when they were younger. His own father had left just before Amelia arrived and he'd felt let down and abandoned, but his mum had been there to get him through it. She'd let him know it wasn't his fault and that his father was simply a shit who cared more about himself than anyone else. Though the pain had been intense at first, it had eased quickly thanks to his mum's care and Amelia's friendship. He hadn't heard from his dad since and had no wish to. He didn't need him and couldn't see that he'd gain anything by getting in touch, but Amelia had never had that.

His anger at her abandonment of their relationship had blinded him for years to the true impact Vera had had on her life. With no Lynne to let her know that her parents' deaths were a horrible act of fate and that Vera's unhappiness was nothing to do with her, she'd internalised all those feelings. Understanding now was like a shaft of bright spring sunshine punctuating dark, gloomy clouds. This explained why she was so interested in the locket and finding out why Vera was so unhappy. If she didn't, it was like Vera's unhappy ghost would be forever following her. Making her feel small. She just wanted to know where she belonged and to whom.

In the silence, as his emotions raged, the room began to close in around them and he searched desperately for something to say. 'Your bedroom hasn't changed much has it?'

It wasn't the smoothest or most comforting thing to say but he had to find some neutral ground before his sentiment ran away with him.

'It's exactly the same as when I left,' Amelia said, shrinking back. 'Vera didn't change anything.'

A large dark wooden wardrobe sat opposite the end of her bed and to the side of it was a small table underneath the window. A tallboy rested against the other wall and on either side of the double bed were short cabinets. One held a lamp; the other was currently stacked high with boxes of tissues and bottles of water. Amelia had never been one for posters on her walls and bare, faded floral wallpaper surrounded her. The only addition had been another painting of Vera's. A scene from the back of the house and out over the rolling fields with Highfield just visible in the corner.

'The place hasn't been redecorated at all,' she said. It was obvious the effort of speaking and moving about had wiped her out and she lay down on the bed, closing her eyes before trying desperately to breathe through her stuffy nose.

The weight of the mattress shifted as he sat down on the edge of the bed. An instinct of love took over and he reached out to brush her hair away from her forehead, tucking it behind her ear. Slowly, she opened her eyes, and his heart somersaulted in his chest. God, he'd missed her. He'd missed her voice, their inane chatter, the joking and laughing that filled their time whenever they were together. He'd missed everything about the girl she'd been and his feelings towards the woman she was now were frighteningly powerful.

'You're quite hot,' he said soothingly. But not half as hot as he was. 'I'm going to get you a cold flannel.' He could get one for himself while he was at it.

Adam headed to the bathroom and took a moment to compose himself. When he returned, he folded the damp cloth and placed it on her head. She closed her eyes again, enjoying the relief.

'Before I go downstairs, I'm going to open the window a little bit. It's really stuffy and hot in here. A bit of fresh air will do you good. I'll close it before I leave though.'

He stood up and she grabbed his hand, pulling him down again. 'Please don't go yet.'

Unsure what to say or do, and frightened by how much the gesture meant, he said, 'Okay, but you'll be fine in a few days, Amelia. I promise.' His eyes rested on her hand clasped over his. She let go and snuggled her hand under the pillow. The moment was lost. He'd pushed her away. He should have just held her hand. What he wouldn't give to have that moment again.

Seconds later, his mum bustled in with Amelia's breakfast and Adam leaped away from the bed. Lynne eyed him warily before focusing on her patient.

'Here you are, poppet. This'll see you through to lunchtime. I've made you a sandwich for lunch and sliced you some cake. And there's hotpot for dinner. Pop it in the oven about an hour before you want to eat on a low heat, and it'll be perfect. I've written you some instructions in case you forget, or do you want me to pop back later?'

'That's fine, Lynne, thanks. I'll need to top my water up, so I can put it on then. I really appreciate you helping me out.' Amelia removed the cold flannel and pushed herself up to sitting. As she ate, the scrambled egg seemed comforting. 'I'd forgotten how much I like scrambled egg. Vera used to make it a lot because of the chickens, especially when I had an upset stomach as a kid.'

'She could be kind sometimes,' Lynne said gently.

'I suppose she could. Vera always pretended Father Christmas existed and put money under my pillow when the Tooth Fairy came. It was as I got older we struggled.'

Lynne tilted her head. 'Perhaps she didn't want to let you go. And don't forget, she was sixty when you arrived. Looking after a lively eight-year-old would have been tiring for her.' Watching his mum speak to Amelia so kindly made Adam even more proud of her and thankful for the way she had brought him up. Amelia was wilting now, her eyelids growing heavier. 'Sophie will pop in tomorrow morning and sort you out for the day, then I'll come back on Monday. She's got Toddler Taps and Tales at the library.'

'Hopefully, I'll feel a lot better by then.'

'Hopefully, but I wouldn't count on it,' Lynne said. 'Mrs Mann down Mill Lane had the flu and she had awful trouble for weeks afterwards. She kept saying it was called chronic fatigue or something. Her husband – miserable old sot that he is – thought she was just trying to get out of doing the washing up, so she got a note from the doctor to prove it. Imagine being married to that type of man. Mine might have run off with another woman but he'd never have dared say something like that to me.'

'I can well believe that,' Adam said, earning a bash on the arm from his mum.

When Amelia had eaten as much as she could, which surprisingly was nearly all of it, Lynne took the tray away and left, closing the window quietly behind her. Lynne was still a little annoyed with Amelia, but her mothering tendencies had got the better of her.

Gently, Adam rested on the edge of the bed once more. He wondered if she'd take his hand again and hope rose in his chest, but she didn't. He could see she was exhausted and tried not to read too much into it but regret snapped at his thoughts. 'I'll see you in a couple of days, okay? But call me if you need anything.'

'I will.' She nodded. 'I promise.'

He went to leave, pulling the door closed.

'Adam?'

'Yeah?'

'I'm sorry.'

He wanted to ask her what for, but she rolled away from him, facing the opposite wall. Could he hope it was the sorry he'd waited years to hear but never had? It was almost too much to hope for.

Chapter 21

Over the days that followed, more food arrived than Amelia could ever eat. Lynne had indeed cleaned out the fridge and it had been packed with all manner of delights from sandwiches made with huge wedges of bread, thick and delicious soups, cakes, biscuits, stews, casseroles, and one-pot meals. Even breakfasts had been catered for with things like kedgeree, porridge and boiled eggs. She had wondered if there'd been a mix-up with the cooking rota because everyone kept bringing her food. Even when she couldn't answer the door, pots were left on the doorstep for her to find when she came downstairs or when Sophie called in, but Amelia had soon learned from all the notes attached that they were gifts to help her feel better, given out of love and consideration for a neighbour. For once, she didn't feel embarrassed or awkward by their kindness, only grateful.

Mr MacMahon had been feeding the chickens and collecting the eggs for her and a basket full sat on the countertop. This morning she'd felt well enough to make the boiled eggs with runny golden yolks and soldiers she'd been craving since her return. Vera had cut the toast up into thin strips for her even as she'd grown into a teenager able to do it herself. Perhaps Lynne had been right. Perhaps Amelia had never given Vera credit for all the things she had done and had only focused on all the things she hadn't.

A sudden image of herself here at the farmhouse, collecting the eggs each morning and making breakfast before she sat down at the kitchen table to work appeared in her mind. She tried to shake it away almost immediately, but it hadn't escaped her notice that in this image she was smiling, whereas when she pictured herself returning to Paris – as she did most evenings – she wasn't smiling at all.

Amelia gazed at the kitchen table now laden with empty pots and dishes to be given back to her kind and compassionate neighbours and she explored the strange feeling growing inside her. For the first time, she felt part of the village, part of its life and community. She wouldn't have had this sort of response from her neighbours in Paris who were strangers to her. Océanè might have stopped by, but she was germ-averse and didn't like the idea of catching anything, giving anyone a wide berth for even sneezing near her.

The day before, feeling good enough to text but not well enough to stop feeling sorry for herself, Amelia sent a message to Océanè saying she was ill. A few minutes later Océanè responded that the English were very dramatic, and she needed to get up and get on with things. She told Amelia not to push her projects back too far or her clients might not wait. There'd been no 'I'm sorry to hear that,' or 'How are you feeling?' Only a brief instruction not to let a cold send her business off track.

Amelia had hoped for more from her only real friend in Paris and couldn't help compare the response to Sophie going out of her way to look after her, even though they'd only known each other a short time. She hadn't realised how cold Océanè could be. Or had she?

Replaying some of their conversations in the past, she realised Océanè could be extremely blunt and she was narrowly focused on her goals. Goals that didn't always match Amelia's. She was, for example, content to marry a man she wasn't passionately in love with simply because he was the most likely man to ask her. Océanè saw their relationship as an investment and saying no, even though she didn't really love Émile, would be a waste of all the effort she'd put in. Amelia's brow crinkled. How had she not realised all this before now?

It was now late Wednesday afternoon and Amelia awaited the arrival of the estate agent. Luckily, she felt human again as her illness subsided to nothing more than a head cold. She'd even managed to work on the farmhouse. She wasn't silly enough to go straight into heavy lifting but there were small bits of tidying and sorting she was more than capable of. The important thing was, after a week of doing nothing other than sleeping, the worst seemed to have passed.

The other morning, Amelia had woken to see Adam from the window, fixing the chicken coop. Knowing he was there had been incredibly comforting. Amelia's cheeks flamed as she remembered reaching out for Adam's hand and him holding hers. Why had she done that? The simple answer was she had no idea why. She'd been overcome with emotion and needed to touch his skin. She hadn't considered the repercussions.

At least Bonnie and Clyde wouldn't be escaping anymore. She'd have to get them a bigger run when she was fully better. Wait, what was she talking about? She'd be leaving soon. It wouldn't be long before she had to put the house on the market and possibly rehome them. Not everyone wanted to keep chickens just because they lived in the country. She had to stop thinking of this place as hers.

Blowing out her cheeks as she perused a tub of leftover stew, trying to decide if she wanted a snack before dinner, a knock at the door drew her attention. It was the estate agent, and for some reason, apprehension fizzed in her stomach. She couldn't quite tell why, and told herself it was simply that she wanted a decent price after all the work she'd put in. Having the table stacked with dishes wasn't exactly how she'd hoped to dress the place, but it couldn't be helped and she'd ensure they were gone before any photos were taken.

Opening the door, she welcomed the middle-aged man in an ill-fitting suit. 'Good afternoon – Mr Simpkins, isn't it?'

'Hello!' he boomed enthusiastically, stepping into the house and wiping his feet on the mat. 'Wow, what can I say. This place looks amazing. I can tell already this'll go quickly. Especially with no chain.'

Amelia tried to smile, but a weight sat heavily on her. Blaming the residual lethargy of the flu for her lack of enthusiasm, or perhaps it was the unsolved mystery still bothering her, she summoned some eagerness. 'I was hoping you'd say that.' Her words rang hollow in her ears. 'As you can see it's been thoroughly redecorated. I'm an interior designer, so I don't know if that'll help sell it.'

'I'm sure it will.' Mr Simpkins opened his leather wallet, pulling out a pen that had been clipped onto the spine. 'It really is gorgeous. When we spoke before, you said you were living in Paris so we should contact you there if you choose to sell with us, is that right?'

'Yes, it is.'

'Then we definitely need to mention that it's been worked on by a Parisian interior designer in the details. People will love that. And I can see you have excellent taste.'

His smile became slightly obsequious and Amelia moved to the kettle. 'Would you like a cup of tea?'

'No, thank you. I just had one in the office before I came out.' He began measuring each room and commenting on various aspects: the open fire, the wide windows. It wasn't until he mentioned Vera's paintings that a fierce stab in Amelia's heart took her breath away.

'Yes, they are lovely,' she replied. 'But no they won't be sold with the house.'

They'd be coming back with her to Paris, though they'd seem out of place there and she had a feeling the constant reminder of Meadowbank would make her melancholy.

Mr Simpkins continued measuring, making his way upstairs and then down again. 'Right, all done. This really is a beautiful house and in such an amazing location, I wouldn't be surprised if we went to sealed bids. I'm valuing the property at …' He typed on the tiny calculator built into his notepad and announced an astonishing figure.

Amelia's jaw dropped. She should have been pleased. She should have been jumping up and down with excitement because the number he gave would support her and her business for a long time. But a voice rang in her head asking, *Are you sure you want to leave?* 'Right, thank you.'

Another knock at the door, made her glance over. It was Adam. 'Shit!'

'Sorry?' Mr Simpkins's eyebrows shot up.

'Bear with me just a second.' Amelia lunged at the door and opened it. Her heart gave a flutter. This would be the first time they'd really spoken since she'd taken his hand. He'd certainly kept his distance, only popping his head around her bedroom door to check she had water and update her on the food that had arrived. He seemed almost as embarrassed as she was as he shuffled his feet. The light outside was fading and the brighter sunshine of day was replaced by a mellow golden glow.

'Hey, look at you,' Adam said happily. 'You look much better.' He stopped short as he spotted Mr Simpkins. 'Sorry, I didn't know you had company.'

'We're all done, actually,' said Mr Simpkins in what Amelia could see was a cheerful, ready-for-the-next-potential-customer demeanour. 'I'm sure you've got other agents coming round, so I've made a note of our rates and valuation here. Like I said, if you choose us, I really don't think it'll take long to sell. We are experts in this area. And this is absolutely top notch. Perfect location, perfect decor.'

'Right, thanks.' Amelia took the piece of paper he offered, the letterhead clear for Adam to see. Just when things were beginning to go well between them, this awkward encounter felt like a giant step backwards. As Mr Simpkins left, a tension mounted between them once more.

'So …' said Adam, but didn't finish the sentence.

Amelia ran her pinched fingers along a fold in the paper. She wanted to shout that she had to sell, that she'd worked too hard to build a successful career in Paris to throw it all away. That even though coming back had been wonderful, she was too scared to admit it to herself. 'I'm feeling much better,' she finally blurted out. 'See.' She waved her hands in front of her body to show that she was fine then dropped them to her sides knowing how ridiculous she looked. 'I've still got a bit of a cold, but I'm definitely over the worst.'

'Great.' He didn't sound pleased and the hurt on his face was almost too much to bear.

Before another intimidating and thick silence could develop, Amelia said, 'What can I do for you, Adam?'

Her words seemed to snap him back to the present. 'I was just—' He scowled as if considering what to say. 'I was wondering if you wanted to maybe go to the pub for dinner?'

'Dinner?' She hadn't been expecting an offer like that and was surprised he'd bothered making it after seeing the estate agent. Adam mistook her surprise as her searching for a polite way to say no and the glimmer of light in his eyes faded.

'If you'd rather not, then I understand.'

'No, I'd really like to.'

Over the last few days of being alone in the creaking old farmhouse, a worming question had niggled at the back of Amelia's mind. How many nights had Vera sat here alone? Isolated? Lonely? Far too many to count, she'd decided, and it was all of her own making. If she hadn't pushed everyone away – for whatever reason – she could have been happy, but she chose not to be. Amelia was crowded with people in Paris but none of them knew her like Adam or Meadowbank did. She was still basically alone there, but that loneliness was not going to touch her tonight. After the way the reality of the estate agent's visit had rocked her, she wanted company.

'I'd definitely like to. Thank you.'

He relaxed and his mouth turned up into an approximation of a grin though it didn't reach his eyes. 'I thought you might have had enough of stew by now.'

'I've definitely eaten every type of stew imaginable this week. I think I've had more vegetables than I could name.' She laughed. 'It's been delicious and I'm sure it's helped me fight this off, but do you know what?'

'What?'

'I must have an iron deficiency because I could murder a steak.'

The scar on his lip creased as he considered her choice. She wanted to reach out and run her finger over it, or even better kiss it. He'd turned his head down and looked at her from under his long brown eyelashes. 'Then let's get going.'

Amelia grabbed her coat and they headed off together. She made sure to leave on the outside light above the front door, knowing it would be dark by the time they returned.

Side by side they strolled through the belt of trees and through the shortcut to the village. It had grown so familiar to her again, and she remembered walks with Vera when she was small. They'd go to the large chestnut tree in the village and search for horse chestnuts to play with. All these memories had been lost after Vera's angry words at their last meeting, but at least she was discovering them again now.

Amelia adjusted the chain of the locket around her neck. She'd neglected her search this last week and essential time had been lost. Time that was running out. Though she still had the upstairs to decorate, it didn't need that much work and she swallowed as an uncomfortable feeling grew inside her. As fonder memories were coming to the fore, having the locket near her and living in the farmhouse made her feel closer to Vera and her parents, while being in the village made her feel less alone.

She'd never minded living on her own in Paris. She'd loved it for so many years, living in exactly the type of place a single young woman should live in and having the type of life a successful single young woman should have. But the farmhouse called out for something different. Hers and Vera's dysfunctional unit had been so at odds with the happy wholesome image the village enjoyed, they'd both felt out of place. Had that caused Vera to become angry and shut herself off from everyone? It wasn't what Amelia wanted for herself, but the idea of anything other than her current life was terrifying. She banished the thoughts as a side effect of too many painkillers – or perhaps not enough – and hoped instead a family like Sophie's would buy the farmhouse.

'Penny for your thoughts?' Adam said, peering at her. He rummaged in his pocket. 'Actually, you looked pretty serious – better made it a fiver.'

'I was just thinking about the locket and Vera,' she replied. She couldn't bear to talk about the estate agent in front of Adam after the way his face had frozen earlier.

'I'm sure we'll find out who he is if we keep searching.'

'I've been thinking about what Mr Hoffelmeyer said.'

'Which bit? He covered quite a lot in a short space of time.'

'That he did,' she replied with a chuckle. 'I meant about his talking to Vera. Do you think his instinct was right and she was hiding something?'

'Like what?'

'I don't know really. A secret of some kind?'

'Possibly. Who knows with Vera. She lived for a long time and must have seen and heard stuff. Try and keep your chin up. There must be other avenues we can explore.'

Without warning, Adam's hand went to the small of her back and his touch sent a comforting warmth through her body. She chanced a glance at him and there was a softness in his fearful smile. It wasn't long before they approached the pub and his hand dropped away, leaving a cold space where it had nestled so perfectly.

The door to the Drunken Duck was wedged open when they

arrived, and chatter spilled out into the street. The water of the duck pond glistened in the early evening light as its inhabitants paddled lazily about. The pub didn't have many seats out front but there was a huge beer garden at the back. Inside it hadn't changed since her visits as a teenager. The bar was still in the same place but had been replaced with something brighter and more rustic. The old swirly carpet had been removed and the flagstones exposed but they were covered with different-sized rugs.

In front of the large inglenook fireplace lay a huge stone hearth with a dog's bowl full of water. Mr MacMahon sat in an armchair with Bobby asleep at his feet. The fire was just beginning to come to life and, warm and content, Mr MacMahon lifted his hand in greeting. Unsure if it was Adam or her he was waving at, she waved back.

A part of her had expected everyone to turn and look at her, just as some had in the café shortly after she arrived, but no one batted an eyelid. They went to the bar and ordered drinks from Dean, the landlord. Though Amelia was feeling better, she couldn't face wine, so she chose a soft drink. While they were waiting to be served, a woman she recognised from school came over.

'Amelia, are you feeling better?'

'I am, thank you.'

'Is it true you're an interior designer now?'

'It is.'

'You're not taking on any work while you're here, are you?'

Amelia tilted her head apologetically. 'No, I'm sorry. I've got enough on with the farmhouse.'

'Oh, that's a shame. My friend's moving to a cottage nearby and wants to hire someone to decorate it so it's really top end.'

'I'm sorry,' she said again, as Adam studied his pint. 'But good luck with your search.'

They made their way to the beer garden festooned with picnic tables and chairs, and seemingly hundreds of flowering pots all painting the border in bright reds and yellows. Heaters dotted around kept them pleasantly warm.

'You know who that was don't you?' Adam said, placing their drinks on the table.

Amelia frowned as she thought. 'I recognise her from school, but I can't remember her name.'

'That was Alison Mann who always had a red nose and never remembered her PE kit.'

'Was it? Gosh she's changed.'

As they settled into an easy reminiscence of school days, Amelia worried that as the evening wore on, they'd run out of things to say or stumble into the dangerous territory of the past. Though her nerves were on high alert, she wouldn't want to be anywhere else right now. Adam had always been a part of her and the time they were spending together now filled a piece that had been missing for the last ten years.

'Is it weird for you?' Amelia asked Adam. 'Having Dean as a dad now?'

'It's not quite like that,' he said with a smile. 'But he and Mum like hanging out together and he makes her happy. I'm just glad she found someone to spend time with. When Dad left, I was so angry with everyone. Don't you remember?'

'You were never angry with me.'

'You helped get me through it.'

Amelia dropped her eyes to her glass, wiping the condensation with her fingertips. He'd helped her through all those years with Vera and their connection with each other had been so strong. She was so ashamed of herself for it all.

As a silence settled between them, she took a moment to enjoy the quiet. There was a low hum of chatter from the other tables, and the pretty chirping of the birds hung on the air. No cars whizzed by. No sirens. She could even hear the odd quack of a duck and bleat of a lamb in the distance. A strange sense of calm slowed the beating of her heart. For so long it had been racing, rushing through life, keeping busy, staying busy, all so she didn't look back. She'd never imagined returning to Meadowbank could be so therapeutic. Her thoughts ran to the spring fair and a question came to her.

'So, what broken heart did Mrs Doyle's carrot cake heal?'

Adam took another sip of his drink. 'My ex-girlfriend, Philippa, left me last Valentine's Day.'

'On Valentine's Day itself?' She was starting to wish she hadn't asked.

'Yep. In the middle of the pub. In front of everyone. She even gave me a card first then said she was sorry, but she'd fallen for someone else.'

'Wow. That's really …'

'Embarrassing?'

'It is a bit. Sorry.'

Adam laughed. 'It is, but it's not as embarrassing as you liking a photo of me in my Speedos.' Amelia's face burned instantly. From Adam's gleeful expression she could tell she looked like a complete idiot. Her mouth fell open like a fish starved of oxygen and her eyes widened. 'Did you think I didn't know?'

'Oh God.' Amelia sank down, hiding her face behind her hands. 'This is so embarrassing. I didn't mean to.'

'Hey! That hurts my feelings even more.'

'I didn't mean that,' she mumbled, unable to lift her head. 'My hand slipped when I was on the train. I wasn't stalking you. I was just …'

'What?'

'I don't know, seeing what you were up to.' There, that was better than nothing. It was definitely better than admitting to lasciviously staring at him with his top off and a bulge in his pants. She chanced a look over her arms. 'How long have you known?'

'That you liked a pervy photo of me?'

'Stop it!'

'Only a couple of days. I hardly ever check it, but Mum's been on at me to get a Facebook page for my sculptures. The pub's got one recently and she's a bit taken with it. After you gave me all those ideas, I decided to start one.'

'That's great, Adam.' Her humiliation faded a little. 'So you got over your heartbreak thanks to Mrs Doyle's carrot cake?'

'Not just carrot cake. You think you got food parcels when you were ill; my farmhouse was full to the rafters with food. I think everyone in the village gave me something. Even the blokes delivered homemade beer "to get me through". Very sadly Mrs Bostock hasn't had her green crockpot back yet. I think she's given up asking.'

Amelia laughed. 'Then maybe I've got some brownie points for already returning mine.'

'You have?'

'Well, not exactly. She must have collected it in the week when she delivered me something else. Or Sophie took it.'

Sitting opposite Adam, she had to force herself not to stare at his handsome face. Every time she saw the scar on his lip she felt a tingle as she imagined his kisses. The wedding dress dream had stayed with her and the emotions it conjured up had felt so real at the time. It was growing harder to separate them from reality.

To keep their conversation flowing, she asked him more about his work and why he'd decided on carpentry and he asked her about interior design. Though the conversation was tinged here and there with tension, most of the time it flew by, their laughter growing so loud the diners at a neighbouring table glanced over once or twice.

The sun fell behind the trees, dappling onto the ground and sending the sky a dusky blue when Sophie and Michael walked into the garden. They were without Isla, holding hands. Though she was enjoying this time with Adam, she wanted to thank Sophie for being so kind to her and as she and Adam were just about to order some food she said, 'Do you mind if we ask Sophie and Michael to join us?'

'Of course not.'

'Sophie? Sophie?' She waved and Sophie glanced at her husband, a wide smile on her face as they headed over.

'Hello, you two.'

'Hi, guys. Drink?' Adam asked, standing up.

'I'll have a white wine, please, Adam,' Sophie replied.

'Top-up?' he asked Amelia. She nodded still not quite ready to make her body fight off the effects of alcohol as well as her cold.

'I'll give you a hand,' Michael said. 'I'd like to see what new beers they've got.'

The men headed off and Sophie slipped into the seat beside Amelia. 'I can't believe how well you're looking. Michael's very impressed with your constitution and Jocelyn was very grateful for your concern. She told Michael to bugger off today when he checked she wasn't showing any symptoms, but she was apparently very complimentary towards you. And Lynne has been talking about you too.'

'Has she? Oh no.' Amelia slumped down and rubbed her forehead. 'I hope she hasn't called me a vulture again.'

Sophie giggled. 'I heard about that. No, it's been nice, this time.'

'Really?' Her kindness when she had the flu had been so unexpected, she'd thought she might have been delirious with fever.

'Well, with donating to the spring fair and then being all pathetically poorly, you're well on your way to being on Lynne's good side now.'

'She was really nice to me the other day. It was … unnerving.'

'Wasn't she nice to you when you were younger? When you and Adam were together?'

Amelia shrugged a shoulder. 'Yeah, but since the first day I arrived back she's not been exactly fond.'

'She is very protective of Adam. But she was the one who organised all the cooking for you. Then everyone just started pitching in of their own accord. You know how this lot are. You and Adam looked pretty cosy when we arrived.'

'We're getting on well again. We used to have a very special connection.'

'I'd say it's still there. My friend once described it as "a look that means you just know that couple are going to make it".' Amelia didn't know what to say but could feel the flush running over her neck. 'I really wish you weren't leaving so soon,' Sophie announced, and her honesty took Amelia aback. 'My friend who paid that compliment is back in Chichester and we text and stuff but we're becoming social media friends, you know. Not proper friends. As soon as I met you, I knew we were alike. I'll miss you when you go. I could see us being true friends. Not the type who come round to check out your furniture or mention your piles of dirty washing.'

Océanè sprang to mind, but Amelia didn't say anything.

'You know the type of friends you have to tidy up for before they come round so they don't make a comment or pull a face. I just knew you weren't one of those.'

That was Océanè all right. She was often judgemental and didn't go out of her way to offer comfort or help when Amelia needed it. She didn't bring wine when she was stressing out over projects. If anything, she encouraged her to work harder. Amelia had always seen that as supportive, not letting her get side-tracked and lose focus, but maybe losing a little focus and kicking back wasn't such a bad thing. Life was about balance and when she pictured hers, the scales were definitely pitched one way.

'I suppose you'll be putting the place on the market soon?' Sophie asked, bringing Amelia back from her thoughts.

'There's still some work to do, but I did have an estate agent round this afternoon. I organised him before I even arrived.'

'What did he say?'

'He quoted an extortionate price and thinks it could even go to sealed bids.'

'That's good isn't it?' Sophie's eyes narrowed on Amelia.

Amelia tried to smile and nodded in reply, but inside, she

found herself searching for reasons to put it off. 'I might wait until after the riddle of the locket is solved before I list it though. I don't want to risk selling the house and someone else finding something.'

'Won't that take time though?'

'It might take a bit longer. I guess I could have another week or two but then I'd have to go back. I've got clients waiting.'

The guys came out of the pub and began to make their way back to the table. Amelia realised that as much as she loved Parisian cafés and bars, the feeling she had sitting in the beer garden of the Drunken Duck with Adam by her side far surpassed it. She'd been an idiot to leave him behind when they could have stayed in touch. Leaving Meadowbank hadn't automatically meant leaving him, though it had felt the only option at the time. She'd given up years of this amazing connection, running away from Vera and the giant gaping hole her parents' deaths had left.

'Where's Isla?' Amelia asked, trying to think about something else.

'The lovely teenage girl next door is babysitting for us tonight, so we get a few hours off.'

'I'm sure you deserve it,' Adam said, glancing at Amelia. They fell into a genial conversation about kids, the lack of lie-ins and how blissful country life was compared to the city. She had a feeling that, if she ever returned to Meadowbank, Sophie was the type of friend she wouldn't have to tidy up for.

By the time they had eaten, the sky was a dark purple-blue and it was nearing ten o'clock. 'We'd better get going,' Amelia said, tiredness swamping her. 'I'm sorry we've taken up your whole evening. You probably wanted to spend time together.'

'We've had a great time,' said Michael, whose eyes were a little unfocused from the number of ales he'd had.

'It's been wonderful,' Sophie said, wrapping her arm around Amelia and kissing her cheek. 'Just what I needed after being Mummy all day. It's nice to sit with friends and remember you're an actual person and not just a food making machine that picks up all their toys.'

It had been just what Amelia had needed too – like the return to Meadowbank had been. Not that she'd really known that before, but her soul felt better for making time in her life for something other than work. Now, she was in desperate need of her bed and fatigue sat heavy on her eyelids.

'Come on, I'll walk you back,' Adam said. 'We can take the shortcut. I'll use my phone as a torch.'

Amelia didn't think twice about walking with Adam through the densely wooded shortcut back to Meadow Farmhouse. They'd left the last of the village behind them and were now in the shade of the tree-lined shortcut. Their steps were absorbed by the earthy path and small blue flowers reached out to tickle their ankles. The ground reached away in places – giving children banks to run down – and thick, sturdy branches arced in front of them, perfect for kids to climb.

'I had a nice time this evening,' she said to Adam. A shiver racked her body and he shrugged off his jacket, placing it around her shoulders. It had grown colder as night descended. 'I haven't spent an evening like that in ages.'

'I thought you had lots of friends in Paris?'

'I do,' she lied. 'But it wasn't the same.'

They exited through the brace of trees to Meadow Farmhouse and Amelia slowed her steps. Adam did the same, swinging his phone around to highlight the way to the house.

'What's wrong?' he asked as she came to a sudden stop.

Her throat closed over in fear. 'Adam, I didn't leave any of the inside lights on.'

Chapter 22

'Why are there lights on?' she asked, instinctively crossing her arms over her chest. 'I only left the outside light on.'

'Maybe you did by accident.'

She shook her head. 'I definitely didn't. I remember checking.'

They edged warily towards the farmhouse, but the silence she'd enjoyed only moments before now terrified her. Every sound that penetrated it rang in her ears as loud as a starter pistol. The hairs on her arms rose in apprehension and her stomach churned. As they approached the front door, a thin shaft of light shone onto the ground. It was ajar.

'Adam,' her voice quivered. 'I didn't leave the door unlocked.'

'Are you absolutely sure?'

'I definitely locked it when I left with you.'

'Right.' From the way Adam swallowed, then scanned around, she could tell he was nervous too. 'You wait here, and I'll take a look inside.'

What? She grabbed his arm before he could walk away. 'Are you joking? I'm not waiting out here on my own for some murderer to come and drag me off into the woods. I'm coming with you.'

'What if there's a murderer in there?' he whispered back, pointing at the house.

'Then I'll run and get help while he's getting you, but I am *not* waiting out here on my own.' Had he never seen a horror movie? She resisted the urge to wail, *I'm too young to die!* and reined in her dramatic tendencies. Though this time the perpetrator was unlikely to be a hedgehog.

'Fine. Just stay behind me, okay?'

A strange sound made her spin around. As it echoed in the darkness she couldn't make out where it was coming from. It sounded like a cross between a bird, a chimp and a car that wouldn't start. And whatever it was, wherever it was coming from, it sounded big. Really, really big. Leaves rustled, the long grass in the fields swayed, and the branches of the trees moved in the wind, gently humming like a distant motorway. The moving shadows crept over the ground, distorting the light. She reached out and grabbed hold of Adam's arm as the strange noise grew louder. 'What the bejesus is that?'

'Foxes,' he whispered.

'Foxes?' She'd forgotten that though they looked most like dogs their call sounded like a bird being murdered by a monkey.

Four eyes glittered at her in the darkness by the wood. 'This is horrible. They look like they want to eat us.'

Adam tutted. 'They're not interested in us, just ignore them.'

She hoped he was right.

Gently, Adam pushed the front door open enough for them to see inside. All the lights were on and the kitchen had been ransacked. They edged in further and saw the living room too had been searched for something. A pane in the large kitchen window at the back of the house had been broken and the side door was barely still intact. They must have tried to kick it in and when they failed, broke the window instead. Whoever *they* were.

Amelia's heart lurched to see all her hard work undone in one fell swoop. Tears sprang to her eyes as she stared around at the mess. Trying to remain calm, she saw that much of the damage was superficial. The sofa cushions were on the floor and the blankets had been tossed aside, but Vera's paintings were intact. In the kitchen, the contents of the cupboards had been tossed about as if a ravenous teenager had searched for food, but again, nothing had been broken. That was something to be grateful for. The intense pain of having her home violated rocked her and she hugged herself.

'I'll check upstairs,' Adam said. 'You stay here.'

'Wait,' she whispered as fear that the intruder may still be here grabbed hold of Amelia's throat. 'Take the broom.'

She handed him the broom and he clutched it with both hands ready to attack. Adam began his ascent of the creaky staircase. Realising she should have got him a knife, she ran to the kitchen and grabbed the largest one she could find. At least if anyone tried to attack Adam, she'd have something more fear-inducing than a broom to defend them both with.

With her eyes, Amelia followed Adam's footsteps, tracing the route along the ceiling. She heard him check the bedrooms and bathroom, then come down the stairs and edge nearer the staircase. He stepped off the last stair, then jumped back up in surprise.

'Jesus, Amelia. Put that knife down.'

'Is it all clear?' It was a stupid question because Adam would have mentioned if it wasn't, or he'd have run out of the house screaming; a sure-fire sign she was to follow.

He pressed a hand to his chest, clearly willing his heart rate to calm down. 'Everything's fine. It doesn't look like anything was taken.'

A sigh escaped Amelia's mouth, then she inhaled another breath quickly. 'The wedding dress!' Pressing the knife into Adam's hands, she ran upstairs and along to Vera's room, opening the wardrobe doors to see it still hanging there in the now empty space. Relief flooded through her. She felt suddenly grateful she'd worn the locket and the photograph of the convalescing soldier was still in her bag.

If nothing was taken, why had someone broken in? Checking the trunk at the foot of Vera's bed she saw the jewellery had been left, as had the television in her room and the living room – all the things of value. A cold chill shot down her spine and she hurried downstairs, eager to stay in Adam's company.

'Are you okay?'

'Yeah, I think so. The dress is fine. But who would break in here and what were they looking for?'

'Let's think about that later, okay? First off, I'll find something to patch that window, then tomorrow we'll sort out getting it fixed. You'd better call the police now.'

'Yes, I suppose I should.'

Amelia called and a policeman came out to take a statement from them both. There were no forensic men in lab coats or dusting for fingerprints, just a quick chat to establish a timeline. He checked the door and window, agreeing with Amelia that it seemed they'd tried to kick the door in first and then, when they had no success due to the heavy oak and sturdy latch, they broke the window. Of course, with no CCTV around the area there was little chance of finding who'd done it and with nothing of value taken it wasn't a priority, but it had shaken Amelia to her core.

Once the policeman had gone, Adam said, 'It is really odd, isn't it? I mean, why wasn't anything taken?'

'I don't know.' Amelia swept up the glass scattered over the counter. 'But I really don't like it.'

In her mind, the faint siren call of Paris told her to come back. Her life was easier there with nothing like this happening. Being alone was better than being somewhere so painful. She shot a glance at Adam who didn't notice her looking and her heart thudded against her chest. Could she walk away from him again? From the light penetrating the gloom that had followed her for all these years.

Unable to find any wood, Adam found a black sack for the window and straightened it out with a flick of his hand. Amelia jumped, her nerves fraught. Swiftly, Adam nailed it tightly across the broken window so no air could get in. He found a screwdriver and tried to refasten the lock onto the door. 'It'll do for tonight, but we'll need to replace it with a new one.'

As Adam washed his hands, Amelia went to the door and ran her hands over the wood. It was probably the same door that had been there since the house was built. The heavy, aged wood was sturdy beneath her fingertips and she pressed her forehead against it, silently thanking it for holding. Perhaps they'd spent so long trying to get in that way, they hadn't had much time to stay in the house once the window was smashed.

'At least I'm just down the road,' Adam said. 'I can be here in two minutes if you need me.'

Two minutes seemed far too long if whoever did this decided to come back. Amelia had never felt so unsettled and on edge. Every noise made her jump and every creak of the ancient house felt like a ghost appearing to haunt her.

'Stay here? Please?' The words escaped from her mouth before she could stop them and braced for his rejection.

Adam started in surprise. 'If you want me to.'

She nodded and emptied the dustpan and brush into the bin. There was a spare room after all. She went to the fridge and pulled out a bottle of wine. Though she hadn't drunk at the pub, she needed something to soothe her tattered nerves and a cup of tea just wasn't going to cut it. Taking two glasses from the cupboard, she went to the living room and sat on the sofa. Adam came to join her.

When she shivered, he pulled a blanket from the back of the chair and wrapped it around her shoulders. 'It's just the shock,' he said gently, his breath fluttering over her skin. 'It'll stop soon. I'll light a fire.'

She watched him on the hearth as he built the fire. Sipping her wine, she allowed the cold, soothing liquid to ease the tension in her throat. As the flames came to life, the room filled with warmth. Despite everything, the break-in, the mystery, the chasm of loss caused by her parents and now, she realised, Vera too, being with Adam at this very moment felt perfect.

Sat in the farmhouse that, even in its current state of disarray, looked how she'd always hoped and dreamed, she realised she'd always run away, first to university then to Paris, all the time with no real friends and no one to share it with. She was like a hamster on a wheel, running on and on only to end up in exactly the same place she had been before – unfulfilled and lonely – pretending everything was fine when she felt hollow and empty inside. A deep loneliness had been buried under work and nights out, and under that loneliness had been the deep, dark loss of her parents. Something she'd fought hard to ignore rather than deal with. Just like her feelings for Adam and the true nature of her difficult, but not altogether horrible, relationship with Vera.

With Adam's shoulder pressing against her, some of the tension released from her shoulders. She was so tired of pushing it all down inside. Of using so much energy to prove to herself and the world she wasn't insignificant and forgettable, that she was something and someone. It was exhausting but here in Meadowbank an inner strength had grown inside her and she knew it was time to finally have the conversation she'd been dreading.

'I'm so sorry I left you, Adam.'

For a time, he stared ahead at his wine glass as if he wasn't sure how to answer. Eventually he glanced over and though his eyes were soft, his jaw was clenched.

'I only ever wanted to leave Vera,' she continued, her voice wavering. 'When I told her I was taking a job in Paris she called me ungrateful and told me never to bother coming back.'

'She—?' He frowned and dropped his eyes. 'I never knew.'

'At first I was so intent on proving Vera wrong that I didn't let myself think about how much it hurt.'

'So it did hurt then? To—' He faltered. 'To leave me behind?'

She held his gaze and though his expression didn't change, she hoped his heart would. 'I always planned to get in touch, but the longer I left it the harder it became. And then I just didn't know how to pick up the pieces. After a while, I convinced myself you'd have forgotten me, and I'd just be being a pain by contacting you.'

Silence filled the room, punctuated here and there by the crackle of the fire. 'That's what hurt more than anything,' he said quietly. 'That you thought I'd forget you. I always thought it was because you'd never loved what we had as much as I did. I know we were young, but it didn't mean it wasn't right. It wasn't until you came back to Meadowbank that I realised not having your parents, only having Vera's bitterness, it made you think you were the problem, that you were just a small, inconvenient part of someone's life.' She listened to his gentle voice absorbing every word. 'I know you're sorry for not saying a proper goodbye.'

'It's not just that, Adam.' Daringly, she moved forwards taking his hand in hers. 'I'm not just sorry I didn't say goodbye or that I let us lose touch. You're right, what we had was special and I should never have let it go.'

As he moved his face closer, her eyes were drawn to his mouth and to the kindness that sprang from his eyes. She so desperately wanted him to forgive her and to love her again as he once had. Her feelings for him were growing stronger every day, and tonight she longed for his love to form a barrier that the world couldn't penetrate. For however short a time, she wanted everything else – her grief over Vera, the agony over her parents – to fade away to nothing. 'Can you forgive me?'

'I can,' he whispered, gently brushing her long dark hair back from her face. 'Don't run away this time. Don't run away from me again. I know I was angry, but I understand it all now. I know how Vera made you feel. I know how you've always associated this place with hurt and pain, but it doesn't have to be that way.' Every cell in Amelia's body pulsed with hope and anticipation. 'You don't have to leave. You could stay here … with me.'

Adam's breath brushed her lips as she continued to reach her head up, sending a thrill through her body. It had been so long since she'd felt like this with someone. Her body yearned for him. When he didn't pull away or move his eyes, she allowed her mouth to meet his and the explosion of emotion nearly blew her off the sofa. It was like being on a roller coaster, her senses swirling and spinning. Every touch of his hand, first on her face, then on her waist, was so charged that she could barely contain it.

When they parted, her eyes still closed, she rested her head on his shoulder, breathing him in. In that moment she felt she could stay at Meadow Farmhouse forever. Adam's arm reached around her, holding her tight, and after another kiss, even more passionate than the first, they fell asleep by the light and warmth of the fire.

Chapter 23

The dawn chorus woke Adam as Amelia lay in his arms, curled into him on the sofa. A sky flooding with pale white light was just visible through the gap in the curtain and birdsong resounded in the silent living room. He moved gently, trying to breathe life into his limbs without waking her. She was so beautiful with her long dark hair cascading over his arm.

The fire had died, and a freezing draught spread over him, but thoughts of the kisses they'd shared soon warmed him up. That first kiss had been like nothing he'd ever known before. Even compared to the kisses they'd shared when they were younger, this was on an entirely different level. It had been emotional, comforting, and above all else, loving. At least, that's how it felt to him.

Amelia stirred and though they were both still fully dressed, an awkwardness rolled up the back of his neck. He felt the warmth of her body against his and closed his eyes, savouring the sensation. If she went back to Paris now, she'd break his heart again, because although he'd tried not to, he loved her as much as he ever had before. But one kiss didn't mean she wanted to stay, or that she wanted to be with him. He'd kissed her before she could respond to his suggestion that she stay in Meadowbank and he knew he was asking a lot. He was asking her to change everything. Was the prospect of being with him enough?

'Hi,' Adam said, gazing down at her.

Amelia's eyes opened and after a second, she nervously moved away from him. 'Hi.' Her voice creaked as she spoke and she cleared her throat.

Unsure as to whether she'd moved away from regret or shyness he stood up from the sofa. 'Are you okay?'

'Yeah, fine. You?'

'Yeah.'

As much as he tried, Adam couldn't read the feelings on her face. When he thought back, even at their best, he hadn't felt this way about Philippa. Amelia had always carried an intensity with her, and the emotions she sparked within him were all-consuming and passionate, but without a hint from her as to how she felt, he was lost.

Did she want him to leave? If he did and had misread her wishes would she think he regretted last night and wanted nothing more than to distance himself? Surely after she suggested he stay there was no misunderstanding. Amelia pushed herself to standing and dashed to the kitchen to put the kettle on. Adam attempted to relax and stretched before following her. He stayed at the other end of the table tapping his fingers on the pine top. All he wanted was a sign that she wanted him to stay.

Amelia said nothing but flashed an embarrassed smile, then pottered around finding cups and milk. He willed her to speak once more. The ground had shifted and he couldn't make out where to go from here. Above all, he worried the kiss had given her closure and meant she wanted nothing more than to leave again. After such an emotional day, it was too dangerous to read too much into her words. The awkward silence they were standing in was deafening and the only sound that broke it was Adam fetching his boots and putting them on. He didn't want to go, but his feet were cold on the flagstone floor.

Amelia shot a look over her shoulder then kept her eyes focused on the kettle. A knock at the door gave some respite from the tension and she went to open it. It was Mr MacMahon with Bobby by his side.

'Morning, Miss Amelia. Everything all right? I come to feed the chickens and saw the window. Wondered what had happened.'

He shot a knowing look at Adam who concentrated on tying his shoelaces.

'Everything's fine, Mr MacMahon. Well, sort of. I was broken into last night.'

'Bobby, get back here.' Bobby strolled into the farmhouse and sniffed Adam's boots. 'Do you know, I've never known a more disobedient sheepdog.'

'Can he have a biscuit?' Amelia asked, pulling one from the jar.

'As long as it don't have dried fruit in. But if you do that, Miss Amelia, he'll be wanting one all the time.'

'Then I'll make sure I've always got one,' she said, smiling down at the dog.

Adam wondered if she realised she was speaking as if she was staying and it was all he could do not to ask her outright. He didn't have the chance to think on it too much before a loud voice from behind Mr MacMahon boomed out and he winced. *Fabulous.* It was his mum.

'What's going on here then? A mothers' meeting?' Mr MacMahon stepped aside and Lynne entered the farmhouse, stopping by Adam's side. Feeling like the world could read the night's events on his face, he tried to frown instead. 'What's going on with your face?' she demanded, pointing at Adam. Amelia sniggered and turned back to the kettle.

'Nothing.' He brought the insides of his cheeks between his teeth to stop them rearing up in a grin at hearing Amelia laugh.

'Now you look like one those pouting catwalk models. What's got into you?'

'Nothing.'

'Don't give me that. A mother can tell.'

After patting Bobby on the head, Adam said, 'I'd better get going.' And gave Amelia an apologetic smile just as she brought his tea to the table.

'Oy!' His mum retracted her elbow from his ribs. 'Are you even listening to me?'

'Yes, of course I am.'

'Then tell me all about this locket and your little trips around the village. I'm surprised you didn't just ask me, Amelia. I might have been able to help.'

'Sorry,' she replied over the rim of her cup. 'We were trying to find out something about Vera, but it was from so long ago it was before your time.'

Mr MacMahon stepped inside directing his speech at Lynne. 'I take it you've heard about the farmhouse being broken into?'

'No!' Lynne gasped. 'The last crime we had around here was Mr Sims driving into the bins after he'd forgotten his glasses. When did this happen?'

'Last night,' Amelia said calmly. 'We got back from the pub and—'

'We? Would *we* be you and Adam?'

'It would,' Adam said, protecting Amelia from answering. He coloured as Lynne turned to look at her.

Amelia continued, staring at her tea. 'We met Sophie and Michael for a drink.'

'Huh.' Lynne's brow crinkled before her voice softened. 'Are you all right?'

'A bit shaken, but I'm fine. Nothing was taken or damaged. It was almost as if they were after food rather than anything of value.'

Lynne ambled forward and sat at the table. 'So tell me about this locket?'

'You are so nosy, Mum.'

'No, I'm not, and if it wasn't for me, no one would know about your tiny stumpy gnome things. Have you sold any more yet?'

'A couple,' he replied begrudgingly.

'See.'

Amelia invited Mr MacMahon to sit down too. 'I found the locket in among Vera's possessions and wondered about it. It's got a picture of an American soldier in it and a baby in a christening gown. I was hoping to find out who the man was and how he was connected with Vera because she never talked about him.'

As Amelia sipped her tea Adam took over the explanation. 'Arthur saw the locket and recognised it, but he wouldn't tell us where or how.'

'Well, I'm not surprised Arthur responded in that way,' Mr MacMahon said. 'Probably brings back bad memories for him.'

Amelia's head shot up. 'What do you mean *bad memories*?'

'He's a Highfield, isn't he? Their land has always bordered Meadow Farm. I heard when he and Vera were young, they used to play together all the time but then one day, both sets of parents had a big falling-out and they were never allowed to speak to each other again.'

Amelia's mouth hung open as did Adam's. Mr MacMahon, his own next-door neighbour, knew all this, and they'd never even thought to ask him because he was only a few years older than his mum. Adam had always assumed he wouldn't know anything about a young Vera, and it seemed Amelia had thought the same.

'But Jennifer Motley,' said Adam, inching forwards, 'and her husband, the millionaire human right's lawyer, bought the place off the last Highfield.'

'That's right,' Amelia added. 'She said she'd bought it off a daughter who didn't live nearby.'

'Probably Arthur's daughter,' Mr MacMahon added.

Amelia had brightened and her voice carried an edge of excitement. 'Maybe that was why Vera had stopped smiling at the age of eighteen? Something to do with this big family row? She was always fiercely proud of her family name.'

'She certainly wasn't the same afterwards, so I'm told,' Mr MacMahon continued. 'But no one knows what happened.'

Amelia turned to Adam. 'But why wouldn't Jocelyn just tell me that?' Adam shrugged. 'Thanks, Mr MacMahon. I don't suppose you know anything else about Vera that might help us?'

'Nothing comes to mind, but if it does, I'll let you know. Come on, Bobby.' He tipped his flat cap. 'I'd best be getting back to work. Nice to know you're all right, Miss Amelia.'

'Thank you, Mr MacMahon.'

'Well,' said Lynne, ruffling like a mother hen. 'I thought I knew all about this village. Must be one of those things that faded from memory. And if her father was anything like Vera, is it surprising there was a falling-out?'

Amelia shook her head. 'I heard her father was a decent man. That's what Jocelyn said, anyway.'

'Well, she should know.' Lynne tucked her chair under the table and turned to Adam, her hands on her hips. 'Now, what did I want you for? Oh, yes, dinner. The pub starts serving at twelve. What do you fancy? Dean's got some lovely scampi on for today. Do you want some or would you like me to make you a one-pot?' Adam couldn't have been more embarrassed if his mum had whacked him in a bib and led him away with a bottle. 'Would you like a plate, Amelia? I can't imagine you fancy cooking after a break-in. I have to admit you've had some bad luck, my girl. Bad luck all your life.'

'I think I'll be fine, Lynne, but thanks for the offer. I've got some leftover stew I can reheat.'

His mum ambled away but not before giving him a meaningful look. A look that said *I know you're falling back in love with her. Be careful.* Or was it just his imagination? When she'd gone, Amelia closed the front door and went back to make a fire. The air was cooler today and whistled through the broken window.

'You don't think …' She took a breath, even though it seemed impossible to even think it. 'Adam, do you think that Arthur might have broken in? Do you think he was after the locket? He's been hanging around and he's been acting strangely. Think how he reacted about the locket when he saw it.' The thoughts in her mind made her cringe. It seemed so improbable, yet someone had broken in and taken nothing of value. Had they merely been searching for something in particular? 'Could he have done it?' she asked. 'Last night was the first time I've been out of the house since we saw him. It would have been his first opportunity to try and find it.' As the question hung in the air, she answered it herself. 'No, he couldn't have, could he? He's not strong enough to kick the door like that and as for breaking the window, he'd have to do that and then scrabble up and in. He couldn't manage that at his age. Could he?'

Adam kept his eyes on the tabletop. 'I don't think so. It would be a lot for an old man like him to do. Plus, he'd have had to sneak out of the care home and get here. It's one thing for him to have a wander around the village during the day, they don't mind him doing that but sneaking out at night? The staff would have spotted him.'

Amelia nodded a silent agreement. 'I just wish I had more information on Vera. Her birth certificate, letters or something, but there's nothing else here. Seeing the locket really bothered him the other day; I don't want to speak to him and be wrong, and upset him for no reason.'

'Where have you looked?'

'I've been through everything down here and had a good search through her room but not the spare rooms. I didn't come across anything in my old room, but there are still two more bedrooms I could check.'

'Then let's go.'

'Really?' Her mug was poised in the air.

'We've come this far, haven't we?'

The joyful look she gave him lit his heart but without the chance to talk about last night and what it meant for them, he was still in an agonising limbo. He felt as if he was teetering on the edge of a precipice and even a slight breeze could blow him over. He couldn't trust himself not to fall even more in love with her, and if he did, he'd be at the bottom of that precipice with no hope of ever climbing out again.

After seeing the estate agent yesterday, no matter how much he wanted to protect his heart, he couldn't waste the chance of spending as much time with her as possible before she left. This time, without the farmhouse or Vera to bring her back, he knew he'd never see her again.

Chapter 24

Amelia had no idea why Vera's birth certificate should be in one of the spare rooms, but it was the only place left to check. The downstairs had been completely stripped and cleared, and Vera's room, although still full of furniture, had been boxed up and sorted. If it wasn't in any of the spare bedrooms then it must have been destroyed. She closed her eyes and prayed that wasn't the case. Surely Vera would have needed it for official things?

'Where do you want to start?' Adam asked, following her up the stairs.

She'd been more than surprised when he wanted to stay and help with the search. As she led the way, the emotions of last night gathered inside her like thunderclouds bringing the storm. She could already imagine Océanè's advice if she called her for support. Her heavy French accent rang around her head. 'It was only a bit of a kiss, Amélie. These small villages are the same the world over. So provincial.' She had said before how everything means so much more in the country than it does in the city. 'In my hometown, a kiss is a declaration of marriage.'

If it had been a declaration of marriage Amelia would have accepted without hesitation. The intensity of that first kiss had cemented the knowledge that she still loved Adam, and though she'd tried her best to ignore it, too scared to look back and accept a mistake that might invalidate all the decisions she'd ever made, he'd always had a special place in her heart and soul. For years now, she'd lived with her regret, knowing she'd never really wanted to leave him behind in the first place. If she hadn't, they could have built a life together and she'd denied them that chance. She was acting like Vera, cutting people out of her life and refusing a chance at happiness.

Amelia clutched the locket around her neck and held it tightly. What the night meant for Adam though, she didn't know. It hadn't escaped her notice that after all the times she'd bailed on morning-after conversations, she desperately wanted one now. This morning, as she'd waited for the kettle to boil, searching for what to say, praying that he'd come and kiss her cheek or give her a sign that last night hadn't been a moment of weakness, he'd instead found his shoes, ready to leave as quickly as possible. Her heart sank in her chest as she thought that was it. Despite what he said last night, he still couldn't truly forgive her. And yet, here he was, helping her with her search. She was more confused than ever, but grateful she had this mystery to occupy her. If she hadn't, there was every chance her heart would break.

'Amelia?' Adam said again. 'Where do you want to start?'

'Oh, sorry.' She hadn't realised she'd been so lost in thought she hadn't answered him and was simply paused at the top of the staircase. 'I know it's not in my room or Vera's. Let's start in the spare room next to the bathroom.'

Amelia opened the door, but it seemed like a waste of time. The room was bare except for a small single wardrobe and a double bed in a black iron bedframe. They entered and Amelia opened the wardrobe to see the stark empty space. Adam began stepping gingerly on the floor, bouncing a little as he did so.

'What are you doing?' Amelia asked with a chuckle as he bobbed along the boards.

'Checking for loose floorboards. You'd be surprised at the number of people who hide things underneath them. I've worked in lots of houses where I've discovered bits and bobs. It's normally older people who do it.'

'There's a squeaky floorboard in Vera's room!' Amelia gasped and ran down the hall.

Adam rushed along behind her and when she stopped abruptly

at the door, he knocked into her. After last night, feeling his body so close to hers again and the warmth that radiated off him, she wanted his arms around her once more. Glancing at him over her shoulder, still in yesterday's clothes, his red hair as dark as autumn leaves, a surge of lust shot through her.

'Which floorboard is it?'

'There,' Amelia replied moving to the side so that he could get through and check it. Sweeping aside the rug that had covered it, the exposed floorboard seemed to Amelia to be as flat as all the others. Adam ran his fingers around the edge of it and pried it up. As he lifted it, he glanced at Amelia and excitement filled the air. She came over and knelt beside him as he moved it away to reveal the small dark space.

Amelia peered over and tentatively put her hand in to pick up the small blue metal money box hiding inside. 'This is it. I bet this has her birth certificate in it and her really personal things.'

'It can't have much else, it's so small. Wait, there's something else under there.'

Amelia leaned over, her brow furrowing as she wiggled the item out, unsure exactly what it was. Under a thick grey layer of dust, the words *photo album* were just visible. Tracing her fingers down the front, they left tracks in the grime and where some sprang into the air it filled her nose.

The album wasn't as old as the other ones she'd found in the wardrobe and she wondered what it could be. As she flipped the first page, her heart bounced in her chest, and instantly her eyes filled. She turned a page, then another, unable to stem the huge teardrops running down her cheeks. The album was full of photographs of her. School photographs and certificates of achievements. Little recognitions of her life. Amelia wiped her nose, aware that tears were pooling at the tip ready to drop into her lap.

'I had no idea she'd kept any of this stuff.'

Adam's voice was soft. 'It shows how much she loved you, in her way.'

As Adam's arms reached around her, she let the tears go. Old school reports were tucked into the pages. Vera had always read them and told her where she needed to improve rather than congratulate her on what she'd done well, and it had hurt at the time, but Amelia had no idea she'd then squirrelled them away and kept them for all these years. Perhaps it had been her way of trying to encourage her. Vera had loved her in her way but had been unable to really show it. Perhaps she'd struggled to acknowledge it herself.

Letting the tears fall, Amelia turned her head into Adam's chest and his soft hushing calmed her. She hadn't been an unimportant burden to Vera, or the village, or to Adam. How had she got it all so wrong?

After a moment, she dried her tears. Answers were at her fingertips and she was eager to check the box and see what it contained.

'Is it locked?' Adam asked.

She tried the lid, but it didn't move. Rather than lurching in disappointment, her stomach jostled with excitement as she remembered the small key in the dressing table that at the time hadn't seemed to have any use. 'Don't worry. I know where the key is.'

Thanking her lucky stars that she hadn't thrown it out, she went to the drawer and took it out, taking the box with her and placing it on the now empty dressing table. Her hands shook as she took the key and tried the lock. Adam came over to her and rested his hand on her shoulder. The key fitted easily into the lock and she turned it, lifting the lid.

The box was empty apart from a small, folded piece of paper. It was thin and torn at the folds but opening it out she could see it was Vera's birth certificate. Relief hit her like a strong gust of wind, but as she read across the columns, the section where the father's name should be written was blank. Her breath left her. Without speaking, she showed the certificate to Adam.

'But … I don't understand.' His eyes widened as he too saw the empty space.

Amelia laid the paper out on the dressing table and put the box next to it so it wouldn't fall from her lap. 'Why wouldn't Margaret Cabot write the father's name when she registered the birth?'

'Perhaps she and Herbert weren't married by then? Shotgun weddings were known to happen.'

'I suppose so. But it's odd, isn't it? I mean, even if they weren't yet married, they must have planned to be.'

'Do you know when exactly they got hitched?'

Amelia shook her head. 'Vera never said. I could check the local church records, but I'd like to talk to Arthur first. He was a Highfield so he's our best chance to find out more about Vera and the soldier.'

'Come on then,' he said eagerly, holding out his hand to pull her up.

She took it, wrapping her fingers around his and a thrill shot through her arm. She wanted to look into Adam's strong, steady gaze every day and wake up to that face every morning, but how could they have any future together? There was no way he would move from Meadowbank. It was in his blood and as she'd always known, a city would choke him. Could she turn her life on its head? If her search was soon to be concluded, she'd have no excuse to stay. Her only hope was to say goodbye properly this time but the thought of that hurt more than any loss she'd experienced so far.

Chapter 25

The short walk to the care home was made in silence as she hoped that Arthur would be there. Seeing Adam glance over as she sighed, she contemplated reaching out for his hand. His arms were swinging by his sides and it would only take a second to make the gesture and show him how much she still cared. How she wanted more contact than the kisses they'd shared last night. Amelia drew on her will, telling herself over and over to just do it, but she couldn't make her arm move and risk him batting it away or worse, allowing his hand to hang limply in hers.

The day grew cold as the sun hid behind heavy clouds. All around the shortcut was alive with birds skittering here and there, in and out of the trees, singing happily to themselves. Meadowbank had gotten under her skin. The fresh air had cleared her lungs and though the weight of this mystery still hung on her shoulders she felt she understood Vera, or at least their relationship, a little better. She still didn't know why Vera had become so unhappy, but at least she knew it wasn't all her fault. Saying goodbye to all this open space and the sense of peace was going to be as much of a hardship as saying goodbye to Adam. She hadn't ever imagined that would be the case when she arrived nearly a month ago.

The care home was a refurbished cottage hospital just the other side of the duck pond. The front garden had a few benches for the residents to sit on and some were gathered there now, enjoying the fresh air. The front door was open, and Adam and Amelia stepped inside.

'Can we speak to Arthur?' Adam asked the lady who met them just inside the doorway.

'Yes, of course. He's in the garden. Though he's a bit tired today. He had a little stroll in the night, and we had to get him back to bed. Goodness knows how he managed to get out. We have staff here all the time and he's never done it before but he's back now, all safe and well.'

Amelia peered at Adam, fear contorting her face. She hooked her arm through his, drawing him back. 'If he did it, Adam, what do we do? I don't want him arrested.'

'I think the police only prosecute if you want to in a case like this. Don't worry, let's just wait and see what he says.'

The lady led them through the bright, cosy care home and into a large back garden. Arthur sat under the shade of a tree, both hands pressed flat against the seat either side of his legs. Like the old gentleman he was, he wore a knitted waistcoat and tie.

'Arthur, dear, Adam and Amelia have come to see you.'

They walked over to him and he shifted uncomfortably. Amelia tried to put him at ease. 'Hello, Arthur. How are you today?'

He didn't reply and the nurse glanced between them all, clearly aware that Arthur wasn't too keen on talking to them. Warily she said, 'Now, I know you're tired, but isn't it nice you've got some visitors? Of course, if you don't feel up to it, I'm sure Amelia and Adam will understand.'

Tension stiffened Amelia's muscles. She didn't want to let go of this chance to find out more information. Arthur was her only hope. She had to convince him to speak to them. Unclipping the locket from around her neck she held it out for him. 'Arthur, please can I ask you some questions about my locket? You recognised it the other day. I wondered if you wanted to look at it?'

His hand shifted as if to reach out, but he hesitated. Amelia sat down by his side and put it in his hand. 'It was Vera's. You do remember Vera, don't you, Arthur?'

'Of course I remember her. I've not lost my marbles yet,' he snapped.

The nurse relaxed, happy the normal Arthur was evident once more. 'I'll leave you to it. Feel free to grab a chair.' She pointed to a stack of plastic garden chairs in the corner and Adam pulled one over.

As she marched away, Amelia glanced at Adam, unsure how to begin. She wasn't going to mention the break-in, it would most likely scare him. Though she glanced at his hands, checking for any cuts. If he had got in through the broken window, he'd have lacerations on his hands or legs but there was nothing. Again, Amelia decided it couldn't have been him. His limbs didn't look capable of dragging him through a window or kicking at the heavy wooden door. 'Do you mind talking to me about Vera? I want to learn a bit more about her before I sell the farmhouse.'

Arthur's head shot up at the word *sell*, alarm clear on his face. How well it mirrored the concern in her own heart and the reticence she felt at letting it all go. It was her family home, she realised now. No matter what had gone before with her parents, Meadow Farmhouse was the home she had known and where her memories were based.

'Is it okay if we talk about Vera?' she asked again. It seemed important to get his agreement before she began. Slowly, Arthur nodded.

Adam sat down and Amelia began.

'Arthur …' Her voice quivered and she did her best to control it as it wasn't just adrenalin pumping through her system but fear too. 'Do you remember you saw me with the locket the other week? Do you remember Vera wearing it?'

He shook his head and disappointment almost floored her.

'But you remember Vera, don't you? Can you tell me how you know her?'

'I was a Highfield, you know,' he replied.

In the garden of the care home, he seemed to relax, and Amelia hoped it would help him answer her questions. He glanced at the sky and his face scrunched up in the light. Deep wrinkles lined his forehead and cheeks. Then he sighed and dropped his gaze.

'I lived there all my life until my daughter put me in this bloody home. It's nice enough, but it's not Highfield. Then she sold it. Told me it was too expensive to run, needed too much work. Bah!'

'It must have been hard leaving your home. I'm sorry that happened to you. But being a Highfield, you lived next door to Vera, didn't you?'

He nodded again, but his face had clouded with sadness. 'We were best friends for a long, long time. From when we were children. Right up until …'

Amelia waited, hoping he'd pick up the thread again, but it was agony. 'I realise this must be hard for you, but I do know how difficult Vera could be. I don't want you to think you'll offend me by saying the truth. I really just want to know about her and, if you remember him, the man in the locket.' She pointed to it, still in his hands and he opened the clasp, his old fingers fumbling but still agile enough to find it. He stared at the picture for a moment. Amelia couldn't tell if he recognised it or not.

'I loved her very much. She was my girl. My first love.'

Amelia was so taken aback she had to remind herself to breathe. 'You loved her?'

Vera had never mentioned any kind of romantic love with anyone. It had always seemed that no one had touched her life in that way. She remembered the photographs of Vera, and Mr MacMahon telling her of the two families falling out. Was the end of her relationship with Arthur the reason for her smile disappearing? 'What happened?' she asked in little more than a whisper.

'We were best friends and eventually, as I grew and became a man, I realised that it wasn't just friendship, but love.' Adam glanced at her and she shifted. 'On one of our walks, I decided to propose, in the coppice.' He closed his eyes as if reliving the memory. 'I thought if my mother objected for any reason it would be because we were so young. I was nineteen; she was eighteen.' He took a long deep breath. 'We were engaged for less than a day.'

'A day? Did Vera break it off?'

He shook his head slowly, sadly. 'Oh, no. That was me. Foolish, stupid Arthur.' His eyes crinkled with anger at himself. While Amelia felt for him, she could only imagine how heart-breaking it must have been for Vera too.

'What happened?'

'I didn't have a ring. I hadn't prepared to ask her, really. I hadn't asked her father's permission, or even spoken to my own parents. I let my heart lead me. When she said yes, she was so happy, but when I told my parents there was uproar. My mother wagged her finger at me, shrieking, "You can't marry the Cabot girl"'. He wagged his finger at them, mimicking what was said to him at the time. '"Of all the people in the village, you chose to ask her? She has no name. It's shameful. Too shameful for a Highfield." She didn't realise how much I loved her, and I wasn't man enough to stand up and fight. We were a proud family. Far too proud. It shouldn't have mattered. And I shouldn't have let it. She was going to wear her mother's wedding dress, you know? She was so happy.'

'Why couldn't you marry the Cabot girl?' Amelia urged, ensuring her tone was level, even though her emotions were roiling inside. Then she remembered the birth certificate and the empty space where her father's name should be. That was what Arthur meant when he, or his mother, said she had no name and that it was shameful.

'Of course,' Amelia said, leaning back a little. 'She was illegitimate, wasn't she? Your mother wouldn't let you marry someone who was illegitimate because it was so disgraceful back then.'

Adam was so shocked his jaw slackened. 'Illegitimate? You mean born out of wedlock?'

'Not just that,' Amelia said, but Arthur continued before she could explain more fully.

'It wasn't her fault,' Arthur said quietly. 'I shouldn't have let it matter. I thought about it all night. Mother had told me to break it off the next day, but I couldn't sleep. That night, I tossed and turned until I couldn't take it anymore. I threw stones at her window. I had to get her attention without waking everyone in the house. She came down as dawn broke. I'll never forget the look on her face as I told her I couldn't marry her.' He sucked in a breath. 'So many tears. When she first told me about her real father, I said it didn't matter, and I should never have let it.'

Amelia's heart tore for them both as she watched it all play out on the old man's face. She felt Adam take her hand and entwine his fingers with hers. She held them tightly, squeezing as if it would help her control her emotions. Arthur dropped his eyes to the picture of the soldier in the locket.

'Is this Vera's father?' Amelia asked. Her finger trembled as she pointed to the locket still in Arthur's hands. He nodded and handed it back to her. All Amelia could do among the raging sea of emotions was hold it tight, the only anchor keeping her in port. A deep sense of regret for Vera rocked her body as she cradled it in her hands.

In Amelia's mind, the pieces of the puzzle fell into place. Jocelyn had said Vera's father was a decent man. Did she think that because he'd taken on another man's child? Jocelyn was of a generation that wouldn't have wanted to discuss such shameful things. As much as she bucked convention by reading *Fifty Shades of Grey* and crushing on handsome TV presenters, Amelia now appreciated her reticence. The American soldier must have recuperated at Highfield and then worked on Meadow Farmhouse when he was well enough. He must have known and fallen in love with Margaret – Vera's mother. Amelia knew she was a beautiful young lady from the photographs she'd seen. She must have slept with him before he left and later found out she was pregnant.

Obviously, he didn't come back from the war, and she married another man. Maybe the soldier had always intended to return and died in battle? As Mr Hoffelmeyer said, they were shipped back as soon as they could fight. Maybe he already had a family back home? She hoped not.

When Vera's mother had registered the birth, she'd been too ashamed to write the name of a man she wasn't married to. How stupid it all was. Why on earth did it matter? Deep down Amelia accepted that was how people thought at that time, but when war raged across the world surely love was more important than any of that. And Amelia was sure that this soldier had loved Vera's mother. Servicemen didn't get that many pictures taken so they wouldn't have been able to give them to every woman who took their fancy. No. It was love; Amelia was sure of it. Maybe that was why Vera was so fiercely proud of her family name, using it as a shield to show she wasn't ashamed, and people couldn't affect her. Suddenly, Amelia understood so much about the angry, reclusive woman who'd taken her in.

What a tangled web of secrets surrounded her home. So much history and heartbreak she could never have imagined. Amelia placed her fingers over her lips, composing herself. 'Do you know the soldier's name?'

Arthur shook his head. 'I'm sorry. He was never spoken of. My mother never told me, and Vera hardly ever spoke of him. Margaret told her the truth of her birth when she was fifteen, but she never told her his name.'

'Do you think he loved Vera's mother?'

'I wish I could tell you for certain,' Arthur said kindly. 'All I can say is that Margaret was a woman of great integrity and wasn't the type to throw herself at every Tom, Dick and Harry.'

Amelia nodded, grateful for his words, but all she could think was that Vera was illegitimate, and that was why the boy from the posh house wasn't allowed to marry her. It must have broken her heart. Had she then taken her anger out on the wedding dress and ripped it? To have kept it for all these years and see it every day – a constant reminder of everything she'd lost that night – must have been torture. At such a young age, it's not surprising it had a huge impact on her. She must have felt so unworthy, so destroyed by it all. An alarm bell rang in Amelia's head. This was all too familiar.

Why had she done it to herself? Tears welled in Amelia's eyes and she flicked one away from the corner before it could escape. Vera had let this one horrible event ruin the rest of her life.

'It was the greatest mistake of my life,' Arthur said earnestly. 'And seeing how it affected Vera as she grew to hate everyone in the village made me even more ashamed. I did love her, you know.'

She reached out a hand and took his. 'I know.'

'After I'd broken it off, Herbert Cabot came to the house to defend Vera. There was a row and my father told him to never step foot on our land again. She never spoke to me after that. Never forgave me.'

'But she could have,' Amelia replied, hoping to ease his burden. Vera could have had so much love and kindness including Amelia's but chose not to; that wasn't Arthur's fault. Yes, he'd broken Vera's heart, but she could have allowed it to heal. Vera chose to hold on to the pain and bitterness, allowing it grow inside her. 'Vera made her choice to stay unhappy rather than move on. That wasn't your fault.'

As a tear escaped from his eye, he squeezed her hand in return. 'Thank you.'

'I'm going to get you some tea, Arthur.' Adam placed a comforting hand on his shoulder. It was just like him to be so caring. Though she'd waited for a sign that he cared about her, perhaps it was time she took her life into her own hands.

Amelia suddenly recognised the crossroads before her. Was she going to continue walking the same path Vera had? She could choose to return to Paris and try again to run away from her painful past, living a life that was both lonely and unfulfilling, or she could be brave and embrace the love that was all around her here in Meadowbank. Her parents had died when she was eight and just like Vera, she'd held on to that grief for far too long. Amelia swallowed. She'd been slowly turning into Vera, seeing the world through her eyes, rather than her own, and it was time to make a change.

Chapter 26

They stepped away from the care home and into the sunshine. A huge honeysuckle bush grew over the garden wall and birds darted in and out of the hedge nearby. Amelia inhaled a deep breath, feeling the air fill her lungs and calm her mind. 'Arthur had a daughter, so I suppose that means he married someone else?' she asked Adam.

'Yes. He married a woman called Samantha.'

'Here in the village?'

Adam nodded.

She was pleased for Arthur. 'That must have been so hard for Vera to see. At least his life has been happier than hers.'

'I'm sorry,' Adam said. 'It still doesn't tell us the name of the soldier.'

'No, it doesn't. But at least now I know who he was and what he meant to Vera. And I understand why she became the way she did. As sad as it is, I'm glad I know. Can you imagine how heart-breaking it must have been for Vera to have lost the man she loved because his parents forbade them marrying, all because she was born out of wedlock? She was still born out of love.'

'It all seems so stupid and insignificant to me.'

Amelia paused. 'It explains why she was so kind to you and your mum even when she hated the rest of the village.'

'Because my dad left, you mean?'

Amelia nodded. 'Your dad abandoned you, just as Arthur abandoned her. Though your mum was a lot braver than Vera was, moving on with her life and now, finding happiness with Dean.'

'Sometimes I wonder if she likes him or his Sunday roasts.'

Amelia gave a small smile.

A ringing sound penetrated her thoughts and she realised it was her phone. At the same time, Lorraine ran over towards Adam, threading her arm through his as soon as she stopped at his side.

'Adam, there you are.'

'Hi, Lorraine. Is it important? Only I'm kind of in the middle of something.'

She glanced at Amelia, narrowing her eyes slightly. 'I have another job for you, and I've decided I'd like some of your little men for the garden.'

'Oh, right. Well perhaps you could swing by the workshop later or I could pop round?'

'Can't you talk now. I mean, I only live over the road. Come and give me a quote for the job now.'

Adam was clearly torn, but Amelia needed to time to think, to process everything she'd just heard and clear her mind of the rambling thoughts and questions mounting inside it. Her phone was still ringing, and she said, 'Adam, I'm going to walk back to the farmhouse.' She waved him off, turned around and grabbed the phone from her pocket and swiped to take the call. 'Hello?'

'Ah, hello, Miss Williams. It's Police Constable Bure here, with an update.'

'Hello, Constable. Thank you for calling.'

'No problem. I just wanted you to know that we've caught the person who broke into your property.'

Amelia held her breath. 'Already? Who was it?'

'A group of youths from the village. You might have seen them whizzing around on their bicycles at all hours. Turns out, they knew that your great-aunt had died and thought it'd be good fun to break into a house where someone had passed on and see what it was like. See if her ghost haunted the place. All very silly and they've had a very stern talking-to about the scare they've given you, as well as wasting police time. I can assure you the parents had no idea and from what I've seen today, those kids won't be going anywhere on their bikes for a while. Now, we weren't planning on pressing charges unless you really want us to?'

Amelia paused for a second. It had been a terrifying night, but if it hadn't happened Adam wouldn't have kissed her. The boys who broke in were just kids. They might be a bit silly on their bikes and a bit inconsiderate of other people's feelings, but did these kids need punishing even more?

'No, thank you, Constable. That's fine. I'm just glad to know what happened.'

'Very nice of you, miss. Thank you.'

'Although ...' An idea occurred to her.

'Yes, miss?'

'How do you feel about unofficial community service, Constable? I've got some gardening that needs doing. Maybe the parents would consent to the kids coming up and helping out for a day? It might teach them a more constructive lesson.'

'Sounds a very good idea to me, miss. I'll speak to the parents and let you know.'

She bid him goodbye and put her phone away. As she glanced over her shoulder, leaving the village behind, Adam was watching her, but Lorraine held him tight. Whilst Amelia didn't really want to leave his side, she needed to think. Hearing Vera's story had made it clear the path she herself was headed down, but to make such a change was asking a lot of herself and she needed to make sure it was the right choice.

The mystery of the locket had become an important way of focusing her attention away from her grief: a coping mechanism. But now it had gained a new, altogether life-changing importance. The death of her parents was a rightfully catastrophic event that had affected her deeply, but how long had she been holding on to that loss? Vera had been a difficult person to live with, unable to give or accept love because she'd closed her heart off. And yet, as Amelia had thought back over their time together, there were occasions when she'd been kind and caring. The photo album had been proof of that. She just found it so hard to show it for fear of getting hurt again. That was why she had reacted so badly to Amelia wanting to move to Paris. The revelation sent a weight from her chest and her breaths grew bigger.

Amelia powered her legs until they almost gave way, and it wasn't long until she'd traversed the shortcut back to Meadow Farmhouse. As she drew level with the farmhouse, she saw Mr Hoffelmeyer waiting at the front door. At her approach, he hurried over, all in a fluster. He was dressed in his usual eccentric attire in a linen suit and enormous straw boater. Under the open jacket she could see an orange silk cravat and matching handkerchief with which he was dabbing at his nose. He was also carrying a battered briefcase. 'Miss Williams? Miss Williams, I'm so glad I've caught you.'

She took in a breath to ensure control of her voice, aware that her emotions were still crashing just below the surface. 'Hello, Mr Hoffelmeyer. How are you today?'

'It's very warm,' he said, sounding slightly annoyed at the beautiful spring day. He glanced at the sun, narrowing his eyes accusingly. 'But never mind. I'm so glad I caught you because some information regarding your family has come to light.'

'My family?' The thought that all the names she'd come across in her search for the man in the locket were members of her family still surprised her.

'Why yes indeed. After you came to see me, I was so enthralled by your tale that I was more determined than ever to find out as much as I could about these men who came to Meadowbank and do you know what I did? So silly of me, really. I don't know why I didn't think of it before.'

'What did you do, Mr Hoffelmeyer?'

'Well, I remembered the shape of the insignia from the photograph you showed me and though we could only see a bit of it, I matched it up to a few possibilities and narrowed it down from there. Eventually, I found out what battalions he could belong to. Then I searched my history books to see if those units came over to Britain – and more specifically to Meadowbank. I also searched the death records. Elsie at the library was particularly helpful with that. Then I cross-referenced those with – no, then I spoke to the oracle of all Meadowbank knowledge – then I cross-referenced that with—'

As her nerves bubbled, Amelia's head pounded. 'Please tell me what you found, Mr Hoffelmeyer. I'm not sure I can take the suspense.'

He took a deep breath and broke out into a smile. Pulling a folder from his briefcase, he handed it over. 'Once I'd found some names, I checked who had died and where. This is for you. I'm sure this is the chap you're looking for. His listed injuries match those from the picture you showed me. Are you all right?'

A tear ran down her face as her feelings grew too much. So he had died. Whoever *he* was. 'Yes, I'm fine. Sorry, it's just a lot to take in.'

'In that case, let me leave this with you, but do call me if you have any questions.' He handed over the file and after patting her arm, left her.

Amelia stared at the farmhouse door, wondering whether to enter or not. The emotions cascading inside her felt too great at the moment. She wasn't ready to face Vera's ghost, aware of how much like her she was becoming. Instead, she clutched the file tightly and carried on towards the coppice. Something in her soul drew her towards it and eventually, as her legs became heavy, she broke her pace and entered the wood. Amelia wiped at the sweat gathering at her temples.

Being away from Meadowbank and the farmhouse gave her space to think and raising her head to the sky she felt the warmth of spring sunshine on her face. Beams of light dappled through the lively green branches that met in a canopy above her head and she took in a deep breath, filling her lungs with fresh, earthy air, allowing it to calm her mind. The smell of damp earth met her as she stepped over the grass and mud underfoot. Mixed with the strange smell of decay were the floral notes of the bluebells beginning to flower on the coppice floor. She came to the clearing where she and Adam had shared their first kiss and where, she now knew, Arthur had proposed to Vera.

Sitting on a tree stump, she opened the file to find various printouts from different books and websites, but one thing caught her eye: his name. Private William Marsh. Her hand went to her lip, stifling her tears. Her heart raced, pressing against her ribcage. He died in combat.

'So he didn't just not bother to come back,' Amelia said to herself. 'He was a hero.' Like so many others.

Tears stung her eyes. His inability to return and marry Vera's mother had wounded Vera so fiercely, but he hadn't abandoned them, and given the fact the locket had remained in her family, Amelia was sure he had loved Vera's mother very much.

She wondered who the oracle of village knowledge was that Mr Hoffelmeyer referred to, but she was pretty sure it was Jocelyn. She'd have to buy her some more biscuits.

Amelia raised her head, studying the patches of sun through the trees, and beams of light passed over her face. When so much love had been lost by war and convention, could she throw away her own chance at happiness?

The way Adam looked at her it was as if he was looking into her soul. Could she really say goodbye to him again? No. She loved him. He'd always been a part of her heart, even though she'd tried to ignore it, hoping that focusing on her career and a new life would help her forget the pain of her past. She couldn't let him go again, or the chance at a life here in Meadowbank. Her happiness lay not only with Adam but with Meadow Farmhouse too.

All the history that her home contained – good and bad – couldn't be forgotten or sold out of her life. It was important. As was Amelia. She wasn't insignificant or inferior as the small voice in her head had always told her. She was worth loving and she had love to give. Belonging somewhere mattered and home wasn't just a place, it was a feeling; one she'd kept pretending was in Paris.

Vera was gone. As were her parents. She let the enormity of the sentence sink in and for once, rather than pushing down the agony, she allowed it to come to the fore. Embracing it for the first time, it consumed her. The tears came again, forcing open all the doors she'd kept shut in her mind. She let misery burn through her, white-hot and blinding, and the salty tears stung her chilled cheeks. How had she never cried like this before over her parents? Over everything? In a final release, she let go of the despair caused by a love she'd never really remembered.

It was time to make a change. And a big one at that.

It was time to let go.

Chapter 27

She had no idea how much time had passed as she sat there crying, but when she looked up the air carried a dampness it hadn't earlier. The coppice was now completely shaded and though some of the sun's rays penetrated through the crown of leaves above her head, her fingers were turning pink from cold. She closed her eyes, enjoying the freshness on her skin. She felt lighter than she had in years. It wasn't so much that a heavy weight had been lifted from her shoulders; this ran much deeper. It was like a giant boulder that had sat on her back had crumbled away and she was now able to stand straighter, breathe deeper and move more freely. There was more space in her mind to think and feel and she knew the decision she'd made was the right one. The one that felt right deep down inside.

A rustling further down the path made her jump and she watched as Adam's frame came into view. Every nerve in her body burned with feeling. 'Adam? What are you doing here?'

'As soon as I could get away from Lorraine I came here. I had a feeling this was where you'd end up.'

'I thought you were busy.'

'Lorraine can take some getting away from, but … I wanted to be with you.' The words sent a bolt of electricity through her. 'What's that?'

Amelia realised he was pointing at the file and she told him about Mr Hoffelmeyer and the information he'd given her.

'So that's it then. You've solved the mystery.' He tried to keep his tone congratulatory, but she could hear the pain ringing through it. Could that mean it wasn't too late for them? That he still felt the way he'd hinted at last night? There was only one way to find out. 'I guess there's nothing to keep you here now.'

'Adam, I need to tell you—'

'That you're leaving?' He shook his head and his eyes filled with sadness. She could tell he was holding back tears. 'I knew you would. I should have known you can't stay. That it'd be too hard for you.'

'Adam—'

'It's okay. I know …' He struggled to get the words but before she could explain he rallied and spoke on. 'I know I'm not enough for you, but you have to know something, Amelia, before you leave.' He stared at her so intently that her brain ceased. Was he about to say the words she longed to hear? 'I should have told you last night, but I was too scared. I love you. I've always loved you. I tried not to after you left. I tried to be angry because it was so hard still loving you and you not being here. But no matter how hard I try, it's always been you. It's only ever been you. I thought after last night, when we kissed – I hoped you felt something for me too – but if you still can't bring yourself to stay—'

'Adam, I'm not leaving.' She took a step forward, closing the distance between them.

'You're – you're not?' His eyes flashed with a hopeful radiance that made her heart burst.

'No. And I don't mean right now, I mean I'm not leaving Meadow Farmhouse. I – I want to stay.'

Adam shook his head. She had to carry on and tell him how she felt before her nerve failed. Her heart broke that he thought he wasn't enough for her. She'd worried too that the kiss had been the end for him rather than the beginning, but she was wrong and the love that exploded inside her filled every cell in her body.

'I want to stay here with you because … because I love you too.'

When Adam's eyes met hers, the brilliance and intensity of his gaze pinned her to the spot. 'You do?'

'Yes. I've been so stupid, Adam.' She pushed her dark hair

from her face. 'I ran away from Meadowbank because I never felt good enough for this place, or you. I honestly thought you'd get over me and that would be that. You'd have forgotten me before you hit twenty. I had no idea I'd hurt you as much as I did and I'm so sorry for that. I didn't mean to. I just couldn't stay back then. But I realise now I've been running away for such a long time. I don't want to end up like Vera. I don't want to let the fact that my parents died make me miss out on a life full of love and friendship and happiness.'

Though his eyes had lightened at her admission, Adam now looked utterly confused. 'But what about Paris? Your life's there. I can't compete with that.'

'Yes, you can.' Whilst she didn't regret her time in Paris, or the career she'd built for herself there, it was clear to her now that her heart belonged somewhere else. 'Paris is beautiful, but it doesn't feel the same as this place. It isn't a home. It isn't where my roots are. And though I love my job, I can do it from anywhere. I've decided to stay here, and I've never been surer of anything in my whole life. I love you, Adam, and I want to be with you, here at Meadow Farmhouse in my family home.'

Amelia held her breath as Adam stepped closer. He was right in front of her now, the light through the trees highlighting the fierce red in his hair. His eyes scanned her face, and she willed him to understand just how much she loved him. Adam slid his hands down her arms, taking her hands in his. Her fingers were still cold but as he stroked them with his thumbs, warmth flooded through her. Adam's mouth moved as he tried to say something. Then on the second attempt the words came. 'I love you.'

Her heartbeat raced as his lips touched hers. The kiss was gentle and intense at the same time and Amelia could barely believe this moment was real. Emotion seemed to flow through her and into him, like the current of a river. Her mouth tingled and it spread through her veins to consume every part of her. Even the other night hadn't been like this and it was all because she'd opened her heart, allowing herself to feel the love he had to give, and to give her love in return.

When they parted, Adam inhaled sharply. 'Are you sure about all this? It means changing everything.'

'I know. But this journey we've been on, finding out about the locket, finding out about Vera, I've realised what I have here. I can't give that up. It's time for a fresh start.'

Her childhood with Vera had been difficult at times, but now she accepted the woman Vera had been. Knowing how she had become so unhappy, it was easier to come to terms with her past. As long as she didn't close her heart off the way Vera had, she could still feel her parents' love. She could have Adam's love too. A whole world of happiness was at her fingertips.

The secrets of Meadow Farmhouse had been revealed and the secret she'd kept from herself was finally out in the open. She was no longer the minor character in her own life. It was time to step into the spotlight and take the lead.

Chapter 28

5th November

The lock of Meadow Farmhouse's front door gently clicked shut and Amelia placed the keys in the pocket of her warmest coat. Though her hands were encased in gloves, she could feel the warmth of Adam's skin as she cupped his face and kissed him. He smiled at her and picked up the present they were taking into the village. It was Bonfire Night and as always, Meadowbank didn't like to miss out on an excuse to celebrate. Over the last few days a fire had been built on the village green and a fireworks display was primed and ready to go.

Mr Simpkins had recently been back with his leather notepad and tiny calculator, but this time it was to value Willow Farm. After missing out on being together for the last ten years, Amelia and Adam weren't wasting any time now and Adam had moved into Meadow Farmhouse. Their evenings were spent together, cosying up on the sofa or talking endlessly at the aged kitchen table as they ate their dinner. Sometimes they'd meet Sophie and Michael in the pub, but Amelia loved her quiet nights in with Adam, and when business forced her to return to Paris, she couldn't wait to get home again.

'Ready?' she asked as she took the other end of the present. It was quite heavy and she should at least make a token effort to help.

'Ready,' he replied. 'But why don't I take this, and you take the torch. I don't fancy stacking it in the dark.'

The cold air nipped at her nose and cheeks as they walked

towards the shortcut, but she couldn't resist glancing back at her new home. The ivy that had grown over the house in dense green vines had been trimmed back, and with a new lick of paint it was the epitome of country chic. Even the sign at the end of the now flower-studded driveway had been replaced. Here and there around Meadow Farm she had also dotted some of Adam's magical sculptures and their cute little Groot-like faces peeped out at the farmhouse's visitors. She'd let go of the ghosts of hers and Vera's pasts and a new life shone from the windows of Meadow Farmhouse.

'This is really heavy you know,' Adam said.

'You're a big strong boy,' she teased. 'You can manage the last little bit. Or do you want me to carry it?'

'Huh! And have you tease me like you did when I couldn't put that new coffee machine together and you could? No thanks.'

Shivering in the cold night air, she pulled her hat further down on her head and wrapped the scarf around her neck. The village green was once again encircled with bunting and stalls and the bright white stars glittered above them. The scent of the bonfire, toffee apples and mulled cider filled her senses as Adam stashed the present behind the bar of the Drunken Duck. As the fireworks lit the sky and children waved their sparklers, the ducks sheltered under the bushes around the duck pond, happily leaving the villagers alone to enjoy themselves.

The queue for Annie's hot chocolates curved around the green and people weaved their way through to get to the stalls. Amelia snuggled into Adam with Sophie, Michael and Isla nearby. The whooshes and bangs made the two-year-old jump, but when the sky filled with starbursts of orange, red and purple, Isla watched with wide eyes.

Six months on and running her interior design business from Meadowbank had become an exciting prospect. Amelia had finished her projects in Paris and was beginning to build up clients in England from her home office in what had been the playroom. The picture of the Metro, a reminder of her time in Paris, sat on the wall above her desk. She didn't regret a second of her life there because it had brought her to this moment, but she was more than happy to start the next chapter of her life.

For a lot of the villagers it seemed Parisian chic was in fashion, especially in this part of Kent, and she was becoming busier than ever. Adam was receiving more and more requests for his sculptures and had even branched out into different designs. Some of his furniture was being stocked at a local garden centre. He was no longer ashamed of his artistic ambitions and was constantly talking about new ideas he had. Some of Amelia's French clients still contacted her and she'd take trips over for a few days now and again, but she was always pleased to come home and found herself smiling on the train back as she remembered the first day she'd arrived back in Meadowbank. The painful memories of her arrival as a child were fading like a picture left out in the sun, and she wasn't sad to see them go as her mind was filled with new, happier ones.

Océanè hadn't been that impressed with Amelia's move to the small 'provincial' village. She'd chastised her and told her she was giving up an amazing career in the fashion and culture capital of the world for a life of jam-making and chicken farming. Her disdain rang the distance between them and though Amelia had texted a few times, hoping to salvage something of their friendship, it didn't seem it was to be. Océanè hadn't responded and the gaps between Amelia's attempts were growing wider. She wasn't going to chase after someone who wouldn't accept her choices. Friends, she had learned, should support each other.

Sophie, on the other hand, had been so happy at Amelia's decision to stay she'd declared they needed another night in the pub to celebrate. Amelia winced at the remembered hangover. It had been one of the worst she'd ever experienced, but one of the best nights of her life. The village had welcomed her, drinks were brought, and Dean the landlord had even given them desserts for free. Sophie had recently applied for a part-time job at the local school. They had a nursery class where Isla could go as soon as she'd turned two, which had just happened, and it would fit in perfectly with Michael's busy hours at the practice. Amelia was happy for her. They were even sharing the eggs Amelia collected daily from the chicken's larger, more extravagant run. There were always far too many for Amelia and Adam to eat on their own. She was even hatching plans for a vegetable patch, as she'd pictured once before, but it was taking a bit more courage to commit to just yet.

After taking Isla to buy a toffee apple, Amelia had whispered to Adam to run into the pub and get the present they had stashed behind the bar for her. Although they'd given her a present for her birthday, Amelia had something special she wanted to give her.

'What's that?' Sophie asked, pointing to the large item behind them, wrapped in brown paper.

'It's a gift,' Amelia replied. 'It's for Isla.'

A huge smile came to Sophie's face. 'What is it?'

'Open it and see.'

Sophie held out her hand to Isla. 'Come on, darling, shall we see what Amelia and Adam have brought for you as a special present?' Isla took two enormous jumps towards it, unable to contain her excitement in single steps. They began removing the paper until Sophie gasped. 'A rocking horse!'

'We used to play on that when we were little,' Adam said, stepping forwards and helping Isla to climb on. She was still a bit young for it, and Adam held on to her waist to make sure she didn't fall off.

'Horsey!' shouted Isla enthusiastically jiggling backwards and forwards. 'Go, horsey.'

Sophie wrapped Amelia in a hug which she eagerly returned. 'You shouldn't have.'

'Rubbish. There's no point in it sitting in Vera's – I mean the spare room – when Isla can make use of it. And look at her face – she loves it.'

'Well we're giving it back when she outgrows it. You should keep it for your own children. It's like a family heirloom.'

'I suppose it is,' Amelia replied, and the thought warmed her heart. 'Do you mind if we nip off for a walk around? I'm dying to get some cake before it runs out.'

'You'd better hurry then; they're going fast.'

'Did you see the look on Isla's face?' she said to Adam as they ambled through the stalls. The smell of smoke filled her nose and excited chatter filled the air.

'The sweat and tears doing it up were no trouble compared to carrying it here. That nearly did me in.'

She jabbed him in the ribs with her elbow. 'Stop complaining, you big wimp. Anyway, I've got a treat for you now.'

He spun her towards him, catching her other hand and holding it tight. 'As long as I've got you, I don't need anything else.'

'How about Mrs Doyle's carrot cake?'

A grin lit up his face. 'Now that sounds good as long as I don't need it for a broken heart.'

'You definitely don't. I just remembered you saying it was your favourite and I wanted to thank you for working on the rocking horse, especially as you wouldn't let me pay you.'

'No chance,' Adam replied. 'Are you sure you're not doing it to get round my mum? Carrot cake is her favourite too, you know.'

'Small steps, I think, Adam.' She patted his hand. 'Small steps.'

Lynne had softened significantly towards Amelia but knowing how she didn't mince her words, Amelia always worried she was going to upset her.

'Hi, Arthur,' Amelia said, as they passed him. She gave him a kiss on the cheek. He was attending the Bonfire Night celebrations with a few other elderly residents. Amelia had been visiting him regularly since she found out about Vera. Sometimes they spoke about how life was for them before the falling-out, and other times they talked about his wife and family. She enjoyed his company and as his daughter was too far away to visit him, she appreciated being the one to make him smile.

The wedding dress in Vera's wardrobe had been sent off to a local seamstress for repairs. It was never going to be as good as new, but the tears would be mended, and it would be given a new lease of life.

'It's lovely to see you, dear,' said Mrs Douglas as they approached the cake stall. 'What can I get you this time? The chocolate cake's already gone, but I've got a lovely red velvet cake if that tickles your fancy?'

'It does, but I'm actually after some of Mrs Doyle's carrot cake, please?' Mrs Douglas didn't seem to mind, but Mrs Doyle was ecstatic and launched out of her chair with vigour. 'How's your bad hip, Mrs Douglas? Sophie said it's been playing up.'

'Oh, it's all right, dear. Bit sore, but it'll ease off. Better to keep moving about than just sit still.'

'Well, if you need anything, do let me know.'

'I will, dear. Thank you.'

'Whole thing or slice?' asked Mrs Doyle, nudging Mrs Douglas over.

'Slice,' said Adam.

'Whole thing, please,' Amelia said, shooting him a glance. 'I want some too, you know. This is our pudding tonight.'

'Whole thing it is,' said Mrs Doyle. 'I'm not arguing with Miss Amelia.'

Amelia flashed her eyes at him as Mrs Doyle manoeuvred the large cake into a box.

'Is that carrot cake?' asked Lynne, appearing at her shoulder. 'Did you know that was my favourite? You're not creeping around me, are you, Amelia? I wouldn't put it past Adam, but you should know better. That sort of thing doesn't work with me.'

'I wouldn't dream of it,' Amelia replied. 'But would you like to join us, Lynne?'

'Oh, go on then, but I'm only having a small slice mind. It's fish night at the pub tonight. Did you two want some haddock? I'll get Dean to save you the biggest fillets.'

Was it Amelia's imagination, or had that been more than one small step with Lynne Noble? She hoped so, because next Valentine's Day she had plans of proposing, that was if Adam didn't get the hint before then.

Amelia wasn't going to wear Vera's wedding dress on her wedding day – it was far too delicate to be used – but the locket would be her something old, or perhaps it should be something borrowed? Whichever one it was, she knew she wanted that little piece of Meadow Farmhouse, and of her family, with her when the time came.

THE END

Acknowledgements

For various reasons, this has been quite an emotional book to write. The story of *The Secrets of Meadow Farmhouse* was inspired by my great-grandparents' heartrending romance, who this book is dedicated to.

My great-grandmother, Marion, was an exceptional and loving woman, not at all like Vera! She fell in love with Billy Davies – a young soldier with the Canadian Expeditionary Force when he passed through Kent as part of his training, and though we don't know the ins and outs of their romance (family history research takes far more time than you think it will!), I know that he loved her dearly, giving her a locket with a picture of him in. Marion passed that locket to my mum who then gave it to me on my wedding day. It was my something old.

At the time, we didn't know who Billy Davies was because my grandmother, Marion's daughter, was born out of wedlock. Marion was cast out of her family and disowned by her mother and sister (her father had already passed away) and because of the shame she felt, she never spoke of Billy, even to my mum, and his name isn't on my grandmother's birth certificate.

When we found out who Billy was, thanks to Ancestry and one of Billy's relatives getting in touch, it was like a piece of a puzzle fell into place, particularly for my mum who truly believed she would never know who her grandfather was, the man her grandmother had loved so much. Marion never met or married anyone else and had he not died at the Battle of Vimy Ridge in 1917, I'm sure Billy would have returned and married her.

It's been both moving and wonderful to use their story as

inspiration for this book and I really hope you've enjoyed it. My mum assures me Marion would have been happy about it!

As usual, I'd like to thank HQ Digital for the glorious cover (it really is BEAUTIFUL!) and to Sarah Goodey, my lovely editor, for helping me bring this story to life.

My family are always amazingly supportive: my parents from afar this time due to lockdown. But on a more positive note, they can be very proud that their grandchildren helped me talk through some plot holes and figure out how Amelia and Adam would act in certain situations! Well done, kids, and thank you!

And thank you to my lovely friends in the book-loving community for reading and reviewing and giving me the confidence to keep going when it gets really, really hard!

Hello bookworms and welcome to Meadowbank!

How did you like your first visit? Doesn't the cover make you want to up sticks and move to the countryside to live in a ramshackle farmhouse?! It did me! I hope you enjoyed reading Amelia and Adam's story and will come back again for the second instalment. I'm working on that book now and can't wait to share it with you! It's based in a library and who doesn't love libraries?!

Thank you so much for choosing to read one of my books. If you enjoyed it, it would be amazing if you'd consider leaving a review wherever you got it from. Reviews really help us to find new readers and I can't tell you how much it means to us to know someone has enjoyed our work.

If you'd like to keep up to date with my progress, you can sign up to my mailing list here: https://bit.ly/3gbqMS0. I send out a newsletter once a month, and only pop into your inbox when I've got something to tell you. I promise I won't bother you all the time!

I'm also really bad (or should that be good?) at procrastinating on social media. So do come and find me on my website: www.keginger.com. Or on Facebook: www.Facebook.com/KatieGAuthor, and Twitter: @KatieGAuthor.

Hopefully I'll see you again soon, and until then, happy reading, everyone!

Lots of love,

Katie

Xxx

ONE PLACE. MANY STORIES

If you enjoyed *The Secrets of Meadow Farmhouse*, then why not try another heartwarming novel from HQ Digital?